The Official NORA ROBERTS Companion

Edited by

DENISE LITTLE AND LAURA HAYDEN

BERKLEY BOOKS
NEW YORK

A Berkley Book
Published by The Berkley Publishing Group
A division of Penguin Group (USA) Inc.
375 Hudson Street
New York, New York 10014

Cover design by Steven Ferlauto
Book design by Pauline Neuwirth

First Edition: October 2003

Library of Congress Cataloging-in-Publication Data

The official Nora Roberts companion / edited by Denise Little and Laura Hayden ; introduction by Nora Roberts.
p. cm.
ISBN 0-425-18344-0
1. Roberts, Nora—Handbooks, manuals, etc. 2. Love stories, American—Handbooks, manuals, etc. 3. Suspense fiction—Handbooks, manuals, etc. I. Little, Denise. II. Hayden, Laura.

PS3568.0243 Z8 2002
813'.54—dc21

2001056599

Printed in the United States of America

10 9 8 7 6 5 4 3 2 1

To the Wyrd Sisters, for their support and the loan of the Nora Roberts rarities we were missing, thank you.

And to our families and friends, voracious readers all, thanks for everything, but most especially for walking around the massive piles of Nora Roberts books everywhere for the last year and not stealing them to read.

A ZILLION RELATIONSHIP BOOKS OUT THERE, AND YOU'RE SAYING I CAN UNDERSTAND WOMEN BETTER BY READING A ROMANCE NOVEL?

IF IT'S BY NORA ROBERTS, YES!
Sigh NEXT THING YOU KNOW I'LL BE JOINING the OPRAH BOOK CLUB
ONE HURDLE AT A TIME...
10-24

acknowledgments

To Nora Roberts, who has given the writers of this book (and millions of fans) volumes and volumes of some of the finest reading available on the planet, thank you for the endless pleasure. And for letting us compile this homage to it, thank you even more!

To Bruce Wilder, who gave us a very good idea of where Nora gets her ideas for heroes, thank you for all the help with the photos.

To Amy Berkower and her staff at Writers House, especially Jodi Reamer, thank you for all the help and support. We couldn't have done it without you.

To Leslie Gelbman, Cindy Hwang, and all the folks at Berkley, thanks for everything.

To Isabel Swift, Lynda Curnyn, Eva Steinberg, and everyone at Silhouette who took the time from their busy schedules to participate, thank you so much for your help, time, and support.

To the publishing and bookselling professionals who gave their time to this project so willingly, thank you all.

—Denise Little and Laura Hayden

Nora's first publicity photo

Nora's latest publicity photo

contents

Foreword *by Julie Garwood* ix
Introduction *by Nora Roberts* xiii

PART ONE: nora—up close and personal 1
"True-Life Romance:
Nora Roberts Revels in the Pleasures of Success"
by Nanci Hellmich 3
Sound Bites from Nora on How to Learn to Write 8
"Nora Roberts: A Celebration of Emotions" *by Judy Quinn* 13

PART TWO: the career 21
A Publisher's Journey: An Interview with Leslie Gelbman 23
From the Beginning: Nora Roberts at Silhouette 38
Timeline of a Career 40
The Mind of an Agent: An Interview with Amy Berkower 52

PART THREE: the books 63
The Nora Roberts Concordance:
A Complete Alphabetical Guide to the
Books of Nora Roberts 65
The Language of Love Reprints 273
From Book to Screen: Nora's Books into Movies 275
On Location with Nora:
A State-by-State and Country-by-Country Title Listing 280

PART FOUR: a.k.a. Robb, J. D. Robb 283
The Life of "In Death":
An In-Depth Look at the J. D. Robb Books 285

J. D. Robb's In Death Books: In Chronological Order 294

PART FIVE: the series 297
The MacGregors: America's Family? 299
The Bonds of Brothers: The Quinns of Chesapeake Bay 308
The Luck of the Irish: The Irish Connection and Nora 311
A Series of Miracles:
A Look at the Rest of Nora Roberts's Series 318

PART SIX: traveling with nora 327
Venice 330
The Cayman Islands 333
Prague 337
Irish Eyes Are Smiling . . . 340
Cork, Ireland 344
Galway, Ireland 347

PART SEVEN: the booksellers 353
The Family Bookstore 355
An Interview with Tommy Dreiling,
Romance Buyer for Barnes & Noble *by Susan C. Stone* 359
Appreciating Nora:
A Talk with Sharon Kelly Roth at Books & Co. 366
Selling Nora:
An Interview with Anne Marie Tallberg,
Former National Romance Buyer for Waldenbooks 371
Bookseller's Corner:
A Talk with Beth Anne Steckiel 378

PART EIGHT: a circle of friends 387
Nora in Their Own Words 389

PART NINE: the fans 401

PART TEN: nora by net 433
Connecting Nora's Fandom 435

PART ELEVEN: a last word from nora 455
The Votes in a Kiss 458

About the Editors 460

foreword

WHEN IT COMES to superlatives, I tend to be rather stubborn. I blame Madison Avenue for my attitude. They insist on touting everything as the whitest, the brightest, the strongest, the most dependable—so I'm careful not to overuse such adjectives myself lest they lose their meanings. But, how can I not use superlatives when it comes to Nora Roberts? She is simply the most remarkable, most prolific writer around. Her body of work boggles the mind. Over one hundred fifty novels to her credit, and she shows no signs of slowing down.

It's a fact. Nora is a publishing dynamo. It's impossible for me to compile a list of her accomplishments because she's adding to them even as I write. An appearance on the *New York Times* bestseller list is a proud achievement for any writer—Nora has had over eighty of them. Getting a book published in another language is praiseworthy—Nora has been translated into twenty-five languages. Selling a million books is a major milestone—Nora has sold more than two hundred million. And by this time next year, all of these numbers will have grown, no doubt, to astounding new heights.

I first met Nora after my second book had been published and I was still a novice to the business. She did a very kind thing for me then, and I'll always be in her debt for it. We were at a writers' conference and I'd been asked to speak at one of the luncheons. I was terrified. After all, I was a writer, not a public speaker. Nevertheless, the organizers of the event had the notion that I should be able to entertain a crowd for twenty minutes. I ran into Nora on my way into the hall. As she greeted me, she evidently could see the abject terror in my eyes because she pulled me aside and said, "Don't worry. This is going to be a piece of cake. I'll be sitting at the front table. If you get nervous, just look at me." I don't know how my legs managed it, but they stayed strong enough to get me to the podium. I looked out at the sea of faces in front of me and searched for Nora's. There she was, as promised, straight ahead at the first table, and she had the biggest grin on her face. I delivered my speech, and each time I would glance at Nora, the grin was firmly plastered. For twenty minutes, it never drooped, never faltered, never moved. As long as I was talking, it was there. It saved me. Since that time I've given dozens of speeches, and now and then I still get a twinge of nerves, but when that happens, I think of Nora and the perpetual grin. The image makes me laugh, and the butterflies disappear.

In the last few years, it's been thrilling to watch Nora's career skyrocket, but it hasn't been a surprise. She's talented and creative . . . that's a given . . . but she's also a crackerjack marketer, a skilled businesswoman, and one of the hardest-working authors in the business. The single quality that I admire most, however, is the attention she pays to the people who buy her books. Her readers are very important to her, and she spends a good part of the year traveling around the country meeting them and signing books. Periodically she hosts events at the bookstore she and her husband, Bruce, own in Boonsboro, Maryland. Last year I was lucky enough to be invited to join her.

As I made the drive from Baltimore, I could definitely see why Nora, despite the fact that she could live anywhere in the world, has chosen to stay put. I'm sure it's part of what keeps her so grounded. The rolling mountains are beautiful, and the Boonsboro area is charming. I drove into town about an hour before the book signing was to begin. The quiet main street looked empty. I began to scan the historic buildings for a sign that read TURN THE PAGE BOOKSTORE, but it didn't take long to discover that a sign wasn't necessary. In the middle of the next block, I could see a crowd of people. They had formed a line that began on the front porch of the storefront, stretched down the steps, along the sidewalk, and then wound around the corner. It was a phenomenal turnout, but I later learned it wasn't an unusual one. As people filed through the store to get their books signed, I heard over and over again how loyal Nora's readers are. Some of them had driven long distances to be there, even from as far away as Canada.

I happened to be a witness to another testimonial to her popularity just a couple of months ago. I was in line to pay at a bookstore when a woman, looking harried, as though she'd just left her office to run an emergency errand, rushed to the counter and asked the clerk, "Is it here yet?" To which the clerk replied, "No, not yet. If it doesn't get here today, it will be in tomorrow." The woman looked immensely disappointed, thanked the clerk, and rushed out of the store. I was curious. As I was paying, I asked the clerk what the woman was so anxious to get. She said, "Oh, she's a Nora Roberts fan. We have lots of them. They're here as soon as her next book comes through the doors." As an author, I can't imagine any higher praise.

Nora has earned such loyalty. Her stories are funny and engaging, intelligent and heartwarming. Whether you pick up a book about the MacGregors or the Stanislaski sisters, you can be sure you're going to meet people who will linger in your memory for a long time. As you will see in

Nora at a book signing with Julie Garwood and Pat Gaffney

the pages that follow, her name printed in bold letters across a book cover means a great adventure awaits within. To those who have watched Nora's career and seen her dedication, it's no wonder that she has earned the devotion of her fans and the admiration of her colleagues.

I recall, a few weeks back, picking up my copy of the *New York Times Book Review*. I don't know if other authors do this, but I thumb to the bestseller page first because I've discovered that it's a good barometer of what's going on in the book world. Poised at the top of the list for that week was a novel by Nora Roberts. Since she's my friend, I smiled and thought, *Way to go, Nora*. And then I glanced at the number two slot. I blinked. There was Nora again. Now I thought, *That's terrific. One* and *two*. I scanned down the other names on the list but came to a screeching halt when Nora Roberts's name appeared for a third time. This time I thought, *Wow. That has to be a record*. But, on the other hand, I have the feeling that one of these days I'll be thinking, *Absolutely incredible*, to another great achievement. Somehow, I don't think Nora has finished amazing us yet.

—JULIE GARWOOD

introduction

WHEN I WAS asked if I'd authorize publication of *The Official Nora Roberts Companion*, I was delighted. Probably the only thing that would have delighted me more was if said companion was—with apologies to both our spouses—say, David Duchovny during a long weekend in Aruba.

But since that was not to be, this is nearly as exciting for me.

It's almost as much of a shock as a thrill to see my professional life compiled, to date, in one volume. A shock because these twenty-some years have gone very quickly, and a thrill because I've had such a wonderful time during them. From that first snowy afternoon in 1979 to the rainy one in 2001 as I write this, I've been blessed to be able to do something I love, to go places I never expected to see, to meet people and forge friendships that have enriched my life more than I can say.

No one makes the trip alone, and I've been incredibly lucky in my travel companions. I'm grateful to the publishing professionals who've worked so hard on my behalf, and who've been springboards, wailing walls, pals, and teachers. My agent, Amy Berkower, who's been my partner, my friend, and my advocate from the beginning, is the most solid of foundations. To Amy, Al Zuckerman, Jodi Reamer, and all the brilliant minds at Writers House, you've made every step of the journey easier, smoother, and special.

Guess who? Kayla wasn't the only beautiful baby girl in the family.

My thanks to Isabel Swift, my editor of nearly two decades at Silhouette, for showing me early on that the creative relationship can also be a warm, funny, and familial one. I owe a tremendous debt to everyone at Harlequin/Silhouette for taking a chance on a very green writer, and making her feel at home.

I owe no less to the marvelous team at Putnam Berkley, headed by the incomparable Phyllis Grann when I came on board. My thanks to her for giving me yet another family, and the priceless gift of Leslie Gelbman as my editor. With Leslie I've been able to try a few new routes, including that leap into the mid-twenty-first century as J. D. Robb.

So much goes into the publication of a book, beyond the book itself. I'm grateful to the sales force, marketing, publicity—even Liz Perl at Berkley who drags me away from home and onto the book-tour circuit every year.

And a very special thanks to Kathy Onorato of Creative Promotions for handling with such cheer and efficiency the details that would make me insane.

I'm forever indebted to the bookseller, my bridge to the reader, for the support, the enthusiasm, the sheer volume of labor it takes to put a book into a reader's hand. I'm sorry I haven't managed to visit every store in every city in every state to thank you personally. Though Liz may manage it yet.

My sons were three and six when I started writing. They grew up with it—they had no choice. Writing allowed me to stay at home with my kids and make a living, a luxury few people manage. I thank my sons, Dan and Jason, for learning the vital rule of a writing household: Don't bother me unless it's blood or fire. And, as they grew more responsible, arterial blood and active fire.

Writers, at least this writer, can be moody, self-absorbed, absentminded, and inexplicably cranky. I warned my husband of these traits before we married, but he didn't run away. Thanks, Bruce.

My parents gave me another foundation—an appreciation for relationships and family and all the chaos that goes with it. My four brothers gave me an understanding of men, whether I wanted it or not! My work would certainly have taken a different tone without them.

Friendships made through the business have been invaluable. I'm not sure what I would have done without the hearts and ears and humor of other writers. They are my jewels. Adding particular glitter to my life are Ruth Langan, Marianne Willman, Patricia Gaffney, and Mary Kay McComas. I love you guys for every laugh, every smart-ass comment, every eye roll behind my back, and for giving me the pure pleasure of the friendship of women.

Last, but certainly far from least, I come to the reader. Without you, I'm talking to myself. While that's not necessarily a bad thing, it's a lot more satisfying to know someone's out there listening. From my first fan letter from the thirteen-year-old girl who hid a copy of *Irish Thoroughbred* under her mattress so her mother wouldn't know she was reading it, to the woman in Astoria, New York, obsessed with black-haired virgins, to the girl from Nairobi who wanted me to find her a pair of red silk pants and a nice Muslim boy, it's been an adventure.

I've enjoyed, laughed over, puzzled over, fumed over, treasured, and wept over countless letters and e-mail posts. It's an amazing thing, this intimate connection made between writer and reader. Certainly not every book discussed in this volume, or yet to be written by me, will connect favorably with every reader. But *we* connect, and that's the beauty of storytelling.

I can only hope that those of you who've read my work have enjoyed the experience half as much as I enjoyed the experience of telling the tale. And that you get some portion of the pleasure out of *The Official Nora Roberts Companion* that I have.

It's not David Duchovny, but there's enough on these pages for you to pick your own fantasy.

—NORA ROBERTS

True to the magician's oath, Roberts reveals no secrets, but the illusion works—in a compelling and detail-rich first hardcover. Good escape reading.

—*Kirkus Reviews* on
HONEST ILLUSIONS

up close

PART ONE

nora—and personal

true-life romance:

Nora Roberts Revels in the Pleasures of Success

by Nanci Hellmich
***USA Today*, March 7, 2000**

BESTSELLING ROMANTIC SUSPENSE writer Nora Roberts, 49, is on a whirlwind shopping spree at The Sky's the Limit boutique in this quaint town. She admires some garnet-and-silver earrings, tries them on and adds them to a growing pile that includes other earrings, pendants, silver chains and freshwater pearls. She spends $429.71 in fifteen minutes.

Her husband once told her that she didn't need any more earrings. Her response: "You can't have too many earrings. They are like orgasms. You can never have too many."

During a day of lunching, shopping and visiting at home, Roberts is always entertaining, often clever and sometimes shocking. The same can be said about her books.

Roberts has published 134 novels and has more than 106 million books in print. She was the fifth bestselling author of 1999 on *USA Today*'s year-end Bestselling Books list. Her romances, including *Homeport* and *The Reef*, dominated the genre on the list.

Her books weave together romance and mystery. The latest, *Carolina Moon* (G. P. Putnam) out this week, is the story of a woman who returns to her South Carolina hometown to try to discover who murdered a childhood friend. While there, she falls in love with a wealthy landowner. *Publishers Weekly* calls it "romantic drama at its best."

Roberts is prolific, sometimes churning out six or more books a year. Besides romantic suspense, she writes futuristic novels about police work under the pen name J. D. Robb.

A redhead with green eyes, Roberts doesn't mince words or dodge challenging questions. She talks forthrightly about everything from the sex scenes in her books to her bitter feelings toward romance writer Janet Dailey, who plagiarized some of her work.

> Shoes are one of the things that separate us from the animals.

Her descriptions of sex are less graphic than the scenes in many romance novels, but they are erotic. She has no problem writing them. "Why should I? Sex is fun. I don't have to practice all these things. I know that Tab A fits into Tab B. Anyway, it's more about emotion than where his hands are."

Roberts is proud of her success and the genre that has made her rich and famous. "At the core, I'm a romance writer," she says in her raspy smoker's voice. "I don't always write straight romance or what a lot of readers, especially those who don't read romance, consider romance. I don't write naked pirate books. There's nothing wrong with a naked pirate, but that's only one avenue. I write relationship books."

Her novels are so popular because they stir the emotions of readers, especially women, and let them celebrate falling in love again, she says. "The romance novel at its core celebrates that rush of emotions you have when you are falling in love, and it's a lovely thing to relive those feelings through a book."

"I want to die at age 120 at my keyboard after having great sex..."

Roberts doesn't look or live like the millionaire she is. She resides in the same unpretentious home she has lived in for twenty-seven years. It's a secluded home near Keedysville, MD, not far from Shepherdstown.

There's a studio office for Roberts on the third floor, an indoor pool on the ground level, a large closet filled with designer clothes and shoes and built-in bookshelves everywhere.

Her home has been added to several times by second husband, Bruce Wilder, forty-eight, a carpenter she met when he came to build bookshelves and remodel a closet in her bedroom about seventeen years ago. The two own a bookstore. "I kept finding him more work to do," she says. "Finally, it was just easier to keep him. He's completely redone the house."

Her seven-figure income allows her to travel abroad, own a Land Rover and a BMW sports car, wear Armani suits and Bruno Magli shoes, and shop whenever she wants. She had no idea that she would ever earn what she pays in taxes now.

Roberts grew up in Silver Spring, MD, just north of Washington, D.C., and about sixty miles from Keedysville. She was the youngest of five children of a TV lighting technician and a homemaker/businesswoman.

Her family members were great readers, and there were books all over the house. She remembers her head always being filled with stories.

She married her high school boyfriend after graduation. They had two boys, Daniel and Jason, now grown. They divorced in the early 1980s.

Early in the marriage, Roberts started reading Harlequin romances in the afternoon while her young sons slept.

Then in February 1979, a blizzard dumped three feet of snow, and Roberts was stuck inside with her boys, then two and five. "I didn't have a four-wheel drive, didn't have enough chocolate. I was just stuck in the house, playing Candy Land incessantly. I thought, 'I have got to do something.'"

She decided to take one of those stories out of her head and write it down. That first book, *Melodies of Love*, was horrible, she says. "There aren't words to describe how bad that book was. But it really taught me that I could do it.

"Editors rejected it soundly, for which I will always be grateful." The book is still tucked away in some "deep, dark drawer."

But Roberts had found her calling. "I was hooked instantly. I loved the process. I opened the dam, and I had all these stories in my head. I wanted desperately to be published."

Roberts continued writing in steno notebooks wherever she went—at her sons' T-ball practices, in the pediatrician's office, in the dentist's office, when the kids slept. She wrote at least six more books before she had the novel *Irish Thoroughbred* published in 1981.

Now she works on a home computer or on a laptop when she's on the road. She pounds out a first draft quickly, then revises several times, "fixing and fiddling" and adding "more description, texture, characterization," she says. In all, she does three or four revisions.

Roberts writes six to eight hours most days, then quits to fix dinner.

She credits her years in Catholic school with giving her self-discipline. "Who teaches guilt and discipline more brilliantly than a nun? I look back, and I would not be where I am without the nuns instilling this work ethic in me. Sister Mary Responsibility is always in the back of my mind."

Roberts has a reputation among editors and fellow romance writers as a great shopper. She shops whenever she has time—when she's in New York meeting with her publisher or on the road on a book tour. "You either shop or you buy. I'm a buyer. All the merchants love me. I like to shop for anything. I like clothes. I like jewelry. I like shoes. I like stuff. I like pretty things to sit around the house that are totally useless."

Most of all, she loves shoes. "Shoes are one of the things that separate us from the animals. It proves that we are a higher being. Otherwise, we could be a golden retriever. They don't wear shoes or accessorize."

Readers often want to know whether her love life is as exciting as that of her book heroines. She says that when she first met and fell in love with Wilder, she realized "This is just like one of my books. It does happen. It can happen. When you are first seeing each other, hormones are driving you."

Over time, she says, love evolves. "You go through phases in a marriage, and you should. If you had to live your whole life in that first rush of love and passion, you'd kill yourself. The relationship develops."

She says she never plans to retire. "Retire from what? I want to die at age 120 at my keyboard after having great sex. Wouldn't that be great?"

sound bites from nora on how to learn to write

N

NORA ROBERTS IS, simply by example, one of the best writing teachers in the field of romance. But Nora does more than teach by example. She is also a wonderful speaker, and very generous in sharing her time and wisdom with writers at every level of experience. She's been a regular at the Romance Writers of America conferences since the organization's earliest days, and she's very open in sharing her methods and manner of writing. Her advice during the course of her talks at these conventions is always concise, well thought out, and useful. Here are some of Nora's words of wisdom for writers:

A writer must understand, appreciate, and enjoy whatever genre he or she is trying to write in. It's a mistake, a really big mistake, to believe that you can write what you wouldn't read for pleasure.

I never know where I'm going when I start a book. I know if I'm writing a romance, then love will conquer all. If I'm writing a suspense book, then good will overcome evil. But that's all I know. Period. Somehow, I'll find a way to get there. My characters will carry me to the end of the book. But I never know how it will all turn out when I start a book. I start with my characters, and a canvas, a setting. Then I get to work.

Did You Know . . .

Despite having written over 150 books, Nora still worries every time she sits down to write a new book that perhaps the words won't come. She says that the fear is a chief motivating factor driving the furious pace with which she creates her prose. The only way she can be sure she'll still find inspiration is to actually write the next novel.

Whatever works for a person is the way they should write—if it takes standing on a ball and juggling for twenty minutes to get you started on writing, then fine. That's what you do.

The most important thing in writing is to have written. I can always fix a bad page. I can't fix a blank one.

A writer never finds the time to write. A writer makes it. If you don't have the drive, the discipline, and the desire, then you can have all the talent in the world, and you aren't going to finish a book. All the talent in the world isn't going to do you any good.

I've never hired a researcher. I do all my own research for a variety of creative and personal reasons. I get ideas for plots out of research that

I don't think a researcher would, because I don't think what I learn would strike the researcher the way it strikes me.

My first drafts are very clean—but very clean bones—they're like a skeleton. For the first draft, I write fairly quickly. I want to get through the story. I don't edit. I know that there are mistakes there. I know I could do something better. There's no texture. There's no zing. But I don't care. I need to get through the story. I need to see if it has an end, if it flows from beginning to end. Then I go back to page one, chapter one, and I start filling out things, fixing them, seeing where I went right, where I went wrong, adding more color, jazzing it up. I know my characters better in the second draft. I understand the point of the story. When I've gone through the whole thing, I go back to page one, chapter one again and I do a polish of the language. I make sure it flows, make sure I haven't made any mistakes, or that I haven't done anything that I could do better another way. Then, hopefully, I instinctively know if I'm done, or if there's anything I should fiddle with a little more. Then it's off to my editor, who tells me if I can do a better job or not.

The middles of my books are often the toughest for me to write. If the pacing flags, I deal with the problem by looking around at all my characters and figuring out which one I can kill.

I work on one book at a time. I need to put all my time, my energy, my affection, and my effort into this story and these people. That's just how I am.

I don't think it matters how long it takes to write a book, as long as it's the best work that I can write at that point in my life.

I can't work with a critique group. I'd rip their throats out. But that's just me. Other writers work with them very successfully. I just don't play well with others when I'm writing.

A corner of Nora's office, with framed book covers on the walls, including the cover she posed for

The shelves in Nora's office where she keeps her RITA statues

When not looking at the gorgeous view, Nora finds inspiration from another source—and it's obvious that The Force is with her!

Nora's desk and computer, and the view she looks out to while she writes

When I'm writing, I don't really worry about readers. It's none of their business what I'm doing. I worry about me and the characters. If I worried about the readers looking over my shoulder, I'd never get anything done. You can't please everyone. This happens to me all the time—I get a postcard from a reader, who'll say, "I hated the book, because of XYZ. Why did you do that?" Then I'll get another postcard from a reader, saying, "I loved the book because of XYZ." Same XYZ for both readers, but it worked for one reader and put another one off. Which reader are you going to believe? The only person you can be sure of pleasing is yourself. The only thing a writer can do is write the best book possible. You can't write, trying to please the readers. They're many, and fickle, and you'll never please them all.

Did You Know . . .

Nora Roberts is an active supporter of foundations promoting literacy, and particularly of the Laubach Literacy International. As she puts it, "Without readers, writers don't have a job."

I don't believe in inspiration. I was educated by nuns. Sister Mary Responsibility kicks the butt out of any artistic muse that mankind ever invented. I write because they pay me and I said I would. Every morning I get up and work out if I'm being good, because I know I'm going to be sitting down for six or eight or however many hours I'm going to write that day. Then I sit down, turn on my computer, and write. It's my job.

To give the reader a sense of place, I imagine it. I research a place; I may even visit it. But then I imagine it: the shadows, the light, the smells, the mood. And I put my characters in the place, and I try to figure out why they are there, why they have that job, what their motivations are. I research the details like flora and fauna. Then it's back to the writing. I just try to make the reader feel what I imagine.

nora roberts: a celebration of emotions

by Judy Quinn
***Publishers Weekly*, February 23, 1998**

THE HOME OF Nora Roberts, hidden among the hills in the rural, western Maryland town of Keedysville, is not the Xanadu-like estate one might expect to be the abode of a bestselling romance author who by the end of 1998 will have written 126 novels, with over 42 million copies in print. It is in fact the same modest country ranch to which Roberts came as a seventeen-year-old bride over thirty years ago.

There have been some improvements, notably a BMW and a Land Rover now parked in the driveway and a fantasy closet full of designer clothes and shoes. But this is the same house in which Roberts, a twenty-eight-year-old stir-crazy housewife stuck indoors with two small sons during a snowstorm in 1979, made her first stab at writing romance fiction. And Roberts isn't going anywhere. "When I came here," she says, "I realized I was home. Sometimes you just recognize it."

Loyalty to her roots is also evident in the way Roberts manages her house of fiction. Although she broke out into hardcover bestsellerdom in 1996 with her fourth hardcover for Putnam, *Montana Sky*, Roberts, unlike some in her genre, continues to write original paperback romances. "I am a popular fiction writer and proud of it," she says. "And I really believe in the category romances. I was there with two young kids, and the shorter format saved my sanity. I remember exactly what it felt like to want to read and not have time to read 200,000 words."

Today, Roberts has no problem with words. She's probably the fastest writer in the business, with an amazingly prolific output that pretty much makes her the Joyce Carol Oates of the romance.

"I just have a fast pace; it's like having green eyes," Roberts says. A petite, auburn-tressed woman with a strong-willed, practical manner, she seems to have always had boundless energy—and a free spirit. The youngest child of five, whose parents ran a lighting company in Silver Spring, MD, Roberts says her mother was ready to lock her into her room rather than let her get married as a teenager. But she was determined. After becoming a Keedysville housewife (she has since divorced and remarried), Roberts tackled leisure-time arts and crafts with extraordinary zeal. "I made jam, did the whole earth mother bit. I could have needlepointed a car."

> I write what I want to know.

But in an awakening that could fit within the pages of Betty Friedan's *The Feminine Mystique*, Roberts soon turned to fiction. "Subconsciously, I was looking for an outlet for creativity. When I started writing, it was like, 'This is it. Why didn't I realize it before?'"

Roberts also says that her work ethic is due to an inherent discipline that "comes from being raised Catholic—if you're not working, there's the near occasion of sin and all that." Indeed, no nun could find fault with Roberts's daily regimen: a morning swim and workout (in the small pool/gym area that used to be the basement of her home) followed by a basically nonstop 9 A.M.–5 P.M. writing stint.

the rise of silhouette

Roberts entered the field at an opportune time. Although it took her a year and a half to break into publishing, she did it with few connections or contacts. A casual acquaintance who worked as a ghostwriter in New York knew she was writing romances and tipped her off to the formation of Silhouette in 1980, an S&S imprint meant to be an American counterpart of Canadian-based Harlequin, which at that time tended to buy only British writers and had already rejected Roberts's early submissions. Roberts quickly sent some manuscripts, unsolicited, to Silhouette, "back when you could do that," and Nancy Jackson, then an acquiring editor for the house, eventually picked *The Irish Thoroughbred* from the slush pile. The manuscript, a horsebreeding tale set in Roberts's own backyard in Maryland, would become her first published romance in 1981. That, in 1984, Silhouette merged with Harlequin "has been a final irony," says Roberts. "I thought, 'Well, now they're writing the check after all.'"

For help with her first contracts, Roberts followed a friend's recommendation and called Amy Berkower, a new agent at Writers House who was looking for clients. Roberts recalls hiring Berkower "over the phone. I guess that wasn't too professional."

But it worked. Berkower remains Roberts's agent today. It was Berkower who assessed when it was time to test the waters with a trade house—Bantam—in 1987. And when that house didn't necessarily publish to Roberts's preferred pace, Berkower facilitated the move to Putnam in 1992. And although Roberts, an avid Mary Stewart fan, immediately wanted to write romantic thrillers, her agent advised her to wait. "Amy said, 'Build a foundation, just keep at the categories and put that away for a while,'" recalls

Roberts. "She was right. When the time came, and I had developed a following, it was just like she said."

Berkower also managed to persuade Roberts to don the J. D. Robb pseudonym for a Berkley mass-market series. Set in the year 2058 and featuring police lieutenant Eve Dallas, newly married to roguish and mysterious high-tech billionaire Roarke, the series was a Putnam response to handling the Roberts output. Although Roberts had already understood the practicality of changing a name (her birth name is actually Robertson), she was reluctant in the case of the Robb books. "I thought it would be a dilution of my readership. But Amy knows me and said, 'Look, it's like having Coke and Caffeine Free Coke.'" Roberts came away convinced of the efficacy of such brand proliferation. The initials J. D. denote her two sons, Jason and Daniel, both now in their twenties, while the surname has a distinct marketing advantage: Robb books almost always appear right next to Roberts books on bookstore shelves.

In all her writing, Roberts is known for her wry humor and the use of different narrators, two devices that were once rarities in a genre that, says Roberts, "was usually about a terrified eighteen-year-old young virgin and all from her point of view." Remarried eighteen years ago to Bruce Wilder, a carpenter who first came into her life when he was hired to oversee her house-expansion project and now owns and operates the local Turn the Page Bookstore Café, Roberts says she could hardly relate to that.

"I never did 'the virgin,'" she says. "My heroine may have problems, she may be vulnerable, but she has to be strong, she has to be intelligent. She has to be independent and so does he, or I'm not interested in telling their stories."

Roberts says she enjoys the short format of category romances, which she calls "charcoal sketches," as much as she does the more fully fleshed-out plots of her hardcovers. Many of her romance series grew out of creating intertwining families and friends whose relationships and subsequent generations expanded beyond the confines of a single book. And along with other writers in the genre, Roberts keeps pushing the envelope of the romance form, writing about a hero with supernatural powers (*Night Shadows*, for Silhouette in 1991) and about witches (the ongoing Donovan

Legacy series for Silhouette). Roberts credits her editors—Silhouette's Isabel Swift, who has worked with Roberts since 1983, and Putnam VP Leslie Gelbman—for allowing her to take such leaps.

But Gelbman did initially worry that her author often relies on surfing the Internet for background research. *Montana Sky*, for example, was crafted without traveling to the state in which it is set, in part because Roberts has an aversion to flying. "I don't believe in the journalistic style," she says. "I don't have time to pop out and go there.

"I know they say, 'Write what you know,'" Roberts continues. "But I write what I want to know." Her characters are as fanciful as her settings. Although *Homeport* heroine Miranda Jones has a determined air as well as "hair the color of a Tonka toy fire engine," Roberts says the resemblance stops there. "She's so much smarter than I. She's got a Ph.D. and all of that. Plus *she's* tall."

Lately, Roberts's on-line research has "become totally addictive," she says, and takes up several hours of her daily regimen. From her gabled top-floor windowed writing room, one of her husband's many renovation projects, Roberts now maintains various subject folders and chat rooms on America Online and other sites. One extremely vocal group of fans have their own "Noraholics" website and came to a signing Roberts held at her husband's bookstore (which has its own website and does a healthy on-line and mail business in orders for Roberts's backlist). "It was wonderful to see how my books helped bring about relationships among these women," she says. And in a Valentine's Day promotion this year, Roberts began a tale on America Online that was completed by readers. It's a project she hopes will inspire some budding writers. "I would have loved to have had that help to get me started," she says.

the plagiarism affair

But Roberts still sees red over the inadvertent "help" she gave Janet Dailey, who admitted in 1997 that her books, *Aspen Gold*, *Tangled Vines*, *Notorious*, and a forthcoming novel now pulled from publication, contained passages from Roberts's works. The shock that Dailey, a prolific romance writer and a longtime acquaintance of Roberts, could pirate her work even caused Roberts to stop writing for a while. "It's like mind rape. To think how far along it's been going . . . it's like being stalked," she says.

As of press time, Roberts was in the pretrial discovery phase of the lawsuit she has filed against Dailey. In lieu of damages, Roberts is asking Dailey to make a donation to the Literacy Volunteers of America, a cause dear to the Romance Writers of America, an organization of which Roberts is a charter member and its first Hall of Fame inductee. Roberts is also requesting that Dailey reveal the full extent of the plagiarism so that all the tainted books can be pulled from the shelves and so that Roberts doesn't have to read through Dailey's entire body of work. "We would like to know the scope of the copying without me having to read until my eyes bleed," says Roberts. The suit estimates that Dailey has lifted from at least thirteen of Roberts's novels. [Editor's note: Since the time of this article, the lawsuit against Janet Dailey has been settled with certain Dailey books having been vetted and Nora donating the settlement amount received from Dailey to Literacy Volunteers of America.]

> "I am a popular writer and proud of it."

While Roberts admits the media attention around the plagiarism has probably increased her name recognition ("I'm sure some people went into stores and said, 'Oh, that's her,' and picked up a book"), she says it also forced her to defend the genre against reporters who implied that all romance writing is interchangeable. "They have no business to sneer," she says. "I don't think it would have happened in any other genre. It was 'It's romance, let's take a shot. Let's talk about heaving bosoms.' Mysteries, for example, have their formulas too."

For Roberts, the romance formula leads to a "celebration of emotions," which she says readers desperately crave. She sees the experience as providing a fix of "that wonderful rush of feeling when you first fall in love." Roberts firmly believes that providing that feeling in a popular genre is an important service. “I get e-mail all the time from people who say, ‘I liked this thriller, but why couldn’t they have put in a love story, too?’” she says. “That’s why it’s always at the core of my work.”

Thanks to her “magic drawer” of stockpiled romance manuscripts, Roberts is working typically a year ahead. And Roberts has no intention of reducing her output in order to focus on her hardcovers. “That would be only one book a year,” she says. “Whatever would I do?”

"Nora Roberts's PRIVATE SCANDALS is right on target. She turns the world of television inside-out, and then outside-in, all the while creating a plot of nailbiting suspense. Oprah, Phil and Sally will need a few days to recover after this!"

—Rex Reed on
PRIVATE SCANDALS

the

PART TWO

career

a publisher's journey

An Interview with Leslie Gelbman

LESLIE GELBMAN IS a powerful figure in publishing, with an unerring eye for beautiful, commercial writing. She's known in the business as a "dream editor"—she has an innate feeling for what makes a good book great, a strong and intuitive sense of how to package a book so it will find the right audience, and she is one of the best in the business at the crazed juggling act of scheduling a full slate of books so that each book performs to the best of its ability. These skills serve her well as the publisher of Berkley. Leslie's been Nora Roberts's editor since Nora came to

Putnam Berkley, and she has been instrumental in charting Nora's single-title publishing program, as Nora's gone from being an author with a good category track record to become one of the bestselling writers in the world. Nora's talent found the perfect match in Leslie's ability to showcase a writer. Leslie talked about her years working with Nora, and here's what she had to say:

DENISE LITTLE: *Why do you think Nora Roberts's books speak to so many people?*

LESLIE GELBMAN: Nora is a natural storyteller—I'm convinced that even if that now-famous snowstorm hadn't occurred and she hadn't been stuck in her house and desperate for a distraction, somehow or other she would still have found herself writing and telling stories. Nora doesn't have to think about how to tell a story—she just does it. This totally organic approach is reflected in her writing style and her characters, both of which are enormously appealing to readers. Her writing is clear and direct, and her characters have a warmth and vitality that's irresistible. Readers feel as if they really *know* Nora's characters, and through them Nora herself. All this stems from her naturalness as a writer—and a person. Nora is one of the warmest and most generous people I know, and her generosity of spirit is in every page she writes. It's no wonder so many people are attracted to her novels.

DENISE LITTLE: *What are Nora's greatest strengths as a writer?*

LESLIE GELBMAN: A reviewer once called Nora a "word artist" and I think this describes perfectly what Nora does best. Nora is able to paint with words, and the images she evokes are so powerful and vivid you actually feel as if you can "see" what Nora is "seeing." More than any other writer Nora is able to evoke this effect in her writing, but she does this without sacrificing any of the pace, action, or characterizations.

Combine this painterly ability with her natural storytelling gifts and you have an amazing talent—Nora Roberts.

Beyond the sheer writing talent, however, is perhaps Nora's greatest strength—her imagination. She has a fertile, limitless imagination that's always exploring new directions, settings, and characters. Nora never thinks, "I can't do that" in her writing—rather it's "How do I make this work?" Her ability to jump over boundaries has been a hallmark of her writing, and the secret weapon in her arsenal.

DENISE LITTLE: *What are some of the high points you've experienced working as Nora Roberts's editor?*

LESLIE GELBMAN: Anyone who's ever worked with Nora knows this is true: Nora is an absolute joy to work with. As an editor, I can't ask for a more professional and enthusiastic author than Nora—every book is equally important to her, and she crafts every word with a lot of love, care, and attention. I've always felt that she and I have always worked together toward the same goal—to publish the best book possible, and to do everything in our power to make it a success. There have been many highlights in our professional relationship—from RITA Awards and nominations to the first time she hit #1 on the *New York Times* list to having *Carolina Moon* garner the #1 spot on the *New York Times* paperback bestseller list for five consecutive weeks—but nothing can surpass the friendship we've developed along the way. It's been wonderful to see success come to such a terrific person, and it's personally as well as professionally gratifying to be a part of helping her achieve that success.

Did You Know . . .

Nora writes every day, usually straight through for six to eight hours, often fueled only by a chocolate and cola break at lunchtime.

DENISE LITTLE: *When a Nora Roberts book comes out, it's an event. You're shipping huge numbers of books, and fans are waiting desperately. How do you prepare for it?*

LESLIE GELBMAN: Just the fact that there is a "new Nora" is an event unto itself. Since we publish many books a year by Nora, in all formats, the publication preparation is ongoing—each novel drives the next. We definitely like to build anticipation for a new release, especially the hardcovers, which is when Nora usually tours. Our marketing and advertising campaigns are multimedia events—in a combination that hits both her loyal fans and new readers. We are constantly challenging ourselves to come up with new and creative packages—many of which have set trends in the industry—that distinguish Nora in such an overwhelmingly crowded marketplace.

DENISE LITTLE: *Nora's a bit more prolific than most writers. How do you adapt to that?*

LESLIE GELBMAN: Nora is indeed prolific, and I've learned to arrange my editing schedule well in advance if I know a manuscript is on the way. I like to read it as soon as I get it, and to give Nora feedback quickly so that she can work on revisions if needed. That way we can put it to rest fairly soon so that I'm not behind on the reading when the next manuscript arrives.

Did You Know . . .

Nora Roberts doesn't believe in writer's block. As she puts it, "Writing is a job. You do your job. People in other professions don't get blocks. Have you ever heard of plumber's block?"

DENISE LITTLE: *Can you talk about the evolution of the J. D. Robb name and the Eve Dallas books? These were a real departure from Nora's mainstream novels. How did you prepare for it as a publisher?*

LESLIE GELBMAN: Well, the J. D. Robb books came about because Nora was eager to write more books but we weren't sure yet of how many Nora Roberts books the marketplace could support. So when her agent suggested she use a pseudonym to write something different from what she was already writing, I agreed. Thus Eve Dallas and Roarke were born. I asked Nora to come up with a name that began with the letter *R* and was close alphabetically to Roberts so the books would be shelved together. Nora easily complied: the *J* and *D* are the initials of her sons' names, and *Robb* seemed to fit. It was entirely Nora's idea to set the novels in the near future, which turned out to be a brilliant stroke because the imaginary setting freed Nora from a lot of conventions and allowed her to create a different universe and to play with the series. Nora has never written another series about the same characters for this number of books, and it has really allowed her to explore their psyches and their relationship in unprecedented depth. Since the books were so different and she was writing them under a pen name we never thought that the audience for them would be so vast, but the series quickly took off, and with each book published the demand for them grew more and more. We've always published them closely together, and when possible included excerpts for future books in the back of the old books, which has really helped fans know when to expect a new J. D. Robb. The first time we didn't include an excerpt I can't tell you the number of panicked phone calls we got from fans fearing that the series was ending!

DENISE LITTLE: *Did the extent of the Eve Dallas books' eventual success surprise you?*

LESLIE GELBMAN: The plan was always to go slow, let the books find their audience and build. And that's just what I did. None of us knew what to expect because not only are these books very different from anything else Nora does, they're very different from anything else in the marketplace. But Nora's always been a trailblazer, and it was no surprise that the books were so original. What has been surprising was the kind of cult following they developed—the readers who love the "In Death" series really *love* it, and are totally addicted to them. I think it even surprised Nora how much she enjoyed writing the series and staying with these characters. I know she has a special place in her heart now for Eve and Roarke, as do I and thousands of her fans.

A Quick Chat With . . .

NORMAN LIDOFSKY,

President and Director of Paperback Sales,
Penguin Group (USA) Inc.

Q: ***Did you have any idea of the kind of success Nora would achieve with Putnam Berkley?***

A: We were all aware of the tremendous success that Nora had at Harlequin/Silhouette and at Bantam when Nora first became a Putnam Berkley author, but there was still a lot of room for potential growth, and I was convinced she was nowhere near her peak yet. And it wasn't an overnight success story—every book became a platform for solid growth, and we never stopped pushing or supporting Nora until her sales exploded and she shot off like a rocket. And even though Nora is in the stratosphere now, I still think her sales haven't reached their peak yet!

Q: ***At what point did you know that Nora would become one of the biggest authors out there, and was there a particular book that stood out?***

A: Originally when we first started working with Nora, she was going to write a book a year for Putnam and we would do the paperback a year later, which is the publishing schedule for most bestselling authors. But Nora isn't like other authors—she could and wanted to write a lot more than a book a year, and, being used to her category romance output, her fans wanted books more quickly. So Nora started writing paperback original romances for us as well as her hard/soft books. Nora was still new on the hardcover scene, but was an established bestseller in paper so we could be really aggressive in our publishing plan in a way that the hardcover sales department couldn't be. Not surprisingly, our original trilogies were all huge bestsellers, and it took the hardcovers six books to catch up with the paperbacks. But absolutely, the paperbacks fueled the growth on the hardcovers, and when Nora's sales finally got in sync on both the paperback and hardcover, that's when her sales really skyrocketed. On the paperback side, her Chesapeake Bay series with the Quinn brothers is the trilogy I remember as selling particularly well—she hit #1 on the *New York Times* list for the first time with *Sea Swept.*

Q: ***What kind of challenges have you faced in getting Nora to the next level?***

A: We never rest on our laurels, so we're always trying to get Nora to the next level—wherever that may be! Right now, the biggest challenge is that there's a lot of Nora books on the market now, between all the different reissues from Harlequin/Silhouette and Bantam—practically a reissue a month. We have to make certain that everyone—from her fans to the bookstores—knows that these reissues are not new books, and that Putnam Berkley is the only publisher publishing new Nora books. Beyond that, our next challenge is building the J. D. Robb name to the level of a Nora Roberts—we're not quite there yet, but we're well on our way.

> "When readers plunk down their money for one of Nora Roberts's novels, they're almost guaranteed to get a well-written romantic suspense story. THE REEF is another good read . . . Roberts has created another page-turning novel."
>
> —*USA Today* on THE REEF

A Quick Chat With . . .

DAN HARVEY,

Senior Vice President, Publishing Director for Penguin Group (USA) Inc.

Q: ***Do you have a favorite promotion or advertising campaign that Putnam has done with one of Nora's books?***

A: For Nora's big 2002 campaign we thought about a slogan for weeks and discarded 125 ideas before going back to the first suggestion: *Nora Roberts writes the books you love.* Which, of course, is true for millions of readers.

Q: ***How closely do you work with the paperback division in planning the campaign?***

A: We're partners all the way, always learning from each other and getting pleasure from each new Nora success.

Q: ***Is there a certain philosophy Putnam has for the marketing and promotion of Nora's books?***

A: We never forget that Nora has built an enormous fan base over the years—and those fans are always there for her, responding to each new book, turning up at autographings, asking questions about what's next. The bond between Nora Roberts and her readers is the key to our marketing success. Nora writes the good books. We do whatever we can to make sure her readers know about them.

Nora with Dan Harvey

DENISE LITTLE: *Many of Nora's books are written as series. How do you think this impacts Nora's career? How is publishing a series different from publishing a stand-alone novel?*

LESLIE GELBMAN: Well, Nora practically created the series concept, and as with most things about Nora, it was natural. Nora had characters that she wanted to visit again, so why not write about them in the books that followed? What's so wonderful is that her fans had the same thought—why can't we see those characters again? So they followed her and specific characters from book to book, and before you knew it, the demand for more books about the same characters became voracious. If reader demand hadn't coincided with Nora's own curiosity about her characters, I doubt we would have seen as many series and connected stories as we have. Because the series have been so successful, it's been a different kind of publishing challenge with stand-alone books—how to interest readers in a new set of characters without having the safety net of guaranteed reader appeal. But what's nice with the stand-alone books is that Nora can try different things and experiment with different stories without worrying about working around already established characters.

Did You Know . . .

Despite her incredible success and the many books she's written, Nora claims that she is still just as scared about what her editor's reaction will be when she mails off her latest manuscript as she was when she mailed her first book. But she doesn't mind the fear. She says it keeps her writing sharp, and drives her to improve her skills with every new book.

DENISE LITTLE: *There's a strong thread of romantic suspense in many of Nora's books. They stand up as mysteries as well as they do as romances. I've always wondered if Nora has picked up a male readership over the course of her career through this element of her work. Do you have any thoughts on that?*

LESLIE GELBMAN: We see lots of fan mail from Nora's readers, and a good percentage of them are men who have read the romantic suspense

nora and diet coke®

IN 1999, Nora was part of a one-of-a-kind crossover promotional campaign launched by Diet Coke® called "The Story Begins with Diet Coke®." Diet Coke® wanted to offer their consumers something extra that the people who bought and drank Diet Coke® already valued, and after extensive marketing research, Diet Coke® realized that Diet Coke® buyers were also avid readers. So Diet Coke® teamed up with four publishers for a special multimillion-dollar merchandising promotion. From February 1, 1999, to April 30, 1999, excerpt booklets from six novels being published in the spring of 1999 were inserted into millions of 12- and 24-packs of Diet Coke® and caffeine-free Diet Coke®. The booklets were 4″ × 6″ in size, up to 32 pages long, and reproduced the book's hardcover jacket. The design of each multipack showed the featured book whose excerpt booklet was in the multipack, as well as the jackets of all six books, so consumers were encouraged to buy more multipacks and collect all six booklets. In addition, there was a consumer contest that asked for 500-word stories about "Living Your Life to the Fullest." The 25 best stories were chosen by the six authors and compiled into a virtual book on www.dietcoke.com, and the first-place winner won a trip to New York City, a visit with publishers, including Putnam Berkley, and a meeting with editors. The six novels chosen for this campaign were Nora's *River's End*, *Be Cool* by Elmore Leonard, *A Sudden Change of Heart* by Barbara Taylor Bradford, *Mistaken Identity* by Lisa Scottoline, *Tara Road* by Maeve Binchy, and *Chicken Soup for the Couple's Soul* by Jack Canfield, et al.

For Nora, this was a match made in heaven. A lifelong drinker of Coke® and Diet Coke®, she was thrilled to be one of the six participating authors. As part of her tour for *River's End*, she visited the Coca-Cola® plant in Atlanta and did a lot of media for the campaign.

novels. Many men read the books either with their wives, or because their wives were reading it and they decided to pick it up and see what the fuss was about. Well, they obviously found out, since they liked her books so much they wrote to tell us about their enjoyment! A lot of men read and enjoy the J. D. Robb books—not surprising since they are grittier and contain more suspense than most of her other work. It doesn't hurt Nora's male readership that the pseudonym is not gender-specific, but I'm sure that once they read a J. D. Robb they'll be back for more even if they find out that J. D. Robb is a woman.

DENISE LITTLE: *Nora's work makes millions of people happy. As one of her publishers, you've been instrumental in helping that happen. Is there anything that stands out in your mind, looking over Nora's career at Berkley/Jove/Putnam, that you can think back on and say, "We did X, and it was a great idea, one that really helped build Nora's popularity"?*

LESLIE GELBMAN: Two things stand out in my mind: the paperback trilogies and *Montana Sky.* The paperback trilogies really helped establish Nora's single-title career—she had a lot of success with her previous single titles, but it wasn't until the paperback trilogies that her audience started to really grow and expand. Nora had always written connected books in her category series romances, but it wasn't until the Born In trilogy that she brought that interconnectedness over to her single titles. And readers were hooked right away—they loved the characters she introduced in *Born in Fire* and followed them to *Born in Ice*, and then *Born in Shame.* And since we had decided to separate the paperback original trilogies from the hardcovers by excluding the suspense element, these books were the first single

Did You Know . . .

Nora Roberts tours every year with the release of her new hardcover novel, often going to 20 or more cities to promote her work. She rarely draws a crowd of less than 200, and her publisher estimates that Nora signs an average of 6,000 books every time they send her out on the road.

titles that Nora wrote that focused almost exclusively on the romantic relationship between the hero and the heroine. So her core romance fans (many of whom may not have read her previous single titles because of the emphasis on suspense) crossed over and fell in love with the trilogies. At the same time, Nora was able to play more and more with suspense in her hardcovers, an element that appealed more to traditionally non-romance readers, including men. So her readership really did expand enormously when she was able to attract both romance readers and mainstream suspense readers at the same time, but with two different kinds of books.

The second thing that stands out in my mind as a kind of seismic shift is *Montana Sky.* This book was a huge step forward for Nora—it was the first hardcover to incorporate the element that was so successful in her trilogies: the interconnected characters. I had been talking with Nora about writing the book that would pull in all her readers, and not just a segment. So I encouraged her to basically write a paperback trilogy, but to contain it in one story and to weave a suspense framework around it strong enough to support all the different characters and their individual relationships. She did, and gave me *Montana Sky*, which was a breakthrough in so many ways—editorially, obviously, but also in sales. *Montana Sky* was Nora's first hardcover *New York Times* bestseller. Nora was already a superstar in romance and women's fiction, but *Montana Sky* established Nora as a major player in the mainstream fiction marketplace as well.

Also being one of six authors chosen by Diet Coke® for their promotion certainly didn't hurt either.

DENISE LITTLE: *What do readers have to look forward to in the future from Nora Roberts and Berkley/Jove/Putnam?*

LESLIE GELBMAN: For all you Eve and Roarke fans, I can promise you many more adventures from the pen of J. D. Robb and a very special book featuring *both* Nora and J.D. in September—*Remember When*. It will mark the first hardcover appearance of J. D. Robb. Another special treat in store is the Key trilogy, a brand-new trilogy, which Nora set in

(L to R) Leslie Gelbman, Nora, and Amy Berkower at a party honoring Nora in New York City, 2002

as close to real time as possible. Each story takes place over the course of four weeks, one story right after the one before, and it involves a quest for three legendary keys. The publishing schedule is exactly like the books, so Jove is publishing *Key of Light* in November 2003, *Key of Knowledge* in December 2003, and *Key of Valor* in January 2004. This is going to be a fabulous event!

DENISE LITTLE: *Is there a Berkley/Jove/Putnam–sponsored place that readers can go on the Internet to check for information on Nora Roberts and her upcoming titles?*

LESLIE GELBMAN: We have a page devoted exclusively to Nora at www.penguin.com. It's on our featured authors page, so you just click on "features" on the homepage and pull down the menu of featured authors for Nora's name.

A Quick Chat With . . .

LIZ PERL,

Vice President, Executive Director of Publicity for Berkley, Riverhead Trade, and New American Library

Q: *Many people probably don't have a clear picture of what you do—can you describe all the things that you work on with Nora?*

A: Basically, my goal is to get exposure for Nora and her books, so that new readers may discover her and fans are made aware of each new book's availability. Together with "Team Nora" (Marianne Patala and Heather Connor—plus Kathy Onorato), I go about this in many ways. We seek to get the books reviewed by sending out early galleys and pitching them to reviewers. We send out press releases to announce forthcoming books.

We also go after media coverage of Nora herself. This includes pitching magazines and newspapers for feature stories on Nora, for example *People* magazine and *USA Today.* We schedule Nora for television and radio interviews as well. This is one area where Nora really shines—she is incredibly mediagenic. Her interviews are fresh, funny, and lively discussions. She has handled some of the worst morning shock jock jerks and never loses her cool. We are always pitching Nora. With everything that she has going on year-round, there's not much downtime.

Probably the most visible aspect of our job is the Nora Mega Tour! Nora usually goes on tour once a year. It is an intense, monthlong tour that takes her from coast to coast. We coordinate all of Nora's appearances and signings, book the media interviews, arrange all transportation (and she *hates* flying), and manage to get her a meal every so often! It is a grueling schedule and there are countless details that must be fine-tuned.

Q: *You've accompanied Nora on many of her tours—do you have any favorite memories or moments to share?*

A: I have a lot of great memories from my travels with Nora; lots of funny things happen on the road.

We were in San Francisco for the launch of *The Villa.* Bruce and Harold (Nora's hairdresser) flew out to meet us there. We had a great wine-tasting party at a beautiful restaurant followed by a great dinner with several of our key book distributors. It was a great, crazy night that ended with us at the

Tonga Lounge at the Fairmont Hotel. If you've never been there, all I can say is—it's a trip. It's a Polynesian-theme club with the world's only indoor rain forest! It was great fun. The next morning, we all convened in Nora's suite for breakfast and to relive stories from the previous night.

There are too many wonderful stories of being with Nora and the readers who come to her book signings. Some people drive hundreds of miles and are just so sweet. It's amazing to see the rapport that Nora has with her readers.

Q: *What are your publicity goals for Nora? And have you reached them yet?*

A: Generally, my goal is always to get the maximum amount of attention paid to Nora and her books. But more specifically, I'm always setting short-term goals and then raising the bar again and again. Having Nora on the *Today* show had been a real goal for me, and she did it for the release of *Three Fates.* That was very gratifying. My goal for next season (well, one of them) is to have her return to the show! I'd also like the cover of *Time* and/or *Newsweek* and a prime time network special devoted to her. So, there's always something more to pursue!

Putnam Berkley Team Nora (L to R): Liz Perl, Heather Connor, Marianne Patala

from the beginning

Nora Roberts at Silhouette

As Nora Roberts's first publisher, Silhouette Books worked with Nora for more than twenty years. In fact, the publication of *Cordina's Crown Jewel* in Silhouette Special Edition marked Nora's one hundredth book for the publisher. A large part of Nora's success in category romance comes from the enormous respect Nora brings to this very particular art. She once said that writing a category romance takes all the elements that writing a mainstream book does—superb characterization, a well-constructed plot, a great sense of pacing, a solid emotional punch, and a happy ending. The only difference is that the writer has to do it with about half the word count. If writing a great mainstream book is like staging an opera successfully, then writing a great series book, she said, is like staging that same opera successfully—but in a phone booth. It's a graphic image that pinpoints both the joys and the challenges of writing series romance perfectly.

Because of Nora's long history with Silhouette, we felt it would be interesting to hear what the people who worked with her there had to say about Nora's career. We've mentioned the title of each person who replied to our questions the first time they responded. So here's what Silhouette's best had to say about Nora Roberts and her books for them:

DENISE LITTLE: *Nora Roberts has been a part of Silhouette almost since its inception (her first book,* Irish Thoroughbred, *was Silhouette Romance #81). How has having Nora Roberts write for you shaped and changed your publishing program through the years?*

ISABEL SWIFT, Vice President, Editorial: Nora Roberts grew up with Silhouette. And just as much as her editors have helped grow her as an author, Nora has helped us grow as a publisher. Through her professionalism, her talent, and her generosity of spirit, Nora Roberts has set the standard for the romance industry at a high mark. Silhouette Books, and the romance industry at large, have benefited immensely from Nora Roberts's contribution. Not only do her books embody all that romance readers come to the shelves to find, but Nora herself is a consummate professional, admired by readers and publishing professionals alike.

LESLIE WAINGER, Executive Editor, Suspense and Adventure Category: I've always been able to count on Nora for editorial variety matched with consistently high quality. She's unafraid to take chances—futuristic time travel, a shape-shifting hero, a true *noir* tone—and unfailingly makes them work. That adds to the strength of the line not only in an immediate way but by demonstrating the boundary-pushing Intimate Moments is capable of, which in turn frees me to take additional editorial chances, keeping the line fresh and the readers happy.

DENISE LITTLE: *In the course of all of those books for Silhouette, Nora has written classic romance, mystery (e.g.,* Storm Warning*), romantic suspense (e.g.,* Partners*), science fiction (e.g.,* Time Was, Times Change*), paranormal crime thrillers (e.g., the Night series), historical novels (e.g.,* Rebellion, Lawless*), glitz (e.g.,* Affaire Royale, Command Performance, The Playboy Prince*), even novels about novelists writing other novels (e.g.,* Loving Jack*), all without losing touch with her hard-core romance fans. Her work for you pretty much puts to rest the theory that category romance is in any way bounded or confined by category conventions. Can you talk a bit about that, including where the impetus for this experimentation comes from, and whether Nora's pushing at the boundaries opened up the way for other writers to take chances in their books for you?*

ISABEL SWIFT: Nora's innate sense of story and understanding of her readers have enabled her to successfully break new ground in a number of areas. *Reflections* and *Dance of Dreams* are two of the very earliest examples of connected stories in category romance, something Nora contin-

timeline
of a career

1979

- **Nora is snowed in and stuck at home with her two small children. After playing enough games of Candy Land to threaten her sanity, she begins writing a novel in a spiral notebook. Though she characterizes that first book as "very bad, terrible, one long cliché," she realizes she has found her calling in life. She continues to write, soon finishing six more books.**

ues to do incredibly well. She was the first to do a cross-line miniseries with *The Calhoun Women*, with the individual volumes appearing first in Silhouette Romance (*Courting Catherine*), then Desire (*A Man for Amanda*), then Special Edition (*For the Love of Lilah*), and then Intimate Moments (*Suzanna's Surrender*). This series gave readers a great sense of the four different Silhouette lines with the four different personalities and stories for each of the Calhoun sisters. Nora was also part of the first romance genre Christmas short story anthology. Now there are hundreds of romance short story collections, but Silhouette's anthology in 1986 was the first, and contained Nora's "Home for Christmas." The book launched the entire genre of romance short stories and novellas.

What exactly makes a story happen can be a creative give-and-take without clear boundaries. The hero in *Night Shift* came from a request of mine that Nora consider a hero like Batman. But the idea really grew from within the two of us. Both Nora and I love comics, and her Special Edition *Local Hero* had a comic creator for a hero and is a favorite of mine. I still think fondly of Commander Zark (brilliantly illustrated by her son Dan). I knew a superhero hero would spark her imagination.

I am sure Nora's families, her connected stories, her magical Donovans, and others have inspired authors, editors, and readers to open their minds to the limitless possibilities of what is often seen as a "lim-

1980

- **Rejection slips mount up, but Nora's first book is accepted by Silhouette in June.**

1981

- **Nora's first book, *Irish Thoroughbred*, is published in May. It appears in the Silhouette Romance line.**
- **Nora attends the first ever Romance Writers of America (RWA) convention. She becomes a charter member of the organization, and will attend every subsequent convention (except one held in Hawaii).**

ited" subgenre of women's fiction. Nora's imagination is wide ranging, but it is the essential humanity of her characters and her keen ear for dialogue that is what makes her stories—no matter how unusual—so effective and so beloved.

DENISE LITTLE: *Why do you think Nora Roberts's books speak to so many people?*

ISABEL SWIFT: Nora writes from her heart. She is a fan and reader of romance and she follows her own sense of what feels right and works and doesn't limit herself by external rules. Her internal drive and fast pace allow her the ability to experiment, be flexible and intuitive, and respond to the demands of the characters or the story.

How does she do it? Well, I think of Nora's writing a story as if she were a runner racing across uncharted territory to a distant goal. She's simply a great athlete, and she's in great shape. She not only has an excellent sense of direction, but she can explore interesting avenues, take detours, climb high to get a view, find and follow the best—the most interesting and beautiful, not necessarily the shortest—path to the goal of telling a compelling story . . . and *still* come in months ahead of anyone else!

1983

- ***Once More with Feeling*** **is published as one of the launch books in the Silhouette Intimate Moments line.**
- ***Reflections*** **and** ***Dance of Dreams*** **are published—Nora's first connected series.**
- **Nora wins her first major writing award—a Golden Medallion from RWA for** ***The Heart's Victory*** **for Best Contemporary Sensual Romance. The Golden Medallion is selected in an open competition among all similar romances of the year, and is judged by fellow romance writers. Because it is given by a writer's peers, it is the most highly prized award in the romance field.**

(L to R) Isabel Swift, Katherine Orr, Nora, and Jodi Reamer

KATHERINE ORR, Vice President, Public Relations: Nora tells her stories from her heart. Her readers are honest, emotional people like her.

DENISE LITTLE: *Silhouette has always been very in touch with its readers, and has often sent writers out to fan events where they mingle with the people who buy the books. Nora has taken part in these events many times and has developed a well-deserved reputation for being generous with her*

1984

- Nora wins Golden Medallions for both *This Magic Moment* (Long Contemporary Romance) and *Untamed* (Traditional Romance).

1985

- *Playing the Odds, Tempting Fate, All the Possibilities,* and *One Man's Art* are published, launching the MacGregor series.
- Nora wins Golden Medallions for both *A Matter of Choice* (Long Contemporary Romance) and *Opposites Attract* (Short Contemporary Romance).
- Nora marries Bruce Wilder, a local carpenter she's hired to build a bookshelf in her bedroom.

fans. Can you tell us about some of these events, and your favorite memories from them?

ISABEL SWIFT: Nora has signed so many books and made time for so many fans, I can't even begin to express her enthusiasm, willingness, and dedication to her readers. Perhaps a good illustration is the number of trips she's gone on across the nation and around the world. She's been to every large metropolis and many small towns across America as well as to England, Ireland, Italy, Finland, the Czech Republic, Australia, and Japan—and she *really* hates to fly.

I was with Nora at a signing once when a reader had a number of requests and suggested Nora get "her people" to take care of it. After graciously responding, Nora looked at me and said, "What people? I am my people!" And for the last two decades, every Christmas the New York Harlequin/Silhouette office is brightened by a tin of home-baked and -decorated Christmas cookies from Nora. Her gifts are really gifts from the heart.

Did You Know . . .

Even though she has a very hectic touring schedule and she writes an average of eight books a year, Nora Roberts still finds time to answer all her own fan mail and e-mail.

1986

- ***Affaire Royale*** **launches the Royal Family of Cordina series.**
- **Nora writes a novella for the very first Christmas romance anthology. In November, *Silhouette Christmas Stories*, anchored by Nora's "Home for Christmas," is published.**

1987

- **In February, Silhouette publishes Daniel and Anna MacGregor's story, *For Now, Forever,* and for the first time the company reissues titles—they reissue the first four MacGregor books to accompany the new title.**
- ***Hot Ice*** **and** ***Sacred Sins*** **are published by Bantam. They are**

DENISE LITTLE: *What are some of the professional high points you've experienced working with Nora Roberts?*

KATHERINE ORR: Nora knows how to give a media person a good piece because she doesn't focus on herself—she talks about stories, *great stories* and how they came about. She respects her fans by thanking them in a subtle way in all her interviews.

DENISE LITTLE: *What are some of your favorite personal memories of Nora?*

KATHERINE ORR: Nora is always right out front when I come to pick her up for her annual Satellite media session in New York. She's always sporting a new Armani suit, a spectacular scarf, Bruno shoes, and a super handbag. She slides into the limo with her huge laugh and says, "Here we go again!" And every time, it is just like it was her first. That's rare.

Did You Know . . .

The very first series romance to ever appear on the *New York Times* list was Nora Roberts's *The Perfect Neighbor,* and how fitting that it is part of the MacGregor Family series.

1988

among Nora's first mainstream single-title books.

- Nora wins the Golden Medallion for Long Contemporary for *One Summer* (Silhouette). With the fourth win in a category, Nora becomes the first author to be inducted into the RWA Hall of Fame.

- The O'Hurley family makes its first appearance in *The Last Honest Woman, Dance to the Piper,* and *Skin Deep.*
- *Rebellion,* a historical romance about the MacGregors, launches the Harlequin Historical line.

Nora with Ruth Ryan Langan at an RWA conference banquet

ISABEL SWIFT: While I've worked with Nora for over eighty books, Nancy Jackson was the editor who acquired Nora's first book, *Irish Thoroughbred.* I was so delighted the day Nancy passed Nora to me. I loved Nora's work. I also vividly remember a lunch with Nora, Karen Solem (then head of Silhouette), and Brian Hickey (then president of Harlequin) when we committed to reissuing the first four MacGregors to go with

publishing *For Now, Forever* in Special Edition. We had never reissued a category romance at the time—it was a revolutionary idea!

Another favorite memory of mine is snorkeling with Nora and Bruce on the Great Barrier Reef in Australia. That was a wonderful event, but some of my favorite times have just been hanging out with Nora and her friends. They are an amazing group.

DENISE LITTLE: *Many of Nora's books are written as series. How do you think this impacts Nora's career? How is publishing a series different from publishing a stand-alone novel?*

ISABEL SWIFT: Nora has taken the multivolume family saga to amazing heights. I was really impressed by the way she threaded past with present and wove a mystery through four wonderful romances with the Calhouns. The way she tied in the follow-up title, *Megan's Mate*, was also beautifully done. Her Civil War backstory in the MacKades is another example of her incredible capability to blend past and present, to create family, different personalities, and relationships, stories that stand alone, yet work together so remarkably. Right after we worked on the MacKades I visited Antietam battlefield with Nora (the setting for those titles) and it was a truly moving and transcendent experience. Nora is a master at creating characters you care about and want to spend time

1991

- **Nora has her first ever *New York Times* bestseller with *Genuine Lies* (Bantam), which appears on the September 8, 1991, list and stays on for one week.**
- **In December 1991, *Carnal Innocence* (Bantam) becomes Nora's second *NYT* bestseller.**
- **Nora's ground-breaking Calhoun Women series is published, with a new book appearing each month for four months, each in a different Silhouette line.**

with. Her miniseries are brilliant, and a natural extension of her special skills. It is something that has set her apart and won her many fans, first in category and now in mainstream.

ALEX OSUSZEK, Vice President, Retail Sales, Harlequin: In publishing her series books I believe Nora clearly differentiates herself from other great writers, and in fact demonstrates the great writer she is. Nora does not constrain her voice and talent to one editorial category nor is she prisoner to the standard hard/soft publishing formula for success that all other major writers with a mass-market following pursue. Nora's approach transcends the norm and in so doing she demonstrates a confidence in her writing and courage of her convictions to be her own voice. The fact that she can write a series

Did You Know . . .

Nora's fondness for writing series springs out of her love for her characters and their families. When asked about the reasons behind her penchant for writing connected novels, she says that, though many of her books were planned as trilogies, it isn't always the case. The MacGregor books, for example, were supposed to be a single title. But according to Nora, "The characters just wouldn't shut up. And I simply fell in love with them."

1992

- **Nora moves her mainstream single-title novels to Putnam Berkley with the publication of *Honest Illusions*, her first hardcover novel.**
- **Nora wins RWA's RITA Award (the new name for the Golden Medallion) for Romantic Suspense for *Night Shift* (Silhouette).**
- **Nora's Donovan Legacy trilogy is published.**

1993

- **Nora wins the RITA for Romantic Suspense for *Divine Evil* (Bantam).**

book, which the industry would suggest speaks to a smaller though most dedicated readership, and achieve bestseller sales recognition is simply unprecedented by any other major author. Writing series strikes me as a way for Nora to hold on to her personal past just as the main characters in her books cherish their history, giving them a richness of character, which is appealing to all Nora's fans. Her publishing integrity is what truly connects Nora to her readers.

DENISE LITTLE: *There's a strong thread of romantic suspense in many of Nora's books. They stand up as mysteries as well as they do as romances. I've always wondered if Nora has picked up a male readership over the course of her career through this element of her work. Do you have any thoughts on that?*

ISABEL SWIFT: She absolutely does have a male readership—not only with her J. D. Robb titles and her mainstreams, but she's always had a select group of male readers for her Silhouette and Harlequin category titles for many years. What's their story? Well, male readers often write in to Nora saying something like, "I never expected to be reading a romance, much less be writing a letter to the author, but I am now a big fan. My wife and I enjoy reading before we go to bed and you are her favorite author." Then they might say they gave their wife a hard time about reading

1994

- **The paperback reprint of *Private Scandals* (Berkley) hits the *New York Times* list for two weeks.**
- ***Born in Fire,* the first book in Nora's first paperback trilogy for Berkley, is published. It too hits the *NYT* paperback list for two weeks.**
- **Nora wins the RITA for Contemporary Single Title for *Private Scandals* and the RITA for Romantic Suspense for *Nightshade.***

1995

- **J. D. Robb makes her first appearance with the publication of *Naked in Death* and *Glory in Death.* The epic story of Eve Dallas and Roarke begins.**
- **The MacKade Brothers series makes its debut with *The Return of Rafe MacKade* and *The Pride of Jared MacKade.* Jared's book is Silhouette Special Edition #1000.**
- ***Hidden Riches* wins the RITA for Romantic Suspense, and with the**

romances and she dared him to read one. Well, you can guess the result. One of my favorites of this sort was the husband who became such an enthusiastic convert that he was turning his entire office—men and women—into Nora fans. The other variation is the husband who gets tired of listening to his wife laugh and cry and so thoroughly enjoy her book (so much more than he is enjoying his!) that once she's done he snatches it up, and voilà, another Nora fan. This was the story for an Ernst & Young accountant who also worked on Harlequin business. He called me one day for help in locating an early Nora title that he wanted to give his wife for a present. We got to talking and he amazed me by quoting whole paragraphs and dialogue of some of his favorite moments in Nora's work.

DENISE LITTLE: *Is there anything you've learned from reading Nora Roberts's work or working with Nora that impacts your personal beliefs and the way you live your life?*

ISABEL SWIFT: No matter how successful Nora has become, she has never lost her sense of self and her humanity. While she is incredibly hard-working, her ambition has never made her less than true to herself or her commitments. I've seen some authors who are usually very nice people get quite grasping and unattractive when they're close to success. That *never* happened with Nora.

fourth win in this category, Nora is inducted again into the RWA Hall of Fame, this time for Romantic Suspense. Nora is the only author to be inducted into the RWA Hall of Fame more than once.

1996

- ***Montana Sky* is Nora's 100th published novel, and is also Nora's first hardcover *New York Times* bestseller.**
- ***Born in Ice* wins the RITA for Contemporary Single Title, and the third win (changed from four) in this category means that Nora is once again inducted into the RWA Hall of Fame.**

DENISE LITTLE: *Partly through Silhouette's worldwide publishing affiliates, Nora Roberts has developed a massive international following. Clearly her work crosses cultural and language boundaries with ease. How many languages is a typical Nora Roberts Silhouette translated into, and how many countries will it typically appear in?*

ISABEL SWIFT: Silhouette and Harlequin are published in over twenty-four languages in over one hundred countries around the world. Nora has fans in Japan, China, Finland, Germany, South America, Sweden, Norway, the Czech Republic, Slovakia, Hungary, Italy, Spain, Greece, Israel, Australia, Portugal, New Zealand, Turkey, the United Kingdom, Brazil, Bulgaria, the Philippines. . . .

Did You Know . . .

Nora is famous for her clever promotional items. She once sent out a box of tissues emblazoned with the words "Don't cry! The MacGregors are back!"

DENISE LITTLE: *Is there a Silhouette-sponsored place that readers can go on the Internet to check for information on Nora Roberts?*

EVERYBODY: Tell the readers to check out eHarlequin.com.

1997

- For the first time, Nora has seven titles on the *New York Times* list in the course of one year. They include *Holding the Dream, Sanctuary, Montana Sky* (reprint), *Sweet Revenge, Finding the Dream, The MacGregor Brides,* and *Sea Swept.*
- Nora receives the RWA Lifetime Achievement Award.

1998

- *Sea Swept* and *Rising Tides*, the first two books in the Chesapeake Bay series, are published. *Sea Swept* becomes Nora's very first #1 *New York Times* bestseller, and *Rising Tides* is Nora's first book to debut at #1 on the *NYT* list.
- *Inner Harbor*, the third book in the Chesapeake Bay series, also hits #1 on the *NYT* list, marking the first time each book in a single Nora trilogy has been a #1 *NYT* bestseller.

the mind of an agent

An Interview with Amy Berkower

AMY BERKOWER, NORA Roberts's literary agent, has been with her from the beginning of Nora's career. Such a long-term partnership between agent and writer is unusual in today's publishing climate—changing agents every few years is fairly common in the writing game, especially among top writers, the kind that agents love to have on their lists. Though poaching clients is professionally frowned upon in the small world of publishing, there's an unspoken understanding among most bestselling writers that they would be welcome at any agency that they chose to grace with their presence. But the partnership between Amy and Nora has not only been exceptionally successful, it has also been one that is extremely loyal and enduring, founded on a mutual respect for the expertise each has in their chosen field of endeavor. Through the years, Amy has seen Nora's career rise from its roots in category romance to today's incredible success. As someone who has been both an active participant in the process and a careful observer of it, she's well placed to shed light on Nora's journey as a writer. Here's what she had to say:

DENISE LITTLE: *Why do you think Nora Roberts's books speak to so many people?*

AMY BERKOWER: Nora's books speak to so many people because they provide an escape into a world populated by likable people whose lives are filled with the kind of romance that may be rooted in fantasy, but isn't so removed from the lives of everyday people.

DENISE LITTLE: *What are Nora's greatest strengths as a writer?*

AMY BERKOWER: I think Nora's greatest gift as a writer is her ability to create likable characters who come alive for her readers. When Nora is writing a book, she often gives me the impression that her characters have moved into her life. From the fan mail Nora receives, I sense that her characters are just as alive to her readers as they are to Nora. They offer a special kind of companionship, which her readers miss so much after they finish a book that

Did You Know . . .

By the end of 2003, Nora Roberts will have published more than 150 books. To date, more than 91 of them have been *New York Times* bestsellers.

they often ask, despite Nora's tremendous output, why she can't write faster.

DENISE LITTLE: *What are some of the professional high points you've experienced working with Nora Roberts?*

AMY BERKOWER: It was especially gratifying to me when Nora became a *New York Times* bestseller in hardcover for the very first time. Though her original paperbacks made the list regularly, there was a time when none of her hardcover books sold over one hundred thousand copies. When I told Phyllis Grann, Nora's publisher at the time, that I was eager to see hardcover growth, Phyllis asked to see a "bigger book with larger scope." Leslie Gelbman, Nora's editor, suggested that Nora write a hardcover with the same kind of story arc as her trilogies, but contained within a single volume. I suggested that Nora set the book in Montana, which was a popular and romantic location at that time. Nora wrote the book. Phyllis gave it a "big" title—*Montana Sky*—and a big corporate push. The book sold twice as many copies as her previous hardcover and was an immediate bestseller. Seeing the book on the *New York Times* hardcover list was proof that Nora was on her way to becoming a "big" bestselling author.

1999

- **Nora is chosen by Diet Coke® to be one of six authors in a special promotion.**
- ***Jewels of the Sun*, the first book in the Gallaghers of Ardmore Irish trilogy, is published.**
- **Every book Nora publishes this year hits the *New York Times* list, including *The Perfect Neighbor,* which becomes the first ever Silhouette category romance to hit the *NYT* list.**

DENISE LITTLE: *What are some of your favorite personal memories of Nora?*

AMY BERKOWER: After Nora had published about a dozen category romances with Silhouette, I told her that an entire manuscript wasn't required in order to secure a contract—she could simply write a proposal. A few weeks later, she sent me a proposal, which I sold. After the contract was signed, Nora confessed that she had written the manuscript before the proposal. She explained to me that there was no way that she could plot a story line without actually writing the book first. Though I knew Nora was an intuitive writer, I had no idea until then of the extent to which she depended on her instinct. She writes directly from her heart, which I think is one of the reasons she has such a large and loyal audience.

Did You Know . . .

Nora Roberts wrote six full manuscripts before her first book was accepted for publication.

DENISE LITTLE: *As Nora's agent, you're a real part of planning for Nora's future books. What do you look at when choosing a publishing path?*

AMY BERKOWER: The process varies, depending on the author I'm

2000

- ***Loyalty in Death* is the first J. D. Robb book to hit the *NYT* list.**
- **On the *USA Today* list of the year's bestselling authors, Nora comes in at #5.**

- ***River's End* is the first reprint of a hardcover to become a #1 *New York Times* bestseller.**
- **For the week of July 16, Nora appears on the *NYT* list four times with four different books.**
- **On the *USA Today* list of the year's bestselling authors, Nora is now at #4.**

working with. I look at the author's particular talents and try to figure out the best way to showcase these talents, given the confines of the market. As Nora is such an intuitive writer, she determines the content of her work. We have, however, worked closely together in planning Nora's career. Questions we've had to deal with range from when to enter the mainstream fiction market and the hardcover market, to whether it was possible to write category romances and achieve mainstream success, to whether Nora should use a pseudonym to satisfy her need to write more books than her publishers could successfully publish under one name.

Did You Know . . .

Every Nora Roberts book published since 1999 has made the *New York Times* list, even the reprints.

DENISE LITTLE: *What triggers the decisions to reprint Nora's early titles, especially in the anthologies from Silhouette? Does reader mail play a part in those decisions, and if so, where can readers lobby for their favorites to appear in the next set of reprints?*

AMY BERKOWER: Reader mail to Nora and Silhouette plays a big role in determining what books are featured in the anthologies. The decision to

2001

- ***Dance upon the Air* and *Heaven and Earth,* the first two books in the Three Sisters Island trilogy, are published, and both debut at #1 on the *New York Times* list.**
- **With *Betrayal in Death,* the twelfth J. D. Robb title, Nora is officially "outed" as J. D. Robb.**
- **For the week of September 21, Nora again has four titles appear on the *NYT* list in a single week.**
- ***Carolina Moon* wins the RITA for Romantic Suspense.**
- ***Midnight Bayou* becomes Nora's first hardcover #1 *NYT* bestseller.**

publish more MacGregor and O'Hurley books was largely based on reader demand, for example.

DENISE LITTLE: *Is there anything that stands out in your mind, looking over Nora's career, that you can think back on and say "We did X, and it was a great idea, one that really helped build Nora's popularity"?*

AMY BERKOWER: When Nora started writing hardcover novels, she was advised to give up writing original paperbacks. It was an unwritten rule in the publishing business that, once you were good enough to be published in hardcover, there was no reason to continue writing paperbacks. Besides being less lucrative, publishers feared that the original paperbacks might somehow undermine the credibility hardcover publication offered a writer. Neither Nora nor I believed that her audience thought this way. Furthermore, from the fan mail that Nora received, I knew that her audience would want more books than a hardcover publication schedule could accommodate. I also knew that Nora enjoyed continuing characters in her category romances and that these books were very popular. So I suggested to Putnam Berkley that they buy a paperback trilogy. Berkley wasn't very enthusiastic about the idea, but they didn't want to turn us down. After Nora delivered all three books, Berkley suggested a publication schedule of one book per year. Since they had

2002

- ***Reunion in Death*** **becomes the first J. D. Robb book to hit #1 on the *New York Times* list.**
- **For the week of April 21, *Three Fates* debuts at #1 on the *NYT* hardcover list and *The Villa*, which also debuted at #1 on the paperback *NYT* list, remains at #1, marking the first time ever Nora has simultaneous #1 *NYT* bestsellers on both hardcover and paperback. Only a handful of authors can claim that honor, and no other romance author has ever accomplished this feat to date.**

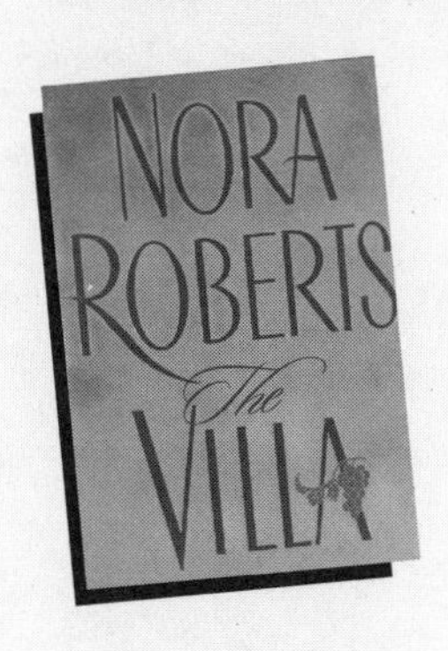

all the manuscripts in hand, I didn't understand why they couldn't publish the books three months apart. Berkley was concerned that Nora would suffer from overexposure if she published more than two books a year. Nora and I believed that the market could tolerate a lot more. So we compromised, and the books were published six months apart. The market proved us right. Now Nora's typical annual publication schedule includes a Putnam hardcover release, a paperback original trilogy from Jove, a Jove paperback reprint of the previous year's Putnam hardcover, two J. D. Robb books from Berkley, an anthology or two or three, and some series books for Silhouette that are usually accompanied by reprint volumes of her older titles for them. And every single book is a bestseller. She had fourteen books on the *New York Times*, the *USA Today*, and/or the *Publishers Weekly* lists in 2000, thirteen books the year before, and it looks like the trend is continuing in 2001. [*Editor's note: This interview was conducted in April 2001.*]

DENISE LITTLE: *Nora's a bit more prolific than most writers. How do you adapt to that?*

AMY BERKOWER: For me it's been both a challenge and a lot of fun trying to figure out a publishing program that takes advantage of Nora's tremendous output and talent. It was very gratifying to watch Nora

2003-2004

- J. D. Robb makes her first hardcover appearance alongside her other half—Nora Roberts—in *Remember When,* published by Putnam in September.

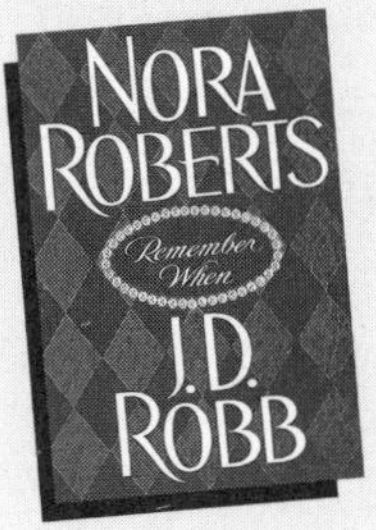

- Nora wins the RITA Award for Best Romantic Suspense for *Three Fates* (beating out *Purity in Death* and *Reunion in Death* among other titles).
- Nora is awarded a special award by Waldenbooks as Bestselling Romance Author of the Year.
- *Divided in Death* becomes the first full-length J. D. Robb novel to be published in hardcover by Putnam in January 2004.

(L to R) Leslie Gelbman, Nora, and Amy Berkower hit the stores in New York City.

prove that she could continue writing category romances, despite the advice of many publishing professionals, and still be a mainstream success. And it was just as gratifying to watch trilogy after trilogy appear on the *New York Times* list. But even though Nora was writing one hardcover, one trilogy, and a few category romances a year, she still wasn't satisfied. She needed to write and publish more books. Though I'd encouraged Putnam Berkley to publish more books than they wanted, I felt that we could push them no further. So we came up with the idea of a pseudonym, something Nora originally resisted. She felt like it would be betraying her fans. But when I explained to her that it was simply a marketing gimmick, like Coke® and Diet Coke®, which would allow her more shelf space in the bookstores, she relented, and J. D. Robb was born. Coping with Nora's insatiable desire to write has forced us to break a lot of rules, and to create a publishing program that has turned out to be as creatively satisfying as it is profitable.

DENISE LITTLE: *How is Nora different as a writer from most romance writers—what sets her apart from the pack and makes her so special?*

AMY BERKOWER: Nora's sense of humor, her ear for dialogue, and her ability to create characters who are impossible not to like are some of the qualities that I think make her such a special writer. Nora is also unusual in that she never complains about writing and she's never missed a due date. In fact, the only time I've ever seen her unhappy is when something is keeping her away from her computer. Love of craft, respect for her audience (she appreciates her fans as much as they adore her), and an ability to stay true to her own voice (which is harder than most people realize) make her a true professional.

DENISE LITTLE: *Many of Nora's books are written as series. How do you think this impacts Nora's career?*

AMY BERKOWER: I've represented many series for kids—Choose Your Own Adventure books, Sweet Valley High books, The Babysitter's Club books. Given the popularity of these series, as well as series television dramas, sitcoms, soaps, and movie sequels, I've never understood why publishers didn't publish more series for adults. Audiences clearly enjoy spending more time with characters they've met before. I think Nora's ability to create a world that her readers look forward to learning more about in successive books is one of the reasons she's been so successful as a writer.

Did You Know . . .

Since 1993, Nora Roberts has offered an annual scholarship to students in her community who want to become writers or teachers. To win the scholarship, seniors from the local high school must submit a writing sample, and Nora judges the contest herself.

DENISE LITTLE: *I would think it would be profoundly satisfying to have been a part of Nora's publishing journey. What do you take home at the end of the workday from working with Nora?*

AMY BERKOWER: Working with Nora is a blessing. It gives me faith that good things can happen to good people.

A Quick Chat With . . .

KATHY ONORATO

of Creative Promotions

Q: ***Liz Perl referred to you as being an important part of "Team Nora." Tell us about Creative Promotions and your relationship with Nora.***

A: Creative Promotions is a full-service, award-winning agency specializing in the promotion of authors and books. I've been working with Nora since 1988—fifteen years and counting!

Q: ***Do you have any favorite promotion among the many you've done for Nora?***

A: It's hard to pick just one. We've worked on so many fun projects over the years. But I have to say the annual magnet we produce listing Nora's upcoming releases gets the most reaction over any other project we have done. Fans and booksellers really look forward to it each year. I'm glad we hit on something that really seems to please the fans!

Q: ***What are some special memories you have of working with Nora?***

A: There are so many, but each "first" is a special memory. The first *New York Times* bestseller . . . the first hardcover . . . the first #1 bestseller . . . the launch of J. D. Robb. Another highlight was planning the party to celebrate the publication of her one hundredth novel, *Montana Sky.* Also, on a personal note, celebrating her son's wedding and birth of her first grandchild. But the main highlight of working with Nora is Nora. She is still the same down-to-earth, real person she was when I first met her over fifteen years ago. All the fame and fortune and success have not changed her—except maybe she shops more than she used to, but she's still Nora.

Nora with Kathy Onorato and Kathy's brother Paul at Nora's annual RWA party in Anaheim, California.

“This latest by Roberts will please her established fans and win her new ones. . . . Employing a story line that is a bit trickier than expected, a lot of witty sexual dialogue, and an endearing assortment of secondary characters—including parents who really care about their adult child's welfare—this book is a sure winner for aficionados of contemporary romantic suspense.”

—*Library Journal* on HIDDEN RICHES

PART THREE

books

the nora roberts concordance

A Complete Alphabetical Guide to the Books of Nora Roberts

IT HAPPENS TO everyone who reads Nora Roberts's books. You see a book in the bestseller rack with Nora's name on it, buy it immediately, and get it home, only to discover that you've got two copies of that story already, with different covers, sometimes even with different titles. Or, worse, you don't buy it, thinking it's a reprint, and discover weeks later that you've missed the next volume in your favorite series, and now the bookseller is sold out. Or you've just read your first couple of Nora's books, and you want the rest of them—now! This section of this volume is your guidebook to the works of Nora Roberts—the hundreds of books, the thousands of editions, the multiple covers . . . whatever you want to know, you'll find it here. Every one of Nora Roberts's books is listed alphabetically by title, and cross-referenced by series and edition. If a book is printed in multiple formats—hardcover, mass market, audio, large print, or electronic text—that information is available, too. To make searching on the Internet easier, we've included the International Standard Book Numbers, or ISBNs. They make it a lot easier to find those out-of-print titles you've been looking for on auction sites. We've also assembled the various covers for each title, so that you can check to see if you've gotten them all (the *serious* Nora collectors do!) or avoid buying more than one version of a single book, as you prefer. This listing includes all of Nora's books scheduled to be published well into 2004. Enjoy looking through the listing, and I hope you find some treasures here that you haven't read. As much fun as rereading Nora's books is, it still doesn't match the thrill of discovering a Nora title that's new to you, just waiting to be opened and read for the first time.

Affaire Royale

Series: Cordina's Royal Family (Bk 1)

For related volumes, see *Command Performance* (Bk 2), *The Playboy Prince* (Bk 3), and *Cordina's Crown Jewel* (Bk 4)

See also the compilation volume: *Cordina's Royal Family*

Editions: Silhouette Intimate Moments #142, May 1986, ISBN: 0-373-07142-6

Language of Love #35 ("Honeysuckle"), ISBN: 0-373-51035-7

Silhouette trade paperback compilation volume, *Cordina's Royal Family*, July 2002, ISBN: 0-373-48483-6

Thorndike Press large print, Oct. 2002, ISBN: 0-786-23793-7

Story: American security expert Reeve McGee travels to the principality of Cordina to guard Her Serene Highness Gabriella from terrorists.

Series Connections: The children of Prince Armand of Cordina and the tiny Monaco-like principality of Cordina form the common threads of this series.

Cover Image(s):

All the Possibilities

Series: The MacGregors (Bk 3)

For related volumes, see *Playing the Odds* (Bk 1), *Tempting Fate* (Bk 2), *One Man's Art* (Bk 4), *For Now, Forever* (Bk 5), *The MacGregor Brides* (Bk 6), *The Winning Hand* (Bk 7), *The MacGregor Grooms* (Bk 8), *The Perfect Neighbor* (Bk 9), *Rebellion*, a novel featuring a story line from Clan MacGregor history, and *Harlequin Historical Christmas Stories 1990*, "In from the Cold," a novella set in pre–Revolutionary War New England

See also the compilation volumes: *The MacGregors: Serena ~ Caine*, *The MacGregors: Alan ~ Grant*, and *The MacGregors: Daniel ~ Ian*

Editions: Silhouette Special Edition #247, July 1985, ISBN: 0-373-09247-4

Silhouette Special Plaid Reissue, Feb. 1987, ISBN: 0-373-48210-8

Language of Love #15 ("Petunia"), ISBN: 0-373-51015-2

Silhouette mass-market compilation volume, *The MacGregors: Alan ~ Grant*, Feb. 1999, ISBN: 0-373-48389-9

Story: Potter Shelby Campbell and U.S. Senator Alan MacGregor match wits in the third installment of the MacGregor clan. Set in D.C.

Series Connections: The children of Daniel MacGregor and his wife, Anna, form the backbone of this series, with a slew of Daniel's grandchildren and great-grandchildren and assorted relatives to fill out the sequels. As Daniel himself would put it, "Good blood. Strong stock."

Cover Image(s):

Art of Deception, The

Series: None

Editions: Silhouette Intimate Moments #131, Feb. 1986, ISBN: 0-373-07131-0
Language of Love #27 ("Love in a Mist"), ISBN: 0-373-51027-6
G. K. Hall & Co. large print hardcover, June 2000, ISBN: 0-7540-4362-2
G. K. Hall & Co. large print paperback, ISBN: 0-7540-4363-0
G. K. Hall & Co. large print hardcover, Dec. 2000, ISBN: 0-7838-9055-9
Silhouette trade paperback compilation volume, *Suspicious*, Nov. 2003, ISBN: 0-373-21873-7

Story: Going undercover in New England, Adam Haines investigates art fraud and prime suspect Kirby Fairchild.

Cover Image(s):

Best Laid Plans

Series: Loving Jack (Bk 2)
For related volumes, see *Loving Jack* (Bk 1) and *Lawless* (Bk 3)
See also the compilation volume: *Love by Design*

Editions: Silhouette Special Edition #511, Mar. 1989, ISBN: 0-373-09511-2
Language of Love #44 ("Dogwood"), ISBN: 0-373-51044-6
John Curley & Associates large print, Nov. 1991, ISBN: 0-373-58119-X
Silhouette trade paperback compilation volume, *Love by Design*, Sept. 2003, ISBN: 0-373-21825-7

Story: Structural engineer Abra Wilson and architect Cody Johnson cross swords as they collaborate on a major building in Arizona, and face sabotage.

Series Connections: In *Loving Jack*, budding novelist Jacqueline MacNamara is conned into renting architect Nathan Powell's home. Nathan is Cody Johnson's partner, and Cody's story is told in *Best Laid Plans. Lawless* is purportedly the book that the character Jack wrote during the course of the series.

Cover Image(s):

Series: "Dream" series, a.k.a. Templeton House (Bks 1, 2, & 3), and *Homeport*

Editions: Countertop Audio audio compilation (Abridged), Jan. 2001, ISBN: 1-8860-8995-7

Story and Series Connections: See *Daring to Dream*, *Holding the Dream*, *Finding the Dream*, and *Homeport*

Cover Image(s):

Betrayal in Death

(writing as J. D. Robb)

Series: In Death (Bk 12)

For related volumes, see *Naked in Death* (Bk 1), *Glory in Death* (Bk 2), *Immortal in Death* (Bk 3), *Rapture in Death* (Bk 4), *Ceremony in Death* (Bk 5), *Vengeance in Death* (Bk 6), *Holiday in Death* (Bk 7), "Midnight in Death" (*Silent Night*, Bk 7.5), *Conspiracy in Death* (Bk 8), *Loyalty in Death* (Bk 9), *Witness in Death* (Bk 10), *Judgment in Death* (Bk 11), "Interlude in Death" (*Out of This World*, Bk 12.5), *Seduction in Death* (Bk 13), *Reunion in Death* (Bk 14), *Purity in Death* (Bk 15), *Portrait in Death* (Bk 16), *Imitation in Death* (Bk 17), *Remember When* (Bk 17.5), *Divided in Death* (Bk 18), and *Visions in Death* (Bk 19)

Editions: Berkley mass market, Mar. 2001, ISBN: 0-425-17857-9
Nova Audio (Abridged), Mar. 2001, ISBN: 1-58788-098-9
Louis Braille Audio (Abridged), Mar. 2001, ISBN: 1-58788-196-9
Thorndike Press large print, July 2001, ISBN: 0-786-23397-4
Gemstar e-book, Berkley, Mar. 2002, ISBN: 0786518979
Adobe Reader e-book, Berkley, Sept. 2001, ISBN: 0786506512
e-book, Berkley, Sept. 2001, ISBN: 0786501170

Story: Eve tries to find a hired killer who is targeting Roarke's employees.

Series Connections: Lt. Eve Dallas is a mid-21st-century cop in a New York City where, despite technological advances, crime still runs rampant. Eve is married to the enigmatic Roarke, a self-made billionaire with a shady past.

Cover Image(s):

Birds, Bees, and Babies '94, "The Best Mistake" novella

Series: None

Editions: Silhouette mass market, May 1994, ISBN: 0-373-48285-X

Story: Sportswriter and confirmed bachelor J. Cooper McKinnon rents an apartment from single mom Zoe Fleming.

Note: This is a multistory collection and also includes novellas by Ann Major and Dallas Schulze.

Cover Image(s):

Birthright

Series: None

Editions: G. P. Putnam's Sons hardcover, Mar. 2003, ISBN: 0-399-14984-8
Jove mass-market reprint, Apr. 2004, ISBN: 0-515-13711-1
BrillianceAudio CD (Unabridged), Mar. 2003, ISBN: 1-59086-399-9
BrillianceAudio (Unabridged), Mar. 2003, ISBN: 1-59086-337-2
BrillianceAudio (Abridged), Mar. 2003, ISBN: 1-59086-341-0
BrillianceAudio (Unabridged), Mar. 2003, ISBN: 1-59086-338-0
Thorndike Press large print, June 2003, ISBN: 0-786-25359-2

Story: Archeologist Callie Dunbrook is on the dig of her life when the secrets of her own past are revealed, throwing her very identity into question.

Cover Image(s):

Blithe Images

Series: None

Editions: Silhouette Romance #127, Jan. 1982, ISBN: 0-671-57127-3
Language of Love #38 ("White Camellia"), ISBN: 0-373-51038-1
Silhouette mass-market reissue, Oct. 2003, ISBN: 0-373-21841-9
Thorndike Press large print, July 2003, ISBN: 0-786-25585-4

Story: Magazine mogul Bret Bardoff signs former Kansas farm girl Hillary Baxter to an exclusive modeling contract, and her world changes forever.

Cover Image(s):

Born in Fire

Series: The Concannan Sisters, a.k.a. the Born In trilogy (Bk 1)
For related volumes, see *Born in Ice* (Bk 2), *Born in Shame* (Bk 3), and compilation volume *Irish Born*

Editions: Jove mass market, Oct. 1994, ISBN: 0-515-11469-3
Nova Audio (Abridged), Aug. 2000, ISBN: 1-58788-190-X
Nova Audio (Abridged), Aug. 2000, ISBN: 1-58788-068-7
Born In Collection (*Born in Fire, Born in Ice, Born in Shame*), BrillianceAudio (Abridged), Feb. 2003, ISBN: 1-59086-537-5
BrillianceAudio (Abridged), Aug. 2001, ISBN: 1-58788-317-1
Thorndike Press large print, Aug. 1995, ISBN: 0-786-20373-0
Putnam hardcover omnibus edition, *Three Complete Novels: Born in Fire, Born in Ice, Born in Shame*, Apr. 1998, ISBN: 0-399-14388-2
Econo-Clad Books, Oct. 1994, ISBN: 0-613-23691-2
Born In Box Set (*Born in Fire, Born in Ice, Born in Shame*), Jove, Nov. 2002, ISBN: 0-515-13496-1
Adobe Reader e-book, Jove, June 2001, ISBN: 078650658X
e-book, Jove, June 2001, ISBN: 0786501197
Berkley trade paperback compilation, *Irish Born*, Nov. 2003, ISBN: 0-425-19589-9

Story: Rogan Sweeney, a wealthy American gallery owner, seeks out Irish glass artist Maggie Concannon, hoping to feature her work.

Series Connections: The three daughters of Irishman Tom Concannon, two born in wedlock, and one the product of a love affair, form the backbone of this series.

Cover Image(s):

Born in Ice

Series: The Concannon Sisters, a.k.a. the Born In trilogy (Bk 2)
For related volumes, see *Born in Fire* (Bk 1), *Born in Shame* (Bk 3), and compilation volume, *Irish Born*

Editions: Jove mass market, Aug. 1995, ISBN: 0-515-11675-0
Nova Audio (Abridged), Sept. 2000, ISBN: 1-58788-191-8
Nova Audio (Abridged), Sept. 2001, ISBN: 1-58788-325-2
Born In Collection (*Born in Fire*, *Born in Ice*, *Born in Shame*), BrillianceAudio (Abridged), Feb. 2003, ISBN: 1-59086-537-5
Putnam hardcover omnibus edition, *Three Complete Novels: Born in Fire, Born in Ice, Born in Shame*, Apr. 1998, ISBN: 0-399-14388-2
Severn House Publishers, Ltd., hardcover British edition, Aug. 1995, ISBN: 0-72784-832-1
Born In Box Set (*Born in Fire*, *Born in Ice*, *Born in Shame*), Jove mass market, Nov. 2002, ISBN: 0-515-13496-1
e-book, Jove, June 2001, ISBN: 0786501200
Adobe Reader e-book, Jove, June 2001, ISBN: 0786506563
Thorndike Press large print, Oct. 1995, ISBN: 0-786-20374-9
Berkley trade paperback compilation, *Irish Born*, Nov. 2003, ISBN: 0-425-19589-9

Story: Brianna Concannon hosts American novelist Grayson Thane at her bed-and-breakfast inn in Ireland.

Series Connections: The three daughters of Irishman Tom Concannon, two born in wedlock, and one the product of a love affair, form the backbone of this series.

Cover Image(s):

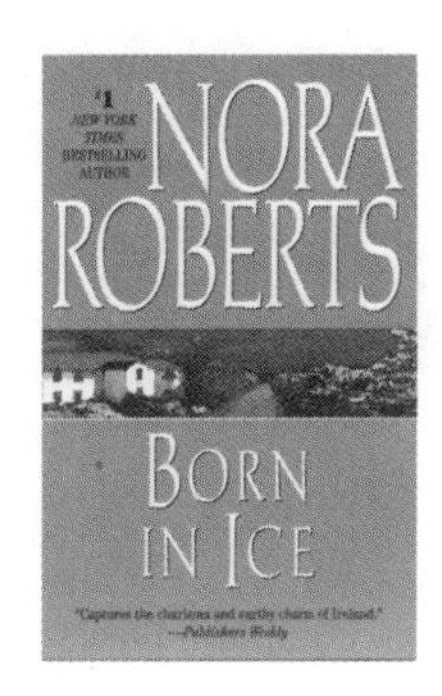

Series: The Concannan Sisters, a.k.a. the Born In trilogy (Bk 3)
For related volumes, see *Born in Fire* (Bk 1), *Born in Ice* (Bk 2), and compilation volume, *Irish Born*

Editions: Jove mass market, Jan. 1996, ISBN: 0-515-11779-X
Nova Audio (Abridged), Nov. 2000, ISBN: 1-58788-192-6
Nova Audio (Abridged), Dec. 2001, ISBN: 1-58788-347-3
Born In Collection (*Born in Fire*, *Born in Ice*, *Born in Shame*), BrillianceAudio (Abridged), Feb. 2003, ISBN: 1-59086-537-5
Thorndike Press large print, Aug. 1995, ISBN: 0-786-20375-7
Severn House Publishers, Ltd., hardcover British edition, ISBN: 0-72784-863-1
Putnam hardcover omnibus edition, *Three Complete Novels: Born in Fire, Born in Ice, Born in Shame*, Apr. 1998, ISBN: 0-399-14388-2
Born In Box Set (*Born in Fire*, *Born in Ice*, *Born in Shame*), Jove mass market, Nov. 2001, ISBN: 0-515-13496-1
Adobe Reader e-book, Jove, June 2001, ISBN: 0786506571
Microsoft Reader e-book, Jove, June 2001, ISBN: B00007EHYP
Berkley trade paperback compilation, *Irish Born*, Nov. 2003, ISBN: 0-425-19589-9

Story: New York advertising exec Shannon Bodine discovers the identity of her biological father. She goes to Ireland to find her roots, where she meets two sisters she didn't know she had, as well as farmer Murphy Muldoon.

Series Connections: The three daughters of Irishman Tom Concannon, two born in wedlock, and one the product of a love affair, form the backbone of this series.

Cover Image(s):

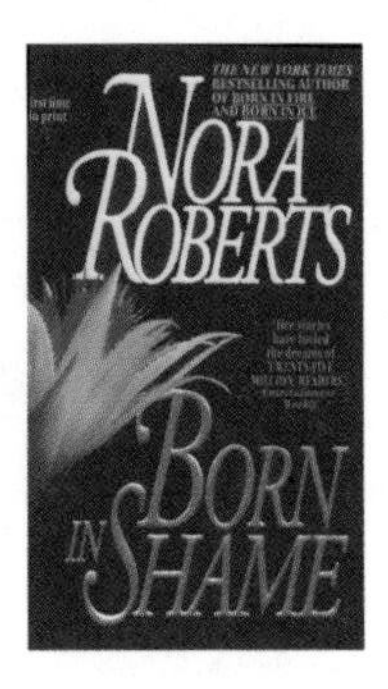

Boundary Lines

Series: None

Editions: Silhouette Intimate Moments #114, Oct. 1985, ISBN: 0-373-07114-0
Language of Love #47 ("Snapdragon"), ISBN: 0-373-51047-0
Silhouette mass-market compilation volume, *Engaging the Enemy*, May 2003, ISBN: 0-373-21819-2

Story: Jullian Baron inherits a Montana ranch and is determined to make a go of it, despite the doubts of her neighbor, cattle baron Aaron Murdock.

Cover Image(s):

Brazen Virtue

Series: Sacred Sins (Bk 2)
For related volumes, see *Sacred Sins* (Bk 1)

Editions: Bantam mass market, May 1988, ISBN: 0-553-27283-7
Bantam hardcover, June 2001, ISBN: 0-553-80212-7
Random House Audio (Abridged), Aug. 2001, ISBN: 0-553-52812-2
Random House Audio CD (Abridged), Aug. 2001, ISBN: 0-553-71436-8
Random House large print hardcover, June 2001, ISBN: 0-375-43112-8

Story: The women behind the Fantasy, Inc., phone-sex service are dying. Detectives Ben Paris and Ed Jackson join forces with mystery novelist Grace McCabe to find the killer.

Series Connections: Detectives Ben Paris and Ed Jackson are partners. As they solve two very different cases, they each find the woman of their dreams.

Cover Image(s):

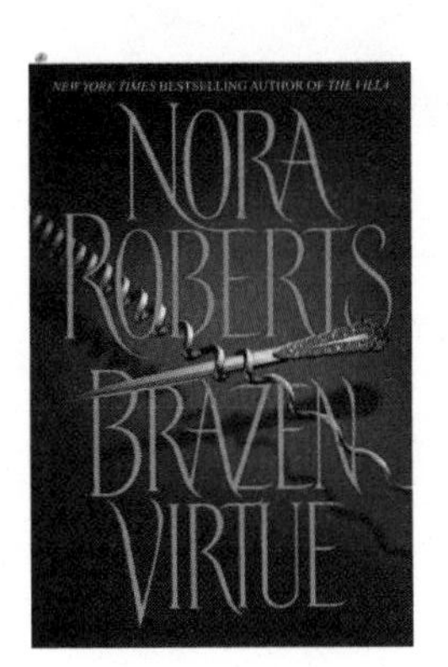

Calhoun Women, The

Series: The Calhoun Women (Bks 1, 2, 3 & 4)

For related volumes, see *Courting Catherine* (Bk 1), *A Man for Amanda* (Bk 2), *For the Love of Lilah* (Bk 3), *Suzanna's Surrender* (Bk 4), and *Megan's Mate* (Bk 5)

See also the compilation volumes: *The Calhoun Women: Catherine and Amanda* and *The Calhoun Women: Lilah and Suzanna*

Editions: Silhouette trade paperback compilation volume, Dec. 1996, ISBN: 0-373-48332-5

Story and Series Connections: See *Courting Catherine* (Bk 1), *A Man for Amanda* (Bk 2), *For the Love of Lilah* (Bk 3), and *Suzanna's Surrender* (Bk 4)

Cover Image(s):

Calhoun Women, The: Catherine and Amanda

Series: The Calhoun Women (Bks 1 & 2)

For related volumes, see *Courting Catherine* (Bk 1), *A Man for Amanda* (Bk 2), *For the Love of Lilah* (Bk 3), *Suzanna's Surrender* (Bk 4), and *Megan's Mate* (Bk 5)

See also the compilation volume: *The Calhoun Women: Lilah and Suzanna*

Editions: Silhouette mass-market compilation volume, Jan. 1998, ISBN: 0-373-48354-6

Silhouette mass-market compilation volume, Sep. 2001, ISBN: 0-373-48495-X

Story and Series Connections: See *Courting Catherine* (Bk 1) and *A Man for Amanda* (Bk 2)

Cover Image(s):

Calhoun Women, The: Lilah and Suzanna

Series: The Calhoun Women (Bks 3 & 4)

For related volumes, see *Courting Catherine* (Bk 1), *A Man for Amanda* (Bk 2), *For the Love of Lilah* (Bk 3), *Suzanna's Surrender* (Bk 4), and *Megan's Mate* (Bk 5)

See also the compilation volume: *The Calhoun Women: Catherine and Amanda*

Editions: Silhouette mass-market compilation volume, Mar. 1998, ISBN: 0-373-48355-4

Silhouette mass-market compilation volume, June 2001, ISBN: 0-373-48498-4

Story and Series Connections: See *For the Love of Lilah* (Bk 3) and *Suzanna's Surrender* (Bk 4)

Cover Image(s):

Captivated

Series: The Donovan Legacy (Bk 1)
For related volumes, see *Entranced* (Bk 2), *Charmed* (Bk 3), and *Enchanted* (Bk 4)
See also the compilation volume: *The Donovan Legacy*

Editions: Silhouette Special Edition #768, Sept. 1992, ISBN: 0-373-09768-9
Silhouette trade paperback compilation volume, *The Donovan Legacy*, Nov. 1999, ISBN: 0-373-48397-X
Thorndike Press large print, June 1993, ISBN: 1-560-54714-6
Silhouette mass-market reissue, Feb. 2004, ISBN: 0-373-28500-0

Story: Screenwriter Nash Kirkland seeks out self-proclaimed witch Morgana Donovan to help him research his next screenplay.

Series Connections: The Donovans share the Donovan Gift—each has special powers that set them apart from ordinary mortals. Their great gifts bring great responsibilities, and even greater rewards.

Cover Image(s):

Captive Star

Series: The Stars of Mithra (Bk 2)
For related volumes, see *Hidden Star* (Bk 1) and *Secret Star* (Bk 3)

Editions: Silhouette Intimate Moments #823, Dec. 1997, ISBN: 0-373-07823-4
Silhouette mass-market reprint, July 2001, ISBN: 0-373-48489-5
Thorndike Press large print, May 2000, ISBN: 0-373-59723-1

Story: Bounty hunter Jack Dakota goes after M. J. O'Leary, only to discover that she's innocent, and that the bad guys who set him up are really after the giant blue diamond hidden in M. J.'s purse.

Series Connections: Three immense blue diamonds in M. J.'s possession form a set of perfectly matched stones once reputed to have been the centerpiece for a pagan altar—the Three Stars of Mithra. One stone represents love, one knowledge, and one generosity. According to the mythology surrounding them, when all three stones sit in a golden triangle as they had in the hands of the god, they confer blessings upon those who possess them. Each novel in the series centers upon one stone and what happens to the woman who holds it.

Cover Image(s):

Carnal Innocence

Series: None

Editions: Bantam mass market, Jan. 1992, ISBN: 0-553-29597-7
Bantam hardcover, Apr. 2001, ISBN: 0-553-11094-2
Bantam Books Audio (Abridged), July 1999, ISBN: 0-553-52637-5
Audible.com (Abridged), Jan. 1999
Wheeler Publishing large print, Dec. 1999, ISBN: 1-56895-810-2
Wheeler Publishing large print, Nov. 2000, ISBN: 1-56895-981-8

Story: Violinist Caroline Waverly arrives at her grandparents' Mississippi home for a vacation, but finds her peace threatened by Tucker Longstreet, and a series of unexplained murders.

Cover Image(s):

Carolina Moon

Series: None

Editions: Putnam hardcover, Mar. 2000, ISBN: 0-399-14592-3
Jove mass market, Apr. 2001, ISBN: 0-515-13038-9
Nova Audio (Abridged), Mar. 2000, ISBN: 1-56740-889-3
Nova Audio (Abridged), Apr. 2001, ISBN: 1-58788-276-0
BrillianceAudio (Unabridged), Mar. 2000, ISBN: 1-56740-494-4
BrillianceAudio, Mar. 2000, ISBN: 1-56749-889-2
BrillianceAudio (Unabridged), Mar. 2000, ISBN: 1-56740-712-9
Thorndike Press large print, June 2000, ISBN: 0-786-22287-5
Thorndike Press large print, June 2001, ISBN: 0-786-22288-3

Story: Tory Bodeen returns to her old hometown in North Carolina, hoping to discover who killed her childhood best friend. The friend's brother, Cade Lavelle, joins in to help track down the murderer before Tory becomes the next victim.

Cover Image(s):

Ceremony in Death

(writing as J. D. Robb)

Series: In Death (Bk 5)

For related volumes, see *Naked in Death* (Bk 1), *Glory in Death* (Bk 2), *Immortal in Death* (Bk 3), *Rapture in Death* (Bk 4), *Vengeance in Death* (Bk 6), *Holiday in Death* (Bk 7), "Midnight in Death" (*Silent Night*, Bk 7.5), *Conspiracy in Death* (Bk 8), *Loyalty in Death* (Bk 9), *Witness in Death* (Bk 10), *Judgment in Death* (Bk 11), *Betrayal in Death* (Bk 12), "Interlude in Death" (*Out of This World*, Bk 12.5), *Seduction in Death* (Bk 13), *Reunion in Death* (Bk 14), *Purity in Death* (Bk 15), *Portrait in Death* (Bk 16), *Imitation in Death* (Bk 17), *Remember When* (Bk 17.5), *Divided in Death* (Bk 18), and *Visions in Death* (Bk 19)

Editions: Berkley mass market, June 1997, ISBN: 0-425-15762-8

Gemstar e-book, Berkley, Mar. 2002, ISBN: 0786519754

Adobe Reader e-book, Berkley, June 2001, ISBN: 0786506385

e-book, Berkley, June 2001, ISBN: 078652197X

Nova Audio (Abridged), Jan. 2002, ISBN: 1-58788-433-X

Nova Audio (Abridged), Jan. 2002, ISBN: 1-58788-434-8

Story: Eve Dallas investigates the death of a fellow police officer. When the cop's granddaughter is killed, too, Eve vows to stop those responsible.

Series Connections: Lt. Eve Dallas is a mid-21st-century cop in a New York City where, despite technological advances, crime still runs rampant. Eve is married to the enigmatic Roarke, a self-made billionaire with a shady past.

Cover Image(s):

Charmed

Series: The Donovan Legacy (Bk 3)

For related volumes, see *Captivated* (Bk 1), *Entranced* (Bk 2), and *Enchanted* (Bk 4)

See also the compilation volume: *The Donovan Legacy*

Editions: Silhouette Special Edition #780, Nov. 1992, ISBN: 0-373-09780-8

Silhouette trade paperback compilation volume, *The Donovan Legacy*, Nov. 1999, ISBN: 0-373-48397-X

Thorndike Press large print, Dec. 1993, ISBN: 1-56054-716-2

Story: A six-year-old girl and her widowed father, writer Boone Sawyer, move in next door to empath and healer Anastasia Donovan, introducing her to a new kind of magic.

Series Connections: The Donovans share the Donovan Gift—each has special powers that set them apart from ordinary mortals. Their great gifts bring great responsibilities, and even greater rewards.

Cover Image(s):

Chesapeake Blue

Series: Chesapeake Bay, a.k.a. The Quinn Brothers (Bk 4)
For related volumes, see *Sea Swept* (Bk 1), *Rising Tides* (Bk 2), and *Inner Harbor* (Bk 3)

Editions: Putnam hardcover, Nov. 2002, ISBN: 0-399-14939-2
Jove mass market, Feb. 2004, ISBN: 0-515-13626-3
Thorndike Press large print hardcover, Feb. 2003, ISBN: 0-786-25128-X
BrillianceAudio (Abridged), Nov. 2002, ISBN: 1-59086-331-3
BrillianceAudio (Abridged), Nov. 2002, ISBN: 1-59086-335-6
BrillianceAudio (Unabridged), Nov. 2002, ISBN: 1-59086-332-1
BrillianceAudio CD (Abridged), Nov. 2002, ISBN: 1-59086-333-X
BrillianceAudio CD (Unabridged), Nov. 2002, ISBN: 1-59086-334-8
BrillianceAudio (Abridged), Jan. 2004, ISBN: 1-59086-336-4

Story: Now a grown man, Seth Quinn must confront his past before he can embrace the future with the woman he loves.

Series Connections: The Quinn brothers were all strays, taken in, adopted, loved, and raised by a very special couple, Ray and Stella Quinn. The death of their parents has left the three brothers coping with the task of caring for the new addition to their family, a tough and wary youngster named Seth.

Cover Image(s):

"Christmas in Ardmore," short story

Series: Irish trilogy, a.k.a. The Gallaghers of Ardmore
For related volumes, see *Jewels of the Sun* (Bk 1), *Tears of the Moon* (Bk 2), and *Heart of the Sea* (Bk 3)

Editions: Jove promotional giveaway volume, Dec. 2000, ISBN: 0-681-51439-6
Note: This short story is no longer in print, but it is available on Nora's official website.

Story: All the Gallaghers celebrate Christmas at the family pub.

Series Connections: The three Gallagher siblings have a gift for hospitality, music, and love. As they each pursue their dreams in the tiny Irish coastal town of Ardmore, the fate of a pair of supernatural lovers rests upon each of the siblings finding and accepting true love.

Cover Image(s):

"Christmas with the Quinns," short story

Series: Chesapeake Bay, a.k.a. The Quinn Brothers
For related volumes, see *Sea Swept* (Bk 1), *Rising Tides* (Bk 2), *Inner Harbor* (Bk 3), and *Chesapeake Blue* (Bk 4)

Editions: Jove promotional giveaway volume, Dec. 2000, ISBN: 0-681-51439-6
- *Note:* This short story is no longer in print, but it is available on Nora's official website.

Story: The tale of Seth's first Christmas with the Quinns, and his joy in having a real family at last.

Series Connections: The Quinn brothers were all strays, taken in, adopted, loved, and raised by a very special couple, Ray and Stella Quinn. The death of their parents has left the three brothers coping with the task of caring for the new addition to their family, a tough and wary youngster named Seth.

Cover Image(s):

Command Performance

Series: Cordina's Royal Family (Bk 2)
For related volumes, see *Affaire Royale* (Bk 1), *The Playboy Prince* (Bk 3), and *Cordina's Crown Jewel* (Bk 4)
See also the compilation volume: *Cordina's Royal Family*

Editions: Silhouette Intimate Moments #198, July 1987, ISBN: 0-373-07198-1
Language of Love #37 ("Crown Imperial"), ISBN: 0-373-51037-3
Silhouette trade paperback compilation volume, *Cordina's Royal Family*, July 2002, ISBN: 0-373-48483-6
Thorndike Press large print hardcover, Nov. 2002, ISBN: 0-786-24239-6

Story: Eve Hamilton returns to Cordina at Prince Alexander's request, where she discovers that the royal family is once again the target of terrorists.

Series Connections: The children of Prince Armand of Cordina and the tiny Monaco-like principality of Cordina form the common threads of this series.

Cover Image(s):

Considering Kate

Series: The Stanislaskis, a.k.a. Those Wild Ukrainians (Bk 6)

For related volumes, see *Taming Natasha* (Bk 1), *Luring a Lady* (Bk 2), *Falling for Rachel* (Bk 3), *Convincing Alex* (Bk 4), and *Waiting for Nick* (Bk 5)

See also the compilation volumes: *The Stanislaski Brothers* and *The Stanislaski Sisters*

Editions: Silhouette Special Edition #1379, Feb. 2001, ISBN: 0-373-24379-0

Thorndike Press large print, Sept. 2001, ISBN: 0-786-23354-0

Story: Ballerina Kate Kimball has left the stage to form her own ballet school. She remodels an historic building in her hometown to accommodate it, with the help of contractor and single father Brody O'Connell.

Series Connections: Ukrainian Americans, and fiercely proud of their heritage, the Stanislaski family brings together the best of two worlds. The Stanislaski siblings and their relations form the core of the series.

Cover Image(s):

Conspiracy in Death

(writing as J. D. Robb)

Series: In Death (Bk 8)

For related volumes, see *Naked in Death* (Bk 1), *Glory in Death* (Bk 2), *Immortal in Death* (Bk 3), *Rapture in Death* (Bk 4), *Ceremony in Death* (Bk 5), *Vengeance in Death* (Bk 6), *Holiday in Death* (Bk 7), "Midnight in Death" (*Silent Night*, Bk 7.5), *Loyalty in Death* (Bk 9), *Witness in Death* (Bk 10), *Judgment in Death* (Bk 11), *Betrayal in Death* (Bk 12), "Interlude in Death" (*Out of This World*, Bk 12.5), *Seduction in Death* (Bk 13), *Reunion in Death* (Bk 14), *Purity in Death* (Bk 15), *Portrait in Death* (Bk 16), *Imitation in Death* (Bk 17), *Remember When* (Bk 17.5), *Divided in Death* (Bk 18), and *Visions in Death* (Bk 19)

Editions: Berkley mass market, Mar. 1999, ISBN: 0-425-16813-1
Nova Audio (Abridged), Nov. 2002, ISBN: 1-58788-443-7
Nova Audio (Abridged), Nov. 2002, ISBN: 1-58788-442-9
Gemstar e-book, Berkley, Jan. 2002, ISBN: 0786519819
Adobe Reader e-book, Berkley, June 2001, ISBN: 0786506768
e-book, Berkley, June 2001, ISBN: 0786500913

Story: After finding a street person's body with a laser hole in his chest and his internal organs missing, Eve Dallas is determined to catch the killer.

Series Connections: Lt. Eve Dallas is a mid-21st-century cop in a New York City where, despite technological advances, crime still runs rampant. Eve is married to the enigmatic Roarke, a self-made billionaire with a shady past.

Cover Image(s):

Convincing Alex

Series: The Stanislaskis, a.k.a. Those Wild Ukrainians (Bk 4)

For related volumes, see *Taming Natasha* (Bk 1), *Luring a Lady* (Bk 2), *Falling for Rachel* (Bk 3), *Waiting for Nick* (Bk 5), and *Considering Kate* (Bk 6)

See also the compilation volumes: *The Stanislaski Sisters* and *The Stanislaski Brothers*

Editions: Silhouette Special Edition #872, Mar. 1994, ISBN: 0-373-09872-3

Silhouette mass-market compilation volume, *The Stanislaski Brothers: Mikhail and Alex*, Nov. 2000, ISBN: 0-373-48422-4

Thorndike Press large print compilation volume, *The Stanislaski Brothers: Mikhail and Alex*, July 2001, ISBN: 0-786-23276-5

Story: Soap opera writer Bess McNee is talking to prostitutes on a New York City street, researching a script, when Detective Alex Stanislaski arrests her for soliciting.

Series Connections: Ukrainian Americans, and fiercely proud of their heritage, the Stanislaski family brings together the best of two worlds. The Stanislaski siblings and their relations form the core of the series.

Cover Image(s):

Cordina's Crown Jewel

Series: Cordina's Royal Family (Bk 4)

For related volumes, see *Affaire Royale* (Bk 1) *Command Performance* (Bk 2), and *The Playboy Prince* (Bk 3)

See also the compilation volume: *Cordina's Royal Family*

Editions: Silhouette Special Edition #1448, Feb. 2002, ISBN: 0-373-24448-7

Thorndike Press large print, June 2002, ISBN: 0-786-24203-5

Story: Her Royal Highness Camilla de Cordina drops her royal identity, ditches her guards, takes off on a road trip, and has to seek shelter from a storm with archeologist Delaney Caine.

Series Connections: The children of Prince Armand of Cordina and the Monaco-like principality of Cordina form the common threads of this series.

Cover Image(s):

Cordina's Royal Family

Series: Cordina's Royal Family (Bks 1, 2, & 3)
For related volumes, see *Affaire Royale* (Bk 1), *Command Performance* (Bk 2), *The Playboy Prince* (Bk 3), and *Cordina's Crown Jewel* (Bk 4)

Editions: Silhouette trade paperback compilation volume, July 2002, ISBN: 0-373-48483-6

Story: See *Affaire Royale* (Bk 1), *Command Performance* (Bk 2), and *The Playboy Prince* (Bk 3)

Series Connections: The children of Prince Armand of Cordina and the tiny Monaco-like principality of Cordina form the common threads of this series.

Cover Image(s):

Courting Catherine

Series: The Calhoun Women (Bk 1)

For related volumes, see *A Man for Amanda* (Bk 2), *For the Love of Lilah* (Bk 3), *Suzanna's Surrender* (Bk 4), and *Megan's Mate* (Bk 5)

See also the compilation volumes: *The Calhoun Women: Catherine and Amanda* and *The Calhoun Women: Lilah and Suzanna*

Editions: Silhouette Romance #801, June 1991, ISBN: 0-373-08801-9

BrillianceAudio (Abridged), May 1998, ISBN: 1-5674-0029-9

Silhouette trade paperback compilation volume, *The Calhoun Women*, Dec. 1996, ISBN: 0-373-48332-5

Silhouette mass-market compilation volume, *The Calhoun Women: Catherine and Amanda*, Jan. 1998, ISBN: 0-373-48354-6

G. K. Hall & Co. large print hardcover, July 1992, ISBN: 0-8161-5403-1

Story: When hotelier Trenton St. James's car breaks down, auto mechanic Catherine "C.C." Calhoun fixes it, only to discover that Trent has come to Maine determined to buy her family's crumbling mansion and convert it into a luxury hotel.

Series Connections: The Calhoun sisters have inherited the family mansion built by Fergus Calhoun in the early 1900s. They've also inherited the family legends about the love affair that Fergus's wife, Bianca, had with an artist, and of the lost Calhoun emeralds, a fabulous set of jewels that vanished when Bianca died young and tragically. As they seek the jewels, they come closer to knowing the truth about Bianca and to finding love for themselves.

Cover Image(s):

Dance of Dreams

Series: Reflections and Dreams, a.k.a. the Davidov series (Bk 2)
For related volumes, see *Reflections* (Bk 1) and a cameo appearance in *Considering Kate*
See also the compilation volume: *Reflections and Dreams*

Editions: Silhouette Special Edition #116, Sept. 1983, ISBN: 0-671-53616-8
Language of Love #8 ("Narcissus"), ISBN: 0-373-51008-X
Silhouette mass-market compilation volume, *Reflections and Dreams*, July 2001, ISBN: 0-373-48442-9
G. K. Hall & Co. large print, ISBN: 0-7838-9043-5

Story: Ruth Bannion, the principal dancer for New York's biggest ballet company, falls in love with the company's director and choreographer, Nickolai Davidov.

Series Connections: Ruth Bannion is the niece of architect Seth Bannion. Seth is married to former prima ballerina Lindsay Dunne, who once danced with Davidov.

Cover Image(s):

Dance to the Piper

Series: The O'Hurleys (Bk 2)

For related volumes, see *The Last Honest Woman* (Bk 1), *Skin Deep* (Bk 3), and *Without a Trace* (Bk 4), with cameo appearances in *Waiting for Nick* and *Considering Kate*, and passing mentions in *Heart of the Sea* and *Tears of the Moon*

See also the compilation volume: *The O'Hurleys: Abby and Maddy*

Editions: Silhouette Special Edition #463, July 1988, ISBN: 0-373-09463-9

Mira mass-market reprint, Nov. 1994, ISBN: 0-373-48232-9

Mira mass-market reprint, Nov. 1998, ISBN: 1-55166-321-X

Mira mass-market reprint, Nov. 1994, ISBN: 1-55166-007-5

Silhouette trade paperback compilation volume, *The O'Hurleys: Abby and Maddy*, Sept. 2004

Story: Maddy O'Hurley, one of Broadway's brightest stars, is in rehearsal for a new musical when a chance meeting with the show's financial backer, recording mogul Reed Valentine, changes her life.

Series Connections: The O'Hurley triplets, Abby, Maddy, and Chantel, and their brother, Trace, form the backbone of this series. The children of veteran performers Frank and Molly O'Hurley, they were born on the road between shows, and raised in hotel rooms and dressing rooms all across America.

Cover Image(s):

Note: The picture of Abby on the back cover of the first edition was painted using Nora Roberts as the model.

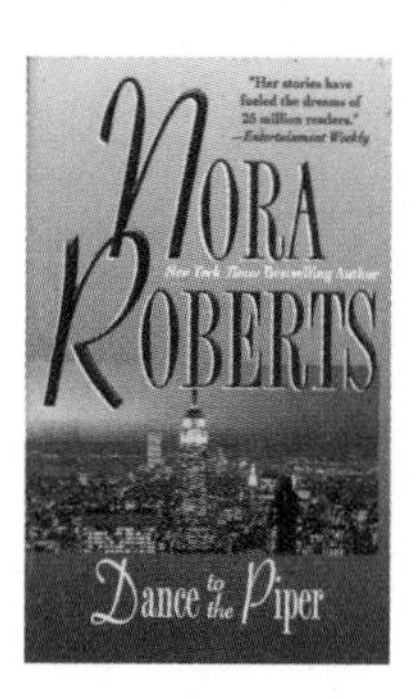

Dance Upon the Air

Series: Three Sisters Island (Bk 1)

For related volumes, see *Heaven and Earth* (Bk 2) and *Face the Fire* (Bk 3)

Editions: Jove mass market, June 2001, ISBN: 0-515-13122-9

Nova Audio (Abridged), July 2001, ISBN: 1-58788-223-X

BrillianceAudio (Unabridged), June 2001, ISBN: 1-58788-222-1

BrillianceAudio (Abridged), June 2002, ISBN: 1-58788-670-7

BrillianceAudio (Unabridged), July 2001, ISBN: 1-58788-221-3

BrillianceAudio (Abridged), June 2001, ISBN: 1-58788-492-5

BrillianceAudio CD (Abridged), July 2001, ISBN: 1-58788-490-9

G. K. Hall & Co. large print, Dec. 2001, ISBN: 0-7838-9619-0

G. K. Hall & Co. large print, July 2002, ISBN:0-7838-9620-4

Gemstar e-book, Jove, Jan. 2002, ISBN: 0786519827

Adobe Reader e-book, Jove, June 2001, ISBN: 078651003X

e-book, Jove, June 2001, ISBN: 0786510021

Story: Nell Channing came to Three Sisters Island seeking refuge from her abusive husband, but her silence about her past leaves the island's sheriff, Zack Todd, wanting to know more about her.

Series Connections: Three Sisters Island suffers under a curse, one that can only be broken by the descendants of the three witches who created the island in 1692. Now three women will unite in friendship and trust to save their home, their lives, and the people they love.

Cover Image(s):

Dangerous

Series: None

Editions: Silhouette trade paperback compilation volume, Dec. 2002, ISBN: 0-373-21854-0

Story: See *Risky Business*, *Storm Warning*, and *The Welcoming.*

Cover Image(s):

Daring to Dream

Series: Dream, a.k.a. Templeton House (Bk 1)
For related volumes, see *Holding the Dream* (Bk 2) and *Finding the Dream* (Bk 3)

Editions: Jove mass market, Aug. 1996, ISBN: 0-515-11920-2
BrillianceAudio (Unabridged), Oct. 1996, ISBN: 1-5610-0738-2
BrillianceAudio (Unabridged), Nov. 1996, ISBN: 1-5610-0813-3
BrillianceAudio (Abridged), Oct. 1997, ISBN: 1-56740-204-6
Countertop Audio compilation audiocassette (Abridged), Jan. 2001, *Best of Nora Roberts* (audio versions of *Daring to Dream*, *Holding the Dream*, *Finding the Dream*, and *Homeport*), ISBN: 1-8860-8995-7
Putnam hardcover omnibus edition, *Three Complete Novels: Daring to Dream, Holding the Dream, Finding the Dream*, Apr. 1999, ISBN: 0-399-14480-3
Jove mass-market boxed set (with *Holding the Dream* and *Finding the Dream*), May 2002, ISBN: 0-515-13457-0
Severn House Publishers, Ltd., hardcover British edition, Apr. 1998, ISBN: 0-7278-53104
e-book, Jove, Jan. 2002, ISBN: 0786519843
Adobe Reader e-book, Jove, June 2001, ISBN: 0786506814
Thorndike Press large print, Jan. 1997, ISBN: 0-786-20894-5

Story: Margo Sullivan lost everything when a man she thought she loved betrayed her. Old friend Josh Templeton steps in to help Margo rebuild her life.
Note: The early working title for *Daring to Dream* was *Willing to Dream.* This title may eventually be recycled, but there are no current plans to do so, and all current mentions on the Internet and in bookstore computers of *Willing to Dream* are artifacts from the early information distributed about the series.

Series Connections: Laura Templeton, Kate Powell, and Margo Sullivan were raised together in Templeton House, high in the Monterey, California, cliffs. Now that they are grown women, the bond they share is in many ways stronger than the one between sisters. They also share a belief in the legend of Seraphina and Felipe, star-crossed lovers who hid a fortune in gold in the cliffs. And as they each seek and find their destiny and their true love, they find a piece of that gold as a blessing on their union.

Cover Image(s):

Divided in Death

Series: In Death (Bk 18)

For related volumes, see *Naked in Death* (Bk 1), *Glory in Death* (Bk 2), *Immortal in Death* (Bk 3), *Rapture in Death* (Bk 4), *Ceremony in Death* (Bk 5), *Vengeance in Death* (Bk 6), *Holiday in Death* (Bk 7), "Midnight in Death" (*Silent Night*, Bk 7.5), *Conspiracy in Death* (Bk 8), *Loyalty in Death* (Bk 9), *Witness in Death* (Bk 10), *Judgment in Death* (Bk 11), *Betrayal in Death* (Bk 12), "Interlude in Death" (*Out of This World*, Bk 12.5), *Seduction in Death* (Bk 13), *Reunion in Death* (Bk 14), *Purity in Death* (Bk 15), *Portrait in Death* (Bk 16), *Imitation in Death* (Bk 17), *Remember When* (Bk 17.5), and *Visions in Death* (Bk 19)

Editions: G. P. Putnam's Sons hardcover, Jan. 2004, ISBN: 0-399-15154-0
Berkley mass market, Sept. 2004

Story: Eve Dallas is on the trail of a killer that leads her to investigate the mysterious Homeland Security Organization.

Series Connections: Lt. Eve Dallas is a mid-21st-century cop in a New York City where, despite technological advances, crime still runs rampant. Eve is married to the enigmatic Roarke, a self-made billionaire with a shady past.

Cover Image(s): Not available

Divine Evil

Series: None

Editions: Bantam mass market, Oct. 1992, ISBN: 0-553-29490-3
Wheeler Publishing large print, Oct. 1998, ISBN: 1-5689-5118-3
Bantam hardcover, Aug. 2004

Story: When sculptor Claire Kimbal goes home to Emmitsboro, Maryland, her return stirs up the deranged mind of a killer. Claire and the sheriff, Cameron Rafferty, must find the murderer.

Cover Image(s):

Donovan Legacy, The

Series: The Donovan Legacy (Bks 1, 2, & 3)
For related volumes, see *Captivated* (Bk 1), *Entranced* (Bk 2), *Charmed* (Bk 3), and *Enchanted* (Bk 4)

Editions: Silhouette trade paperback compilation volume, Nov. 1999, ISBN: 0-373-48397-X

Story and Series Connections: See *Captivated* (Bk 1), *Entranced* (Bk 2), and *Charmed* (Bk 3)

Cover Image(s):

Dual Image

Series: None

Editions: Silhouette Intimate Moments #123, Dec. 1985, ISBN: 0-373-07123-X
Language of Love #29 ("Red Carnation"), ISBN: 0-373-51029-2
Silhouette mass-market compilation volume, *Truly Madly Manhattan*, Jan. 2003, ISBN: 0-373-21803-6
Thorndike Press large print, Nov. 2000, ISBN: 0-786-22605-6

Story: Actress Ariel Kirkwood gets a part in screenwriter Booth DeWitt's semiautobiographical new film, portraying his cold and calculating ex-wife.

Series Connections: Characters from this book have fleeting mentions in several subsequent books, notably *Convincing Alex.*

Cover Image(s):

Enchanted

Series: The Donovan Legacy (Bk 4)
For related volumes, see *Captivated* (Bk 1), *Entranced* (Bk 2), and *Charmed* (Bk 3)
See also the compilation volume: *The Donovan Legacy*

Editions: Silhouette Intimate Moments #961, Nov. 1999, ISBN: 0-373-07961-3
Thorndike Press large print, July 2000, ISBN: 0-786-22599-8

Story: When Rowan Murray seeks the peace of a cabin in the Oregon woods, she finds herself drawn to neighbor Liam Donovan.

Series Connections: The Donovans share the Donovan Gift—each has special powers that set them apart from ordinary mortals. Their great gifts bring great responsibilities, and even greater rewards.

Cover Image(s):

Endings and Beginnings

Series: None

Editions: Silhouette Intimate Moments #33, Jan. 1984, ISBN: 0-671-46157-5

Note: From the Heart, a single-volume collection of three unrelated early books (*Tonight and Always*, *A Matter of Choice*, and *Endings and Beginnings*), is the only version of these works currently in print. These titles are only available in the Berkley edition of *From the Heart.* These titles have reverted to the author and are no longer available from Harlequin.

Jove mass market, *From the Heart*, Nov. 1996, ISBN: 0-515-11965-2

Berkley trade paperback, *From the Heart*, June 2000, ISBN: 0-425-17616-9

Thorndike Press large print, Apr. 1997, ISBN: 0-786-21046-X

Adobe Reader e-book, June 2001, ISBN: 0-786-50709-8

Story: Washington, D.C.–based reporter and anchorperson Liv Carmichael clashes with highly regarded national reporter T. C. Thorpe over stories, airtime, and love.

Series Connections: Myra Ditmyer, from the MacGregor series, has a notable cameo in this book.

Cover Image(s):

Engaging the Enemy

Series: None

Editions: Silhouette mass-market compilation volume, May 2003,
ISBN: 0-373-21819-2

Story and Series Connections: See *A Will and a Way* and *Boundary Lines.*

Cover Image(s):

Entranced

Series: The Donovan Legacy (Bk 2)

For related volumes, see *Captivated* (Bk 1), *Charmed* (Bk 3), and *Enchanted* (Bk 4)

See also the compilation volume: *The Donovan Legacy*

Editions: Silhouette Special Edition #774, Oct. 1992, ISBN: 0-373-09774-3

Silhouette compilation trade paperback volume, *The Donovan Legacy*, Nov. 1999, ISBN: 0-373-48397-X

Silhouette mass-market reissue, June 2004, ISBN: 0-373-28501-9

Story: Sebastian Donovan is a witch and a seer, and private investigator Mary Ellen "Mel" Sutherland needs his help to find a kidnapped baby.

Series Connections: The Donovans share the Donovan Gift—each has special powers that set them apart from ordinary mortals. Their great gifts bring great responsibilities, and even greater rewards.

Cover Image(s):

Face the Fire

Series: Three Sisters Island (Bk 3)

For related volumes, see *Dance Upon the Air* (Bk 1) and *Heaven and Earth* (Bk 2)

Editions: Jove mass market, June 2002, ISBN: 0-515-13287-X

BrillianceAudio (Unabridged), June 2002, ISBN: 1-58788-227-2

BrillianceAudio CD (Abridged), June 2002, ISBN: 1-58788-967-6

BrillianceAudio CD (Abridged), June 2002, ISBN: 1-58788-968-4

Nova Audio (Abridged), June 2002, ISBN: 1-58788-229-9

BrillianceAudio Collector's Case edition, June 2002, ISBN: 1-58788-228-0

BrillianceAudio (Abridged), Apr. 2003, ISBN: 1-59086-992-3

G. K. Hall & Co. large print, Aug. 2003, ISBN: 0-7838-9627-1

Thorndike Press large print hardcover, Aug. 2003, ISBN: 0-783-89623-9

Adobe Reader e-book, Jove, Aug. 2002

Story: Mia Devlin and Sam Logan had once shared what Mia thought was the love of a lifetime, until Sam left Three Sisters Island, and Mia. Now Sam's back, and he's determined to win Mia's love again.

Series Connections: Three Sisters Island suffers under a curse, one that can only be broken by the descendents of the three witches who created the island in 1692. Now three women will unite in friendship and trust to save their home, their lives, and the people they love.

Cover Image(s):

Fall of Shane MacKade, The

Series: The MacKade Brothers (Bk 4)

For related volumes, see *The Return of Rafe MacKade* (Bk 1), *The Pride of Jared MacKade* (Bk 2), and *The Heart of Devin MacKade* (Bk 3)

Editions: Silhouette Special Edition #1022, Apr. 1996, ISBN: 0-373-24022-8

Harlequin large print trade paperback, May 1998, ISBN: 0-373-59863-7

Silhouette trade paperback compilation volume, *The MacKade Brothers: Devin and Shane*, June 2004, ISBN: 0-373-21885-0

Story: When Dr. Rebecca Knight shows up to go ghost hunting on Shane MacKade's land, he might scoff at her mission, but he finds the woman quite appealing.

Series Connections: The four MacKade brothers lost their parents early and struggled to raise each other, save the family farm, and find their fortunes. But they were never so tired or so busy that they couldn't go looking for trouble . . . and find it.

Cover Image(s):

Falling for Rachel

Series: The Stanislaskis, a.k.a. Those Wild Ukrainians (Bk 3)
For related volumes, see *Taming Natasha* (Bk 1), *Luring a Lady* (Bk 2), *Convincing Alex* (Bk 4), *Waiting for Nick* (Bk 5), and *Considering Kate* (Bk 6)
See also the compilation volumes: *The Stanislaski Brothers* and *The Stanislaski Sisters*

Editions: Silhouette Special Edition #810, Apr. 1993, ISBN: 0-373-09810-3
Silhouette mass-market compilation volume, *The Stanislaski Sisters: Natasha and Rachel*, Feb. 2001, ISBN: 0-373-48423-2
Silhouette mass-market compilation volume, *The Stanislaski Sisters: Rachel and Natasha*, Apr. 1997, ISBN: 0-373-20134-6
Thorndike Press large print hardcover compilation volume, *The Stanislaski Sisters: Natasha and Rachel*, ISBN: 0-786-23366-4

Story: When Zach Muldoon's kid brother, Nick, gets in trouble, public defender Rachel Stanislaski comes to their rescue.

Series Connections: Ukrainian Americans, and fiercely proud of their heritage, the Stanislaski family brings together the best of two worlds. The Stanislaski siblings and their relations form the core of the series.

Cover Image(s):

Finding the Dream

Series: Dream, a.k.a Templeton House (Bk 3)
For related volumes, see *Daring to Dream* (Bk 1) and *Holding the Dream* (Bk 2)

Editions: Doubleday hardcover edition, July 1997, ISBN: 1-56865-422-7
Jove mass market, Aug. 1997, ISBN: 0-515-12087-1
BrillianceAudio (Unabridged), July 1997, ISBN: 1-56100-740-4
BrillianceAudio (Unabridged), Aug. 1997, ISBN: 1-56100-815-X
Nova Audio (Abridged), Aug. 1997, ISBN: 1-56100-929-6
Nova Audio (Abridged), May 1998, ISBN: 1-5674-0205-4
Countertop Audio compilation audiocassette (Abridged), Jan. 2001, *The Best of Nora Roberts* (audio version of *Daring to Dream*, *Holding the Dream*, *Finding the Dream*, and *Homeport*), ISBN: 1-8860-8995-7
Putnam hardcover omnibus edition, *Three Complete Novels: Daring to Dream, Holding the Dream, Finding the Dream*, Apr. 1999, ISBN: 0-399-14480-3
Jove mass-market boxed set (with *Daring to Dream* and *Holding the Dream*), May 2002, ISBN: 0-515-13457-0
Severn House Publishers, Ltd., British hardcover edition, ASIN: 0-7278-2295-0
Thorndike Press large print, Jan. 1998, ISBN: 0-786-21130-X
e-book, Jove, Sept. 2001, ISBN: 0786501340
Adobe Reader e-book, Jove, Sept. 2001, ISBN: 0786507055

Story: Laura Templeton's husband divorces and betrays her, leaving Laura and her two children shattered. Then Laura's childhood flame, Michael Fury, returns to her life, hoping to finally win her heart.

Series Connections: Laura Templeton, Kate Powell, and Margo Sullivan were raised together in Templeton House, high in the Monterey, California, cliffs. Now that they are grown women, the bond they share is in many ways stronger than the one between sisters. They also share a belief in the legend of Seraphina and Felipe, star-crossed lovers who hid a fortune in gold in the cliffs. And as they each seek and find their destiny and their true love, they find a piece of that gold as a blessing on their union.

Cover Image(s):

First Impressions

Series: None

Editions: Silhouette Special Edition #162, Apr. 1984, ISBN: 0-671-53662-1
Language of Love #5 ("Foxglove"), ISBN: 0-373-51005-5
Silhouette hardcover edition, June 2003, ISBN: 0-373-21863-X

Story: When Vance Banning, a wealthy construction company president, moves in next door to Shane Abbott, he's amused when his new neighbor thinks he's an out-of-work carpenter.

Cover Image(s):

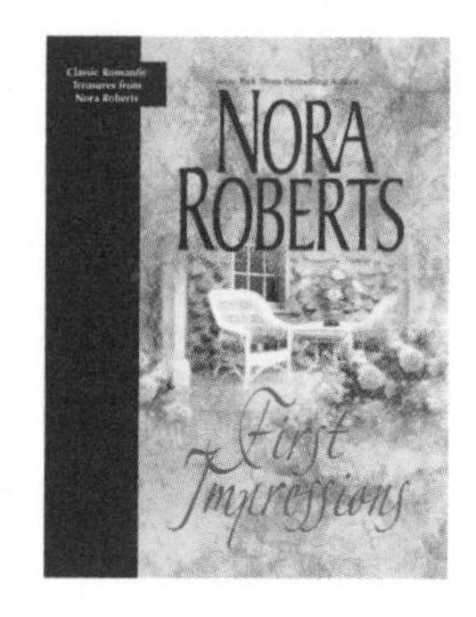

For Now, Forever

Series: The MacGregors (Bk 5)

For related volumes, see *Playing the Odds* (Bk 1), *Tempting Fate* (Bk 2), *All the Possibilities* (Bk 3), *One Man's Art* (Bk 4), *The MacGregor Brides* (Bk 6), *The Winning Hand* (Bk 7), *The MacGregor Grooms* (Bk 8), *The Perfect Neighbor* (Bk 9), *Rebellion*, a novel featuring a story from Clan MacGregor history, and *Harlequin Historical Christmas Stories 1990*, "In from the Cold," a novella set in pre–Revolutionary War New England

See also the compilation volumes: *The MacGregors: Serena ~ Caine*, *The MacGregors: Alan ~ Grant*, and *The MacGregors: Daniel ~ Ian*

Editions: Silhouette Special Edition #361, Feb. 1987, ISBN: 0-373-09361-6

Language of Love #19 ("White Periwinkle"), ISBN: 0-373-51019-5

Silhouette mass-market compilation volume, *The MacGregors: Daniel ~ Ian*, Apr. 1999, ISBN: 0-373-48390-2

Story: Daniel MacGregor's survival is in question after a car accident. Daniel's wife of forty years, surgeon Anna MacGregor, remembers their courtship as she waits to find out if Daniel will live.

Note: The original publication of this book was accompanied by the re-release of the first four MacGregor books, the first such re-release in Silhouette's history.

Series Connections: The children of Daniel MacGregor and his wife, Anna, form the backbone of this series, with a slew of Daniel's grandchildren and great-grandchildren and assorted relatives to fill out the sequels. As Daniel himself would put it, "Good blood. Strong stock."

Cover Image(s):

For the Love of Lilah

Series: The Calhoun Women (Bk 3)

For related volumes, see *Courting Catherine* (Bk 1), *A Man for Amanda* (Bk 2), *Suzanna's Surrender* (Bk 4), and *Megan's Mate* (Bk 5)

See also the compilation volumes: *The Calhoun Women: Catherine and Amanda* and *The Calhoun Women: Lilah and Suzanna*

Editions: Silhouette Special Edition #685, Aug. 1991, ISBN: 0-373-09685-2

Silhouette trade paperback compilation volume, *The Calhoun Women*, Dec. 1996, ISBN: 0-373-48332-5

Silhouette mass-market compilation volume, *The Calhoun Women: Lilah and Suzanna*, Mar. 1998, ISBN: 0-373-48355-4

G. K. Hall & Co. large print, May 1993, ISBN: 0-8161-5725-1

Story: Lilah Calhoun is looking along the beach for the lost Calhoun emeralds, but instead finds Cornell professor Maxwell Quartermain drowning in the ocean, and rescues him.

Series Connections: The Calhoun sisters have inherited the family mansion built by Fergus Calhoun in the early 1900s. They've also inherited the family legends about the love affair that Fergus's wife, Bianca, had with an artist, and of the lost Calhoun emeralds, a fabulous set of jewels that vanished when Bianca died young and tragically. As they seek the jewels, they come closer to knowing the truth about Bianca and to finding love for themselves.

Cover Image(s):

Series: The MacGregors

For related volumes, see *Playing the Odds* (Bk 1), *Tempting Fate* (Bk 2), *All the Possibilities* (Bk 3), *One Man's Art* (Bk 4), *For Now, Forever* (Bk 5), *The MacGregor Brides* (Bk 6), *The Winning Hand* (Bk 7), *The MacGregor Grooms* (Bk 8), *The Perfect Neighbor* (Bk 9), and *Harlequin Historical Christmas Stories 1990*, "In from the Cold," a novella set in pre–Revolutionary War New England

See also the compilation volumes: *The MacGregors: Serena ~ Caine*, *The MacGregors: Alan ~ Grant*, and *The MacGregors: Daniel ~ Ian*

Editions: Harlequin Romance Novel trade paperback anthology edition, *Forever Mine*, (with *Rebellion* by Nora Roberts, *Reckless Love* by Elizabeth Lowell, and *Dark Stranger* by Heather Graham Pozzessere), Apr. 1999, ISBN: 0-373-83400-4

Story and Series Connections: See *Rebellion*

Cover Image(s):

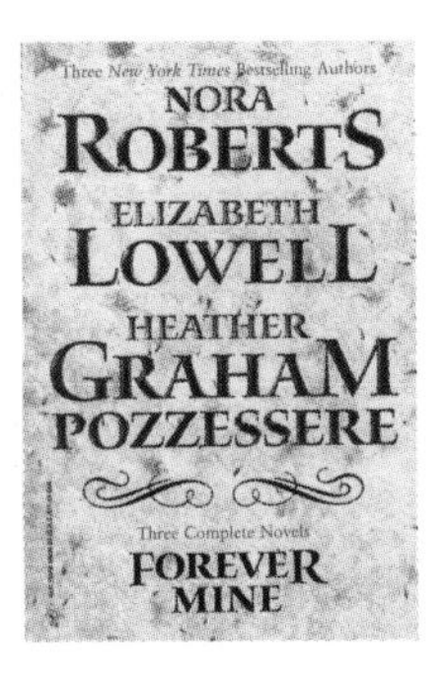

From the Heart

Series: None

Editions: Jove mass market, Nov. 1996, ISBN: 0-515-11965-2
Berkley trade paperback, June 2000, ISBN: 0-425-17616-9
Thorndike Press large print, Apr. 1997, ISBN: 0-786-21046-X
Adobe Reader e-book, June 2001, ISBN: 0786507098
e-book, June 2001, ISBN: 0786503084

Story: See *Tonight and Always*, *A Matter of Choice*, and *Endings and Beginnings.*
Note: These titles are only available in the Berkley edition of *From the Heart.*
These titles have reverted to the author and are no longer available from Harlequin.

Series Connections: Myra Ditmyer, of the MacGregor books, makes a notable cameo appearance in *Endings and Beginnings.*

Cover Image(s):

Series: None

Editions: Silhouette Romance #199, Jan. 1983, ISBN: 0-671-57199-0
Language of Love #14 ("Forget-Me-Not"), ISBN: 0-373-51014-4
G. K. Hall & Co. large print, Jan. 1985, ISBN: 0-8161-3743-9
Silhouette mass-market reissue, Oct. 2003, ISBN: 0-373-21842-7

Story: B. J. Clark, the manager of a quaint Lakeside Inn in New England, faces off with its new owner, hotelier Taylor Reynolds.

Cover Image(s):

Gabriel's Angel

Series: None

Editions: Silhouette Intimate Moments #300, Aug. 1989, ISBN: 0-373-07300-3
Language of Love #32 ("Wisteria"), ISBN: 0-373-51032-2
Harlequin large print, Apr. 1993, ISBN: 0-373-58806-2
Harlequin large print, Apr. 1993, ISBN: 0-373-58906-9
Silhouette hardcover edition, Sept. 2003, ISBN: 0-373-21869-9

Story: Artist Gabriel Bradley found the total isolation he'd sought at his mountain cabin, until the day a spring blizzard landed the beautiful and very pregnant Laura Malone on his front porch, in desperate need of help.

Series Connections: None

Cover Image(s):

Genuine Lies

Series: None

Editions: Bantam mass market, Sept. 1991, ISBN: 0-553-29078-9
Bantam hardcover edition, July 1998, ISBN: 0-553-10834-4
Wheeler Publishing large print, Nov. 1998, ISBN: 1-5689-5678-9

Story: When Hollywood star Eve Benedict tells her story to biographer Julia Summers, it soon becomes clear that someone is willing to kill to prevent the book's release.

Cover Image(s):

Glory in Death

(writing as J. D. Robb)

Series: In Death (Bk 2)

For related volumes, see *Naked in Death* (Bk 1), *Immortal in Death* (Bk 3), *Rapture in Death* (Bk 4), *Ceremony in Death* (Bk 5), *Vengeance in Death* (Bk 6), *Holiday in Death* (Bk 7), "Midnight in Death" (*Silent Night*, Bk 7.5), *Conspiracy in Death* (Bk 8), *Loyalty in Death* (Bk 9), *Witness in Death* (Bk 10), *Judgment in Death* (Bk 11), *Betrayal in Death* (Bk 12), "Interlude in Death" (*Out of This World*, Bk 12.5), *Seduction in Death* (Bk 13), *Reunion in Death* (Bk 14), *Purity in Death* (Bk 15), *Portrait in Death* (Bk 16), *Imitation in Death* (Bk 17), *Remember When* (Bk 17.5), *Divided in Death* (Bk 18), and *Visions in Death* (Bk 19)

Editions: Berkley mass market, Dec. 1995, ISBN: 0-425-15098-4
Recorded Books (Unabridged), Dec. 1995, ISBN: 0-7887-4374-0
Nova Audio (Abridged), Apr. 2001, ISBN: 1-58788-100-4
BrillianceAudio (Abridged), Apr. 2001, ISBN: 1-58788-197-7
Putnam hardcover, June 2004, ISBN: 0-399-15158-3
Gemstar e-book, Berkley, Jan. 2002, ISBN: 0786520183
Adobe Reader e-book, Berkley, June 2001, ISBN: 0786507136
e-book, Berkley, June 2001, ISBN: 0786506008

Story: Lt. Eve Dallas must find out who is killing a series of high-powered women before he can kill again.

Series Connections: Lt. Eve Dallas is a mid-21st-century cop in a New York City where, despite technological advances, crime still runs rampant. Eve is married to the enigmatic Roarke, a self-made billionaire with a shady past.

Cover Image(s):

Going Home

Series: None

Editions: Silhouette trade paperback compilation volume, Oct. 2002, ISBN: 0-373-21848-6

Story and Series Connections: See *Mind over Matter*, *Unfinished Business*, and *Island of Flowers*.

Cover Image(s):

Harlequin Historical Christmas Stories 1990, "In from the Cold" novella

Series: The MacGregors

For related volumes, see *Playing the Odds* (Bk 1), *Tempting Fate* (Bk 2), *All the Possibilities* (Bk 3), *One Man's Art* (Bk 4), *For Now, Forever* (Bk 5), *The MacGregor Brides* (Bk 6), *The Winning Hand* (Bk 7), *The MacGregor Grooms* (Bk 8), *The Perfect Neighbor* (Bk 9), and *Rebellion*, a novel featuring a story line from Clan MacGregor history.

See also the compilation volumes: *The MacGregors: Serena ~ Caine*, *The MacGregors: Alan ~ Grant*, and *The MacGregors: Daniel ~ Ian*

Editions: Harlequin Historical Christmas Stories 1990, Nov. 1990, ISBN: 0-373-83218-4

Silhouette mass-market compilation volume, *The MacGregors: Daniel ~ Ian*, Apr. 1999, ISBN: 0-373-48390-2

Story: After the Boston Tea Party, Minuteman Ian MacGregor flees into the wilderness with a musket ball in his shoulder, finally finding shelter in widow Allanna Flynn's barn.

Note: This is a multistory collection and also includes novellas by Patricia Potter and Ruth Ryan Langan.

Series Connections: The children of Daniel MacGregor and his wife, Anna, form the backbone of this series, with a slew of Daniel's grandchildren and great-grandchildren and assorted relatives to fill out the sequels. As Daniel himself would put it, "Good blood. Strong stock."

Cover Image(s):

Heart of Devin MacKade, The

Series: The MacKade Brothers (Bk 3)
For related volumes, see *The Return of Rafe MacKade* (Bk 1), *The Pride of Jared MacKade* (Bk 2), and *The Fall of Shane MacKade* (Bk 4)

Editions: Silhouette Intimate Moments #697, Mar. 1996, ISBN: 0-373-07697-5
Silhouette trade paperback compilation volume, *The MacKade Brothers: Devin and Shane*, June 2004, ISBN: 0-373-21885-0
Thorndike Press large print, Apr. 1998, ISBN: 0-373-59859-9

Story: Sheriff Devin MacKade has loved Cassie Dolin since they were kids together. Now that her abusive marriage is ending, he is finally free to reach out to her.

Series Connections: The four MacKade brothers lost their parents early and struggled to raise each other, save the family farm, and find their fortunes. But they were never so tired or so busy that they couldn't go looking for trouble . . . and find it.

Cover Image(s):

Heart of the Sea

Series: Irish trilogy, a.k.a. The Gallaghers of Ardmore (Bk 3)
For related volumes, see *Jewels of the Sun* (Bk 1) and *Tears of the Moon* (Bk 2)

Editions: Jove mass market, Dec. 2000, ISBN: 0-515-12855-4
Nova Audio (Abridged), Jan. 2001, ISBN: 1-56740-871-0
BrillianceAudio (Unabridged), Dec. 2000, ISBN: 1-56740-693-9
BrillianceAudio (Unabridged), Jan. 2001, ISBN: 1-56740-470-7
BrillianceAudio (Abridged), Nov. 2001, ISBN: 1-58788-341-4
Jove mass-market boxed set (with *Jewels of the Sun* and *Tears of the Moon*), Apr. 2001, ISBN: 0-515-13164-4
G. K. Hall & Co. large print, Feb. 2001, ISBN: 0-7838-8987-9
G. K. Hall & Co. large print, Apr. 2001, ISBN: 0-7838-8988-7
Nora Roberts Irish Jewels Trilogy, BrillianceAudio compilation (Abridged), June 2003, ISBN: 1-59086-541-3
e-book, Jove, Sept. 2001, ISBN: 0786501413
Adobe Reader e-book, Jove, Sept. 2001, ISBN: 0786507195

Story: Darcy Gallagher meets her match when entertainment mogul Trevor McGee arrives in Ardmore.

Series Connections: The three Gallagher siblings have a gift for hospitality, music, and love. As they each pursue their dreams in the tiny Irish coastal town of Ardmore, the fate of a pair of supernatural lovers rests upon each of the siblings finding and accepting true love.

Cover Image(s):

Heart's Victory, The

Series: None

Editions: Silhouette Special Edition #59, Nov. 1982, ISBN: 0-671-53559-5
Language of Love #16 ("Tuberose"), ISBN: 0-373-51016-0
Silhouette Classics #24, Oct. 1988, ISBN: 0-373-04624-3
Thorndike Press large print hardcover, Aug. 2002, ISBN: 0-786-23979-4
Silhouette hardcover edition, May 2003, ISBN: 0-373-21861-3
Thorndike Press large print, Feb. 2003, ISBN: 0-7540-7403-X

Story: Cynthia "Foxy" Fox made a play for racecar driver Lance Matthews as a teenager, but Lance rebuffed her. Now she's all grown up, a professional photographer on assignment to cover the racing season.

Cover Image(s):

Heaven and Earth

Series: Three Sisters Island (Bk 2)

For related volumes, see *Dance Upon the Air* (Bk 1) and *Face the Fire* (Bk 3)

Editions: Jove mass market, Dec. 2001, ISBN: 0-515-13202-0
Nova Audio (Abridged), Dec. 2001, ISBN: 1-58788-226-4
Nova Audio (Abridged), Nov. 2002, ISBN: 1-58788-674-X
BrillianceAudio CD (Abridged), Nov. 2001, ISBN: 1-58788-965-X
BrillianceAudio (Unabridged), Nov. 2001, ISBN: 1-58788-225-6
BrillianceAudio CD (Abridged), Nov. 2001, ISBN: 1-58788-966-8
BrillianceAudio (Unabridged), Dec. 2001, ISBN: 1-58788-224-8
G. K. Hall & Co. large print, Apr. 2002, ISBN: 0-7838-9618-2
G. K. Hall & Co. large print, Dec. 2002, ISBN: 0-7838-9621-2
Adobe Reader e-book, Jove, Feb. 2003

Story: Deputy Sheriff Ripley Todd has ignored her unusual powers for years. Then MacAllister Booke, a visiting scientist researching witchcraft on Three Sisters Island, forces her to confront them.

Series Connections: Three Sisters Island suffers under a curse, one that can only be broken by the descendents of the three witches who created the island in 1692. Now three women will unite in friendship and trust to save their home, their lives, and the people they love.

Cover Image(s):

Her Mother's Keeper

Series: None

Editions: Silhouette Romance #215, Apr. 1983, ISBN: 0-671-57215-6
Language of Love #20 ("Pansy"), Nov. 1992, ISBN: 0-373-51020-9

Story: Gwen Lacrosse heads home to Louisiana to save her mother from the wiles of younger man Luke Powers, only to have her assumptions challenged, and to discover that she, too, is attracted to him.

Cover Image(s):

Hidden Riches

Series: None

Editions: G. P. Putnam's Sons hardcover, July 1994, ISBN: 0-399-13948-6

Jove mass market, May 1995, ISBN: 0-515-11606-8
Media Books Audio (Abridged), Apr. 1999, ISBN: 1-57815-011-6
BrillianceAudio (Unabridged), June 1994, ISBN: 1-56100-554-1
Bookcassette Sales (Abridged), June 1994, ISBN: 1-56100-180-5
Nova Audio (Abridged), June 1994, ISBN: 1-56100-362-X
G. P. Putnam's Sons hardcover omnibus edition, *Three Complete Novels: Honest Illusions*, *Private Scandals*, *Hidden Riches*, July 2000, ISBN: 0-399-14627-X
Jove mass-market boxed set (with *Homeport* and *True Betrayals*), May 2002, ISBN: 0-515-13456-2
Thorndike Press large print, Oct. 1994, ISBN: 0-786-20272-6
e-book, Jove, June 2001, ISBN: 0786502614
Adobe Reader e-book, Jove, June 2001, ISBN: 0786507535

Story: When Dora Conroy buys some trinkets for her Philadelphia antiques shop, she doesn't realize that she's buying a hidden treasure trove. Her impulsive purchase makes Dora and her tenant, former cop Jed Skimmerhorn, the targets of dangerous thieves.

Cover Image(s):

Hidden Star

Series: The Stars of Mithra (Bk 1)
For related volumes, see *Captive Star* (Bk 2) and *Secret Star* (Bk 3)

Editions: Silhouette Intimate Moments #811, Oct. 1997, ISBN: 0-373-07811-0
Silhouette reprint, July 2001, ISBN: 0-373-48488-7
Thorndike Press large print, ISBN: 0-373-59712-6

Story: When Bailey James wakes up alone in a hotel room with amnesia, a sack full of hundred-dollar bills, a gun, and a mysterious blue diamond, she asks private investigator Cade Parris for help.

Series Connections: Three immense blue diamonds form a set of perfectly matched stones once reputed to have been the centerpiece for a pagan altar—the Three Stars of Mithra. One stone represents love, one knowledge, and one generosity. According to the mythology surrounding them, when all three stones sit in a golden triangle, as they had in the hands of the god, they confer blessings upon those who hold them. Each novel in the series centers upon one stone and what happens to the woman who holds it.

Cover Image(s):

Holding the Dream

Series: Dream, a.k.a. Templeton House (Bk 2)
For related volumes, see *Daring to Dream* (Bk 1) and *Finding the Dream* (Bk 3)

Editions: Jove mass market, Jan. 1997, ISBN: 0-515-12000-6
BrillianceAudio (Unabridged), Dec. 1996, ISBN: 1-5610-0739-0
BrillianceAudio (Unabridged), Jan. 1997, ISBN: 1-5610-0814-1
BrillianceAudio (Abridged), June 1997, ISBN: 1-5674-0203-8
Severn House Publishers, Ltd., British hardcover edition, Apr. 1999, ISBN: 0-7278-2215-2
G. P. Putnam's Sons hardcover omnibus edition, *Three Complete Novels: Daring to Dream, Holding the Dream, Finding the Dream*, Apr. 1999, ISBN: 0-399-14480-3
Jove mass-market boxed set (with *Daring to Dream* and *Finding the Dream*), May 2002, ISBN: 0-515-13457-0
Countertop Audio compilation audiocassette (Abridged), *The Best of Nora Roberts* (audio versions of *Daring to Dream*, *Holding the Dream*, *Finding the Dream*, and *Homeport*), Jan. 2001, ISBN: 1-8860-8995-7
Thorndike Press large print, July 1997, ISBN: 0-786-21053-2
Gemstar e-book, Jove, Jan. 2002, ISBN: 0786520507
Adobe Reader e-book, Jove, Sept. 2001, ISBN: 0786507543

Story: Kate Powell has always been ambitious and proud of her achievements, so when she's accused of embezzling and fired, she's devastated. Byron DeWitt helps Kate clear her name and rebuild her life.

Note: The early working title for *Holding the Dream* was *Waiting to Dream.* This title may eventually be recycled, but there are no current plans to do so, and all current mentions of *Waiting to Dream* on the Internet and in bookstore computers are artifacts from the early information distributed about the series.

Series Connections: Laura Templeton, Kate Powell, and Margo Sullivan were raised together in Templeton House, high in the Monterey, California, cliffs. Now that they are grown women, the bond they share is in many ways stronger than the one between sisters. They also share a belief in the legend of Seraphina and Felipe, star-crossed lovers who hid a fortune in gold in the cliffs. And as they each seek and find their destiny and their true love, they find a piece of that gold as a blessing on their union.

Cover Image(s):

Holiday in Death

(writing as J. D. Robb)

Series: In Death (Bk 7)

For related volumes, see *Naked in Death* (Bk 1), *Glory in Death* (Bk 2), *Immortal in Death* (Bk 3), *Rapture in Death* (Bk 4), *Ceremony in Death* (Bk 5), *Vengeance in Death* (Bk 6), "Midnight in Death" (*Silent Night*, Bk 7.5), *Conspiracy in Death* (Bk 8), *Loyalty in Death* (Bk 9), *Witness in Death* (Bk 10), *Judgment in Death* (Bk 11), *Betrayal in Death* (Bk 12), "Interlude in Death" (*Out of This World*, Bk 12.5), *Seduction in Death* (Bk 13), *Reunion in Death* (Bk 14), *Purity in Death* (Bk 15), *Portrait in Death* (Bk 16), *Imitation in Death* (Bk 17), *Remember When* (Bk 17.5), *Divided in Death* (Bk 18), and *Visions in Death* (Bk 19)

Editions: Berkley mass market, June 1998, ISBN: 0-425-16371-7
BrillianceAudio (Abridged), Oct. 2001, ISBN: 1-58788-440-2
Nova Audio (Abridged), Oct. 2001, ISBN: 1-58788-439-9
Gemstar e-book, Berkley, Jan. 2002, ISBN: 0786520515
Adobe Reader e-book, Berkley, June 2001, ISBN: 0786507551
e-book, Berkley, June 2001, ISBN: 0786500921

Story: Eve Dallas tracks a serial killer who is using New York's poshest dating service, Personally Yours, to find his victims.

Series Connections: Lt. Eve Dallas is a mid-21st-century cop in a New York City where, despite technological advances, crime still runs rampant. Eve is married to the enigmatic Roarke, a self-made billionaire with a shady past.

Cover Image(s):

Series: None

Editions: G. P. Putnam's Sons hardcover, Mar. 1998, ISBN: 0-399-14387-4
Jove mass market, Apr. 1999, ISBN: 0-515-12489-3
BrillianceAudio (Unabridged), Apr. 1998, ISBN: 1-56740-565-7
BrillianceAudio (Abridged), Jan. 1999, ISBN: 1-56740-283-6
Bookcassette Sales Audio (Unabridged), Mar. 1998, ISBN: 1-56100-786-2
Nova Audio (Abridged), Mar. 1998, ISBN: 1-56740-761-7
Countertop Audio compilation audiocassette (Abridged), *The Best of Nora Roberts* (audio versions of *Daring to Dream*, *Holding the Dream*, *Finding the Dream*, and *Homeport*), Jan. 2001, ISBN: 1-8860-8995-7
Jove mass-market boxed set (with *Hidden Riches* and *True Betrayals*), May 2002, ISBN: 0-515-13456-2
Thorndike Press large print, July 1998, ISBN: 0-786-21426-0
Thorndike Press large print, Mar. 1999, ISBN: 0-786-21427-9
BrillianceAudio CD (Abridged), Feb. 2003, ISBN: 1-59086-518-9
BrillianceAudio CD (Abridged), Feb. 2003, ISBN: 1-59086-536-1
Adobe Reader e-book, June 2001, ISBN: 0786507578
e-book, June 2001, ISBN: 0786501456

Story: Art expert Dr. Miranda Jones is in Italy to authenticate a Renaissance bronze when she's accused of leaking news of the piece's existence to the press. She recruits art thief Ryan Boldari to help find the piece after it is stolen.

Cover Image(s):

Honest Illusions

Series: None

Editions: Putnam hardcover, July 1992, ISBN: 0-399-13761-0
Jove mass market, Aug. 1993, ISBN: 0-515-11097-3
Berkley trade paperback, Sept. 2002, ISBN: 0-425-18619-9
BrillianceAudio (Unabridged), Oct. 1992, ISBN: 1-56100-479-0
BrillianceAudio (Unabridged), Sept. 2001, ISBN: 1-58788-770-3
Nova Audio (Abridged), June 2001, ISBN: 1-58788-404-6
Nova Audio (Abridged), Aug. 2002, ISBN: 1-58788-406-2
Putnam hardcover omnibus edition, *Three Complete Novels: Honest Illusions, Private Scandals, Hidden Riches*, July 2000, ISBN: 0-399-14627-X
Thorndike Press large print, Jan. 1993, ISBN: 1-56054-561-5
Adobe Reader e-book, June 2001, ISBN: 0786507586
e-book, June 2001, ISBN: 0786502622

Story: Roxy Nouvelle and Luke Callahan worked together seamlessly as magicians, thieves, and lovers until Luke vanished without a trace. Five years later, Luke is back and Roxy must work with him—even if she doesn't trust him.

Cover Image(s):

Hot Ice

Series: None

Editions: Bantam mass market, Aug. 1987, ISBN: 0-553-26461-3
Bantam hardcover, Aug. 2002, ISBN: 0-553-80274-7
Random House Audio (Abridged), Aug. 2002, ISBN: 0-553-71328-0
Random House large print hardcover, Aug. 2002, ISBN: 0-375-43167-5
G. K. Hall & Co. large print, Jan. 1989, ISBN: 0-8161-4489-3

Story: Socialite Whitney MacAllister's world changed forever when jewel thief Doug Lord burst into her life with a map to a fortune in gems taped to his chest and a trio of killers on his heels.

Cover Image(s):

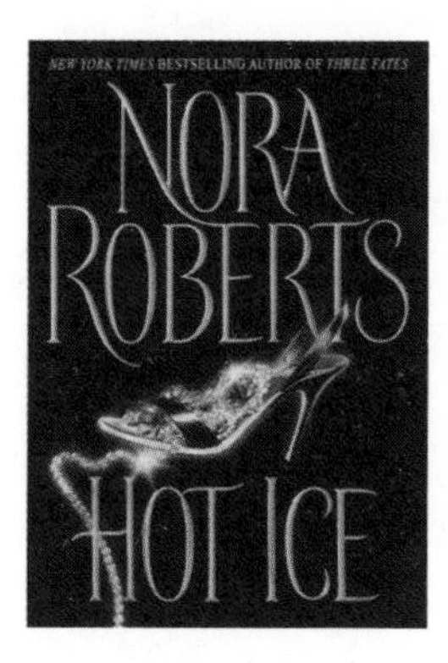

Imitation in Death

(writing as J. D. Robb)

Series: In Death (Bk 17)

For related volumes, see *Naked in Death* (Bk 1), *Glory in Death* (Bk 2), *Immortal in Death* (Bk 3), *Rapture in Death* (Bk 4), *Ceremony in Death* (Bk 5), *Vengeance in Death* (Bk 6), *Holiday in Death* (Bk 7), "Midnight in Death" (*Silent Night*, Bk 7.5), *Conspiracy in Death* (Bk 8), *Loyalty in Death* (Bk 9), *Witness in Death* (Bk 10), *Judgment in Death* (Bk 11), *Betrayal in Death* (Bk 12), "Interlude in Death" (*Out of This World*, Bk 12.5), *Seduction in Death* (Bk 13), *Reunion in Death* (Bk 14), *Purity in Death* (Bk 15), *Portrait in Death* (Bk 16), *Remember When* (Bk 17.5), *Divided in Death* (Bk 18), and *Visions in Death* (Bk 19)

Editions: Berkley mass market, Sept. 2003, ISBN: 0-425-19158-3
BrillianceAudio (Unabridged), Aug. 2003, ISBN: 1-59086-723-8
BrillianceAudio (Abridged), Aug. 2003, ISBN: 1-59086-725-4
BrillianceAudio (Unabridged), Aug. 2003, ISBN: 1-59086-724-6

Story: Lt. Eve Dallas pursues a killer who is finding inspiration in the crimes of the most infamous serial killers in history.

Series Connections: Lt. Eve Dallas is a mid-21st-century cop in a New York City where, despite technological advances, crime still runs rampant. Eve is married to the enigmatic Roarke, a self-made billionaire with a shady past.

Cover Image(s):

Immortal in Death

(writing as J. D. Robb)

Series: In Death (Bk 3)

For related volumes, see *Naked in Death* (Bk 1), *Glory in Death* (Bk 2), *Rapture in Death* (Bk 4), *Ceremony in Death* (Bk 5), *Vengeance in Death* (Bk 6), *Holiday in Death* (Bk 7), "Midnight in Death" (*Silent Night*, Bk 7.5), *Conspiracy in Death* (Bk 8), *Loyalty in Death* (Bk 9), *Witness in Death* (Bk 10), *Judgment in Death* (Bk 11), *Betrayal in Death* (Bk 12), "Interlude in Death" (*Out of This World*, Bk 12.5), *Seduction in Death* (Bk 13), *Reunion in Death* (Bk 14), *Purity in Death* (Bk 15), *Portrait in Death* (Bk 16), *Imitation in Death* (Bk 17), *Remember When* (Bk 17.5), *Divided in Death* (Bk 18), and *Visions in Death* (Bk 19)

Editions: Berkley mass market, July 1996, ISBN: 0-425-15378-9
Nova Audio (Abridged), June 2001, ISBN: 1-58788-101-2
BrillianceAudio (Abridged), June 2001, ISBN: 1-58788-198-5
Putnam hardcover, Nov. 2004, ISBN: 0-399-15159-1
Adobe Reader e-book, Berkley, June 2001, ISBN: 0786507659
e-book, Berkley, June 2001, ISBN: 0786501499

Story: Lt. Eve Dallas is getting married and the complications are already piling up. Supermodel Pandora turns up dead, Eve's friends Mavis and Leonardo are the most likely suspects in the murder, and even Eve's fiancé, Roarke, could be implicated.

Note: The early working title for *Immortal in Death* was *Profit in Death.* Because some information about the book was released under the *Profit in Death* title, it still turns up in various lists and on the Internet. *Profit in Death* may eventually be recycled for another J. D. Robb book, but there are no current plans to do so (as of summer 2002), and all mentions on the Internet and in bookstore computers of this title are artifacts of that early information.

Series Connections: Lt. Eve Dallas is a mid-21st-century cop in a New York City where, despite technological advances, crime still runs rampant. Eve is married to the enigmatic Roarke, a self-made billionaire with a shady past.

Cover Image(s):

Inner Harbor

Series: Chesapeake Bay, a.k.a. The Quinn Brothers (Bk 3)
For related volumes, see *Sea Swept* (Bk 1), *Rising Tides* (Bk 2), and *Chesapeake Blue* (Bk 4)

Editions: Jove mass market, Jan. 1999, ISBN: 0-515-12421-4
Bookcassette Sales Audio (Unabridged), Dec. 1998, ISBN: 1-56100-780-3
Bookcassette Sales Audio (Abridged), Dec. 1998, ISBN: 1-56740-758-7
Bookcassette Sales Audio (Abridged), Oct. 1999, ISBN: 1-56740-323-9
BrillianceAudio (Unabridged), Dec. 1998, ISBN: 1-56740-559-2
Nova Audio compilation (Abridged), *The Quinn Brothers*, Aug. 2002, ISBN: 1-5908-6120-5
Jove mass-market boxed set (with *Sea Swept* and *Rising Tides*), Oct. 2000, ISBN: 0-515-12992-5
Thorndike Press large print, Aug. 1999, ISBN: 0-786-21442-2
e-book, Jove, June 2001, ISBN: 0786501502
Adobe Reader e-book, Jove, June 2001, ISBN: 0786507683

Story: Ad exec Phillip Quinn already has his hands full with his job, taking care of young Seth, and helping his brothers start their new business, but he just can't resist Dr. Sybill Griffin, even though he knows she's keeping something secret from him.

Series Connections: The Quinn brothers were all strays, taken in, adopted, loved, and raised by a very special couple, Ray and Stella Quinn. The death of their parents has left the brothers coping with the task of caring for the new addition to their family, a tough and wary youngster named Seth.

Cover Image(s):

Irish Born

Series: The Concannon Sisters, a.k.a. the Born In trilogy (Bks 1, 2, & 3)

Editions: Berkley trade paperback compilation volume, Nov. 2003, ISBN: 0-425-19589-9

Story and Series Connections: See *Born in Fire*, *Born in Ice*, and *Born in Shame*

Cover Image(s):

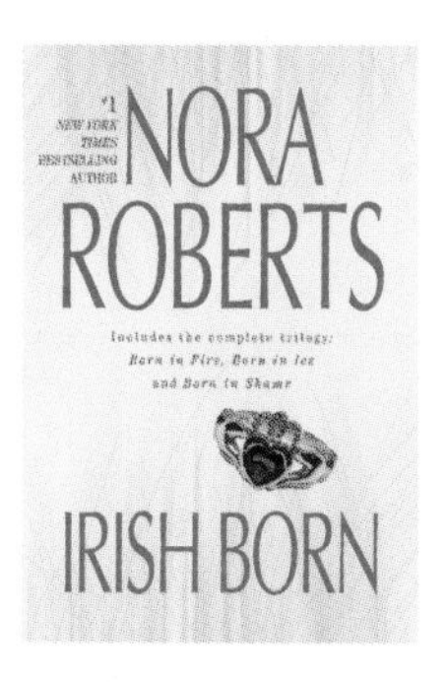

Irish Hearts

Series: Irish Hearts (Bks 1 & 2)
For related volumes, see *Irish Rebel* (Bk 3)

Editions: Silhouette mass-market compilation volume, June 2000, ISBN: 0-373-48400-3
Thorndike Press large print, Dec. 2000, ISBN: 0-786-22966-7
Thorndike Press large print, Dec. 2001, ISBN: 0-786-22967-5

Story and Series Connections: See *Irish Thoroughbred* and *Irish Rose*

Cover Image(s):

Irish Rebel

Series: Irish Hearts (Bk 3)
For related volumes, see *Irish Thoroughbred* (Bk 1) and *Irish Rose* (Bk 2)
See also the compilation volume: *Irish Hearts*

Editions: Silhouette Special Edition #1328, June 2000, ISBN: 0-373-24328-6
Harlequin reprint, Jan. 2002, ISBN: 0-373-23993-9
Thorndike Press large print, ISBN: 0-786-22968-3

Story: Trainer Brian Donnelly comes from Ireland to work at the Thoroughbred farm Royal Meadows, where he meets the owner's daughter, Keeley Grant.

Series Connections: Adelia Cunnane came from Ireland to America to stay with her uncle Paddy, who was a horse trainer at Royal Meadows. She married the farm's owner, Travis Grant, in *Irish Thoroughbred.* Her cousin Erin McKinnon's story is told in *Irish Rose. Irish Rebel* is Travis and Dee's daughter Keeley's story.

Cover Image(s):

Irish Rose

Series: Irish Hearts (Bk 2)

For related volumes, see *Irish Thoroughbred* (Bk 1) and *Irish Rebel* (Bk 3)

See also the compilation volume: *Irish Hearts*

Editions: Silhouette Intimate Moments #232, Mar. 1988, ISBN: 0-373-07232-5

Language of Love #3 ("Cabbage Rose"), ISBN: 0-373-51003-9

Silhouette mass-market compilation volume, *Irish Hearts* (with *Irish Thoroughbred*), June 2000, ISBN: 0-373-48400-3

John Curley & Associates large print, July 1990, ISBN: 0-373-58456-3

Story: When Travis Grant takes his family to visit Dee's home village in Ireland, he brings his friend, gambler and horse breeder Burke Logan, along to look at the horses. What interests Burke most, though, is Dee's cousin Erin McKinnon.

Series Connections: Adelia Cunnane came from Ireland to America to stay with her uncle Paddy, who was a horse trainer at Royal Meadows. She married the farm's owner, Travis Grant, in *Irish Thoroughbred.* Her cousin Erin McKinnon's story is told in *Irish Rose. Irish Rebel* is Travis and Dee's daughter Keeley's story.

Cover Image(s):

Irish Thoroughbred

Series: Irish Hearts (Bk 1)
For related volumes, see *Irish Rose* (Bk 2) and *Irish Rebel* (Bk 3)
See also the compilation volume: *Irish Hearts*

Editions: Silhouette Romance #81, May 1981, ISBN: 0-671-57081-1
Language of Love #1 ("Lily of the Valley"), ISBN: 0-373-51001-2
Silhouette mass-market compilation volume, *Irish Hearts* (with *Irish Rose*), June 2000, ISBN: 0-373-48400-3
G. K. Hall & Co. large print, May 1985, ISBN: 0-8161-3828-1

Story: Adelia Cunnane comes from Ireland to America to stay with her uncle Paddy, the horse trainer at Royal Meadows, where the stable's owner, Travis Grant, catches her eye.
Note: This was Nora Roberts's first published book.

Series Connections: Adelia Cunnane came from Ireland to America to stay with her uncle Paddy, who was a horse trainer at Royal Meadows. She married the farm's owner, Travis Grant, in *Irish Thoroughbred*. Her cousin Erin McKinnon's story is told in *Irish Rose*. *Irish Rebel* is Travis and Dee's daughter Keeley's story.

Cover Image(s):

Island of Flowers

Series: None

Editions: Silhouette Romance #180, Oct. 1982, ISBN: 0-671-57180-X
Language of Love #10 ("Amaryllis"), ISBN: 0-373-51010-1
Silhouette trade paperback compilation volume, *Going Home*, Oct. 2002, ISBN: 0-373-21848-6
Thorndike Press large print hardcover, Nov. 2002, ISBN: 0-786-24218-3

Story: When Laine Simmons comes to Hawaii to visit her long-estranged father, her father's partner, Dillon O'Brian, is determined to mistrust her.

Cover Image(s):

Jewels of the Sun

Series: Irish trilogy, a.k.a. The Gallaghers of Ardmore (Bk 1)
For related volumes, see *Tears of the Moon* (Bk 2) and *Heart of the Sea* (Bk 3)

Editions: Jove mass market, Nov. 1999, ISBN: 0-515-12677-2
BrillianceAudio (Abridged), Dec. 2000, ISBN: 1-5878-8038-5
BrillianceAudio (Unabridged), Nov. 1999, ISBN: 1-5674-0691-2
Bookcassette Sales Audio (Unabridged), Nov. 1999, ISBN: 1-5674-0468-5
Nova Audio (Abridged), Nov. 1999, ISBN: 1-5674-0869-9 Jove mass-market boxed set (with *Tears of the Moon* and *Heart of the Sea*), Apr. 2001, ISBN: 0-515-131614-4
G. K. Hall & Co. large print, May 2000, ISBN: 0-7838-8989-5
G. K. Hall & Co. large print, Apr. 2001, ISBN: 0-7838-8990-9
Nora Roberts Irish Jewels Trilogy, BrillianceAudio compilation (Abridged), June 2003, ISBN: 15908-6541-3
e-book, Jove, Sept. 2001, ISBN: 0786501529
Adobe Reader e-book, Jove, Sept. 2001, ISBN: 0786507713
Gemstar e-book, Jove, Jan. 2002, ISBN: 0786520590

Story: College professor Jude Murray comes to Ardmore, Ireland, to spend some time in her grandmother's ancestral home, and meets local pub owner Aidan Gallagher.

Series Connections: The three Gallagher siblings have a gift for hospitality, music, and love. As they each pursue their dreams in the tiny Irish coastal town of Ardmore, the fate of a pair of supernatural lovers rests upon each of the siblings finding and accepting true love.

Cover Image(s):

Jingle Bells, Wedding Bells, "All I Want for Christmas" novella

Series: None

Editions: Silhouette mass market, Nov. 1994, ISBN: 0-373-48331-7

Story: Five-year-old identical twins Zack and Zeke Taylor get their Christmas wish to Santa early—they want bicycles and a mom. Now they just have to convince their dad to cooperate.

Note: This is a multistory collection and also includes novellas by Barbara Boswell, Myrna Temte, and Elizabeth August.

Series Connections: The boys' dog is named Commander Zark (see *Local Hero*).

Cover Image(s):

Judgment in Death

(writing as J. D. Robb)

Series: In Death (Bk 11)

For related volumes, see *Naked in Death* (Bk 1), *Glory in Death* (Bk 2), *Immortal in Death* (Bk 3), *Rapture in Death* (Bk 4), *Ceremony in Death* (Bk 5), *Vengeance in Death* (Bk 6), *Holiday in Death* (Bk 7), "Midnight in Death" (*Silent Night*, Bk 7.5), *Conspiracy in Death* (Bk 8), *Loyalty in Death* (Bk 9), *Witness in Death* (Bk 10), *Betrayal in Death* (Bk 12), "Interlude in Death" (*Out of This World*, Bk 12.5), *Seduction in Death* (Bk 13), *Reunion in Death* (Bk 14), *Purity in Death* (Bk 15), *Portrait in Death* (Bk 16), *Imitation in Death* (Bk 17), *Remember When* (Bk 17.5), *Divided in Death* (Bk 18), and *Visions in Death* (Bk 19)

Editions: Berkley mass market, Sept. 2000, ISBN: 0-425-17630-4
Nova Audio (Abridged), Sept. 2000, ISBN: 1-58788-079-2
BrillianceAudio (Abridged), Sept. 2000, ISBN: 1-58788-174-8
G. K. Hall & Co. large print, Feb. 2001, ISBN: 0-7838-9334-5
G. K. Hall & Co. large print, Jan. 2002, ISBN: 0-7838-9335-3
Adobe Reader e-book, Berkley, June 2001, ISBN: 0786507721
e-book, Berkley, June 2001, ISBN: 0786502649

Story: When a dirty cop is bludgeoned to death in a joint called Purgatory, Eve knows that hell might soon follow. One cop's sins are about to put innocent people's lives at risk, unless Eve can find the killer fast.

Series Connections: Lt. Eve Dallas is a mid-21st-century cop in a New York City where, despite technological advances, crime still runs rampant. Eve is married to the enigmatic Roarke, a self-made billionaire with a shady past.

Cover Image(s):

Key of Knowledge

Series: Key trilogy (Bk 2)
For related volumes, see *Key of Light* (Bk 1) and *Key of Valor* (Bk 3)

Editions: Jove mass market, Dec. 2003, ISBN: 0-515-13637-9
BrillianceAudio (Abridged), Dec. 2003, ISBN: 1-59086-904-4
BrillianceAudio (Abridged), Dec. 2003, ISBN: 1-59086-323-2
BrillianceAudio (Abridged), Dec. 2003, ISBN: 1-59086-903-6
BrillianceAudio (Unabridged), Dec. 2003, ISBN: 1-59086-325-9

Story: Dana has always found comfort and knowledge in books, but she will need more to find the truth and the second key.

Series Connections: Three women are on a quest to find three mystical keys that will free the souls of three goddesses.

Cover Image(s):

Key of Light

Series: Key trilogy (Bk 1)
For related volumes, see *Key of Knowledge* (Bk 2) and *Key of Valor* (Bk 3)

Editions: Jove mass market, Nov. 2003, ISBN: 0-515-13628-X
BrillianceAudio (Abridged), Nov. 2003, ISBN: 1-59086-320-8
BrillianceAudio (Abridged), Nov. 2003, ISBN: 1-59086-901-X
BrillianceAudio (Abridged), Nov. 2003, ISBN: 1-59086-902-8
BrillianceAudio (Unabridged), Nov. 2003, ISBN: 1-59086-319-4

Story: Malory, Dana, and Zoe accept the challenge, but it is Malory's task to find the first key.

Series Connections: Three women are on a quest to find three mystical keys that will free the souls of three goddesses.

Cover Image(s):

Key of Valor

Series: Key trilogy (Bk 3)
For related volumes, see *Key of Light* (Bk 1) and *Key of Knowledge* (Bk 2)

Editions: Jove mass market, Jan. 2004, ISBN: 0-515-13653-0

Story: Zoe must find the strength and courage to find the third and final key.

Series Connections: Three women are on a quest to find three mystical keys that will free the souls of three goddesses.

Cover Image(s):

Last Honest Woman, The

Series: The O'Hurleys (Bk 1)

For related volumes, see *Dance to the Piper* (Bk 2), *Skin Deep* (Bk 3), *Without a Trace* (Bk 4), with cameo appearances in *Waiting for Nick* and *Considering Kate*, and passing mentions in *Heart of the Sea* and *Tears of the Moon*

See also the compilation volume: *The O'Hurleys: Abby and Maddy*

Editions: Silhouette Special Edition #451, May 1988, ISBN: 0-373-09451-5

Harlequin reprint, Oct. 1990, ISBN: 0-373-48231-0

Mira mass market, Feb. 1995, ISBN: 1-551-66020-2

Mira mass market, Jan. 1999, ISBN: 1-551-66507-7

John Curley & Associates large print, Jan. 1991, ISBN: 0-373-58030-4

Silhouette paperback compilation volume, *The O'Hurleys: Abby and Maddy*, Sept. 2004

Story: Biographer Dylan Crosby wants to do a book on Abby O'Hurley Rockwell's dead husband. Abby agrees to be interviewed, even though she knows Dylan's questions might bring the secrets of her past to light.

Series Connections: The O'Hurley triplets, Abby, Maddy, and Chantel, and their brother, Trace, form the backbone of this series. The children of veteran performers Frank and Molly O'Hurley, they were born on the road between shows, and raised in hotel rooms and dressing rooms all across America.

Cover Image(s):

Note: The paintings of Abby on the front cover of the first edition of this book and the back covers of all the O'Hurley original editions use Nora Roberts as the model, in celebration of *The Last Honest Woman* being Nora's fiftieth book for Silhouette.

Law Is a Lady, The

Series: None

Editions: Silhouette Special Edition #175, July 1984, ISBN: 0-671-53675-3
Language of Love #2 ("Hollyhock"), ISBN: 0-373-51002-0
Silhouette hardcover edition, July 2003, ISBN: 0-373-21866-4

Story: When Sheriff Victoria Ashton busted director Phillip Kincaid for speeding in Friendly, New Mexico, Phillip realized that the tiny town was the perfect location for his new movie.

Cover Image(s):

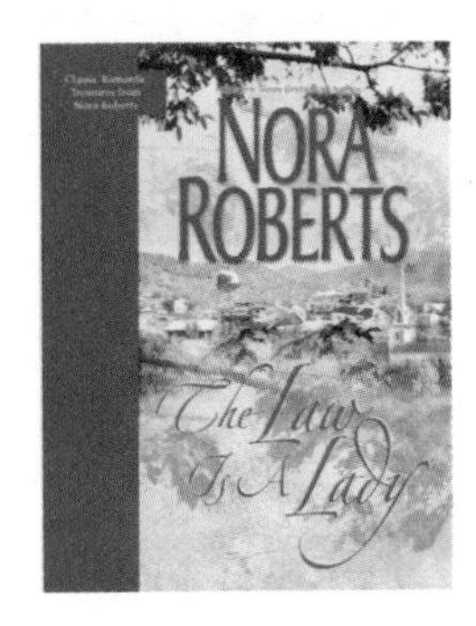

Lawless

Series: Loving Jack (Bk 3)

For related volumes, see *Loving Jack* (Bk 1) and *Best Laid Plans* (Bk 2)

See also the compilation volume: *Love by Design*

Editions: Harlequin Historical #21, May 1989, ISBN: 0-373-28621-X

Silhouette mass-market reissue, Oct. 2003, ISBN: 0-373-83592-2

Story: Half-Apache drifter Jake Redman takes genteel Sarah Conway under his wing after she journeys to Arizona territory in 1875 to find that her miner father has been killed in a "mining accident" that may be something much more sinister.

Series Connections: In *Loving Jack*, budding novelist Jacqueline MacNamara is conned into renting architect Nathan Powell's home. Nathan is Cody Johnson's partner, and Cody's story is told in *Best Laid Plans. Lawless* is purportedly the book that the character Jack wrote during the course of the series.

Note: A lead role in a movie based on *Lawless* is mentioned in *The Last Honest Woman* and *Skin Deep* as Chantel O'Hurley's first big break as an actress.

Cover Image(s):

Less of a Stranger

Series: None

Editions: Silhouette Romance #299, June 1984, ISBN: 0-671-57299-7
Language of Love #36 ("Spring Crocus"), ISBN: 0-373-51036-5
Thorndike Press large print, Dec. 2002, ISBN: 0-786-24004-0
Silhouette mass-market reissue, Sept. 2003, ISBN: 0-373-21895-8
Chivers North American large print, June 2003, ISBN: 0-754-08893-6
Chivers North American large print, June 2003, ISBN: 0-754-08894-4

Story: David Katcherton comes to a small coastal resort town to buy Megan Miller's family's amusement park.

Cover Image(s):

Lessons Learned

Series: Great Chefs (Bk 2)
For related volumes, see *Summer Desserts* (Bk 1)
See also the compilation volume: *Table for Two*

Editions: Silhouette Special Edition #318, June 1986, ISBN: 0-373-9318-7
Language of Love #25 ("Pink"), ISBN: 0-373-51025-X
Silhouette mass-market compilation volume, *Table for Two*, Nov. 2002, ISBN: 0-373-21840-0

Story: Publicist Juliet Trent escorts superstar Italian chef Carlo Franconi on a two-week publicity tour of the United States.

Series Connections: Italy's most famous chef, Carlo Franconi, had a small part in *Summer Desserts* and demanded an encore performance as the star.

Cover Image(s):

Little Magic, A

Series: Once Upon anthologies

For related volumes, see *Once Upon a Castle*, *Once Upon a Star*, *Once Upon a Rose*, *Once Upon a Dream*, *Once Upon a Kiss*, and *Once Upon a Midnight.*

Editions: Berkley trade paperback, Jan. 2002, ISBN: 0-425-18318-1

Jove mass-market edition, June 2004, ISBN: 0-515-13524-0

Story: See *Once Upon a Castle*, *Once Upon a Star*, and *Once Upon a Dream.*

Note: This book features three of the novellas from Nora's Once Upon books, compiled into a single volume.

Series Connections: The Once Upon novellas all involve a touch of magic, though the focus of that magic varies from story to story in the series.

Cover Image(s):

Local Hero

Series: None

Editions: Silhouette Special Edition #427, Jan. 1988, ISBN: 0-373-09427-2
Language of Love #48 ("Morning Glory"), ISBN: 0-373-51048-9
Silhouette mass-market compilation volume, *Truly, Madly Manhattan*, Jan. 2003, ISBN: 0-373-21803-6

Story: After a big promotion, Hester Wallace moves to uptown Manhattan with her son, Radley. Comic book creator Mitch Dempsey, Hester's new neighbor, soon becomes an essential part of both their lives.

Note: The book includes a drawing of Commander Zark rendered by Nora's son Dan.

Cover Image(s):

Love by Design

Series: Loving Jack (Bks 1, 2, & 3)

Editions: Silhouette trade paperback compilation volume, Sept. 2003, ISBN: 0-373-21825-7

Story and Series Connections: See *Best Laid Plans* and *Loving Jack.*

Cover Image(s):

Loving Jack

Series: Loving Jack (Bk 1)
For related volumes, see *Best Laid Plans* (Bk 2) and *Lawless* (Bk 3)
See also the compilation volume: *Love by Design*

Editions: Silhouette Special Edition #499, Jan. 1989, ISBN: 0-373-09499-X
Language of Love #42 ("Red Tulip"), ISBN: 0-373-51042-X
Silhouette trade paperback compilation volume, *Love by Design*, Sept. 2003, ISBN: 0-373-21825-7

Story: Jacqueline MacNamara moves into a beautiful house, only to discover that the place wasn't her cousin Fred's to lease when the home's real owner, architect Nathan Powell, returns from an extended business trip.

Series Connections: *Lawless* is purportedly the book that Jacqueline MacNamara wrote during the course of *Loving Jack.* Cody Johnson is Nathan's partner, and Cody's story is told in *Best Laid Plans.* A lead role in a movie based on *Lawless* is mentioned in *The Last Honest Woman* and *Skin Deep* as Chantel O'Hurley's first big break as an actress.

Cover Image(s):

Loyalty in Death

(writing as J. D. Robb)

Series: In Death (Bk 9)

For related volumes, see *Naked in Death* (Bk 1), *Glory in Death* (Bk 2), *Immortal in Death* (Bk 3), *Rapture in Death* (Bk 4), *Ceremony in Death* (Bk 5), *Vengeance in Death* (Bk 6), *Holiday in Death* (Bk 7), "Midnight in Death" (*Silent Night*, Bk 7.5), *Conspiracy in Death* (Bk 8), *Witness in Death* (Bk 10), *Judgment in Death* (Bk 11), *Betrayal in Death* (Bk 12), "Interlude in Death" (*Out of This World*, Bk 12.5), *Seduction in Death* (Bk 13), *Reunion in Death* (Bk 14), *Purity in Death* (Bk 15), *Portrait in Death* (Bk 16), *Imitation in Death* (Bk 17), *Remember When* (Bk 17.5), *Divided in Death* (Bk 18), and *Visions in Death* (Bk 19)

Editions: Berkley mass market, Oct. 1999, ISBN: 0-425-17140-X
Nova Audio (Abridged), Jan. 2003, ISBN: 1-58788-445-3
Thorndike Press large print, May 2000, ISBN: 0-786-22443-6
Thorndike Press large print, May 2001, ISBN: 0-786-22444-4
e-book, Berkley, Sept. 2001, ISBN: 0786500905
Adobe Reader e-book, Berkley, Sept. 2001, ISBN: 0786507403
BrillianceAudio (Abridged), Jan. 2003, ISBN: 1-58788-446-1

Story: When a terrorist group called Cassandra commits a series of murders, Eve Dallas is determined to take them down.

Series Connections: Lt. Eve Dallas is a mid-21st-century cop in a New York City where, despite technological advances, crime still runs rampant. Eve is married to the enigmatic Roarke, a self-made billionaire with a shady past.

Cover Image(s):

Luring a Lady

Series: The Stanislaskis, a.k.a. Those Wild Ukrainians (Bk 2)
For related volumes, see *Taming Natasha* (Bk 1), *Falling for Rachel* (Bk 3), *Convincing Alex* (Bk 4), *Waiting for Nick* (Bk 5), and *Considering Kate* (Bk 6)
See also the compilation volumes: *The Stanislaski Brothers* and *The Stanislaski Sisters*

Editions: Silhouette Special Edition #709, Dec. 1991, ISBN: 0-373-09709-3
Silhouette mass-market compilation volume, *The Stanislaski Brothers: Mikhail and Alex*, Nov. 2000, ISBN: 0-373-48422-4
Silhouette large print edition, Oct. 1994, ISBN: 0-373-58894-1
Thorndike Press large print compilation volume, *The Stanislaski Brothers: Mikhail and Alex*, July 2001, ISBN: 0-786-23276-5

Story: Carpenter and sculptor Mikhail Stanislaski barges into Sydney Hayward's uptown Manhattan office to complain of neglect and irresponsibility on the part of her family's corporation. Sydney puts her job and her honor on the line to correct things.

Series Connections: Ukrainian Americans, and fiercely proud of their heritage, the Stanislaski family brings together the best of two worlds. The Stanislaski siblings and their relations form the core of the series.

Cover Image(s):

MacGregor Brides, The

Series: The MacGregors (Bk 6)

For related volumes, see *Playing the Odds* (Bk 1), *Tempting Fate* (Bk 2), *All the Possibilities* (Bk 3), *One Man's Art* (Bk 4), *For Now, Forever* (Bk 5), *The Winning Hand* (Bk 7), *The MacGregor Grooms* (Bk 8), *The Perfect Neighbor* (Bk 9), *Rebellion*, a novel featuring a story line from Clan MacGregor history, and *Harlequin Historical Christmas Stories 1990*, "In from the Cold," a novella set in pre–Revolutionary War New England

See also the compilation volumes: *The MacGregors: Serena ~ Caine*, *The MacGregors: Alan ~ Grant*, and *The MacGregors: Daniel ~ Ian*

Editions: Silhouette mass market, Nov. 1997, ISBN: 0-373-48350-3

Harlequin reprint, July 2002, ISBN: 0-373-21847-8

Wheeler Publishing large print, Mar. 2002, ISBN: 1-58724-191-9

Story: Laura, Gwen, and Julia are MacGregor cousins, perfect subjects for their grandfather Daniel to hone his matchmaking techniques upon.

Series Connections: The children of Daniel MacGregor and his wife, Anna, form the backbone of this series, with a slew of Daniel's grandchildren and great-grandchildren and assorted relatives to fill out the sequels. As Daniel himself would put it, "Good blood. Strong stock."

Cover Image(s):

MacGregor Grooms, The

Series: The MacGregors (Bk 8)

For related volumes, see *Playing the Odds* (Bk 1), *Tempting Fate* (Bk 2), *All the Possibilities* (Bk 3), *One Man's Art* (Bk 4), *For Now, Forever* (Bk 5), *The MacGregor Brides* (Bk 6), *The Winning Hand* (Bk 7), *The Perfect Neighbor* (Bk 9), *Rebellion*, a novel featuring a story line from Clan MacGregor history, and *Harlequin Historical Christmas Stories 1990*, "In from the Cold," a novella set in pre–Revolutionary War New England

See also the compilation volumes: *The MacGregors: Serena ~ Caine*, *The MacGregors: Alan ~ Grant*, and *The MacGregors: Daniel ~ Ian*

Editions: Silhouette mass market, Nov. 1998, ISBN: 0-373-48369-4
Wheeler Publishing large print, Oct. 2002, ISBN: 1-58724-279-6
Silhouette mass-market reissue, Nov. 2002, ISBN: 0-373-21855-9

Story: Daniel MacGregor continues to play matchmaker, this time with his three grandsons—former First Son D. C. MacGregor, Duncan Blade, and Ian MacGregor.

Series Connections: The children of Daniel MacGregor and his wife, Anna, form the backbone of this series, with a slew of Daniel's grandchildren and great-grandchildren and assorted relatives to fill out the sequels. As Daniel himself would put it, "Good blood. Strong stock."

Cover Image(s):

MacGregors, The: Alan ~ Grant

Series: The MacGregors (Bks 3 & 4)

For related volumes, see *Playing the Odds* (Bk 1), *Tempting Fate* (Bk 2), *All the Possibilities* (Bk 3), *One Man's Art* (Bk 4), *For Now, Forever* (Bk 5), *The MacGregor Brides* (Bk 6), *The Winning Hand* (Bk 7), *The MacGregor Grooms* (Bk 8), *The Perfect Neighbor* (Bk 9), *Rebellion*, a novel featuring a story line from Clan MacGregor history, and *Harlequin Historical Christmas Stories 1990*, "In from the Cold," a novella set in pre–Revolutionary War New England

See also the compilation volumes: *The MacGregors: Serena ~ Caine* and *The MacGregors: Daniel ~ Ian*

Editions: Silhouette mass-market compilation volume, Feb. 1999, ISBN: 0-373-48389-9

Story and Series Connections: See *All the Possibilities* (Alan) and *One Man's Art* (Grant)

Cover Image(s):

MacGregors, The: Daniel ~ Ian

Series: The MacGregors (Bk 5) and the novella "In from the Cold"

For related volumes, see *Playing the Odds* (Bk 1), *Tempting Fate* (Bk 2), *All the Possibilities* (Bk 3), *One Man's Art* (Bk 4), *For Now, Forever* (Bk 5), *The MacGregor Brides* (Bk 6), *The Winning Hand* (Bk 7), *The MacGregor Grooms* (Bk 8), *The Perfect Neighbor* (Bk 9), *Rebellion*, a novel featuring a story line from Clan MacGregor history, and *Harlequin Historical Christmas Stories 1990*, "In from the Cold," a novella set in pre–Revolutionary War New England

See also the compilation volumes: *The MacGregors: Serena ~ Caine* and *The MacGregors: Alan ~ Grant*

Editions: Silhouette mass-market compilation volume, Apr. 1999, ISBN: 0-373-48390-2

Story and Series Connections: See *For Now, Forever* (Daniel) and "In from the Cold" (*Harlequin Historical Christmas Stories 1990*) (Ian)

Cover Image(s):

MacGregors, The: Serena ~ Caine

Series: The MacGregors (Bks 1 & 2)

For related volumes, see *Playing the Odds* (Bk 1), *Tempting Fate* (Bk 2), *All the Possibilities* (Bk 3), *One Man's Art* (Bk 4), *For Now, Forever* (Bk 5), *The MacGregor Brides* (Bk 6), *The Winning Hand* (Bk 7), *The MacGregor Grooms* (Bk 8), *The Perfect Neighbor* (Bk 9), *Rebellion*, a novel featuring a story line from Clan MacGregor history, and *Harlequin Historical Christmas Stories 1990*, "In from the Cold," a novella set in pre–Revolutionary War New England

See also the compilation volumes: *The MacGregors: Alan ~ Grant* and *The MacGregors: Daniel ~ Ian*

Editions: Silhouette mass-market compilation volume, Dec. 1998, ISBN: 0-373-48388-0

Story and Series Connections: See *Playing the Odds* (Serena) and *Tempting Fate* (Caine)

Cover Image(s):

Man for Amanda, A

Series: The Calhoun Women (Bk 2)

For related volumes, see *Courting Catherine* (Bk 1), *For the Love of Lilah* (Bk 3), *Suzanna's Surrender* (Bk 4), and *Megan's Mate* (Bk 5)

See also the compilation volumes: *The Calhoun Women: Catherine and Amanda*, and *The Calhoun Women: Lilah and Suzanna*

Editions: Silhouette Desire #649, July 1991, ISBN: 0-373-05649-4

Silhouette trade paperback compilation volume, *The Calhoun Women*, Dec. 1996, ISBN: 0-373-48332-5

Silhouette mass-market compilation volume, *The Calhoun Women: Catherine and Amanda*, Jan. 1998, ISBN: 0-373-48354-6

BrillianceAudio (Abridged), Jan. 1999, ISBN: 1-5674-0042-6

G. K. Hall & Co. large print, Jan. 1993, ISBN: 0-8161-5415-5

Story: Amanda Calhoun is already juggling working, hunting for the lost family jewels, and planning her sister's wedding when Sloan O'Riley, Oklahoma cowboy and head architect for the Calhoun mansion renovation, complicates her life.

Series Connections: The Calhoun sisters have inherited the family mansion built by Fergus Calhoun in the early 1900s. They've also inherited the family legends about the love affair that Fergus's wife, Bianca, had with an artist, and of the lost Calhoun emeralds, a fabulous set of jewels that vanished when Bianca died young and tragically. As they seek the jewels, they come closer to knowing the truth about Bianca and to finding love for themselves.

Cover Image(s):

Matter of Choice, A

Series: None

Editions: Silhouette Intimate Moments #49, May 1984, ISBN: 0-671-50295-6

Note: From the Heart, a single-volume collection of three unrelated early books (*Tonight and Always*, *A Matter of Choice*, and *Endings and Beginnings*) is the only version of these works currently in print. These titles are only available in the Berkley edition of *From the Heart.* These titles have reverted to the author and are no longer available from Harlequin.

Jove mass market, *From the Heart*, Nov. 1996, ISBN: 0-515-11965-2

Berkley trade paperback, *From the Heart*, June 2000, ISBN: 0-425-17616-9

Story: Sgt. James "Slade" Sladerman makes it his mission to protect antique-shop owner Jessica Winslow from the smugglers using her shop.

Cover Image(s):

Megan's Mate

Series: The Calhoun Women (Bk 5)

For related volumes, see *Courting Catherine* (Bk 1), *A Man for Amanda* (Bk 2), *For the Love of Lilah* (Bk 3), and *Suzanna's Surrender* (Bk 4)

See also the compilation volumes: *The Calhoun Women: Catherine and Amanda* and *The Calhoun Women: Lilah and Suzanna*

Editions: Silhouette Intimate Moments #745, Nov. 1996, ISBN: 0-373-07745-9

Harlequin large print edition, June 1999, ISBN: 0-373-59990-0

Story: When Megan O'Riley's brother Sloan marries Amanda Calhoun, Megan moves with her nine-year-old son to Maine to help out with the Calhoun family business. Calhoun family friend Nathaniel Fury is determined to get to know the wary newcomer.

Series Connections: The Calhoun sisters have inherited the family mansion built by Fergus Calhoun in the early 1900s. They've also inherited the family legends about the love affair that Fergus's wife, Bianca, had with an artist, and of the lost Calhoun emeralds, a fabulous set of jewels that vanished when Bianca died young and tragically. As they seek the jewels, they come closer to knowing the truth about Bianca and to finding love for themselves.

Cover Image(s):

Melodies of Love

(written as Jill March)

Series: None

Editions: This story, which Nora wrote very early in her career, appeared in 1982 in a periodical, a tabloid that is no longer in business. It has never been reprinted.

Story: Not available

Cover Image(s): Not available

Midnight Bayou

Series: None

Editions: G. P. Putnam's Sons hardcover, Nov. 2001, ISBN: 0-399-14824-8
Jove mass market, Dec. 2002, ISBN: 0-515-13397-3
Nova Audio (Abridged), Nov. 2001, ISBN: 1-5788-780-0
Nova Audio (Abridged), Nov. 2002, ISBN: 1-5788-781-9
BrillianceAudio CD (Abridged), Oct. 2001, ISBN: 1-5878-8782-7
BrillianceAudio (Unabridged), Oct. 2001, ISBN: 1-5878-8779-7
BrillianceAudio CD (Abridged), Oct. 2001, ISBN: 1-5878-8783-5
BrillianceAudio (Unabridged), Nov. 2001, ISBN: 1-58788-778-9
Chivers North American large print, Aug. 2002, ISBN: 0-754-01731-1
Thorndike Press large print, Jan. 2002, ISBN: 0-786-23739-2
Thorndike Press large print, Dec. 2002, ISBN: 0-786-23737-6
Walker and Co. large print, Nov. 2002, ISBN: 1-41040-052-2

Story: Declan Fitzgerald buys a dilapidated mansion on the outskirts of New Orleans, planning to restore it. Declan and his friend Angelina Simone become convinced the house is haunted.

Cover Image(s):

Mind over Matter

Series: None

Editions: Silhouette Intimate Moments #185, Apr. 1987, ISBN: 0-373-07185-X
Language of Love #45 ("Clematis"), ISBN: 0-373-51045-4
Silhouette trade paperback compilation volume, *Going Home*, Oct. 2002, ISBN: 0-373-21848-6
Thorndike Press large print, Oct. 2000, ISBN: 0-786-22604-8

Story: Theatrical agent Aurora Fields books a very special client to appear on producer David Brady's documentary about paranormal phenomena.

Cover Image(s):

Montana Sky

Series: None

Editions: G. P. Putnam's Sons hardcover, Mar. 1996, ISBN: 0-399-14122-7
Jove mass market, May 1997, ISBN: 0-515-12061-8
BrillianceAudio (Unabridged), Apr. 1996, ISBN: 1-56100-314-X
BrillianceAudio (Unabridged), Apr. 1996, ISBN: 1-56100-689-0
BrillianceAudio (Abridged), Mar. 1997, ISBN: 1-56740-161-9
Nova Audio (Abridged), Apr. 1996, ISBN: 1-56100-892-3
Nova Audio (with *True Betrayals* and *Sanctuary*), July 2001, ISBN: 1-58788-720-7
Putnam hardcover omnibus edition, *Three Complete Novels: True Betrayals, Montana Sky, Sanctuary*, June 2001, ISBN: 0-399-14731-4
Thorndike Press large print, June 1996, ISBN: 0-786-20672-1
Adobe Reader e-book, Jove, June 2001, ISBN: 0786507810
e-book, Jove, June 2001, ISBN: 0786501553

Story: When Montana cattle baron Jack Mercy died, he left behind a ranch worth almost $20 million, three daughters, and a will stating that before any of them can inherit a share in the ranch, they must all live together on it for one year.

Cover Image(s):

Mysterious

Series: None

Editions: Silhouette trade paperback compilation volume, Aug. 2003,
ISBN: 0-373-21812-5

Story and Series Connections: See *The Right Path*, *This Magic Moment*, and *Search for Love*

Cover Image(s):

Naked in Death

(writing as J. D. Robb)

Series: In Death (Bk 1)

For related volumes, see *Glory in Death* (Bk 2), *Immortal in Death* (Bk 3), *Rapture in Death* (Bk 4), *Ceremony in Death* (Bk 5), *Vengeance in Death* (Bk 6), *Holiday in Death* (Bk 7), "Midnight in Death" (*Silent Night*, Bk 7.5), *Conspiracy in Death* (Bk 8), *Loyalty in Death* (Bk 9), *Witness in Death* (Bk 10), *Judgment in Death* (Bk 11), *Betrayal in Death* (Bk 12), "Interlude in Death" (*Out of This World*, Bk 12.5), *Seduction in Death* (Bk 13), *Reunion in Death* (Bk 14), *Purity in Death* (Bk 15), *Portrait in Death* (Bk 16), *Imitation in Death* (Bk 17), *Remember When* (Bk 17.5), *Divided in Death* (Bk 18), and *Visions in Death* (Bk 19)

Editions: Berkley mass market, July 1995, ISBN: 0-425-14829-7
Putnam hardcover, Mar. 2004, ISBN: 0-399-15157-5
Nova Audio (Abridged), Jan. 2001, ISBN: 1-58788-080-6
BrillianceAudio (Abridged), Dec. 2000, ISBN: 1-58788-195-0
Thorndike Press large print, Mar. 2000, ISBN: 0-786-22415-0
e-book, Berkley, Feb. 2002, ISBN: 0786522321
Adobe Reader e-book, Berkley, Feb. 2002, ISBN: 078652233X

Story: New York detective Lt. Eve Dallas's main suspect in the death of a high-profile prostitute is the enigmatic Irish billionaire, Roarke.

Note: The original cover flats for this book were produced with the author's name as D. J. MacGregor. The pseudonym came from the first names of Nora's sons—Dan and Jason—and the last name of her most extensive series characters. But someone pointed out that this would mean that Nora's Eve Dallas books would be shelved half an alphabet away from her work under her own name, and the pseudonym was changed to J. D. Robb prior to the book's publication.

Series Connections: Lt. Eve Dallas is a mid-21st-century cop in a New York City where, despite technological advances, crime still runs rampant. Eve is married to the enigmatic Roarke, a self-made billionaire with a shady past.

Cover Image(s):

Name of the Game, The

Series: None

Editions: Silhouette Intimate Moments #264, Nov. 1988, ISBN: 0-373-07264-3
Language of Love #33 ("Trumpet Flower"), ISBN: 0-373-51033-0
Silhouette hardcover edition, Aug. 2003, ISBN: 0-373-21868-0

Story: Game show producer Johanna Patterson fights her attraction to famous actor Sam Weaver.

Cover Image(s):

Night Moves

Series: None

Editions: Harlequin Intrigue #19, June 1985, ISBN: 0-373-22019-7
Language of Love #7 ("Marigold"), ISBN: 0-373-51007-1
Silhouette trade paperback compilation, *Suspicious*, Nov. 2003, ISBN: 0-373-21873-7

Story: Homeowner Maggie Fitzgerald hires Cliff Delaney to bring new life to the property she has just purchased, but instead he discovers a dead body.

Series Connections: None (despite the similar title, this is *not* part of the Night Tales series).
Note: This is Nora's only Harlequin Intrigue.

Cover Image(s):

Night Shadow

Series: Night Tales (Bk 2)

For related volumes, see *Night Shift* (Bk 1), *Nightshade* (Bk 3), *Night Smoke* (Bk 4), and *Night Shield* (Bk 5)

See also the compilation volume: *Night Tales*

Editions: Silhouette Intimate Moments #373, Mar. 1991, ISBN: 0-373-07373-9

Silhouette trade paperback compilation volume, *Night Tales*, Sept. 2000, ISBN: 0-373-48410-0

Thorndike Press large print, July 1991, ISBN: 1-560-54175-X

Story: ADA Deborah O'Roarke finds herself torn between a masked crime fighter, Nemesis, and a wealthy businessman, Gage Guthrie.

Series Connections: Policeman Boyd Fletcher, his family, and his close friends provide the connection between the Night series books. In *Night Shift*, Cilla O'Roarke meets Detective Boyd Fletcher and his partner, Althea Grayson. In *Night Shadow*, the attention shifts to Deborah O'Rourke, Cilla's sister. In *Nightshade*, the action follows Boyd's partner, Althea Grayson. *Night Smoke* centers on Boyd's sister, Natalie Fletcher. *Night Shield* follows the romance of Allison Fletcher, Boyd's daughter.

Cover Image(s):

Night Shield

Series: Night Tales (Bk 5)

For related volumes, see *Night Shift* (Bk 1), *Night Shadow* (Bk 2), *Nightshade* (Bk 3), and *Night Smoke* (Bk 4)

See also the compilation volume: *Night Tales*

Editions: Silhouette Intimate Moments #1027, Sept. 2000, ISBN: 0-373-27097-6

Thorndike Press large print, Feb. 2001, ISBN: 0-786-23050-9

Chivers North American large print, June 2001, ISBN: 0-754-04454-8

Story: Detective Allison Fletcher works with a nightclub owner, Jonah Blackhawk, to solve a high-profile burglary case.

Series Connections: Policeman Boyd Fletcher, his family, and his close friends provide the connection between the Night series books. In *Night Shift*, Cilla O'Roarke meets Detective Boyd Fletcher and his partner, Althea Grayson. In *Night Shadow*, the attention shifts to Deborah O'Rourke, Cilla's sister. In *Nightshade*, the action follows Boyd's partner, Althea Grayson. *Night Smoke* centers on Boyd's sister, Natalie Fletcher. *Night Shield* follows the romance of Allison Fletcher, Boyd's daughter.

Cover Image(s):

Night Shift

Series: Night Tales (Bk 1)
For related volumes, see *Night Shadow* (Bk 2), *Nightshade* (Bk 3), *Night Smoke* (Bk 4), and *Night Shield* (Bk 5)
See also the compilation volume: *Night Tales*

Editions: Silhouette Intimate Moments #365, Jan. 1991, ISBN: 0-373-07365-8
Silhouette trade paperback compilation volume, *Night Tales*, Sept. 2000, ISBN: 0-373-48410-0

Story: Detective Boyd Fletcher is assigned to protect DJ Cilla O'Roarke after she receives a series of threatening phone calls.

Series Connections: Policeman Boyd Fletcher, his family, and his close friends provide the connection between the Night series books. In *Night Shift*, Cilla O'Roarke meets Detective Boyd Fletcher and his partner, Althea Grayson. In *Night Shadow*, the attention shifts to Deborah O'Rourke, Cilla's sister. In *Nightshade*, the action follows Boyd's partner, Althea Grayson. *Night Smoke* centers on Boyd's sister, Natalie Fletcher. *Night Shield* follows the romance of Allison Fletcher, Boyd's daughter.

Cover Image(s):

Night Smoke

Series: Night Tales (Bk 4)
For related volumes, see *Night Shift* (Bk 1), *Night Shadow* (Bk 2), *Nightshade* (Bk 3), and *Night Shield* (Bk 5)
See also the compilation volume: *Night Tales*

Editions: Silhouette Intimate Moments #595, Oct. 1994, ISBN: 0-373-07595-2
Silhouette trade paperback compilation volume, *Night Tales*, Sept. 2000, ISBN: 0-373-48410-0
Thorndike Press large print hardcover, Oct. 1998, ISBN: 0-373-59929-3

Story: Businesswoman Natalie Fletcher needs help from arson inspector Ryan Piasecki when someone torches her warehouse.
Note: This book features guest appearances from all previous Night series characters, including some pivotal help from Nemesis (see *Night Shadow*).

Series Connections: Policeman Boyd Fletcher, his family, and his close friends provide the connection between the Night series books. In *Night Shift*, Cilla O'Roarke meets Detective Boyd Fletcher and his partner, Althea Grayson. In *Night Shadow*, the attention shifts to Deborah O'Rourke, Cilla's sister. In *Nightshade*, the action follows Boyd's partner, Althea Grayson. *Night Smoke* centers on Boyd's sister, Natalie Fletcher. *Night Shield* follows the romance of Allison Fletcher, Boyd's daughter.

Cover Image(s):

Night Tales

Series: Night Tales (Bks 1, 2, 3, & 4)
For related volumes, see *Night Shift* (Bk 1), *Night Shadow* (Bk 2), *Nightshade* (Bk 3), *Night Smoke* (Bk 4), and *Night Shield* (Bk 5)

Editions: Silhouette trade paperback compilation volume, Sept. 2000,
ISBN: 0-373-48410-0

Story and Series Connections: See *Night Shift*, *Night Shadow*, *Nightshade*, and *Night Smoke*

Cover Image(s):

Nightshade

Series: Night Tales (Bk 3)

For related volumes, see *Night Shift* (Bk 1), *Night Shadow* (Bk 2), *Night Smoke* (Bk 4), and *Night Shield* (Bk 5)

See also the compilation volume: *Night Tales*

Editions: Silhouette Intimate Moments #529, Nov. 1993, ISBN: 0-373-07529-4

Silhouette trade paperback compilation volume, *Night Tales*, Sept. 2000, ISBN: 0-373-48410-0

Thorndike Press large print hardcover, Aug. 1996, ISBN: 0-373-59740-1

Story: Lt. Althea Grayson and private investigator Colt Nightshade put aside their philosophical differences to find a missing girl.

Series Connections: Policeman Boyd Fletcher, his family, and his close friends provide the connection between the Night series books. In *Night Shift*, Cilla O'Roarke meets Detective Boyd Fletcher and his partner, Althea Grayson. In *Night Shadow*, the attention shifts to Deborah O'Rourke, Cilla's sister. In *Nightshade*, the action follows Boyd's partner, Althea Grayson. *Night Smoke* centers on Boyd's sister, Natalie Fletcher. *Night Shield* follows the romance of Allison Fletcher, Boyd's daughter.

Cover Image(s):

Once More with Feeling

Series: None

Editions: Silhouette Intimate Moments #2, May 1983, ISBN: 0-671-47781-1
Silhouette Classic, ISBN: 0-373-15311-2
Silhouette Two in One, *Once More with Feeling* and *Song of the West*, May 1991, ISBN: 0-373-48238-8
Wheeler Publishing large print, May 2002, ISBN: 1-58724-221-4
Silhouette hardcover reissue, May 2003, ISBN: 0-373-21862-1

Story: Musician Brandon Carstairs seeks to win back the trust and the heart of singer Raven Williams.

Cover Image(s):

Note: The cover image appearing on the two-in-one volume did not appear originally on either of the books it contains. It is instead from the cover of the original edition of *Boundary Lines.*

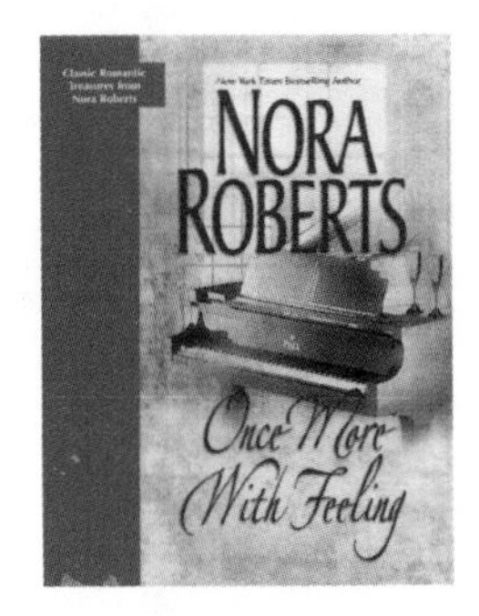

Once Upon a Castle, "Spellbound" novella

Series: Once Upon anthologies

For related volumes, see *Once Upon a Star*, *Once Upon a Dream*, *Once Upon a Rose*, *Once Upon a Kiss*, and *Once Upon a Midnight*

See also the compilation volume: *A Little Magic*, containing Nora's novellas from *Once Upon a Castle*, *Once Upon a Star*, *Once Upon a Dream*, and *Once Upon a Kiss*

Editions: Jove mass market, Mar. 1998, ISBN: 0-515-12241-6

Berkley trade paperback compilation volume, *A Little Magic*, Jan. 2002, ISBN: 0-425-18318-1

Jove mass-market compilation volume, *A Little Magic*, June 2004. ISBN: 0-515-13524-0

Story: Under a spell cast thousands of years ago, photographer Colin Farrell is haunted by dreams of Irish lass Bryna Torrance.

Note: This volume also features novellas by Jill Gregory, Ruth Ryan Langan, and Marianne Willman.

Series Connections: All of the Once Upon books involve a touch of magic, though the focus of that magic varies from book to book in the series.

Cover Image(s):

Once Upon a Dream, "In Dreams" novella

Series: Once Upon anthologies

For related volumes, see *Once Upon a Castle*, *Once Upon a Star*, *Once Upon a Rose*, *Once Upon a Kiss*, and *Once Upon a Midnight*

See also the compilation volume: *A Little Magic*, containing Nora's novellas from *Once Upon a Castle*, *Once Upon a Star*, and *Once Upon a Dream*

Editions: Jove mass market, Nov. 2000, ISBN: 0-515-12947-X

Berkley trade paperback compilation volume, *A Little Magic*, Jan. 2002, ISBN: 0-425-18318-1

Jove mass-market compilation volume, *A Little Magic*, June 2004 ISBN: 0-515-13524-0

Story: During a trip to Ireland, Kayleen Brennan visits a castle where she meets Flynn, a man cursed to live forever with only his dreams.

Note: This volume also features novellas by Jill Gregory, Ruth Ryan Langan, and Marianne Willman.

Series Connections: All of the Once Upon books involve a touch of magic, though the focus of that magic varies from book to book in the series.

Cover Image(s):

Once Upon a Kiss, "A World Apart" novella

Series: Once Upon anthologies

For related volumes, see *Once Upon a Castle*, *Once Upon a Star*, *Once Upon a Dream*, *Once Upon a Rose*, and *Once Upon a Midnight*

See also the compilation volume: *A Little Magic*, containing Nora's novellas from *Once Upon a Castle*, *Once Upon a Star*, and *Once Upon a Dream*

Editions: Jove mass market, Oct. 2002, ISBN: 0-515-13386-8

Thorndike Press large print, Apr. 2003, ISBN: 0-786-25161-1

Story: Demon slayer Kadra is transported from her world to modern-day New York to fight a demon.

Note: This volume also features novellas by Jill Gregory, Ruth Ryan Langan, and Marianne Willman.

Cover Image(s):

Once Upon a Midnight, "The Witching Hour" novella

Series: Once Upon anthologies

For related volumes, see *Once Upon a Castle*, *Once Upon a Star*, *Once Upon a Dream*, *Once Upon a Rose*, and *Once Upon a Kiss*

See also the compilation volume: *A Little Magic*, containing Nora's novellas from *Once Upon a Castle*, *Once Upon a Star*, and *Once Upon a Dream*

Editions: Jove mass market, Oct. 2003, ISBN: 0-515-13619-0

Story: In a war-torn kingdom, Aurora learns she is the warrior queen foretold in a legendary prophecy.

Note: This volume also features novellas by Jill Gregory, Ruth Ryan Langan, and Marianne Willman.

Cover Image(s):

Once Upon a Rose, "Winter Rose" novella

Series: Once Upon anthologies

For related volumes, see *Once Upon a Castle*, *Once Upon a Star*, *Once Upon a Dream*, *Once Upon a Kiss*, and *Once Upon a Midnight*

See also the compilation volume: *A Little Magic*, containing Nora's novellas from *Once Upon a Castle*, *Once Upon a Star*, and *Once Upon a Dream*

Editions: Jove mass market, Oct. 2001, ISBN: 0-515-13166-0

Thorndike Press large print, Mar. 2002, ISBN: 0-786-24048-2

Story: After Deirdre, the cursed Queen of the Winter Isle, heals the injured Prince Kylar, he becomes determined to find a way to warm her heart.

Note: This volume also features novellas by Jill Gregory, Ruth Ryan Langan, and Marianne Willman.

Series Connections: All of the Once Upon books involve a touch of magic, though the focus of that magic varies from book to book in the series.

Cover Image(s):

Once Upon a Star, "Ever After" novella

Series: Once Upon anthologies

For related volumes, see *Once Upon a Castle*, *Once Upon a Dream*, *Once Upon a Rose*, *Once Upon a Kiss*, and *Once Upon a Midnight*

See also the compilation volume: *A Little Magic*, containing Nora's novellas from *Once Upon a Castle*, *Once Upon a Star*, and *Once Upon a Dream*

Editions: Jove mass market, Dec. 1999, ISBN: 0-515-12700-0

Berkley trade paperback compilation volume, *A Little Magic*, Jan. 2002, ISBN: 0-425-18318-1

Jove mass-market compilation volume, *A Little Magic*, June 2004, ISBN: 0-515-13524-0

Story: Allena buys an enchanted pendant and is transported to a mysterious island where she meets Conal, who is suspicious of all women.

Note: This volume also features novellas by Jill Gregory, Ruth Ryan Langan, and Marianne Willman.

Series Connections: All of the Once Upon books involve a touch of magic, though the focus of that magic varies from book to book in the series.

Cover Image(s):

One Man's Art

Series: The MacGregors (Bk 4)

For related volumes, see *Playing the Odds* (Bk 1), *Tempting Fate* (Bk 2), *All the Possibilities* (Bk 3), *For Now, Forever* (Bk 5), *The MacGregor Brides* (Bk 6), *The Winning Hand* (Bk 7), *The MacGregor Grooms* (Bk 8), *The Perfect Neighbor* (Bk 9), *Rebellion*, a novel featuring a story line from Clan MacGregor history, and *Harlequin Historical Christmas Stories 1990*, "In from the Cold," a novella set in pre–Revolutionary War New England

See also the compilation volumes: *The MacGregors: Serena ~ Caine*, *The MacGregors: Alan ~ Grant*, and *The MacGregors: Daniel ~ Ian*

Editions: Silhouette Special Edition #259, Sept. 1985, ISBN: 0-373-09259-8

Silhouette Special Plaid Reissue, Feb. 1987, ISBN: 0-373-48211-6

Language of Love #17 ("Red Poppy"), ISBN: 0-373-51017-9

Silhouette mass-market compilation volume, *The MacGregors: Alan ~ Grant*, Feb. 1999, ISBN: 0-373-48389-9

Story: Artist Gennie Grandeau finds cartoonist Grant Campbell a confusing yet attractive distraction from her grief over her sister's death.

Series Connections: The children of Daniel MacGregor and his wife, Anna, form the backbone of this series, with a slew of Daniel's grandchildren and great-grandchildren and assorted relatives to fill out the collection of sequels. As Daniel himself would put it, "Good blood. Strong stock."

Cover Image(s):

One Summer

Series: *Celebrity* Magazine (Bk 1)
For related volumes, see *Second Nature* (Bk 2)
See also the compilation volume: *Summer Pleasures*

Editions: Silhouette Special Edition #306, Apr. 1986, ISBN: 0-373-09306-3
Language of Love #31 ("Red and White Roses"), ISBN: 0-373-51031-4
Silhouette mass-market compilation volume, *Summer Pleasures*, Aug. 2002, ISBN: 0-373-21839-7

Story: *Celebrity* photographer Shane Colby and photojournalist Bryan Mitchell become unwilling traveling partners on their special assignment.

Series Connections: *Celebrity* magazine and its contributors form the connection between the books in this series. Bryan Mitchell shows up for a cameo appearance in *Skin Deep*, to photograph Chantel O'Hurley.

Cover Image(s):

Opposites Attract

Series: None

Editions: Silhouette Special Edition #199, Nov. 1984, ISBN: 0-671-53699-0
Language of Love #9 ("China Aster"), ISBN: 0-373-51009-8
Silhouette hardcover reissue, July 2003, ISBN: 0-373-21865-6

Story: Even though ice princess Asher Wolfe and hotheaded Ty Starbuck were opposites on the tennis court, Asher is ready to rekindle their love affair.

Cover Image(s):

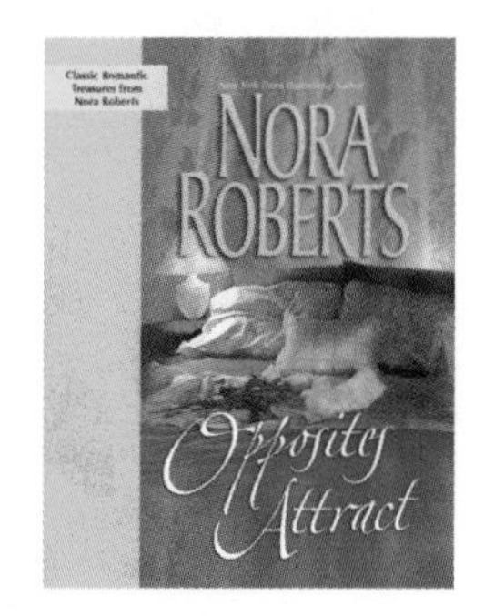

Out of This World, "Interlude in Death" novella

(writing as J. D. Robb)

Series: In Death (Bk 12.5)

For related volumes, see *Naked in Death* (Bk 1), *Glory in Death* (Bk 2), *Immortal in Death* (Bk 3), *Rapture in Death* (Bk 4), *Ceremony in Death* (Bk 5), *Vengeance in Death* (Bk 6), *Holiday in Death* (Bk 7), "Midnight in Death" (*Silent Night*, Bk 7.5), *Conspiracy in Death* (Bk 8), *Loyalty in Death* (Bk 9), *Witness in Death* (Bk 10), *Judgment in Death* (Bk 11), *Betrayal in Death* (Bk 12), *Seduction in Death* (Bk 13), *Reunion in Death* (Bk 14), *Purity in Death* (Bk 15), *Portrait in Death* (Bk 16), *Imitation in Death* (Bk 17), *Remember When* (Bk 17.5), *Divided in Death* (Bk 18), and *Visions in Death* (Bk 19)

Editions: Jove mass market, Aug. 2001, ISBN: 0-515-13109-1
Thorndike Press large print, Jan. 2002, ISBN: 0-786-23844-5

Story: Eve Dallas's off-planet vacation with Roarke is interrupted when a rogue ex-cop threatens Roarke's life.

Note: This volume also features novellas by Maggie Shayne, Laurell K. Hamilton, and Susan Krinard.

Series Connections: Lt. Eve Dallas is a mid-21st-century cop in a New York City where, despite technological advances, crime still runs rampant. Eve is married to the enigmatic Roarke, a self-made billionaire with a shady past.

Cover Image(s):

Partners

Series: None

Editions: Silhouette Intimate Moments #94, May 1985, ISBN: 0-373-07094-2
Language of Love #21 ("Orchid"), ISBN: 0-373-51021-7
Thorndike Press large print, June 2001, ISBN: 0-786-22612-9
Silhouette trade paperback compilation, *Suspicious*, Nov. 2003, ISBN: 0-373-21873-7

Story: Reporters Matthew Bates and Laurel Armand go from rivals to partners to lovers when they investigate a murder case.

Cover Image(s):

Perfect Neighbor, The

Series: The MacGregors (Bk 9)

For related volumes, see *Playing the Odds* (Bk 1), *Tempting Fate* (Bk 2), *All the Possibilities* (Bk 3), *One Man's Art* (Bk 4), *For Now, Forever* (Bk 5), *The MacGregor Brides* (Bk 6), *The Winning Hand* (Bk 7), *The MacGregor Grooms* (Bk 8), *The Perfect Neighbor* (Bk 9), *Rebellion*, a novel featuring a story line from Clan MacGregor history, and *Harlequin Historical Christmas Stories 1990*, "In from the Cold," a novella set in pre–Revolutionary War New England

See also the compilation volumes: *The MacGregors: Serena ~ Caine*, *The MacGregors: Alan ~ Grant*, and *The MacGregors: Daniel ~ Ian*

Editions: Silhouette Special Edition #1232, Mar. 1999, ISBN: 0-373-24232-8
Harlequin Mills & Boon large print, May 2002, ISBN: 0-373-04788-6

Story: Matchmaking Daniel MacGregor invites writer Preston McQuinn to move into the apartment building of his granddaughter Cybil Campbell.

Series Connections: The children of Daniel MacGregor and his wife, Anna, form the backbone of this series, with a slew of Daniel's grandchildren and great-grandchildren and assorted relatives to fill out the sequels. As Daniel himself would put it, "Good blood. Strong stock."

Cover Image(s):

Playboy Prince, The

Series: Cordina's Royal Family (Bk 3)
For related volumes, see *Affaire Royale* (Bk 1), *Command Performance* (Bk 2), and *Cordina's Crown Jewel* (Bk 4)
See also the compilation volume: *Cordina's Royal Family*

Editions: Silhouette Intimate Moments #212, Oct. 1987, ISBN: 0-373-07212-0
Language of Love #39 ("Cyclamen"), ISBN: 0-373-51039-X
Silhouette trade paperback compilation volume, *Cordina's Royal Family*, July 2002, ISBN: 0-373-48483-6
Thorndike Press large print hardcover, Dec. 2002, ISBN: 0-786-23980-8
Thorndike Press large print, June 2003, ISBN: 0-7540-8974-6
Thorndike Press large print, June 2003, ISBN: 0-7540-8973-8

Story: Lady Hannah Rothchild's "shy" demeanor attracts rather than protects her from Prince Bennett's amorous advances.

Series Connections: The children of Prince Armand of Cordina and the tiny Monaco-like principality of Cordina form the common threads of this series.

Cover Image(s):

Playing the Odds

Series: The MacGregors (Bk 1)

For related volumes, see *Tempting Fate* (Bk 2), *All the Possibilities* (Bk 3), *One Man's Art* (Bk 4), *For Now, Forever* (Bk 5), *The MacGregor Brides* (Bk 6), *The Winning Hand* (Bk 7), *The MacGregor Grooms* (Bk 8), *The Perfect Neighbor* (Bk 9), *Rebellion*, a novel featuring a story line from Clan MacGregor history, and *Harlequin Historical Christmas Stories 1990*, "In from the Cold," a novella set in pre–Revolutionary War New England

See also the compilation volumes: *The MacGregors: Serena ~ Caine*, *The MacGregors: Alan ~ Grant*, and *The MacGregors: Daniel ~ Ian*

Editions: Silhouette Special Edition #225, Mar. 1985, ISBN: 0-373-09225-3

Language of Love #12 ("Hyacinth"), ISBN: 0-373-51012-8

Silhouette Special Plaid Reissue, Feb. 1987, ISBN: 0-373-48208-6

Silhouette mass-market compilation volume, *The MacGregors: Serena ~ Caine*, Dec. 1998, ISBN: 0-373-48388-0

Story: Matchmaker Daniel MacGregor arranges for gambler Justin Blade to travel on the same cruise ship as MacGregor's blackjack-dealing granddaughter, Serena.

Series Connections: The children of Daniel MacGregor and his wife, Anna, form the backbone of this series, with a slew of Daniel's grandchildren and great-grandchildren and assorted relatives to fill out the sequels. As Daniel himself would put it, "Good blood. Strong stock."

Cover Images(s):

Portrait in Death

(writing as J. D. Robb)

Series: In Death (Bk 16)

For related volumes, see *Naked in Death* (Bk 1), *Glory in Death* (Bk 2), *Immortal in Death* (Bk 3), *Rapture in Death* (Bk 4), *Ceremony in Death* (Bk 5), *Vengeance in Death* (Bk 6), *Holiday in Death* (Bk 7), "Midnight in Death" (*Silent Night*, Bk 7.5), *Conspiracy in Death* (Bk 8), *Loyalty in Death* (Bk 9), *Witness in Death* (Bk 10), *Judgment in Death* (Bk 11), *Betrayal in Death* (Bk 12), "Interlude in Death" (*Out of This World*, Bk 12.5), *Seduction in Death* (Bk 13), *Reunion in Death* (Bk 14), *Purity in Death* (Bk 15), *Imitation in Death* (Bk 17), *Remember When* (Bk 17.5), *Divided in Death* (Bk 18), and *Visions in Death* (Bk 19)

Editions: Berkley mass market, Mar. 2003, ISBN: 0-425-18903-1
BrillianceAudio (Unabridged), Feb. 2003, ISBN: 1-59086-719-X
BrillianceAudio (Abridged), Feb. 2003, ISBN: 1-59086-721-1
BrillianceAudio (Unabridged), Feb. 2003, ISBN: 1-59086-720-3

Story: Eve Dallas hunts a killer who likes to pose his victims for a final, deadly portrait.

Series Connections: Lt. Eve Dallas is a mid-21st-century cop in a New York City where, despite technological advances, crime still runs rampant. Eve is married to the enigmatic Roarke, a self-made billionaire with a shady past.

Cover Image(s):

Pride of Jared MacKade, The

Series: The MacKade Brothers (Bk 2)

For related volumes, see *The Return of Rafe MacKade* (Bk 1), *The Heart of Devin MacKade* (Bk 3), and *The Fall of Shane MacKade* (Bk 4)

Editions: Silhouette Special Edition #1000, Dec. 1995, ISBN: 0-373-24000-7

G. K. Hall & Co. large print, Dec. 1997, ISBN: 0-373-59829-7

Silhouette trade paperback compilation, *The MacKade Brothers: Rafe and Jared*, Apr. 2004, ISBN: 0-373-21857-5

Story: Savannah Morningstar is attracted to Jared MacKade, the attorney who informs her of an unexpected inheritance.

Series Connections: The MacKade brothers lost their parents early and struggled to raise each other, save the family farm, and find their fortunes. But they were never so tired or so busy that they couldn't go looking for trouble . . . and find it every time.

Cover Image(s):

Private Scandals

Series: None

Editions: G. P. Putnam's Sons hardcover, July 1993, ISBN: 0-399-13828-5

Jove mass market, July 1994, ISBN: 0-515-11400-6

BrillianceAudio (Unabridged), July 1993, ISBN: 1-56100-509-6

BrillianceAudio (Unabridged), Aug. 1993, ISBN: 1-56100-142-2

G. P. Putnam's Sons hardcover omnibus edition, *Three Complete Novels: Honest Illusions, Private Scandals, Hidden Riches*, July 2000, ISBN: 0-399-14627-X

Thorndike Press large print, Jan. 1994, ISBN: 0-786-20040-5

Berkley trade paperback, Aug. 2003, ISBN: 0-425-19038-2

Adobe Reader e-book, June 2001, ISBN: 0786508159

e-book, June 2001, ISBN: 0786501634

Story: Talk show host Deanna Reynolds dates foreign correspondent Finn Riley and receives "love" notes from a killer.

Cover Image(s):

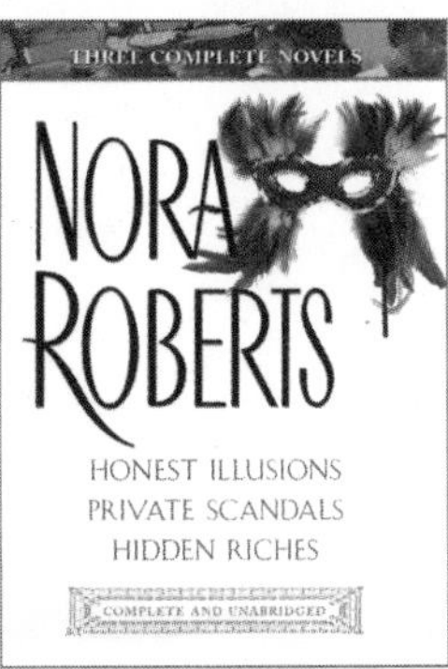

Promise Me Tomorrow

Series: None

Editions: Pocket mass market, Feb. 1984, ISBN: 0-671-47019-1

Story: Architect Sarah Lancaster finds her career threatened by her attraction to Byron Lloyd, who offers passion without promise.
Note: This was Nora's first single-title release.

Cover Image(s): Not available

Public Secrets

Series: None

Editions: Bantam mass market, July 1990, ISBN: 0-553-28578-5
Bantam hardcover, July 1997, ISBN: 0-553-10655-4
Wheeler Publishing large print paperback, Jan. 1995, ISBN: 1-56895-055-1

Story: Detective Michael Kesselring wants to help Emma McAvoy reconstruct her missing memories concerning the death of her half-brother.

Cover Image(s):

Purity in Death

(writing as J. D. Robb)

Series: In Death (Bk 15)

For related volumes, see *Naked in Death* (Bk 1), *Glory in Death* (Bk 2), *Immortal in Death* (Bk 3), *Rapture in Death* (Bk 4), *Ceremony in Death* (Bk 5), *Vengeance in Death* (Bk 6), *Holiday in Death* (Bk 7), "Midnight in Death" (*Silent Night*, Bk 7.5), *Conspiracy in Death* (Bk 8), *Loyalty in Death* (Bk 9), *Witness in Death* (Bk 10), *Judgment in Death* (Bk 11), *Betrayal in Death* (Bk 12), "Interlude in Death" (*Out of This World*, Bk 12.5), *Seduction in Death* (Bk 13), *Reunion in Death* (Bk 14), *Portrait in Death* (Bk 16), *Imitation in Death* (Bk 17), *Remember When* (Bk 17.5), *Divided in Death* (Bk 18), and *Visions in Death* (Bk 19)

Editions: Berkley mass market, Sept. 2002, ISBN: 0-425-18630-X
Nova Audio (Abridged), Sept. 2002, ISBN: 1-58788-691-X
BrillianceAudio (Unabridged), Sept. 2002, ISBN: 1-58788-689-8
BrillianceAudio (Unabridged), Sept. 2002, ISBN: 1-58788-690-1

Story: Lt. Eve Dallas battles a virulent new computer virus that can infect man and machine alike.

Series Connections: Lt. Eve Dallas is a mid-21st-century cop in a New York City where, despite technological advances, crime still runs rampant. Eve is married to the enigmatic Roarke, a self-made billionaire with a shady past.

Cover Image(s):

Rapture in Death

(writing as J. D. Robb)

Series: In Death (Bk 4)

For related volumes, see *Naked in Death* (Bk 1), *Glory in Death* (Bk 2), *Immortal in Death* (Bk 3), *Ceremony in Death* (Bk 5), *Vengeance in Death* (Bk 6), *Holiday in Death* (Bk 7), "Midnight in Death" (*Silent Night*, Bk 7.5), *Conspiracy in Death* (Bk 8), *Loyalty in Death* (Bk 9), *Witness in Death* (Bk 10), *Judgment in Death* (Bk 11), *Betrayal in Death* (Bk 12), "Interlude in Death" (*Out of This World*, Bk 12.5), *Seduction in Death* (Bk 13), *Reunion in Death* (Bk 14), *Purity in Death* (Bk 15), *Portrait in Death* (Bk 16), *Imitation in Death* (Bk 17), *Remember When* (Bk 17.5), *Divided in Death* (Bk 18), and *Visions in Death* (Bk 19)

Editions: Berkley mass market, Oct. 1996, ISBN: 0-425-15518-8
Nova Audio (Abridged), Nov. 2001, ISBN: 1-58788-102-0
BrillianceAudio (Abridged), Nov. 2001, ISBN: 1-58788-199-3
Gemstar e-book, Jan. 2002, ISBN: 0786520361
Adobe Reader e-book, June 2001, ISBN: 0786508175
e-book, June 2001, ISBN: 0786501650

Story: Eve Dallas's honeymoon is interrupted by the apparent suicide of one of Roarke's employees, leading Eve to explore the deadly side of virtual reality.

Series Connections: Lt. Eve Dallas is a mid-21st-century cop in a New York City where, despite technological advances, crime still runs rampant. Eve is married to the enigmatic Roarke, a self-made billionaire with a shady past.

Cover Image(s):

Series: The MacGregors

For related volumes, see *Playing the Odds* (Bk 1), *Tempting Fate* (Bk 2), *All the Possibilities* (Bk 3), *One Man's Art* (Bk 4), *For Now, Forever* (Bk 5), *The MacGregor Brides* (Bk 6), *The Winning Hand* (Bk 7), *The MacGregor Grooms* (Bk 8), *The Perfect Neighbor* (Bk 9), and *Harlequin Historical Christmas Stories 1990*, "In from the Cold," a novella set in pre–Revolutionary War New England

See also the compilation volumes: *The MacGregors: Serena ~ Caine*, *The MacGregors: Alan ~ Grant*, and *The MacGregors: Daniel ~ Ian*

Editions: Harlequin Historical #4, Aug. 1988, ISBN: 0-373-28604-X

Harlequin mass-market reprint, July 1999, ISBN: 0-373-83428-4

Harlequin Romance anthology edition, *Forever Mine* (including *Rebellion* by Nora Roberts, *Reckless Love* by Elizabeth Lowell and *Dark Stranger* by Heather Graham Pozzessere), Apr. 1999, ISBN: 0-373-83400-4

Story: Englishman Brigham Langston is determined to win the heart of Scottish wildcat Serena MacGregor, who hates everything English.

Note: This book takes a look at the MacGregor clan in eighteenth-century Scotland.

Series Connections: The children of Daniel MacGregor and his wife, Anna, form the backbone of this series, with a slew of Daniel's grandchildren and great-grandchildren and assorted relatives to fill out the sequels. As Daniel himself would put it, "Good blood. Strong stock."

Cover Image(s):

Series: None

Editions: G. P. Putnam's Sons hardcover, Sept. 1998, ISBN: 0-399-1441-2
Jove mass market, Oct. 1999, ISBN: 0-515-12608-X
BrillianceAudio (Unabridged), Oct. 1998, ISBN: 1-56740-405-7
BrillianceAudio (Abridged), Oct. 1999, ISBN: 1-56740-320-4
Nova Audio (Abridged), Oct. 1998, ISBN: 1-56740-802-8
Bookcassette Sales (Unabridged), Oct. 1998, ISBN: 1-56740-607-6
Econo-Clad Books hardcover, Oct. 1999, ISBN: 0-613-22257-1
Thorndike Press large print, Feb. 1999, ISBN: 0-786-21698-0
Thorndike Press large print, Jan. 2000, ISBN: 0-786-21699-9
e-book, Jove, June 2001, ISBN: 0786501669
Adobe Reader e-book, Jove, June 2001, ISBN: 0786509503

Story: Salvage diver Matthew Lassiter comes back into Tate Beaumont's life in hopes of finding a treasure and love.

Cover Image(s):

Reflections

Series: Reflections and Dreams, a.k.a. the Davidov series (Bk 1)
For related volumes, see *Dance of Dreams* (Bk 2), and a cameo appearance in *Considering Kate*
See also the compilation volume: *Reflections and Dreams*

Editions: Silhouette Special Edition #100, June 1983, ISBN: 0-671-53600-1
Language of Love #6 ("Yellow Jasmine"), ISBN: 0-373-51006-3
Silhouette mass-market compilation volume, *Reflections and Dreams*, July 2001, ISBN: 0-373-48442-9

Story: Architect Seth Bannion appreciates how much his niece adores dancer Lindsay Dunne, because he's falling for the ballet teacher, too.

Series Connections: Ruth Bannion is architect Seth Bannion's niece. Seth Bannion is married to former prima ballerina Lindsay Dunne, who once danced with Nickolai Davidov. These characters make a cameo appearance in *Considering Kate.*

Cover Image(s):

Reflections and Dreams

Series: Reflections and Dreams, a.k.a. the Davidov series (Bks 1 & 2)
For related volumes, see *Reflections* (Bk 1), *Dance of Dreams* (Bk 2), and a cameo appearance in *Considering Kate*

Editions: Silhouette mass-market compilation volume, July 2001,
ISBN: 0-373-48442-9

Story and Series Connections: See *Dance of Dreams* and *Reflections*

Cover Image(s):

Remember When

(Part 1 by Nora Roberts; Part 2 by J. D. Robb)

Series: Stand-alone Nora Roberts story and In Death series (Bk 17.5)
For related volumes, see *Naked in Death* (Bk 1), *Glory in Death* (Bk 2), *Immortal in Death* (Bk 3), *Rapture in Death* (Bk 4), *Ceremony in Death* (Bk 5), *Vengeance in Death* (Bk 6), *Holiday in Death* (Bk 7), "Midnight in Death" (*Silent Night*, Bk 7.5), *Conspiracy in Death* (Bk 8), *Loyalty in Death* (Bk 9), *Witness in Death* (Bk 10), *Judgment in Death* (Bk 11), *Betrayal in Death* (Bk 12), "Interlude in Death" (*Out of This World*, Bk 12.5), *Seduction in Death* (Bk 13), *Reunion in Death* (Bk 14), *Purity in Death* (Bk 15), *Portrait in Death* (Bk 16), *Imitation in Death* (Bk 17), *Divided in Death* (Bk 18), and *Visions in Death* (Bk 19)

Editions: G. P. Putnam's Sons hardcover, Sept. 2003, ISBN: 0-399-15106-0
Berkley mass market, May 2004, ISBN: 0-425-19547-3
BrillianceAudio (Unabridged), Sept. 2003, ISBN: 1-59355-184-3
BrillianceAudio (Unabridged), Sept. 2003, ISBN: 1-59355-187-8
BrillianceAudio (Unabridged), Sept. 2003, ISBN: 1-59355-188-6
BrillianceAudio (Abridged), Sept. 2003, ISBN: 1-59355-186-X
BrillianceAudio (Unabridged), Sept. 2003, ISBN: 1-59355-185-1

Story: A diamond heist brings together an insurance investigator and the daughter of one of the thieves. Nearly sixty years later, some of the diamonds are still missing, and Eve Dallas investigates when it looks like someone is willing to kill to find them.
Note: These are two connected stories that begin in the present with the Nora Roberts story and then continue into the future with the J. D. Robb story. This is the first hardcover appearance by J. D. Robb.

Series Connections: Lt. Eve Dallas is a mid-21st-century cop in a New York City where, despite technological advances, crime still runs rampant. Eve is married to the enigmatic Roarke, a self-made billionaire with a shady past.

Cover Image(s):

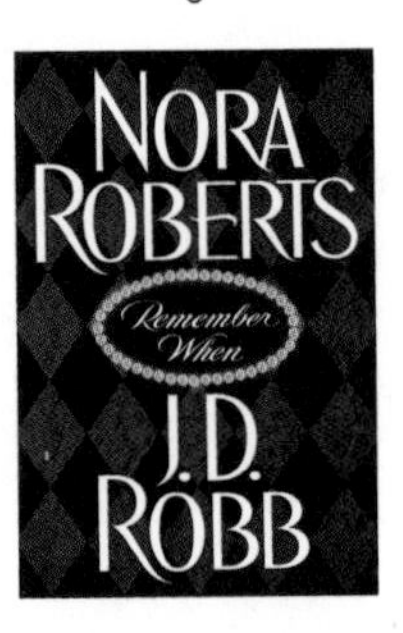

Return of Rafe MacKade, The

Series: The MacKade Brothers (Bk 1)

For related volumes, see *The Pride of Jared MacKade* (Bk 2), *The Heart of Devin MacKade* (Bk 3), and *The Fall of Shane MacKade* (Bk 4)

Editions: Silhouette Intimate Moments #631, Apr. 1995, ISBN: 0-373-07631-2

Thorndike Press large print, Apr. 1997, ISBN: 0-373-59766-5

Silhouette trade paperback compilation volume, *The MacKade Brothers: Rafe and Jared*, Apr. 2004, ISBN: 0-373-21857-5

Story: Antique dealer Regan Bishop is reluctant to work with contractor Rafe MacKade in furnishing his Civil War–era mansion because of his bad-boy reputation.

Series Connections: The MacKade brothers lost their parents early and struggled to raise each other, save the family farm, and find their fortunes. But they were never so tired or so busy that they couldn't go looking for trouble . . . and find it every time.

Cover Image(s):

Reunion in Death

(writing as J. D. Robb)

Series: In Death (Bk 14)

For related volumes, see *Naked in Death* (Bk 1), *Glory in Death* (Bk 2), *Immortal in Death* (Bk 3), *Rapture in Death* (Bk 4), *Ceremony in Death* (Bk 5), *Vengeance in Death* (Bk 6), *Holiday in Death* (Bk 7), "Midnight in Death" (*Silent Night*, Bk 7.5), *Conspiracy in Death* (Bk 8), *Loyalty in Death* (Bk 9), *Witness in Death* (Bk 10), *Judgment in Death* (Bk 11), *Betrayal in Death* (Bk 12), "Interlude in Death" (*Out of This World*, Bk 12.5), *Seduction in Death* (Bk 13), *Purity in Death* (Bk 15), *Portrait in Death* (Bk 16), *Imitation in Death* (Bk 17), *Remember When* (Bk 17.5), *Divided in Death* (Bk 18), and *Visions in Death* (Bk 19)

Editions: Berkley mass market, Mar. 2002, ISBN: 0-425-18397-1
Nova Audio (Abridged), Mar. 2002, ISBN:1-58788-687-1
BrillianceAudio (Unabridged), Mar. 2002, ISBN: 1-58788-685-5
BrillianceAudio (Unabridged), Mar. 2002, ISBN: 1-58788-686-3

Story: A string of poisonings leads Eve Dallas to Julianna Dunne, a killer whom Eve put away, but who now has been released on "good behavior."

Series Connections: Lt. Eve Dallas is a mid-21st-century cop in a New York City where, despite technological advances, crime still runs rampant. Eve is married to the enigmatic Roarke, a self-made billionaire with a shady past.

Cover Image(s):

Right Path, The

Series: None

Editions: Silhouette Intimate Moments #85, Mar. 1985, ISBN: 0-373-07085-3
Language of Love #26 ("Lavender"), ISBN: 0-373-51026-8
Silhouette trade paperback compilation volume, *Mysterious*, Aug. 2003, ISBN: 0-373-21812-5
Thorndike Press large print, July 2002, ISBN: 0-786-24221-3

Story: Morgan James's Greek vacation takes an unexpected turn when she finds a knife at her throat. But her "attacker," Nicolas Gregoras, insists that he is innocent.

Cover Image(s):

Rising Tides

Series: Chesapeake Bay, a.k.a. The Quinn Brothers (Bk 2)
For related volumes, see *Sea Swept* (Bk 1), *Inner Harbor* (Bk 3), and *Chesapeake Blue* (Bk 4)

Editions: Jove mass market, Aug. 1998, ISBN: 0-515-12317-X
BrillianceAudio (Abridged), Aug. 1999, ISBN: 1-56740-304-2
Bookcassette Sales (Unabridged), Aug. 1998, ISBN: 1-56100-779-X
Bookcassette Sales (Unabridged), Aug. 1998, ISBN: 1-56740-558-4
Nova Audio (Abridged), Aug. 1998, ISBN: 1-56740-757-9
Nova Audio compilation (Abridged), *The Quinn Brothers*, Aug. 2002, ISBN: 1-59086-120-5
Jove boxed set (with *Sea Swept* and *Inner Harbor*), Oct. 2000, ISBN: 0-515-12992-5
Thorndike Press large print hardcover, Jan. 1999, ISBN: 0-786-21441-4
Gemstar e-book, Jove, Mar. 2002, ISBN: 0786518952
Adobe Reader e-book, Jove, June 2001, ISBN: 0786508248
e-book, Jove, June 2001, ISBN: 0786501677

Story: Ethan Quinn's memories of being abused as a child affect his relationship with his ward, Seth, and with Grace Monroe, the Quinns' housekeeper.

Series Connections: The Quinn brothers were all strays, taken in, adopted, loved, and raised by a very special couple, Ray and Stella Quinn. The death of their parents has left the brothers coping with the task of caring for the new addition to their family, a tough and wary youngster named Seth.

Cover Image(s):

Risky Business

Series: None

Editions: Silhouette Intimate Moments #160, Sept. 1986, ISBN: 0-373-07160-4

Language of Love #41 ("White Daisy"), ISBN: 0-373-51041-1

Silhouette trade paperback compilation volume, *Dangerous*, Dec. 2002, ISBN: 0-373-21854-0

Thorndike Press large print, June 2003, ISBN: 0-786-25384-3

Story: Attorney Jonas Sharpe comes to the Mexican island of Cozumel and joins forces with Liz Palmer to find the drug smugglers who murdered Jonas's twin brother.

Cover Image(s):

River's End

Series: None

Editions: G. P. Putnam's Sons hardcover, Mar. 1999, ISBN: 0-399-14470-6
Berkley mass market, May 2000, ISBN: 0-515-12783-3
BrillianceAudio (Unabridged), Mar. 1999, ISBN: 1-56740-412-X
BrillianceAudio (Abridged), June 2000, ISBN: 1-56740-986-5
Bookcassette Sales (Unabridged), Mar. 1999, ISBN: 1-56740-640-8
Thorndike Press large print, May 1999, ISBN: 0-786-21861-4
Thorndike Press large print, May 1999, ISBN: 0-786-21862-2
e-book, Jove, June 2001, ISBN: 0786501685
Adobe Reader e-book, Jove, June 2001, ISBN: 0786508507
Gemstar e-book, Jan. 2002, ISBN: 0786511575

Story: True-crime writer Noah Brady wants to write about the murder of Olivia MacBride's mother at the hands of her father.

Cover Image(s):

Rules of the Game

Series: None

Editions: Silhouette Intimate Moments #70, Oct. 1984, ISBN: 0-671-50299-9
Language of Love #18 ("Gladiola"), ISBN: 0-373-51018-7
Thorndike Press large print hardcover, Dec. 2002, ISBN: 0-786-24003-2
Silhouette hardcover edition, June 2003, ISBN: 0-373-21864-8

Story: Baseball player Park Jones hopes that television director Brooke Gordon can turn him into the perfect commercial spokesman.

Cover Image(s):

Sacred Sins

Series: Sacred Sins (Bk 1)
For related volumes, see *Brazen Virtue* (Bk 2)

Editions: Bantam mass market, Dec. 1987, ISBN: 0-553-26574-1
Bantam hardcover, July 2000, ISBN: 0-553-80116-3
Bantam Books Audio (Abridged), July 2000, ISBN: 0-553-52730-4
Bantam Doubleday Dell Downloadable Audio
Random House large print hardcover, July 2000, ISBN: 0-375-43066-0
Thorndike Press large print, Jan. 1988, ISBN: 0-896-21118-5

Story: Detective Ben Paris finds it hard to put any faith in the psychological profile of a serial killer that Dr. Tess Court has created.

Series Connections: Detectives Ben Paris and Ed Jackson are partners. As they solve two very different cases, they each find the woman of their dreams.

Cover Image(s):

Sanctuary

Series: None

Editions: G. P. Putnam's Sons hardcover, Mar. 1997, ISBN: 0-399-14240-1
Jove mass market, May 1998, ISBN: 0-515-12273-4
BrillianceAudio (Abridged), Jan. 1998, ISBN: 1-56740-247-X
BrillianceAudio (Unabridged), Apr. 1997, ISBN: 1-56100-729-3
Bookcassette Sales (Unabridged), Apr. 1997, ISBN: 1-5610-0804-4
Nova Audio (Abridged), May 1997, ISBN: 1-56100-967-9
Nova Audio (with *Montana Sky* and *True Betrayals*), July 2001, ISBN: 1-58788-720-7
Thorndike Press large print, May 1997, ISBN: 0-786-20969-0
Putnam hardcover omnibus edition, *Three Complete Novels: True Betrayals, Montana Sky, Sanctuary*, June 2001, ISBN: 0-399-14731-4
e-book, Jove, Sept. 2001, ISBN: 0786501707
Adobe Reader e-book, Jove, Sept. 2001, ISBN: 0786508574
Gemstar e-book, Jan. 2002, ISBN: 078652040X

Story: Photographer Jo Ellen Hathaway works with family friend Nathan Delany to learn the truth about the tragedies that have struck both families.

Note: Sanctuary was adapted as a made-for-TV movie. It aired on CBS on Feb. 28, 2001.

Cover Image(s):

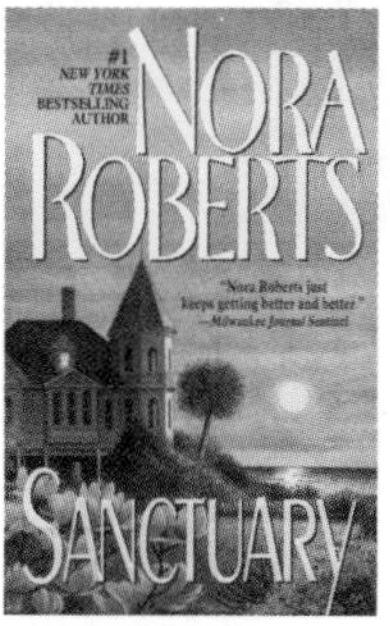

Sea Swept

Series: Chesapeake Bay, a.k.a. The Quinn Brothers (Bk 1)
For related volumes, see *Rising Tides* (Bk 2), *Inner Harbor* (Bk 3), and *Chesapeake Blue* (Bk 4)

Editions: Jove mass market, Jan. 1998, ISBN: 0-515-12184-3
Bookcassette Sales, Jan. 1998, ISBN: 1-5674-0557-6
BrillianceAudio (Abridged), Dec. 1997, ISBN: 1-56740-756-0
BrillianceAudio (Unabridged), Jan. 1998, ISBN: 1-56100-778-1
Nova Audio (Abridged), Sept. 1998, ISBN: 1-56740-271-2
Nova Audio compilation (Abridged), *The Quinn Brothers*, Aug. 2002, ISBN: 1-5908-6120-5
Jove boxed set (with *Rising Tides* and *Inner Harbor*), Oct. 2000, ISBN: 0-515-12992-5
Thorndike Press large print, July 1998, ISBN: 0-786-21433-3
e-book, Jove, Sept. 2001, ISBN: 0786501693
Adobe Reader e-book, Jove, Sept. 2001, ISBN: 0786508582
Gemstar e-book, Jove, Jan. 2002, ISBN: 0786511532

Story: Social worker Anna Spinelli must investigate Cameron Quinn and his brothers to determine if their home is an appropriate place for a child.

Series Connections: The Quinn brothers were all strays, taken in, adopted, loved, and raised by a very special couple, Ray and Stella Quinn. The death of their parents has left the brothers coping with the task of caring for the new addition to their family, a tough and wary youngster named Seth.

Cover Image(s):

Search for Love

Series: None

Editions: Silhouette Romance #163, July 1982, ISBN: 0-671-57163-X
Language of Love #11 ("Great Yellow Daffodil"), ISBN: 0-373-51011-X
Silhouette trade paperback compilation volume, *Mysterious*, Aug. 2003, ISBN: 0-373-21812-5

Story: When Serenity Smith flies to France to meet her long-lost grandmother, she finds herself under the scrutiny of the woman's grandson, the dark and complex Christophe de Kergallen.

Cover Image(s):

Second Nature

Series: *Celebrity* Magazine (Bk 2)
For related volumes, see *One Summer* (Bk 1)
See also the compilation volume: *Summer Pleasures*

Editions: Silhouette Special Edition #288, Jan. 1986, ISBN: 0-373-09288-1
Language of Love #30 ("Bluebell"), ISBN: 0-373-51030-6
Silhouette mass-market compilation volume, *Summer Pleasures*, Aug. 2002, ISBN: 0-373-21839-7

Story: Journalist Lee Radcliffe ambushes reclusive horror writer Hunter Brown for an interview and finds the price for cooperation is one very passionate kiss.

Series Connections: *Celebrity* magazine and its contributors form the connection between the books in this series.

Cover Image(s):

Secret Star

Series: The Stars of Mithra (Bk 3)
For related volumes, see *Hidden Star* (Bk 1) and *Captive Star* (Bk 2)

Editions: Silhouette Intimate Moments #835, Feb. 1998, ISBN: 0-373-07835-8
Silhouette reprint, July 2001, ISBN: 0-373-48490-9
Thorndike Press large print, ISBN: 0-373-59733-9

Story: When Grace Fontaine walks into the room, Lt. Seth Buchanan is shocked—because he's investigating her "murder."

Series Connections: Three immense blue diamonds form a set of perfectly matched stones once reputed to have been the centerpiece for a pagan altar—the Three Stars of Mithra. One stone represents love, one knowledge, and one generosity. According to the mythology surrounding them, when all three stones sit in a golden triangle, as they had in the hands of the god, they confer blessings upon those who hold them. Each novel in the series centers upon one stone and what happens to the woman who holds it.

Cover Image(s):

Seduction in Death

(writing as J. D. Robb)

Series: In Death (Bk 13)

For related volumes, see *Naked in Death* (Bk 1), *Glory in Death* (Bk 2), *Immortal in Death* (Bk 3), *Rapture in Death* (Bk 4), *Ceremony in Death* (Bk 5), *Vengeance in Death* (Bk 6), *Holiday in Death* (Bk 7), "Midnight in Death" (*Silent Night*, Bk 7.5), *Conspiracy in Death* (Bk 8), *Loyalty in Death* (Bk 9), *Witness in Death* (Bk 10), *Judgment in Death* (Bk 11), *Betrayal in Death* (Bk 12), "Interlude in Death" (*Out of This World*, Bk 12.5), *Reunion in Death* (Bk 14), *Purity in Death* (Bk 15), *Portrait in Death* (Bk 16), *Imitation in Death* (Bk 17), *Remember When* (Bk 17.5), *Divided in Death* (Bk 18), and *Visions in Death* (Bk 19)

Editions: Berkley mass market, Sept. 2001, ISBN: 0-425-18146-4
Nova Audio (Abridged), Sept. 2001, ISBN: 1-5878-8683-9
BrillianceAudio (Unabridged), Sept. 2001, ISBN: 1-5878-8681-2

Story: Eve Dallas investigates "Dante," a serial murderer who courts his victims in cyberspace for weeks before finally making a date where he wines, dines, drugs, rapes, and kills them.

Series Connections: Lt. Eve Dallas is a mid-21st-century cop in a New York City where, despite technological advances, crime still runs rampant. Eve is married to the enigmatic Roarke, a self-made billionaire with a shady past.

Cover Image(s):

Silent Night,
"Midnight in Death" novella
(writing as J. D. Robb)

Series: In Death (Bk 7.5)

For related volumes, see *Naked in Death* (Bk 1), *Glory in Death* (Bk 2), *Immortal in Death* (Bk 3), *Rapture in Death* (Bk 4), *Ceremony in Death* (Bk 5), *Vengeance in Death* (Bk 6), *Holiday in Death* (Bk 7), *Conspiracy in Death* (Bk 8), *Loyalty in Death* (Bk 9), *Witness in Death* (Bk 10), *Judgment in Death* (Bk 11), *Betrayal in Death* (Bk 12), "Interlude in Death" (*Out of This World*, Bk 12.5), *Seduction in Death* (Bk 13), *Reunion in Death* (Bk 14), *Purity in Death* (Bk 15), *Portrait in Death* (Bk 16), *Imitation in Death* (Bk 17), *Remember When* (Bk 17.5), *Divided in Death* (Bk 18), and *Visions in Death* (Bk 19)

Editions: Jove mass market, Nov. 1998, ISBN: 0-515-12385-4

Story: Eve Dallas is on the trail of an escaped sociopathic murderer who is systematically killing all the people who once put him behind bars.

Note: This anthology also features novellas by Susan Plunkett, Dee Holmes, and Claire Cross.

Series Connections: Lt. Eve Dallas is a mid-21st-century cop in a New York City where, despite technological advances, crime still runs rampant. Eve is married to the enigmatic Roarke, a self-made billionaire with a shady past.

Cover Image(s):

Silhouette Christmas Stories, "Home for Christmas" novella

Series: None

Editions: Silhouette mass market, Nov. 1986, ISBN: 0-373-48207-8

Story: When Jason Law returns to Quiet Valley, he knows that Faith Monroe didn't wait for him as she had promised, and he's determined to prove it doesn't matter.

Note: This was the first series romance Christmas anthology, and its success launched a flood of seasonal anthologies in the romance genre. This anthology also features novellas by Debbie Macomber, Maura Seger, and Tracy Sinclair.

Cover Image(s):

Silhouette Summer Sizzlers, "Impulse" novella

Series: None

Editions: Silhouette mass market, June 1989, ISBN: 0-373-48217-5

Story: Rebecca Malone makes two impulsive decisions: to go to Greece for fun and adventure and to fall in love with a handsome stranger, Stephen Nickodemus.

Note: This anthology also features novellas by Parris Afton Bonds and Kathleen Korbel.

Cover Image(s):

Skin Deep

Series: The O'Hurleys (Bk 3)

For related volumes, see *The Last Honest Woman* (Bk 1), *Dance to the Piper* (Bk 2), *Without a Trace* (Bk 4), with cameo appearances in *Waiting for Nick* and *Considering Kate*, and passing mentions in *Heart of the Sea* and *Tears of the Moon*

See also compilation volume: *The O'Hurleys: Chantel and Trace*, Nov. 2004

Editions: Silhouette Special Edition #475, Sept. 1988, ISBN: 0-373-09475-2

Mira mass market, Oct. 1995, ISBN: 1-55166-050-4

John Curley & Associates large print, May 1991, ISBN: 0-373-58042-8

Silhouette paperback compilation volume, *The O'Hurleys: Chantel and Trace*, Nov. 2004

Story: Actress Chantel O'Hurley is desperate to prove to P. I. Quinn Doran that she hasn't encouraged her obsessed fans, including the one who is threatening her.

Series Connections: The O'Hurley triplets, Abby, Maddy, and Chantel, and their brother, Trace, form the backbone of this series. The children of veteran performers Frank and Molly O'Hurley, they were born on the road between shows, and raised in hotel rooms and dressing rooms all across America. A lead role in a movie based on *Lawless* is mentioned in *Skin Deep* as Chantel O'Hurley's first big break as an actress. Bryan Mitchell from *One Summer* shows up for a cameo appearance in *Skin Deep*, to photograph Chantel.

Cover Image(s):

Song of the West

Series: None

Editions: Silhouette Romance #143, Apr. 1982, ISBN: 0-671-57143-5
Silhouette Two in One, *Once More with Feeling* and *Song of the West*, May 1991, ISBN: 0-373-48238-8

Story: Former Olympic gymnast Samantha Evans goes to Wyoming to help her pregnant twin sister and meets wealthy cattle baron Jake Tanner.

Cover Image(s):

Note: The cover image appearing on the two-in-one volume did not appear originally on either of the books it contains. It is instead from the cover of the original edition of *Boundary Lines.*

Stanislaski Brothers, The: Mikhail and Alex

Series: The Stanislaskis, a.k.a. Those Wild Ukrainians (Bks 2 & 4)
For related volumes, see *Taming Natasha* (Bk 1), *Luring a Lady* (Bk 2), *Falling for Rachel* (Bk 3), *Convincing Alex* (Bk 4), *Waiting for Nick* (Bk 5), and *Considering Kate* (Bk 6)
See also the compilation volume: *The Stanislaski Sisters: Natasha and Rachel*

Editions: Silhouette mass-market compilation volume, Nov. 2000,
ISBN: 0-373-48422-4
Thorndike Press large print compilation volume, July 2001,
ISBN: 0-786-23276-5

Story and Series Connections: See *Luring a Lady* and *Convincing Alex.*

Cover Image(s):

Stanislaski Sisters, The: Natasha and Rachel

Series: The Stanislaskis, a.k.a. Those Wild Ukrainians (Bks 1 & 3)

For related volumes, see *Taming Natasha* (Bk 1), *Luring a Lady* (Bk 2), *Falling for Rachel* (Bk 3), *Convincing Alex* (Bk 4), *Waiting for Nick* (Bk 5), and *Considering Kate* (Bk 6)

See also the compilation volume: *The Stanislaski Brothers: Mikhail and Alex*

Editions: Silhouette mass-market compilation volume, May 1997, ISBN: 0-373-20134-6

Silhouette mass-market compilation volume, Feb. 2001, ISBN: 0-373-48423-2

Thorndike Press large print compilation volume, Dec. 2001, ISBN: 0-786-23366-4

Story and Series Connections: See *Taming Natasha* and *Falling for Rachel*

Cover Image(s):

Storm Warning

Series: None

Editions: Silhouette Romance #274, Feb. 1984, ISBN: 0-671-57274-1
Language of Love #4 ("Wallflower"), ISBN: 0-373-51004-7
Silhouette trade paperback compilation volume, *Dangerous*, Dec. 2002, ISBN: 0-373-21854-0

Story: Autumn Gallagher arrives at a remote inn, where she finds a dead body and learns that the other guests are all the deceased's blackmail victims, including Lucas McLean, a man she once loved.

Cover Image(s):

Sullivan's Woman

Series: None

Editions: Silhouette Romance #280, Mar. 1984, ISBN: 0-671-57280-6
Language of Love #22 ("Stock"), ISBN: 0-373-51022-5
Silhouette mass-market reissue, Aug. 2003, ISBN: 0-373-21896-6

Story: Just when everything seems impossible for the unemployed Cassidy St. John, artist Colin Sullivan offers her a job as a model for his next painting.

Cover Image(s):

Summer Desserts

Series: Great Chefs (Bk 1)
For related volumes, see *Lessons Learned* (Bk 2)
See also the compilation volume: *Table for Two*

Editions: Silhouette Special Edition #271, Nov. 1985, ISBN: 0-373-09271-7
Language of Love #23 ("Dahlia"), ISBN: 0-373-51023-3
Silhouette mass-market compilation volume, *Table for Two*, Nov. 2002, ISBN: 0-373-21840-0

Story: Blake Cocharan wants a superb pastry chef, and Summer Lyndon is the perfect choice as well as a potentially tasty one.

Series Connections: Italy's most famous chef, Carlo Franconi, had a small part in *Summer Desserts* and demanded an encore performance as the star.

Cover Image(s):

Summer Pleasures

Series: *Celebrity* Magazine (Bks 1 & 2)
For related volumes, see *Second Nature* (Bk 1) and *One Summer* (Bk 2)

Editions: Silhouette mass-market compilation volume, Aug. 2002,
ISBN: 0-373-21839-7

Story and Series Connections: See *Second Nature* and *One Summer*

Cover Image(s):

Suspicious

Series: none

Editions: Silhouette trade compilation volume, Nov. 2003, ISBN: 0-373-21873-7

Story: See *Partners*, *The Art of Deception*, and *Night Moves.*

Cover Image(s):

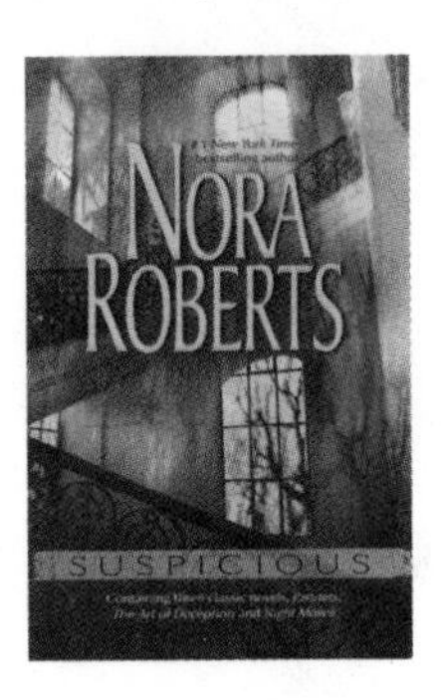

Suzanna's Surrender

Series: The Calhoun Women (Bk 4)

For related volumes, see *Courting Catherine* (Bk 1), *A Man for Amanda* (Bk 2), *For the Love of Lilah* (Bk 3), and *Megan's Mate* (Bk 5)

See also the compilation volumes: *The Calhoun Women: Catherine and Amanda* and *The Calhoun Women: Lilah and Suzanna*

Editions: Silhouette Intimate Moments #397, Sept. 1991, ISBN: 0-373-07397-6

Silhouette trade paperback compilation volume, *The Calhoun Women*, Dec. 1996, ISBN: 0-373-48332-5

Silhouette mass-market paperback compilation volume, *The Calhoun Women: Lilah and Suzanna*, Mar. 1998, ISBN: 0-373-48355-4

G. K. Hall & Co. large print, Feb. 1994, ISBN: 0-8161-5872-X

Story: During their search for the Calhoun emeralds, Suzanna and her sisters discover that ex-cop Holt Bradford is the grandson of the man who loved their grandmother.

Series Connections: The Calhoun sisters have inherited the family mansion built by Fergus Calhoun in the early 1900s. They've also inherited the family legends about the love affair that Fergus's wife, Bianca, had with an artist, and of the lost Calhoun emeralds, a fabulous set of jewels that vanished when Bianca died young and tragically. As they seek the jewels, they come closer to knowing the truth about Bianca and to finding love for themselves.

Cover Image(s):

Sweet Revenge

Series: None

Editions: Bantam mass market, Jan. 1989, ISBN: 0-553-27859-2
Bantam hardcover, Sept. 1996, ISBN: 0-553-10514-0
Wheeler Publishing large print, Feb. 1998, ISBN: 1-5689-5531-6
Thorndike Press large print, Aug. 1989, ISBN: 0-8962-1913-5

Story: Disillusioned by her royal father's cruelty, Adrianne plots to steal his most precious possession, with or without the enigmatic Philip Chamberlain's help.

Cover Image(s):

Table for Two

Series: Great Chefs (Bks 1 & 2)
For related volumes, see *Summer Desserts* (Bk 1) and *Lessons Learned* (Bk 2)

Editions: Silhouette mass-market compilation volume, Nov. 2002,
ISBN: 0-373-21840-0
Thorndike Press large print, May 2003, ISBN: 0-786-25258-8

Story and Series Connections: See *Summer Desserts* and *Lessons Learned*

Cover Image(s):

Taming Natasha

Series: The Stanislaskis, a.k.a Those Wild Ukrainians (Bk 1)

For related volumes, see *Luring a Lady* (Bk 2), *Falling for Rachel* (Bk 3), *Convincing Alex* (Bk 4), *Waiting for Nick* (Bk 5), and *Considering Kate* (Bk 6)

See also the compilation volumes: *The Stanislaski Brothers* and *The Stanislaski Sisters*

Editions: Silhouette Special Edition #583, Mar. 1990, ISBN: 0-373-09583-X

Silhouette mass-market compilation volume, *The Stanislaski Sisters: Rachel and Natasha*, May 1997, ISBN: 0-373-20134-6

Silhouette mass-market compilation volume, *The Stanislaski Sisters: Natasha and Rachel*, Feb. 2001, ISBN: 0-373-48423-2

Chivers North American large print, Oct. 1992, ISBN: 0-373-58577-2

Thorndike Press large print compilation volume, Dec. 2001, ISBN: 0-786-23366-4

Story: Former dancer Natasha Stanislaski opens a toy store, where she meets composer Spence Kimball and his little girl, Freddie.

Series Connections: Ukrainian Americans, and fiercely proud of their heritage, the Stanislaski family brings together the best of two worlds. The Stanislaski siblings and their relations form the core of the series.

Cover Image(s):

Tears of the Moon

Series: Irish trilogy, a.k.a. The Gallaghers of Ardmore (Bk 2)
For related volumes, see *Jewels of the Sun* (Bk 1) and *Heart of the Sea* (Bk 3)

Editions: Jove mass market, July 2000, ISBN: 0-515-12854-6
BrillianceAudio (Unabridged), July 2000, ISBN: 1-56740-469-3
BrillianceAudio (Abridged), June 2001, ISBN: 1-58788-308-2
Bookcassette Sales (Unabridged), July 2000, ISBN: 1-56740-692-0
Nova Audio (Abridged), June 2001, ISBN: 1-56740-870-2
Jove mass-market boxed set (with *Jewels of the Sun* and *Heart of the Sea*), Apr. 2001, ISBN: 0-515-131647-4
G. K. Hall & Co. large print paperback, Sept. 2001, ISBN: 0-7838-8992-5
G. K. Hall & Co. large print hardcover, Sept. 2000, ISBN: 0-7838-8991-7
e-book, Jove, June 2001, ISBN: 078650174-X
Adobe Reader e-book, Jove, June 2001, ISBN: 0786508361

Story: Shawn Gallagher, the cook at his family pub, is caught by surprise when his childhood friend Brenna O'Toole decides to act on her crush on him.

Series Connections: The three Gallagher siblings have a gift for hospitality, music, and love. As they each pursue their dreams in the tiny Irish coastal town of Ardmore, the fate of a pair of supernatural lovers rests upon each of the siblings finding and accepting true love.

Cover Image(s):

Series: None

Editions: Silhouette Romance #529, Sept. 1987, ISBN: 0-373-08529-X
Language of Love #43 ("Apple Blossom"), ISBN: 0-373-51043-8
G. K. Hall & Co. large print, July 1988, ISBN: 0-8161-4509-1
Silhouette mass-market reissue, Oct. 2003, ISBN: 0-373-21897-4

Story: Socialite Eden Carlbough finds that running a girls' camp is just as hard as resisting Chase Elliot, the handsome orchard owner next door.

Cover Image(s):

Tempting Fate

Series: The MacGregors (Bk 2)

For related volumes, see *Playing the Odds* (Bk 1), *All the Possibilities* (Bk 3), *One Man's Art* (Bk 4), *For Now, Forever* (Bk 5), *The MacGregor Brides* (Bk 6), *The Winning Hand* (Bk 7), *The MacGregor Grooms* (Bk 8), *The Perfect Neighbor* (Bk 9), *Rebellion*, a novel featuring a story line from Clan MacGregor history, and *Harlequin Historical Christmas Stories 1990*, "In from the Cold," a novella set in pre–Revolutionary War New England

See also the compilation volumes: *The MacGregors: Serena ~ Caine*, *The MacGregors: Alan ~ Grant*, and *The MacGregors: Daniel ~ Ian*

Editions: Silhouette Special Edition #235, May 1985, ISBN: 0-373-09235-0

Silhouette Special Plaid Reissue, Feb. 1987, ISBN: 0-373-48209-4

Language of Love #13 ("Gloxinia"), ISBN: 0-373-51013-6

Silhouette mass-market compilation volume, *The MacGregors: Serena ~ Caine*, Dec. 1998, ISBN: 0-373-48388-0

Story: When their siblings marry, Caine MacGregor and Diana Blade can no longer ignore each other.

Series Connections: The children of Daniel MacGregor and his wife, Anna, form the backbone of this series, with a slew of Daniel's grandchildren and great-grandchildren and assorted relatives to fill out the sequels. As Daniel himself would put it, "Good blood. Strong stock."

Cover Image(s):

This Magic Moment

Series: None

Editions: Silhouette Intimate Moments #25, Nov. 1983, ISBN: 0-671-47482-0
Language of Love #24 ("Iris"), ISBN: 0-373-51024-1
Silhouette Classics #3, Dec. 1987, ISBN: 0-373-04603-0
Arena Films video, *Magic Moments* (made-for-TV movie), (Apr. 1995 video release date), ASIN: 6303257593
Silhouette trade paperback compilation volume, *Mysterious*, Aug. 2003, ISBN: 0-373-21812-5

Story: Producer Ryan Swan realizes that magician Pierce Atkins is masking his memories of his unhappy childhood by performing seemingly impossible escapes.

Cover Image(s):

Three Complete Novels: Born in Fire, Born in Ice, Born in Shame

Series: The Concannan Sisters, a.k.a. the Born In trilogy (Bks 1, 2, & 3)
For related volumes, see *Born in Fire* (Bk 1), *Born in Ice* (Bk 2), and *Born in Shame* (Bk 3)

Editions: G. P. Putnam's Sons hardcover omnibus edition, Apr. 1998, ISBN: 0-399-14388-2

Story and Series Connections: See *Born in Fire*, *Born in Ice*, and *Born in Shame*

Cover Image(s):

Three Complete Novels:

Daring to Dream, Holding the Dream, Finding the Dream

Series: Dream, a.k.a. Templeton House (Bks 1, 2, & 3)
For related volumes, see *Daring to Dream* (Bk 1), *Holding the Dream* (Bk 2), and *Finding the Dream* (Bk 3)

Editions: G. P. Putnam's Sons hardcover omnibus edition, Apr. 1999, ISBN: 0-399-14480-3

Story and Series Connections: See *Daring to Dream* (Bk 1), *Holding the Dream* (Bk 2), and *Finding the Dream* (Bk 3)

Cover Image(s):

Three Complete Novels: Honest Illusions, Private Scandals, Hidden Riches

Series: None

Editions: G. P. Putnam's Sons hardcover omnibus edition, July 2000, ISBN: 0-399-14627-X

Story: See *Honest Illusions*, *Private Scandals*, and *Hidden Riches*

Cover Image(s):

Three Complete Novels: True Betrayals, Montana Sky, Sanctuary

Series: None

Editions: G. P. Putnam's Sons hardcover omnibus edition, June 2001, ISBN: 0-399-14731-4
Nova Audio (Abridged), July 2001, ISBN: 1-58788-720-7

Story: See *True Betrayals*, *Montana Sky*, and *Sanctuary*

Cover Image(s):

Three Fates

Series: None

Editions: G. P. Putnam's Sons hardcover, Apr. 2002, ISBN: 0-399-14840-X
Jove mass market, Apr. 2003, ISBN: 0-515-13506-2
Nova Audio (Abridged), Apr. 2002, ISBN: 1-5878-8695-2
BrillianceAudio (Unabridged), Apr. 2002, ISBN: 1-5878-8693-6
BrillianceAudio CD (Unabridged), Apr. 2002, ISBN: 1-5878-8696-0
BrillianceAudio (Unabridged), Apr. 2002, ISBN: 1-58788-694-4
BrillianceAudio CD library edition, Apr. 2002, ISBN: 1-58788-697-9
Thorndike Press large print, Dec. 2002, ISBN: 0-786-23839-9
Thorndike Press large print, June 2002, ISBN: 0-786-23835-6
Wheeler Publishing large print, Apr. 2003, ISBN: 1-41040-098-0

Story: Three siblings—Malachi, Gideon, and Rebecca—search for a family heirloom, a silver statue, as well as its matching two pieces.

Cover Image(s):

Time and Again

Series: Time and Again, a.k.a. the Hornblower Brothers (Bks 1 & 2)
For related volumes, see *Time Was* (Bk 1) and *Times Change* (Bk 2)

Editions: Silhouette mass market, Sept. 2001, ISBN: 0-373-48441-0

Story and Series Connections: See *Time Was* and *Times Change*

Cover Image(s):

Time Was

Series: Time and Again, a.k.a. the Hornblower Brothers (Bk 1)
For related volumes, see *Times Change* (Bk 2)
See also the compilation volume: *Time and Again*

Editions: Silhouette Special Edition #313, Dec. 1989, ISBN: 0-373-07313-5
Silhouette mass-market compilation volume, *Time and Again*, Sept. 2001, ISBN: 0-373-48441-0

Story: Thanks to a time gateway, Caleb Hornblower travels in time from 2252 to 1989, where he meets and falls in love with Liberty Stone.

Series Connections: Caleb and Jacob Hornblower are brothers from the 23rd century who travel back in time to meet their perfect mates, who are sisters.

Cover Image(s):

Times Change

Series: Time and Again, a.k.a. the Hornblower Brothers (Bk 2)
For related volumes, see *Time Was* (Bk 1)
See also the compilation volume: *Time and Again*

Editions: Silhouette Intimate Moments #317, Jan. 1990, ISBN: 0-373-07317-8
Silhouette mass-market compilation volume, *Time and Again*, Sept. 2001, ISBN: 0-373-48441-0

Story: Jacob Hornblower comes back in time to the 20th century to find his brother Caleb, but instead runs into Sunny Stone.

Series Connections: Caleb and Jacob Hornblower are brothers from the 23rd century who travel back in time to meet their perfect mates, who are sisters.

Cover Image(s):

Tonight and Always

Series: None

Editions: Silhouette Intimate Moments #12, July 1983, ISBN: 0-671-46156-7

Note: From the Heart, a single-volume collection of three unrelated early books (*Tonight and Always*, *A Matter of Choice*, and *Endings and Beginnings*) is the only version of these works currently in print. These titles are only available in the Berkley edition of *From the Heart.* These titles have reverted to the author and are no longer available from Harlequin.

Jove mass market, *From the Heart*, Nov. 1996, ISBN: 0-515-11965-2

Berkley trade paperback, *From the Heart*, June 2000, ISBN: 0-425-17616-9

Story: Bestselling writer Jordan Taylor needs the expertise of renowned anthropologist Kasey Wyatt to help him write his new book.

Cover Image(s):

Treasures Lost, Treasures Found

Series: None

Editions: Silhouette Intimate Moments #150, July 1986, ISBN: 0-373-07150-7
Language of Love #40 ("Purple Lilac"), ISBN: 0-373-51040-3
Silhouette hardcover reissue, Aug. 2003, ISBN: 0-373-21867-2

Story: The only way Kate Hardesty can find a sunken treasure is to join forces with Ky Silver, a diver she once loved.

Cover Image(s):

True Betrayals

Series: None

Editions: Jove mass market, May 1996, ISBN: 0-515-11855-9

G. P. Putnam's Sons hardcover omnibus edition, *Three Complete Novels: True Betrayals, Montana Sky, Sanctuary*, June 2001, ISBN: 0-399-14731-4

G. P. Putnam's Sons hardcover, June 1995, ISBN: 0-399-14059-X

BrillianceAudio CD (Abridged), June 2003, ISBN: 1-59086-524-3

Bookcassette Sales (Unabridged), July 1995, ISBN: 1-56100-628-9

BrillianceAudio (Abridged), Sept. 1996, ISBN: 1-56740-121-X

BrillianceAudio (Abridged), July 1995, ISBN: 1-56100-421-9

BrillianceAudio (Unabridged), Sept. 2001, ISBN: 1-58788-769-X

BrillianceAudio (Unabridged), Jan. 1995, ISBN: 1-56100-253-4

Nova Audio (with *Montana Sky* and *Sanctuary*), July 2001, ISBN: 1-58788-720-7

Jove mass-market boxed set (with *Homeport* and *Hidden Riches*), ISBN: 0-515-13456-2

e-book, Jove, June 2001, ISBN: 0786501839

Adobe Reader e-book, Jove, June 2001, ISBN: 0786509295

Thorndike Press large print, Nov. 1995, ISBN: 0-786-20505-9

Story: At her mother's horse farm, Kelsey Byden meets Gabe Slater, a racing stable owner. Together, they discover that some people will do anything to win.

Cover Image(s):

Truly, Madly Manhattan

Series: None

Editions: Silhouette mass-market compilation volume, Jan. 2003,
ISBN: 0-373-21803-6

Story and Series Connections: See *Dual Image* and *Local Hero*

Cover Image(s):

Two of a Kind

Series: none

For related volumes, see *Silhouette Summer Sizzlers* "Impulse" and *Birds, Bees, and Babies '94* "The Best Mistake"

Editions: Silhouette hardcover compilation, Sept. 2003, ISBN: 0-373-21870-2

Story: See *Silhouette Summer Sizzlers* "Impulse" and *Birds, Bees, and Babies '94* "The Best Mistake"

Cover Image(s): Not available

Unfinished Business

Series: None

Editions: Silhouette Intimate Moments #433, June 1992, ISBN: 0-373-07433-6
Thorndike Press large print, Mar. 1993, ISBN: 1-5605-4634-4
Silhouette trade paperback compilation volume, *Going Home*, Oct. 2002, ISBN: 0-373-21848-6

Story: Returning home as an adult, Vanessa Sexton learns that her old boyfriend Brady Tucker has grown from a reckless teenager into a pillar of the community.

Cover Image(s):

Untamed

Series: None

Editions: Silhouette Romance #252, Oct. 1983, ISBN: 0-671-57252-0
Language of Love #28 ("Azalea"), ISBN: 0-373-51028-4
Silhouette mass-market reissue, June 2003, ISBN: 0-373-21843-5
Thorndike Press large print, Oct. 2003, ISBN: 0-786-25610-9

Story: Lion trainer Jo Wilder believes in the magic the circus brings to its audience. After watching her perform, circus owner Keane Prescott believes in magic, too.

Cover Image(s):

Vengeance in Death

(writing as J. D. Robb)

Series: In Death (Bk 6)

For related volumes, see *Naked in Death* (Bk 1), *Glory in Death* (Bk 2), *Immortal in Death* (Bk 3), *Rapture in Death* (Bk 4), *Ceremony in Death* (Bk 5), *Holiday in Death* (Bk 7), "Midnight in Death" (*Silent Night*, Bk 7.5), *Conspiracy in Death* (Bk 8), *Loyalty in Death* (Bk 9), *Witness in Death* (Bk 10), *Judgment in Death* (Bk 11), *Betrayal in Death* (Bk 12), "Interlude in Death" (*Out of This World*, Bk 12.5), *Seduction in Death* (Bk 13), *Reunion in Death* (Bk 14), *Purity in Death* (Bk 15), *Portrait in Death* (Bk 16), *Imitation in Death* (Bk 17), *Remember When* (Bk 17.5), *Divided in Death* (Bk 18), and *Visions in Death* (Bk 19)

Editions: Berkley mass market, Oct. 1997, ISBN: 0-425-16039-4
BrillianceAudio (Abridged), June 2002, ISBN: 1-58788-437-2
Nova Audio (Abridged), June 2002, ISBN: 1-58788-436-4
e-book, Berkley, June 2001, ISBN: 078650093X
Adobe Reader e-book, Berkley, June 2001, ISBN: 0786509406

Story: Eve Dallas realizes the person who is killing former acquaintances of Roarke is sadistic, brilliant, and quite possibly lives in her house.

Series Connections: Lt. Eve Dallas is a mid-21st-century cop in a New York City where, despite technological advances, crime still runs rampant. Eve is married to the enigmatic Roarke, a self-made billionaire with a shady past.

Cover Image(s):

Villa, The

Series: None

Editions: Jove mass market, Apr. 2002, ISBN: 0-515-13218-7
G. P. Putnam's Sons hardcover, Mar. 2001, ISBN: 0-399-14712-8
BrillianceAudio (Unabridged), Mar. 2001, ISBN: 1-58788-137-3
BrillianceAudio (Abridged), Mar. 2001, ISBN: 1-58788-139-X
Bookcassette Sales (Abridged), Mar. 2001, ISBN: 1-58788-188-8
Bookcassette Sales (Unabridged), Mar. 2001, ISBN: 1-58788-138-1
BrillianceAudio CD (Abridged), Mar. 2001, ISBN: 1-58788-140-3
Random House large print hardcover, Mar. 2001, ISBN: 0-375-43103-9
e-book, Jove, Jan. 2002, ISBN: 0786517816
Adobe Reader e-book, Jove, Jan. 2002, ISBN: 0786517824
BrillianceAudio (Abridged), Feb. 2002, ISBN: 1-58788-653-7

Story: When two wineries merge, Tyler MacMillan's management techniques clash with Sophia Giambelli's style, but they put aside their differences when Sophia's father is murdered.

Cover Image(s):

Visions in Death

(writing as J. D. Robb)

Series: In Death (Bk 19)

For related volumes, see *Naked in Death* (Bk 1), *Glory in Death* (Bk 2), *Immortal in Death* (Bk 3), *Rapture in Death* (Bk 4), *Ceremony in Death* (Bk 5), *Vengeance in Death* (Bk 6), *Holiday in Death* (Bk 7), "Midnight in Death" (*Silent Night*, Bk 7.5), *Conspiracy in Death* (Bk 8), *Loyalty in Death* (Bk 9), *Witness in Death* (Bk 10), *Judgment in Death* (Bk 11), *Betrayal in Death* (Bk 12), "Interlude in Death" (*Out of This World*, Bk 12.5), *Seduction in Death* (Bk 13), *Reunion in Death* (Bk 14), *Purity in Death* (Bk 15), *Portrait in Death* (Bk 16), *Imitation in Death* (Bk 17), *Remember When* (Bk 17.5), and *Divided in Death* (Bk 18)

Editions: G. P. Putnam's Sons hardcover, Aug. 2004

Story: When the police department is approached by a psychic who claims to have witnessed a murder in a vision, Eve must decide what is fact and what is fiction in time to catch a killer before he strikes again.

Series Connections: Lt. Eve Dallas is a mid-21st-century cop in a New York City where, despite technological advances, crime still runs rampant. Eve is married to the enigmatic Roarke, a self-made billionaire with a shady past.

Cover Image(s): Not available

Waiting for Nick

Series: The Stanislaskis, a.k.a Those Wild Ukrainians (Bk 5)

For related volumes, see *Taming Natasha* (Bk 1), *Luring a Lady* (Bk 2), *Falling for Rachel* (Bk 3), *Convincing Alex* (Bk 4), and *Considering Kate* (Bk 6)

See also the compilation volumes: *The Stanislaski Brothers* and *The Stanislaski Sisters*

Editions: Silhouette Special Edition #1088, Mar. 1997, ISBN: 0-373-24088-0

Silhouette large print, Dec. 1999, ISBN: 0-373-59651-0

Story: Broadway composer Nick LeBeck learns that Freddie Kimball is no longer a child, but an attractive woman who has been in love with him for ten years.

Series Connections: Ukrainian Americans, and fiercely proud of their heritage, the Stanislaski family brings together the best of two worlds. The Stanislaski siblings and their relations form the core of the series. The four O'Hurleys and their families make an appearance in this book.

Cover Image(s):

Welcoming, The

Series: None

Editions: Silhouette Special Edition #553, Oct. 1989, ISBN: 0-373-09553-8
Language of Love #46 ("Garden Anemone"), ISBN: 0-373-51046-2
Silhouette trade paperback compilation volume, *Dangerous*, Dec. 2002, ISBN: 0-373-21854-0
John Curley & Associates large print, ISBN: 0-373-58235-8

Story: Federal agent Roman DeWinter comes to Orcas Island to catch a criminal, yet his instincts tell him that inn owner Charity Ford is innocent.

Cover Image(s):

Will and a Way, A

Series: None

Editions: Silhouette Special Edition #345, Nov. 1986, ISBN: 0-373-09345-4
Language of Love #34 ("Purple Columbine"), ISBN: 0-373-51034-9
Silhouette mass-market compilation volume, *Engaging the Enemy*, May 2003, ISBN: 0-373-21819-2

Story: In order to collect an inheritance, Pandora McVie must spend six months with Michael Donahue in an isolated mansion.

Cover Image(s):

Winning Hand, The

Series: MacGregors (Bk 7)

For related volumes, see *Playing the Odds* (Bk 1), *Tempting Fate* (Bk 2), *All the Possibilities* (Bk 3), *One Man's Art* (Bk 4), *For Now, Forever* (Bk 5), *The MacGregor Brides* (Bk 6), *The MacGregor Grooms* (Bk 8), *The Perfect Neighbor* (Bk 9), *Rebellion*, a novel featuring a story line from Clan MacGregor history, and *Harlequin Historical Christmas Stories 1990*, "In from the Cold," a novella set in pre–Revolutionary War New England

See also the compilation volumes: *The MacGregors: Serena ~ Caine*, *The MacGregors: Alan ~ Grant*, and *The MacGregors: Daniel ~ Ian*

Editions: Silhouette Special Edition #1202, Oct. 1998, ISBN: 0-373-24202-6
Harlequin large print, Aug. 2001, ISBN: 0-373-04698-7

Story: When Kansas girl Darcy Wallace hits it big in Las Vegas, casino owner Robert "Mac" MacGregor wants to make sure that no one takes advantage of her.

Series Connections: The children of Daniel MacGregor and his wife, Anna, form the backbone of this series, with a slew of Daniel's grandchildren and great-grandchildren and assorted relatives to fill out the sequels. As Daniel himself would put it, "Good blood. Strong stock."

Cover Image(s):

Without a Trace

Series: The O'Hurleys (Bk 4)

For related volumes, see *The Last Honest Woman* (Bk 1), *Dance to the Piper* (Bk 2), *Skin Deep* (Bk 3), with cameo appearances in *Waiting for Nick* and *Considering Kate*, and passing mentions in *Heart of the Sea* and *Tears of the Moon.* See also *The O'Hurleys: Chantel and Trace.*

Editions: Silhouette Special Edition #625, Oct. 1990, ISBN: 0-373-09625-9
Chivers North American large print, July 1993, ISBN: 0-373-58817-8
Mira reprint, Feb. 1996, ISBN: 1-55166-059-8
Silhouette mass-market compilation volume, *The O'Hurleys: Chantel and Trace*, Nov. 2004

Story: Spy Trace O'Hurley is planning on retiring, but he can't say no when Gillian Fitzpatrick asks for his help.

Series Connections: The O'Hurley triplets, Abby, Maddy, and Chantel, and their brother, Trace, form the backbone of this series. The children of veteran performers Frank and Molly O'Hurley, they were born on the road between shows, and raised in hotel rooms and dressing rooms all across America.

Cover Image(s):

Witness in Death

(writing as J. D. Robb)

Series: In Death (Bk 10)

For related volumes, see *Naked in Death* (Bk 1), *Glory in Death* (Bk 2), *Immortal in Death* (Bk 3), *Rapture in Death* (Bk 4), *Ceremony in Death* (Bk 5), *Vengeance in Death* (Bk 6), *Holiday in Death* (Bk 7), "Midnight in Death" (*Silent Night*, Bk 7.5), *Conspiracy in Death* (Bk 8), *Loyalty in Death* (Bk 9), *Judgment in Death* (Bk 11), *Betrayal in Death* (Bk 12), "Interlude in Death" (*Out of This World*, Bk 12.5), *Seduction in Death* (Bk 13), *Reunion in Death* (Bk 14), *Purity in Death* (Bk 15), *Portrait in Death* (Bk 16), *Imitation in Death* (Bk 17), *Remember When* (Bk 17.5), *Divided in Death* (Bk 18), and *Visions in Death* (Bk 19)

Editions: Berkley mass market, Mar. 2000, ISBN: 0-425-17363-1
BrillianceAudio (Abridged), Apr. 2003, ISBN: 1-58788-448-8
Thorndike Press large print, Aug. 2000, ISBN: 0-786-22715-X
Thorndike Press large print, Aug. 2001, ISBN: 0-786-22716-8
e-book, Berkley, Sept. 2001, ISBN: 078650188X
Adobe Reader e-book, Berkley, Sept. 2001, ISBN: 078650949X

Story: Eve Dallas and Roarke go to the theater, where they witness a bizarre onstage death.

Series Connections: Lt. Eve Dallas is a mid-21st-century cop in a New York City where, despite technological advances, crime still runs rampant. Eve is married to the enigmatic Roarke, a self-made billionaire with a shady past.

Cover Image(s):

the language of love reprints

LANGUAGE OF LOVE titles, reissues of forty-eight of Nora Roberts's early Silhouette books, were published over the course of the early 1990s by Silhouette. The books in the series are listed in order of publication here:

1. lily of the valley—*Irish Thoroughbred*
2. hollyhock—*The Law Is a Lady*
3. cabbage rose—*Irish Rose*
4. wallflower—*Storm Warning*
5. foxglove—*First Impressions*
6. yellow jasmine—*Reflections*
7. marigold—*Night Moves*
8. narcissus—*Dance of Dreams*

9. china aster—*Opposites Attract*
10. amaryllis—*Island of Flowers*
11. great yellow daffodil—*Search for Love*
12. hyacinth—*Playing the Odds*
13. gloxinia—*Tempting Fate*
14. forget-me-not—*From This Day*
15. petunia—*All the Possibilities*
16. tuberose—*The Heart's Victory*
17. red poppy—*One Man's Art*
18. gladiola—*Rules of the Game*
19. white periwinkle—*For Now, Forever*
20. pansy—*Her Mother's Keeper*
21. orchid—*Partners*
22. stock—*Sullivan's Woman*
23. dahlia—*Summer Desserts*
24. iris—*This Magic Moment*
25. pink—*Lessons Learned*
26. lavender—*The Right Path*
27. love in a mist—*The Art of Deception*
28. azalea—*Untamed*
29. red carnation—*Dual Image*
30. bluebell—*Second Nature*
31. red and white roses—*One Summer*
32. wisteria—*Gabriel's Angel*
33. trumpet flower—*The Name of the Game*
34. purple columbine—*A Will and a Way*
35. honeysuckle—*Affaire Royale*
36. spring crocus—*Less of a Stranger*
37. crown imperial—*Command Performance*
38. white camellia—*Blithe Images*
39. cyclamen—*The Playboy Prince*
40. purple lilac—*Treasures Lost, Treasures Found*
41. white daisy—*Risky Business*
42. red tulip—*Loving Jack*
43. apple blossom—*Temptation*
44. dogwood—*Best Laid Plans*
45. clematis—*Mind over Matter*
46. garden anemone—*The Welcoming*
47. snapdragon—*Boundary Lines*
48. morning glory—*Local Hero*

from book to screen

Nora's Books into Movies

SO FAR, ONLY two of Nora's books have been made into movies, although many have been optioned (including *Montana Sky*, *Sacred Sins*, *Private Scandals*, and *The Reef*). Fox 2000 optioned the rights for Mel Gibson and Bruce Davey's studio-based Icon Productions for Roberts's In Death series (under the pen name J. D. Robb) to produce along with Susan Landau. The two that were made were TV movies, one for cable and the other for CBS. The first movie made from Nora's books was *Magic Moments*, which was an adaptation of *This Magic Moment*, a Silhouette Intimate Moments book. The movie first aired on

March 19, 1989, and starred John Shea (who went on to star as the seductive Lex Luthor in *Lois and Clark: The Adventures of Superman*) and Jenny Seagrove (well known for her role in the miniseries *A Woman of Substance*). Another well-known actor also had a small role in *Magic Moments*—Eric La Salle, who would gain fame on the TV series *ER*.

magic moments
movie credits

Directed by: Lawrence Gordon Clark

Written by: Charlotte Bingham and Terence Brady

Produced by: David Conroy, Jonathan Dana, John Goldstone, Eric Rattray, and Keith Richardson

Production company: Arena Films

Cast: John Shea as Troy Gardner
Jenny Seagrove as Melanie James
Paul Freeman as Brian Swann
Eric La Salle as Dancing Guy

The other movie made from one of Nora's books is *Sanctuary*, which was made for CBS and aired on CBS on February 28, 2001. CBS billed it as "Nora Roberts's *Sanctuary*," and it starred Melissa Gilbert (famous for *Little House on the Prairie* as well as other TV work) and Costas Mandylor (known for his work on the TV series *Secret Agent Man* and *Picket Fences*). This was a very faithful adaptation—in fact, Nora received a writing credit for the movie. Nora visited the set of *Sanctuary* in Canada where she got to meet and hang out with the cast and crew.

Nora with Melissa Gilbert and Costas Mandylor, the star of the TV movie Sanctuary

sanctuary
movie credits

Directed by: Katt Shea

Written by: Nora Roberts (book), Katt Shea, and Vivienne Radkoff

Produced by: Andrew Adelson, Tracey Alexander, Vivienne Radkoff, and Frank Siracusa

Production company: Adelson Entertainment, CBS Productions, CBS Television, and Tracey Alexander Productions

Cast: Melissa Gilbert as Jo Ellen Hathaway
Costas Mandylor as Nathan Delaney
Kathy Baker as Aunt Kate
Leslie Hope as Kirby Fitzsimmons
Kenneth Walsh as Sam Hathaway
Chris Martin as Brian Hathaway

Nora on the set of Sanctuary *with director Katt Shea*

Nora on the set of Sanctuary *with Melissa Gilbert*

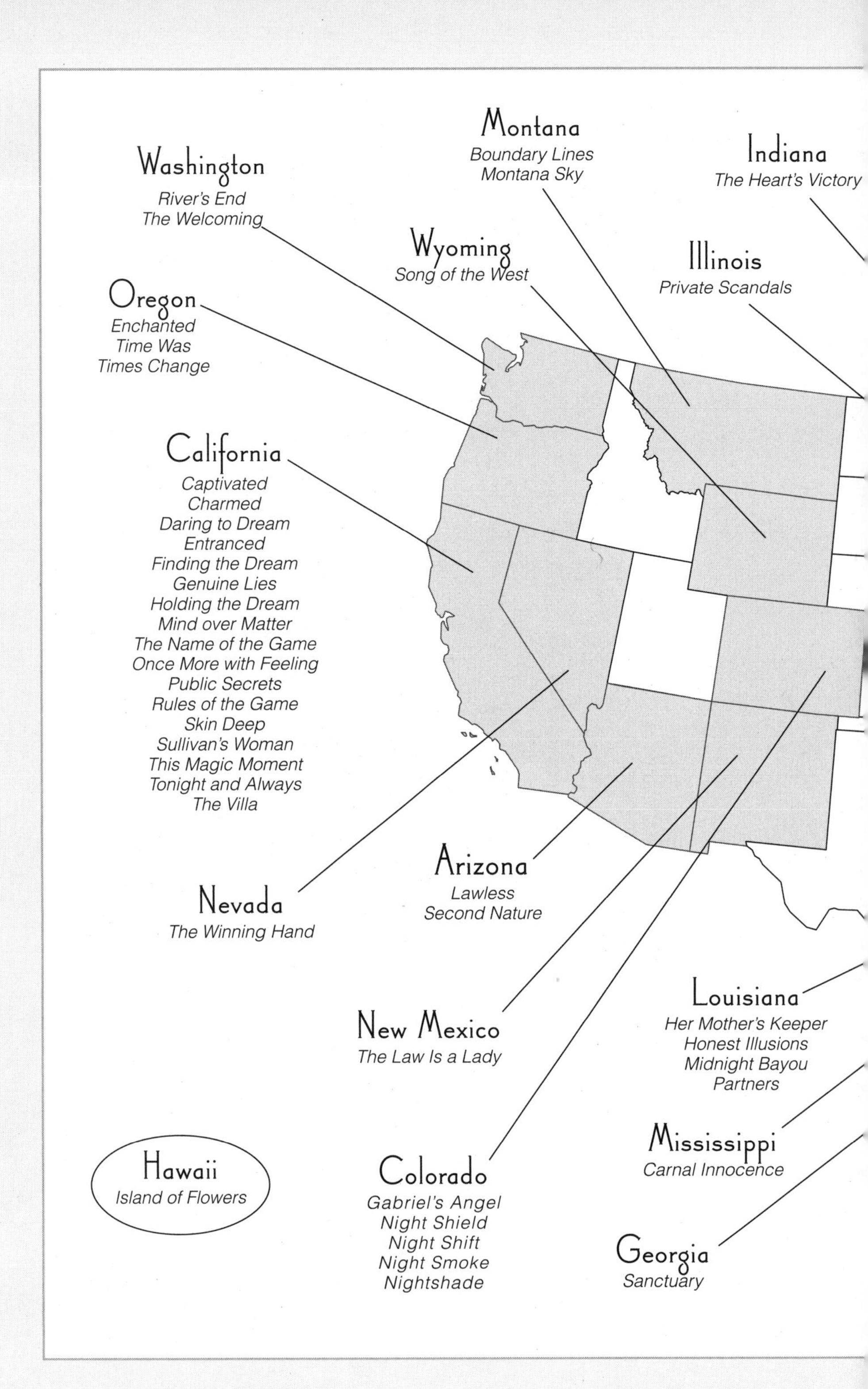

Montana
Boundary Lines
Montana Sky
Indiana
The Heart's Victory
Washington
River's End
The Welcoming
Wyoming
Song of the West
Illinois
Private Scandals
Oregon
Enchanted
Time Was
Times Change
California
Captivated
Charmed
Daring to Dream
Entranced
Finding the Dream
Genuine Lies
Holding the Dream
Mind over Matter
The Name of the Game
Once More with Feeling
Public Secrets
Rules of the Game
Skin Deep
Sullivan's Woman
This Magic Moment
Tonight and Always
The Villa
Arizona
Lawless
Second Nature
Nevada
The Winning Hand
Louisiana
Her Mother's Keeper
Honest Illusions
Midnight Bayou
Partners
New Mexico
The Law Is a Lady
Mississippi
Carnal Innocence
Hawaii
Island of Flowers
Colorado
Gabriel's Angel
Night Shield
Night Shift
Night Smoke
Nightshade
Georgia
Sanctuary

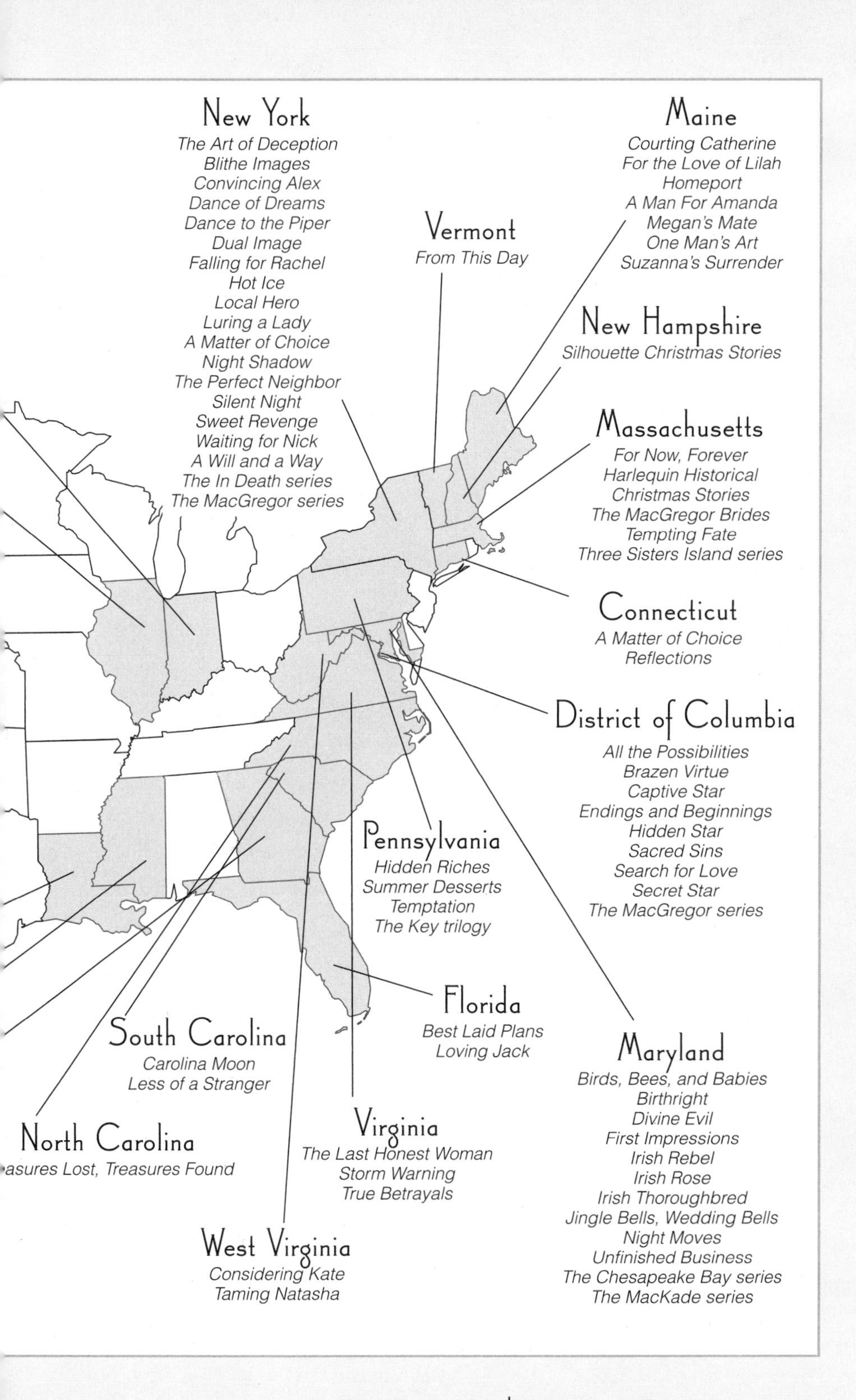
New York
The Art of Deception
Blithe Images
Convincing Alex
Dance of Dreams
Dance to the Piper
Dual Image
Falling for Rachel
Hot Ice
Local Hero
Luring a Lady
A Matter of Choice
Night Shadow
The Perfect Neighbor
Silent Night
Sweet Revenge
Waiting for Nick
A Will and a Way
The In Death series
The MacGregor series
Vermont
From This Day
Maine
Courting Catherine
For the Love of Lilah
Homeport
A Man For Amanda
Megan's Mate
One Man's Art
Suzanna's Surrender
New Hampshire
Silhouette Christmas Stories
Massachusetts
For Now, Forever
Harlequin Historical
Christmas Stories
The MacGregor Brides
Tempting Fate
Three Sisters Island series
Connecticut
A Matter of Choice
Reflections
District of Columbia
All the Possibilities
Brazen Virtue
Captive Star
Endings and Beginnings
Hidden Star
Sacred Sins
Search for Love
Secret Star
The MacGregor series
Pennsylvania
Hidden Riches
Summer Desserts
Temptation
The Key trilogy
Florida
Best Laid Plans
Loving Jack
South Carolina
Carolina Moon
Less of a Stranger
North Carolina
asures Lost, Treasures Found
Virginia
The Last Honest Woman
Storm Warning
True Betrayals
West Virginia
Considering Kate
Taming Natasha
Maryland
Birds, Bees, and Babies
Birthright
Divine Evil
First Impressions
Irish Rebel
Irish Rose
Irish Thoroughbred
Jingle Bells, Wedding Bells
Night Moves
Unfinished Business
The Chesapeake Bay series
The MacKade series

on location with nora

A State-by-State and Country-by-Country Title Listing

arizona *Lawless* • *Second Nature* **california** *Captivated* • *Charmed* • *Daring to Dream* • *Entranced* • *Finding the Dream* • *Genuine Lies* • *Holding the Dream* • *Mind over Matter* • *The Name of the Game* • *Once More with Feeling* • *Public Secrets* • *Rules of the Game* • *Skin Deep* • *Sullivan's Woman* • *This Magic Moment* • *Tonight and Always* • *The Villa* **colorado** *Gabriel's Angel* • *Night Shield* • *Night Shift* • *Night Smoke* • *Nightshade* **connecticut** *A Matter of Choice* • *Reflections* **district of columbia** *All the Possibilities* • *Brazen Virtue* • *Captive Star* • *Endings and Beginnings* • *Hidden Star* • *Sacred Sins* • *Search for Love* • *Secret Star* • *The MacGregor series* **florida** *Best Laid Plans* • *Loving Jack* **georgia** *Sanctuary* **hawaii** *Island of Flowers* **illinois** *Private Scandals* **indiana** *The Heart's Victory* **louisiana** *Her Mother's Keeper* • *Honest Illusions* • *Midnight Bayou* • *Partners* **maine** *Courting Catherine* • *For the Love of Lilah* • *Homeport* • *A Man for Amanda* • *Megan's Mate* • *One Man's Art* • *Suzanna's Surrender* **maryland** *Birds, Bees, and Babies* • *Birthright* • *Divine Evil* • *First Impressions* • *Irish Rebel* • *Irish Rose* • *Irish Thoroughbred* • *Jingle Bells, Wedding Bells* • *Night Moves* • *Unfinished Business* • *The Chesapeake Bay series* • *The MacKade series* **massachusetts** *For Now, Forever* • *Harlequin Historical Christmas Stories* • *The MacGregor Brides* • *Tempting Fate* • *Three Sisters Island series* **mississippi** *Carnal Innocence* **montana** *Boundary Lines* •

Montana Sky ▸**nevada** *The Winning Hand* ▸**new hampshire** *Silhouette Christmas Stories* ▸**new mexico** *The Law Is a Lady* ▸**new york** *The Art of Deception* • *Blithe Images* • *Convincing Alex* • *Dance of Dreams* • *Dance to the Piper* • *Dual Image* • *Falling for Rachel* • *Hot Ice* • *Local Hero* • *Luring a Lady* • *A Matter of Choice* • *Night Shadow* • *Once Upon a Kiss* • *The Perfect Neighbor* • *Silent Night* • *Sweet Revenge* • *Waiting for Nick* • *A Will and a Way* • *The In Death series* • *The MacGregor series* ▸**north carolina** *Treasures Lost, Treasures Found* ▸**oregon** *Enchanted* • *Time Was* • *Times Change* ▸**pennsylvania** *Hidden Riches* • *Summer Desserts* • *Temptation* • *The Key trilogy* ▸**south carolina** *Carolina Moon* • *Less of a Stranger* ▸**vermont** *From This Day* ▸**virginia** *The Last Honest Woman* • *Storm Warning* • *True Betrayals* ▸**washington** *River's End* • *The Welcoming* ▸**west virginia** *Considering Kate* • *Taming Natasha* ▸**wyoming** *Song of the West*

INTERNATIONAL LOCATIONS

▸**caribbean** *The Reef* ▸**cordina** (fictional Mediterranean Europe) *Affaire Royale* • *Command Performance* • *The Playboy Prince* ▸**france** *Promise Me Tomorrow* • *Search for Love* ▸**greece** *The Right Path* • *Silhouette Summer Sizzlers* ▸**ireland** *Born in Fire* • *Born in Ice* • *Born in Shame* • *Heart of the Sea* • *Jewels of the Sun* • *Once Upon a Castle* • *Once Upon a Dream* • *Tears of the Moon* • *Vengeance in Death* ▸**italy** *Homeport* ▸**madagascar** *Hot Ice* ▸**mexico** *Risky Business* • *Without a Trace* ▸**morocco** *Without a Trace* ▸**scotland** *Rebellion* ▸**multiple locations** *Charmed* • *Lessons Learned* • *The MacGregor Grooms* • *One Summer* • *Opposites Attract* • *Playing the Odds* • *Three Fates* • *Untamed*

FICTIONAL LOCATIONS

Once Upon a Midnight • *Once Upon a Rose* • *Once Upon a Star* • *Sweet Revenge (Jaquir, in the Middle East)*

OFF-PLANET

Out of this World • *Rapture in Death*

"The publishing world might be hard-pressed to find an author with a more diverse style or fertile imagination than Roberts, writing here as J. D. Robb. . . . This latest addition is a perfect balance of suspense, futuristic police procedure and steamy romance. In short, it is truly fine entertainment."

—*Publishers Weekly* on
VENGEANCE IN DEATH

J. D.

PART FOUR

a.k.a. Robb, Robb

the life of "in death"

An In-Depth Look at the J. D. Robb Books

SPOILER ALERT: IF YOU HAVEN'T READ THE BOOKS IN THE SERIES, RUN AWAY NOW, AND DON'T COME BACK UNTIL YOU'VE READ THEM ALL!

The year is 2058 . . .

The mean streets of New York have grown meaner with age and it takes a new breed of cop to keep them safe. Lt. Eve Dallas is that kind of a cop—dedicated, smart, and tough. With ten years on the force, she's considered a veteran, defending the innocent, identifying the guilty, and bringing criminals to justice.

The reader's first introduction to Eve (*Naked in Death*) provides a brief but telling glimpse into the inner woman as she's haunted by the failures of the night before, by her inability to save a child from being killed. In this book and subsequent ones, the reader realizes that the "lost child" is a recurring theme, reflecting Eve's own childhood, destroyed at the hands of her abusive father. Despite her insecurities, she has forged a tough exterior in order to protect her vulnerable heart.

Did You Know . . .

Nora Roberts resisted getting a pseudonym for years, despite the advice of her agent and publisher. It was only when her agent, Amy Berkower, pointed out that it was just like having Coke® and Diet Coke® that Nora created the J. D. Robb series.

The first time we see Eve in action, she's investigating a case about a serial killer who is murdering "licensed companions." In the not too distant yet dingy future, human vices like prostitution have been legalized. The chief suspect for the murders is an enigmatic Irish billionaire who goes only by the name of Roarke. He is the last person Eve should be attracted to: He's filthy rich, lives a luxurious lifestyle, has a collection of antique firearms (just like the murder weapon), and can have any woman in the world if he so desires. At first, she wonders if their mutual attraction is something he manufactured—to distract her from her professional duties. But she eventually responds, albeit initially reluctantly, to his overtures.

> *". . . Sex isn't high on my priority list. It's distracting."*
>
> *The temper in his eyes lighted to a laugh. "Damn right it is. When it's done well. Isn't it time you let me show you?"*
>
> —From *Naked in Death*

This scene starts a love affair, which to date, has extended over nineteen full novels and three novellas, an unparalleled structure in comparison with Nora's romances or the books of other romance authors. By necessity, romance readers have been used to a story structure in which the romance progresses over the course of a single book, but not over more than one.

At best, lead characters in one book might make a secondary appearance in other books within a trilogy or a limited series. But Nora's Eve Dallas books brought back her characters to be the stars of a series that shows every sign of continuing as long as Nora cares to write about them.

However, those readers who read mysteries, specifically mystery series, are very familiar with this sort of multibook structure, savoring the ability to slip back into the world of their favorite mystery series characters and watching the slower progression of their personal lives as opposed to the faster-paced environment of the criminal investigation.

Nora did not pioneer the concept of the lead investigator exonerating a lead suspect and then developing a personal relationship with him or her. It's a popular plot device utilized by many mystery series authors. But what makes Nora's approach unique is twofold: The roles are reversed—the female investigative lead exonerates the nonprofessional male—and, even more important, Nora is using her well-honed romance skills to develop a highly erotic yet character-driven romance that fulfills the requirements of the typical romance reader. It's one of the first times an author has dovetailed two genres so well and with such commercial success and acceptance from readers of both genres. To add even a higher degree of difficulty, Nora set the entire series in the future, which has attracted science fiction readers as well, who comment on the believability of this mid-twenty-first-century world.

Did You Know . . .

Of all the things Nora's invented for her novels, the thing she'd most like to have in real life is an AutoChef.

It was a real coup to pull this off in a single book, but Nora takes it a step further by keeping the relationship both inventive and center stage for all subsequent books, continuing to engineer complex, no-holds-barred homicide investigations and continuing to build this world of the not-too-distant future.

Throughout the series, Eve and Roarke continue to explore their thoughts and feelings, their instincts, and their relationship with each other. In *Glory in Death*, the reader sees returning secondary characters and becomes willing to invest some time in their lives since it appears they may return in subsequent books. We are again presented with Mavis Freestone, Eve's effervescent best friend; Summerset, Roarke's disapproving butler; Whitney, Eve's gruff commander; Feeney, the department's computer whiz; Nadine, the nosy vid reporter; and Dr. Mira, the shrink who actually knows what she's doing. We also meet for the first time Officer Delia Peabody, who will become Eve's protégée. The relationship between Eve and Roarke progresses in *Glory in Death* until the closing scene, where Roarke pops "the question." Eve responds:

> *"We're standing here, beat to shit, walking away from a crime scene where either or both of us could have bought it, and you're asking me to marry you?"*
>
> *[Roarke] tucked his arm around her waist again, nudged her forward. "Perfect timing."*

In the next book, *Immortal in Death*, Eve's prewedding jitters affect her professional life. But both her professional and private lives cross when her best friend, Mavis, is the chief suspect in a love triangle murder. At the end, Eve figures out not only who the killer is, but how she can deal with her own upcoming wedding. She explains to Roarke:

> *"I figured it out. . . . It's a formality. And it's not a contract. . . . It's a promise. It's not so hard to promise to do something you really want, anyway. And if I'm lousy at being a wife, you'll just have to live with it. I don't break my promises."*

Rapture in Death picks up around three weeks after the wedding, with Eve and Roarke on their off-planet honeymoon. The first mysterious death happens at their honeymoon resort and two more follow them once they're back on Earth. Eve, usually cold and calculating in her professional life, demonstrates a surprisingly different side of her personality when she realizes that Roarke is the next intended victim. After battling with the villain, Eve runs to save her husband, running into Peabody along the way.

"Roarke, oh God, oh God, please." Tears were streaming, scalding her, blinding her. Panic sweat flooded out of her pores, soaking her skin. "She's killing him. She's going to kill him."

This honest outpouring of emotion is a new twist to Eve's heretofore tightly regimented personality and very evidently a result of the depth of her feelings for her husband. In *Ceremony in Death*, the situation is reversed, with Roarke saving his wife at the end of the book. Because the readers of the series are very aware of his feelings for his wife through his actions and his words in the various books, it's his actions that speak the loudest in this situation.

As the door slid open, he crouched and, baring his teeth, prepared to spring. . . . He came in like a wolf, with a snarl and a lunge. The force of Roarke's attack sent [the villain] flying back. . . . Roarke's fist flew up and cracked against his face. [to Eve] "Get the hell back," Roarke demanded. "He's mine."

Vengeance in Death brings Summerset into a more pivotal position and offers some explanation for the relationship between Roarke and his butler. Also, the character of computer whiz-kid McNab is introduced. More details are revealed about Roarke's veiled past as Eve figures out he's the point of commonality in a series of grisly murders: All the victims had assisted Roarke in one way or another in his quest to get vengeance for the murder of a young girl years ago in Ireland—a young girl who was Summerset's daughter. At the end, there's a rare interchange between Eve and Summerset. Eve, injured by a blast meant for Summerset, is being tended to tenderly by the butler.

His hands were as gentle as a mother's with an infant. . . . "You saved my life. You stepped in front of me. Why?"

"It's my job, don't take it personally. . . ."

The relationship between Summerset and Eve eventually gets back to its usual venomous overtones, but in *Holiday in Death* there are still some traces of a truce in place. When Summerset offers to help Eve find a rare book for Roarke's Christmas present, she contemplates how much she'd hate owing him for the favor. But the holidays also bring back unsettling memories for Eve. Her current case brings suppressed memories of her abusive father closer to the surface than ever before. As Eve works to solve the Twelve Days of Christmas murders, the relationship between McNab and Peabody heads off in an interesting direction.

In *Conspiracy in Death*, Eve's professional reputation takes a hit when a fellow officer accuses her of improprieties and she's investigated by the Internal Affairs Bureau, complicating her pursuit of a possible serial killer. As her professional world is turned upside down, she continues to have uncontrolled flashes of memories from her forgotten childhood. Her relationship with Roarke seems to be the only stable footing she has in her life until she passes the invasive Level Three psychiatric questioning exonerating her from IAB charges. Then she's at last free to figure out who is killing people and stealing their internal organs, and why.

Marital discord threatens Eve and Roarke in *Loyalty in Death.* To further complicate things, when Eve learns that McNab and Peabody have taken their relationship to a more personal level, Eve unleashes the following rare interchange when Roarke inquires as to why it won't work:

> *"Because it won't. It doesn't. Your energies and your focus get all split up when they need to be channeled on the job. You start mixing sex and romance and Christ knows what into it, everything gets tilted. They've got no business having sex. Cops aren't supposed to—"*
>
> *"Have a personal life? . . . Personal feelings and choices?"*

In addition to Peabody and McNab's relationship, Peabody shows her more maternal side when her brother Zeke comes to New York. Despite Peabody's mother-hen tendencies, Zeke becomes a murder suspect. In addition to Zeke's woes, a group of terrorists are planting bombs all over the city and the tension is palpable as Eve and Roarke race the clock in hopes of disarming the explosives.

Witness in Death leaves explosive plots behind and pays homage to Agatha Christie's *Witness for the Prosecution* by having Eve and Roarke witness the death of an actor while in the midst of a live theatrical production. Eve suffers more memory flashes, this time not about her abusive father, but concerning her absent mother. Peabody vacillates between McNab and Charles, the licensed companion who is paying her attention. Officer Trueheart, first onstage in *Conspiracy in Death*, returns in *Witness.*

Did You Know . . .

The *J* and *D* in Nora's J. D. Robb pseudonym stand for the names of her sons, Jason and Dan.

The past haunts Roarke in *Judgment in Death* when an old partner turned adversary seems to be at the center of a cop's murder in a club owned by Roarke. Eve and Roarke disagree on how to protect the other from danger, but it serves as a great source of tension, which they overcome to work together. The relationship between McNab and Peabody stays in the background in this book, as the focus is on Roarke's past and some of his less than legal activities.

Betrayal in Death takes a different tack from earlier books by revealing the identity of the villain early in the book, turning the mystery elements into suspense elements as Eve fights the clock to stop the man from killing more people, all of whom are associated with Roarke. The big question becomes: who hired the hit man and why? Another case of role reversal occurs as Eve becomes the one who comforts and helps Roarke deal with his emotional conflicts, not as a cop, but as his wife. The relationship between Peabody and McNab falters as McNab decides he doesn't want to take a backseat to the other man in Peabody's life—Charles. As the hit man chooses victims who are progressively closer to Roarke, they all realize that both Eve and Summerset are in danger. Eve offers an insightful revelation concerning Summerset's role in Roarke's world:

> *"You're the only thing he brought with him from the past that he values."*

What she doesn't say is that she represents Roarke's future, something else his tormentor would likely try to rob from him.

These first twelve books in the series represent the first year of Eve and Roarke's life together. As this series continues, readers have faith that the relationship between Eve and Roarke will never grow stale. Nor will the other characters. Under Nora's deft hand, the secondary characters have never been relegated to merely set dressing but are three-dimensional people who act as sounding boards and mirrors to the main characters as well as leading their own lives. Although many readers (especially those from the romance camp) clamor for the transition of Eve into a mother, Nora has reportedly said she will never do this. But what we can be sure she will do is continue the adventures of Lt. Eve Dallas and her Irish billionaire husband, embroiling them in mystery and suspense and entertaining readers for years to come.

you've been **betrayed!**

FOR THE PUBLICATION of the twelfth J. D. Robb novel, *Betrayal in Death,* Leslie Gelbman, Amy Berkower, and Nora all agreed that it was time to "out" J. D. Robb as Nora Roberts. For years many readers already knew of Nora's alter ego, but this official unveiling would make it known to everybody. Berkley made it into a huge event, with an innovative marketing and publicity campaign playing up the "betrayal" aspect in the new title and in the unveiling. First, booksellers were sent postcards stating that they'd been "betrayed" by a *New York Times* bestselling author, and a silhouette of Nora appeared on the postcard. The next round of postcards sent had clues to who this author could be. The third and final round of postcards revealed Nora as J. D. Robb, and the silhouette of Nora was replaced with Nora's photo. The "two sides of Nora" idea was played up in the special riser created for *Betrayal in Death,* and then in the print ads, and of course Nora's name was added to the cover of *Betrayal in Death.* Nora was officially "out"!

DISCOVER BOTH SIDES OF
NORA ROBERTS
photos: John Earle
#1 NEW YORK TIMES BESTSELLING AUTHOR
NORA ROBERTS
WRITING AS
J.D.
ROBB
FIRST TIME IN PRINT
BETRAYAL IN DEATH
NORA ROBERTS
J.D.
ROBB
NAKED IN DEATH
Get *Naked* first... discover where the Eve Dallas series began!
The *New York Times* bestselling author of *The Villa* has been leading a double life. But now the secret is out: **Nora Roberts is J.D. Robb**—and you won't feel *betrayed* with her latest supenseful novel featuring New York detective Eve Dallas.
Available wherever books are sold.
Berkley Member of Penguin Putnam Inc.
Visit Berkley online at www.penguinputnam.com
Writing too good to keep secret...

J. D. Robb's
In Death books

In Chronological Order

UNLIKE MOST OF Nora Roberts's works, the J. D. Robb novels should be read in chronological order for maximum enjoyment of the series, so they are presented here in order of publication, rather than alphabetical by title. Alphabetical-by-title listings for the In Death books can be found mingled in the previous section of this book.

Naked in Death (July 1995)
Glory in Death (Dec. 1995)
Immortal in Death (July 1996)
Rapture in Death (Oct. 1996)
Ceremony in Death (June 1997)
Vengeance in Death (Oct. 1997)
Holiday in Death (June 1998)
"Midnight in Death" novella from *Silent Night* (Nov. 1998)
Conspiracy in Death (Mar. 1999)
Loyalty in Death (Oct. 1999)
Witness in Death (Mar. 2000)
Judgment in Death (Sept. 2000)
Betrayal in Death (Mar. 2001)
"Interlude in Death" novella from *Out of This World* (Aug. 2001)
Seduction in Death (Sept. 2001)
Reunion in Death (Mar. 2002)
Purity in Death (Sept. 2002)
Portrait in Death (Mar. 2003)
Imitation in Death (Sept. 2003)
Remember When (Sept. 2003)
Divided in Death (Mar. 2004)
Visions in Death (Aug. 2004)

Mary Kay McComas, Nora, and Pat Gaffney share fun moments with the customers of That Bookstore in Danville.

Nora, Pat Gaffney, and Mary Kay McComas in front of That Bookstore in Danville.

"Exciting, romantic, great fun."

—*Cosmopolitan* on MONTANA SKY

"Roberts has a warm feel for her characters and an eye for the evocative detail."

—*Chicago Tribune*

PART FIVE

series

the macgregors

America's Family?

SPOILER ALERT: THIS ARTICLE ASSUMES THAT THE READER HAS READ AND ENJOYED ALL OF THE MACGREGOR BOOKS—AND IF YOU HAVEN'T, YOU SHOULD, SO GO OUT AND DO SO BEFORE READING THIS!

FAMILY RELATIONSHIPS ARE central to the world of Nora Roberts. Whether her characters love their relatives, hate them, or have never met them, it's a given that those characters are going to have to learn to deal, for better or for worse, with their assorted relations in the course of one of Nora's novels. In fact, that's one of the secret pleasures of reading Nora's books—the chance to appreciate family life in all of its infinite variation. And of all the families she has created so far, the biggest and most complex clan lives in the pages of her many MacGregor novels.

The MacGregors, despite the fact that they exist only in the pages of fiction, embody the virtues of the perfect family, the one we all wish we had. They're loving, close-knit, supportive, sometimes a little too "in your face" for comfort but always willing to lend a hand when needed, maddening, and meddling—but always with the best of intentions. And every MacGregor, tall or small, is so interesting that a family reunion is something to be rejoiced in, not dreaded. The family patriarch and matriarch, Daniel and Anna MacGregor, are exactly the sort of relatives a sane person would both yearn for and fear having. With each succeeding generation of MacGregors, Daniel's matchmaking escapades get more outlandish and more successful, and his quirks and vices get more amusing. And Anna's calm competence in the face of chaos gets more amazing. The MacGregor books are as addictive as any recreational drug—not surprisingly, since they tap into our deep emotional need for family ties.

Nora with her father, Bernard Robertson Senior, a.k.a. Pop

Did You Know . . .

Nora Roberts's characters are as real to her as they are to her readers. When asked about why she keeps adding to the MacGregor series, Nora is very clear on who is to blame. She says, "Daniel MacGregor just never stops nagging."

Through ten novels, a novella, at least four generations, and hitting the high points of more than two hundred years of history, the MacGregors make a splash in Nora's books, flamboyantly asserting themselves in the fictional plane of existence. From their first appearance in *Playing the Odds*, it was clear that the MacGregors were a family to be reckoned with. Even as Serena MacGregor fought against the preordained path her father had laid for her, we as readers knew she was doomed to fall in love with Justin Blade. We rooted for the couple's happiness and then waited with bated breath to see what tricks Daniel had up his sleeve to ensnare his next child in a "suitable" marriage. Of course, Daniel's definition of a suitable mate bears little resemblance to society's—in fact, his methods have a lot more in common with the tricks top horse breeders use to ensure the vigor of a racing dynasty, right down to his mutters of "Good blood, strong stock."

Which isn't to say that it's all clear sailing for Daniel. In fact, in that very first book, Serena takes her revenge for having been so neatly manipulated:

> *There was a huge bookshelf along the east wall. Stomping to it, Serena pulled out a volume titled* Constitutional Convention. *She flipped it open, revealing the hollow where six cigars were secreted. Watching her father, she scooped them out and broke them in half.*
>
> *"Rena!" he said in quiet horror.*
>
> *"It's the next best thing to poisoning you," she told him. . . .*

But seeing his little girl happy is worth any price, even the loss of his beloved cigars. Daniel isn't interested in having quiet, dutiful descendants, even if it costs him in peace of mind and tobacco. He wants his loved ones to have fine minds, independent spirits, challenging goals—and marriages filled with passion. His relationship with Anna is the basis for what he wants for his children and grandchildren, and while it may be blissful, it's anything but peaceful. As Anna says to Serena in *Playing the Odds:*

> *"When I met your father, I thought he was a conceited, loud-mouthed ox . . . I fell for him anyway. . . . The only thing we both agreed on was that we couldn't, and wouldn't, live without each other."*

Nora's own growing clan (L to R): husband Bruce; Nora with her first grandchild, Kayla; Dan; daughter-in-law Stacie; and Jason

Daniel and Anna don't expect their offspring to settle for anything less. Even when Alan brings home a Campbell, of all things, Daniel proves to be elastic enough to adapt and enthusiastic enough to prod for more grandbabies.

By the time he's got all the children married off safely, it's time to start working on the next generation. The grandchildren, though warned by their parents of their imposing relative's matchmaking tendencies, are no match for Daniel. In *The MacGregor Brides*, *The Winning Hand*, *The MacGregor Grooms*, and *The Perfect Neighbor*, Daniel looms large, and his ploys are as varied as they are successful. Ranging from telling his namesake D. C. that Layna Drake would never suit him, to conspiring with an old friend to pretend illness long enough to throw their grandchildren together and let proximity take its course, to sending his beloved granddaughters an alarm system with a remarkably attractive security expert attached, Daniel's even more interfering and irresistible with the second generation than he was with the first. As Shelby Campbell says, "No offense to Alan, or to your wife, but I think if I were going to marry a MacGregor, he'd have to be you."

The joy of watching three generations of MacGregors deal with Daniel and each other is matched only by the sense of love and family pride that is at the core of the MacGregor books. The clan that Nora has captured on paper is one that every reader of the books becomes a part of. And now that millions of Americans have shared the fun of MacGregor watching, it seems to make us a family to each other as well. Certainly, when fans get together, we discuss MacGregor exploits as happily and with as much interest as we do our own family foibles. The Clan MacGregor lives in our minds and our hearts; it joins us together until we all become part of the MacGregors—America's family.

Bruce, Kathy Onorato, and Nora behind the counter at Turn the Page

The MacGregor Family Tree

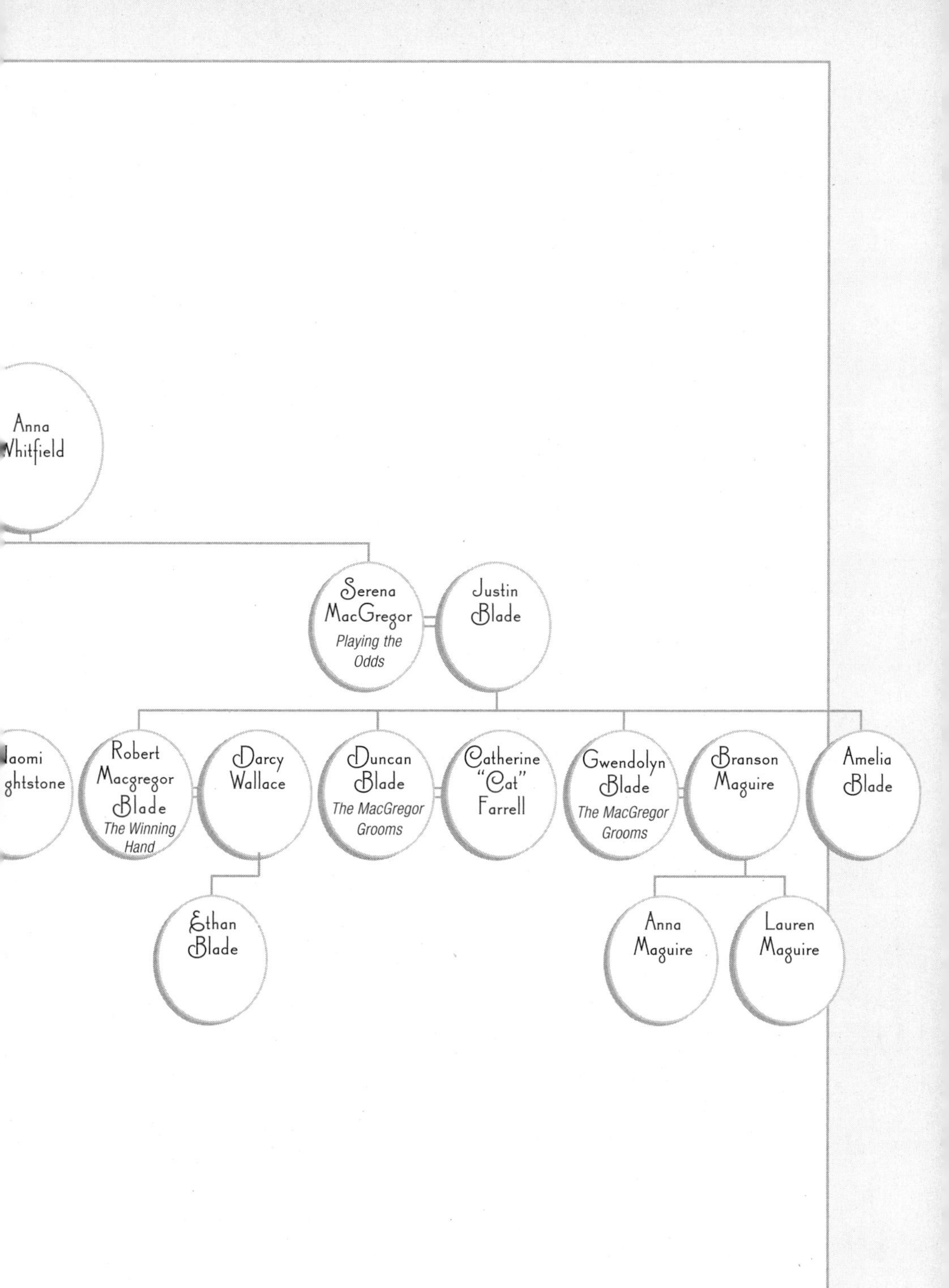
Anna
Whitfield
Serena
MacGregor
Playing the
Odds
Justin
Blade
aomi
ghtstone
Robert
Macgregor
Blade
The Winning
Hand
Darcy
Wallace
Duncan
Blade
The MacGregor
Grooms
Catherine
"Cat"
Farrell
Gwendolyn
Blade
The MacGregor
Grooms
Branson
Maguire
Amelia
Blade
Ethan
Blade
Anna
Maguire
Lauren
Maguire

The MacGregor Family Tree (part 2)

the grandeau branch

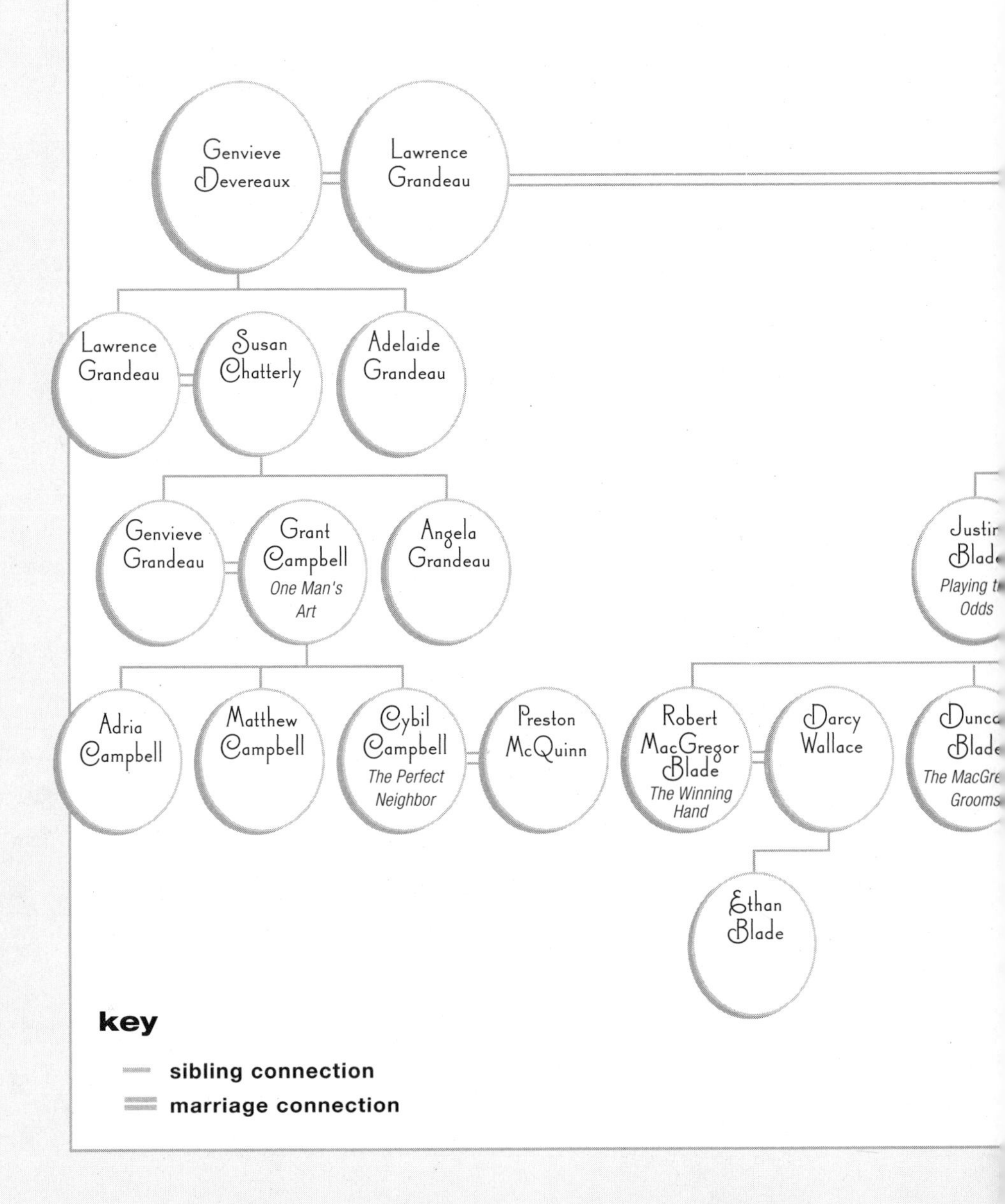

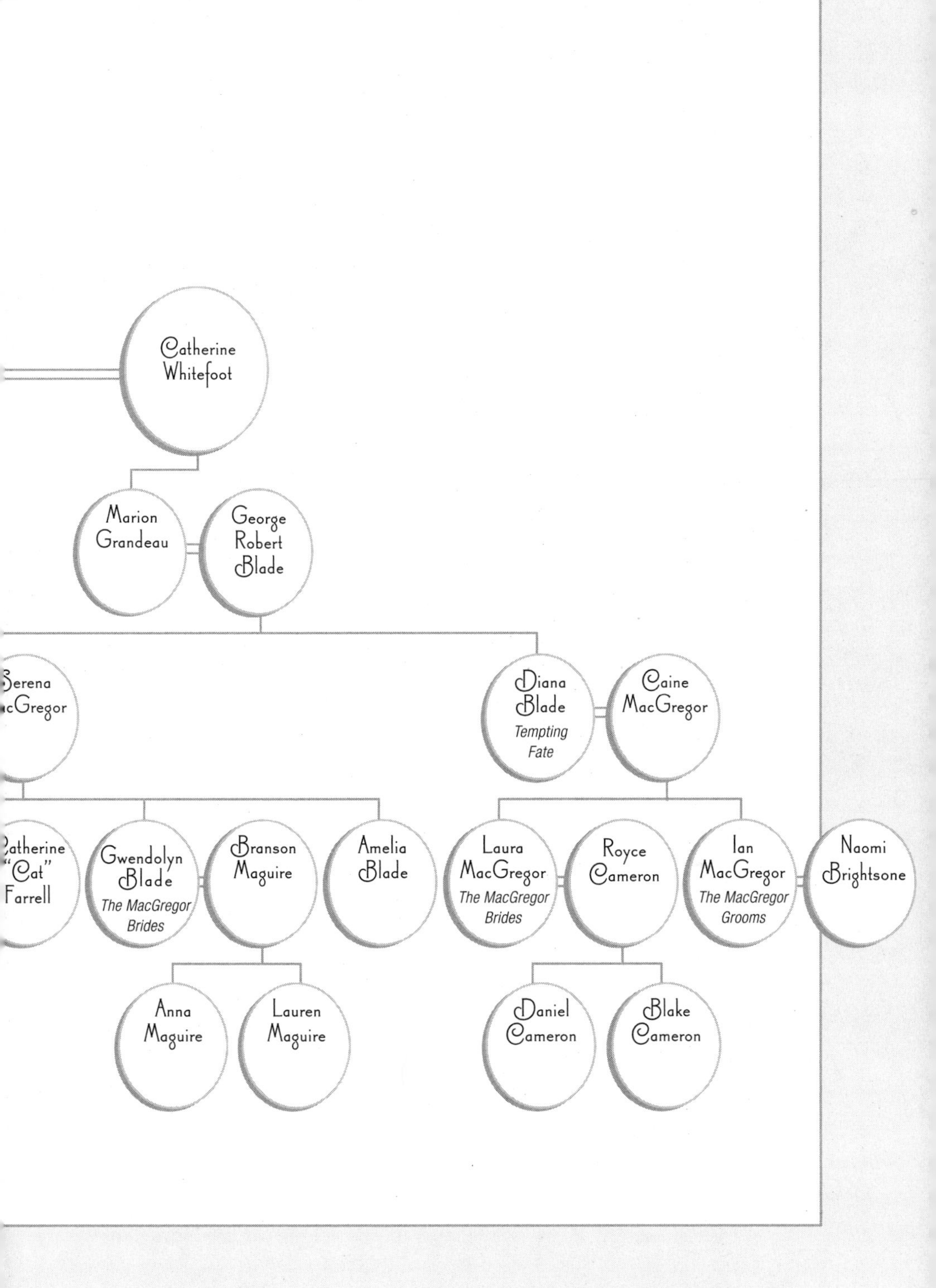
Catherine Whitefoot
Marion Grandeau
George Robert Blade
Serena
cGregor
Diana Blade
Tempting Fate
Caine MacGregor
atherine
"Cat"
Farrell
Gwendolyn Blade
The MacGregor Brides
Branson Maguire
Amelia Blade
Laura MacGregor
The MacGregor Brides
Royce Cameron
Ian MacGregor
The MacGregor Grooms
Naomi Brightsone
Anna Maguire
Lauren Maguire
Daniel Cameron
Blake Cameron

the bonds of brothers:

The Quinns of Chesapeake Bay

SPOILER WARNING FOR THOSE WHO HAVEN'T READ THE CHESAPEAKE BAY SERIES: BE SURE TO READ THE BOOKS FIRST!

NORA WRITES MEN well. She should—she was the only girl in her family with four older brothers, and then she went and had two sons of her own. So as Nora once said, "It was either like them, appreciate them, and do my best to understand them, or run screaming." Nowhere is her understanding and appreciation of them on better display than in her series about the Quinn brothers of the eastern shore of Chesapeake Bay. This wasn't Nora's first series centered on a family of men (that distinction goes to the MacKade series) but the novels about the Quinn brothers gave Nora the room to really explore in depth the bonds between men—between father and son, between brothers, and between friends.

Before they were adopted by Ray and Stella Quinn, Cam, Ethan, and Phillip were lost boys—they lived on the streets, with all of the horror and brutality that entailed. They were well on their way to dying young from either drugs or violence—whatever home or family they had before was even worse than the streets, so they chose the streets. But all that changed once they met Ray and Stella. A couple without children of their own, Ray and Stella opened their hearts and home to three sullen, scared boys. And as a result of their love and generosity, the bonds within the Quinn family became as strong as those of any family bound by blood—and in many cases, stronger.

In *Sea Swept*, Cameron Quinn has the world on a string—he lives fast, with fast women and even faster cars and boats. But the world he forged for himself comes crashing down when he finds out that his father, Ray, is dying. He comes home to the tiny town of St. Christopher on Maryland's eastern shore to say good-bye to the only father he's ever known, and to promise him that he and his brothers will take care of Seth, the last lost boy taken in by Ray Quinn. The Quinns were a family, and although Ray had been the core of the Quinn family, Ray knew that his sons would need each other—and Seth would need them—in the difficult time to follow.

> *"Don't let the boy go. You're brothers. Remember you're brothers. So proud of you. All of you. Quinns." He smiled a little, and stopped fighting. "You have to let me go now."*

Cam, Ethan, and Phillip all swear to take care of Seth and finish the adoption procedures begun by Ray. But there are rumors about Seth and

Newlyweds Nora and Bruce, circa 1985

who he really is, rumors that only Ray knew the answers to. The rumors and the scandal that threatens could tear the brothers apart and pit them against Seth, but that's not what happens. Instead, the Quinn brothers band together to protect Seth and forge even deeper bonds with each other. Seth was a Quinn now, and to attack one Quinn means taking on all the others.

But this closed circle isn't exclusive to the boys—in *Rising Tides* and *Inner Harbor* the circle of love begun by Ray and Stella is flexible enough to allow in the women the Quinn brothers would love, and even a dog. And just because Ray has died it doesn't mean he is gone—his spirit remains (both his spirit of love and acceptance and his literal spirit—his ghost speaks to his sons on more than one occasion).

Although the mystery of Seth's parentage was revealed in *Inner Harbor*, this didn't mean that the story of the Quinns was over. Many readers had fallen in love with Seth and clamored for Nora to write his story. At first Nora resisted, since Seth was still a boy at the end of *Inner Harbor* and that was how Nora saw him. But pleas for Seth continued, and slowly Nora came up with an idea for Seth's story, and for the kind of man he grew into. So Seth's story, *Chesapeake Blue*, was published by Putnam in hardcover in November 2002, and readers once again could visit with the Quinns of Maryland's eastern shore.

A formal portrait of Mr. and Mrs. Bruce Wilder

the luck of the irish

The Irish Connection and Nora

SPOILER WARNING FOR THOSE WHO HAVEN'T READ ANY OF NORA'S BOOKS WITH IRISH SETTINGS: BE SURE TO READ THE BOOKS FIRST!

IRELAND AND THE Irish have an allure for Nora that's almost unmatched among her books—from her very first book, *Irish Thoroughbred*, to her more recent book *Three Fates* and even in the J. D. Robb books, she has visited Ireland and created countless unforgettable Irish and Irish American characters. And why not—Nora's own family roots are there, and that heritage is a big part of who she is—as an individual and as a writer. Nora has said, "I knew I was home the moment I landed at Shannon Airport." There's music and magic in Irish lore and language—a richness of words and images that has inspired storytellers through the ages. And Nora is nothing if not a born storyteller.

But although Nora has touched upon her Irish heritage in many books, it wasn't until the two Irish trilogies—the Born In trilogy and the Gallaghers of Ardmore trilogy—that it became clear how much Ireland and the Irish have fired Nora's imagination. These books rank among her most popular novels ever. Although the heart of both series is family—the Concannon sisters in one and the Gallagher siblings in the other—Nora takes them in different directions. About the Born In trilogy, Nora says,

> "Setting a story in Ireland was a natural decision. Both the land and its people inspire, as well as thrive on, stories. The idea, for me, was to write of Ireland, and of family, as they intertwined in my heart. In each book in this new trilogy I chose to feature one of three sisters, different in type but bound by blood. Their lives have each taken a different course, yet it is Ireland that inspires them, as it inspires me."

So in *Born in Fire* we meet Maggie and Brianna Concannon, sisters but as different as night and day. Maggie is proud and quick-tempered—an artist who works with glass, she has ambitions that rival her talent. Born of parents who have a difficult marriage, Maggie and Brianna have dealt with their situation and their parents in different ways. Always closer to her father, Maggie was devastated when he died suddenly of a heart attack and she blames her mother for the unhappiness of the marriage.

Brianna, whose story is told in *Born in Ice*, is less confrontational than Maggie by both nature and choice. She chose a different path: A natural homemaker, Brianna deals with her bitter mother by creating a soothing, comfortable environment that nourishes both body and soul.

Nora in Ireland—and the bit of Irish land that's hers

In *Born in Shame* we, along with Maggie and Brianna, meet Shannon Bodine, an Irish American who is Maggie and Brianna's half sister—the product of an adulterous love affair between Tom Concannon and Shannon's mother. But no matter how resistant Shannon and Maggie are to the idea at first, Shannon is family—Concannon blood runs in her veins. And Ireland calls to Shannon as strongly as it does to Maggie and Brianna.

With the Gallagher family of Ardmore, Nora decided to borrow from the wealth of Irish folklore and legends, and create her own. The tale of Prince Carrick and his lady Gwen give the trilogy its frame (and the books their titles), and although each novel stands on its own, with its own unique situation and love story, all are enhanced by the poignant and lyrical legend. By the end of the third book, *Heart of the Sea*, readers are rooting as much for Carrick and his Gwen as they are for the Gallagher siblings and their loves: Aidan and Jude Murray, Shawn and Brenna O'Toole, and Darcy and Trevor McGee. And how appropriate that the Gallagher family business is the local pub, which has traditionally been the center of social life in Irish towns and where many a storyteller has spun a tale. So join Nora in Ireland as she brings you through the doors of Gallagher's Pub, where the fire's burning low and the pints are waiting. She has a story to tell you.

the legend of prince garrick and lady gwen

as told by Aidan Gallagher

"THERE WAS A maid known as Gwen. She was of humble birth, but a lady in her heart and manner. She had hair as pale as winter sunlight and eyes as green as moss. Her beauty was known throughout the land and though she carried herself with pride (for she had a slim and pleasing form), she was a modest maid who, as her blessed mother had died in the birthing of her, kept the tidy cottage for her aging father. She did as she was bid, and what was expected, and was never heard to complain. Though she was seen from time to time walking on the cliffs of an evening, and staring out over the sea, as if she wished to grow wings and fly.

"I can't say what was in her heart. Perhaps this is something she didn't know herself. But she kept the cottage, cared for her father, and walked the cliffs alone. One day, when she was taking flowers to the grave of her mother, for she was buried near the well of St. Declan, she met a man—what she thought was a man. He was tall and straight, with dark hair waving to his shoulders and eyes as blue as the bluebells she carried in her arms. By her name he called her, and his voice was like music in her head and set her heart to dancing. And in a flash, like a lightning strike, they fell in love over her dear mother's grave with the breeze sighing through the tall trees like faeries whispering.

"Well, however heart recognized heart, it was not the simple matter of a maid and a man taking hands and joining lives, for he was Carrick, the faerie prince who lived in the silver palace under the hill where her cottage sat. She feared a spell, and she doubted both his heart and her own. And the more her heart yearned, the more she doubted, for she'd been taught to beware of the faeries and the rafts where they gathered.

"Even so, one night, when the moon was ripe and full, Carrick lured Gwen from the cottage and onto his great winged horse to fly with her over the land and sea and show her the wonders he would give her if only she would pledge to him. His heart was hers, and all he had he would give her.

Nora and Bruce by an Irish cottage

"And it happened that her father, wakeful with aches in his bones, saw his young Gwen swirl out of the sky on the white winged horse with the faerie prince behind her. In his fear and lack of understanding he thought only to save her from the spell he was sure she was under. So he forbade her to have truck with Carrick again, and to ensure her safety he betrothed her to a steady young man who made his living on the water. And Lady Gwen, a maid with great respect for her father, dutifully tucked her heart away, ceased her walking, and prepared to be wed, as was bid her.

"On first hearing, Carrick gave way to a black temper and sent the lightning and thunder and wind to whip and crash over the hills and down to the sea. And the villagers, farmers, and fishermen trembled, but Lady Gwen sat quiet in her cottage and saw to her mending.

"At dawn Carrick mounted his winged horse and flew up to the sun. He gathered fire from it, formed dazzling diamonds from it, and put them in a silver sack. And these flaming and magic jewels he brought to her at her cottage. When she went out to meet him, he spilled them at her feet, and said to her, 'I've brought you jewels from the sun. These are my passion for you. Take them, and me, for I will give you all I have, and more.'

"But she refused, telling him she was promised to another. Duty held her and pride him as they parted, leaving the jewels lying among the flowers. And so they became flowers.

"On the day she married the fisherman, her father died. It was as if he'd held on to his life, with all its pains, until he was assured his Gwen was safe and cared for. So her husband moved into the cottage, and left her before the sun rose every day to go out and cast his nets. And their lives settled into a contentment and order. But Carrick, he could not forget her. She was in his heart. While Gwen was living her life as was expected of her, Carrick lost his joy in music and in laughter. One night, in great despair, he mounted his horse again and flew up to the moon,

Nora by the Pullman Restaurant in Galway

gathering its light, which turned to pearls in his silver bag. Once more, he went to her, and though she carried her first child in her womb, she slipped out of her husband's bed to meet him.

" 'These are tears of the moon,' he told her. 'They are my longing for you. Take them, and me, for I will give you all I have, and more.' Again, though tears of her own spilled onto her cheeks, she refused him. For she belonged to another, had his child inside her, and would not betray her vow. Once more they parted, duty and pride, and the pearls that lay on the ground became moonflowers.

"So the years passed, with Carrick grieving and Lady Gwen doing what was expected of her. She birthed her children, and took joy in them. She tended her flowers, and she remembered love. For though her husband was a good man, he had never touched her heart in its deepest chambers. And she grew old, her face and body aging, while her heart stayed young with the wistful wishes of a maid.

"As time is different for faeries than for mortals, one day Carrick mounted his winged horse and flew out over the sea and dived deep, deep into it, to find its heart. There, the pulse of it flowed into his silver bag and became sapphires. These he took to Lady Gwen, whose children had children now, whose hair had gone white, and whose eyes had grown dim. But all the faerie prince saw was the maid he loved and longed for. At her feet, he spilled the sapphires. 'These are the heart of the sea. They are my constancy. Take them, and me, for I will give you all I have, and more.'

"And this time, with the wisdom of age, she saw what she had done by turning away love for duty. For never once trusting her heart. And what he had done, for offering jewels, but not giving her the one thing that may have swayed her to him.

"And it was the words of love—rather than passion, rather than longing, even rather than constancy—she needed. But now she was old and bent, and she knew as the faerie prince couldn't, not being mortal, that it was too late. She wept the bitter tears of an old woman and told him that her life was ended. And she said that if he had brought her love rather than jewels, had spoken of love rather than passion and longing and constancy, her heart might have won over duty. He had been too proud, she said, and too blind to see her heart's desire.

"Her words angered him, for he had brought her love, again and again, in the only way he knew. And this time, before he walked away from her, he cast a spell. She would wonder and she would wait, as he had, year after year, alone and lonely, until true hearts met and accepted the gifts he had offered her. Three times to meet, three times to accept, before the spell could be broken. He mounted and flew into the night, and the jewels at her feet again became flowers. She died that very night, and on her grave flowers spring up, season to season, while the spirit of Lady Gwen, lovely as the young maid, waits and weeps for love lost."

Nora sitting by the Irish Sea

a series of miracles

A Look at the Rest of Nora Roberts's Series

ONE OF THE joys of reading Nora Roberts's series books is the chance to visit a favorite world again and again, each story a small miracle of characterization and setting. Whether it's the clan in Ardmore or the Quinn brothers of Chesapeake Bay or the supernaturally gifted Donovans or the crime fighters in the Night Tales books, through the course of writing her many novels, Nora has built a number of unique universes that readers love to return to.

At home in the kitchen with Nora and Bruce

Nora essentially pioneered the idea of doing linked series of novels in mainstream women's publishing, and she continues to dominate it. While the idea was common in other areas of fiction (mystery, science fiction/fantasy, children's books, and so on all had long traditions of series work, and books like the Nancy Drew Series, *The Lord of the Rings,* and the many adventures of Miss Marple and Travis McGee were staples of publishing) it hadn't been tried on a regular basis in contemporary romance publishing. In the arena of women's fiction, where each novel centers on a relationship that has to begin, develop, mature, and come to an appropriate conclusion in the course of a single novel, series work was rare, and never at the bestseller levels. Nora Roberts changed all that.

Nora's first series for Silhouette was *Reflections* and *Dance of Dreams*, published in 1983. Her first mainstream series, *Sacred Sins* and *Brazen Virtue*, was originally published in 1987. Many more followed, in category romance and in single-title release.

Nora's series are as addictive as French fries (appropriately one of Nora's favorite foods), but what's even more amazing than their power to charm is the variety of worlds that she has penned. It's clear that Nora doesn't worry about her readers being narrow-minded. In fact, she trusts them implicitly to enjoy her stories for what they are, great tales well told, no matter where and when she sets them.

Nora's series are built around all kinds of families, real or created—from extended families or siblings bound by blood to groupings of people bound together by love or childhood friendships or their jobs. In Nora's world, relationships of all kinds center the universe. The self-absorbed loner doesn't exist, with the exception of an occasional villain, for very long. Before the end of chapter one, that character is up to his or her eyeballs in relatives, nosy neighbors, or interfering friends. Or, more often, all of the above. Nora's series books just take that central theme and carry it to its logical conclusion—that there is simply no ducking the people you love, no matter how irritating they are, even through the course of a whole bunch of novels.

Did You Know . . .

A copy of a Nora Roberts book is sold somewhere in America every four minutes.

In Nora's world, nobody makes a better audience for major upheavals in a character's life than the people who love him or her. In these series, rather like a demented Greek chorus, brothers and sisters watch with glee as their siblings take a dive into the chaos of love. Police officers grin as their partners get embroiled with members of the opposite sex. Parents hold their breath as their offspring embark on adventures of the heart. The common thread that holds each book to the rest in a series is the simple glue of humans caring for each other as a community. It's the kind of world we all want to live in, so the series' popularity is really no surprise.

Nora's series keep growing. Each new one has its rabid fans ready to swear it's

Nana with Kayla

Opening Christmas gifts with Nora, Stacie, and Kayla. Guess who gets most of the presents this year?

the best thing Nora's ever written, while some fans remain faithful to old favorites as the greatest ever (though they gobble up the new books just as fast as the rabid ones do). At any gathering of romance readers, in person or on-line, somewhere there will be a discussion of the relative merits of Eve Dallas versus the Quinn Brothers, or the MacGregors versus the MacKades. If you want to join in—and it's amazingly good fun—be prepared for the fights to become heated. Personally, I'm not picky. I love them all—though I will admit to a slight partiality for the Eve and Roarke books (the editors of *this* book fought over who would get to write about them—the matter was settled civilly with a coin toss).

For Nora Roberts's readers who have not yet discovered all of the many linked books that Nora has penned, here is a listing of the various series by Nora Roberts, in alphabetical order:

Christmas 2002 with Nora, Bruce, and Kayla

the calhoun women *Courting Catherine, A Man for Amanda, For the Love of Lilah, Suzanna's Surrender, Megan's Mate*

celebrity magazine *One Summer, Second Nature*

chesapeake bay *Sea Swept, Rising Tides, Inner Harbor, Chesapeake Blue*

the concannon sisters *Born in Fire, Born in Ice, Born in Shame*

cordina's royal family *Affaire Royale, Command Performance, The Playboy Prince, Cordina's Crown Jewel*

the donovan legacy *Captivated, Entranced, Charmed, Enchanted*

dream series *Daring to Dream, Holding the Dream, Finding the Dream*

great chefs *Summer Desserts, Lessons Learned*

in death series *Naked in Death, Glory in Death, Immortal in Death, Rapture in Death, Ceremony in Death, Vengeance in Death, Holiday in Death,* "Midnight in Death" *Silent Night, Conspiracy in Death, Loyalty in Death, Witness in Death, Judgment in Death, Betrayal in Death,* "Interlude in Death" *Out of This World, Seduction in Death, Reunion in Death, Purity in Death, Portrait in Death, Imitation in Death, Remember When, Divided in Death, Visions in Death*

irish hearts *Irish Thoroughbred, Irish Rose, Irish Rebel*

irish trilogy *Jewels of the Sun, Tears of the Moon, Heart of the Sea*

key trilogy *Key of Light, Key of Knowledge, Key of Valor*

loving jack *Loving Jack, Best Laid Plans, Lawless*

the macgregors *Playing the Odds; Tempting Fate; All the Possibilities; One Man's Art; For Now, Forever; The MacGregor Brides; The Winning Hand; The MacGregor Grooms; The Perfect Neighbor; Rebellion;* "In from the Cold" *Harlequin Historical Christmas Stories 1990*

the mackade brothers *The Return of Rafe MacKade, The Pride of Jared MacKade, The Heart of Devin MacKade, The Fall of Shane MacKade*

night tales *Night Shift, Night Shadow, Nightshade, Night Smoke, Night Shield*

the o'hurleys *The Last Honest Woman, Dance to the Piper, Skin Deep, Without a Trace*

reflections and dreams *Reflections, Dance of Dreams*

sacred sins *Sacred Sins, Brazen Virtue*

the stanislaskis *Taming Natasha, Luring a Lady, Falling for Rachel, Convincing Alex, Waiting for Nick, Considering Kate*

the stars of mithra *Hidden Star, Captive Star, Secret Star*

three sisters island *Dance Upon the Air, Heaven and Earth, Face the Fire*

time and again *Time Was, Times Change*

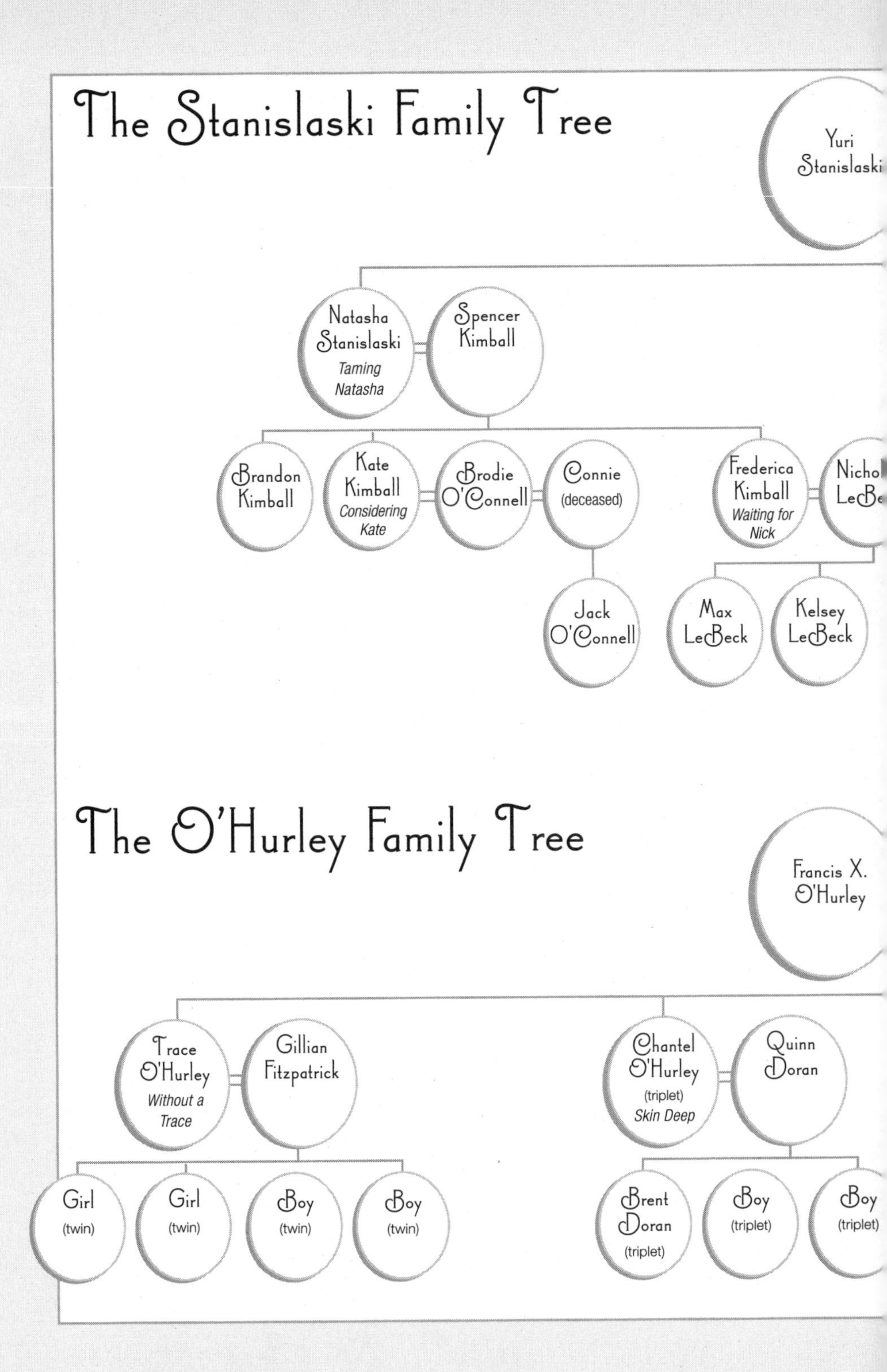
The Stanislaski Family Tree
Yuri Stanislaski
Natasha Stanislaski
Taming Natasha
Spencer Kimball
Brandon Kimball
Kate Kimball
Considering Kate
Brodie O'Connell
Connie
(deceased)
Frederica Kimball
Waiting for Nick
Nicho
LeBe
Jack O'Connell
Max LeBeck
Kelsey LeBeck
The O'Hurley Family Tree
Francis X. O'Hurley
Trace O'Hurley
Without a Trace
Gillian Fitzpatrick
Chantel O'Hurley
(triplet)
Skin Deep
Quinn Doran
Girl
(twin)
Girl
(twin)
Boy
(twin)
Boy
(twin)
Brent Doran
(triplet)
Boy
(triplet)
Boy
(triplet)

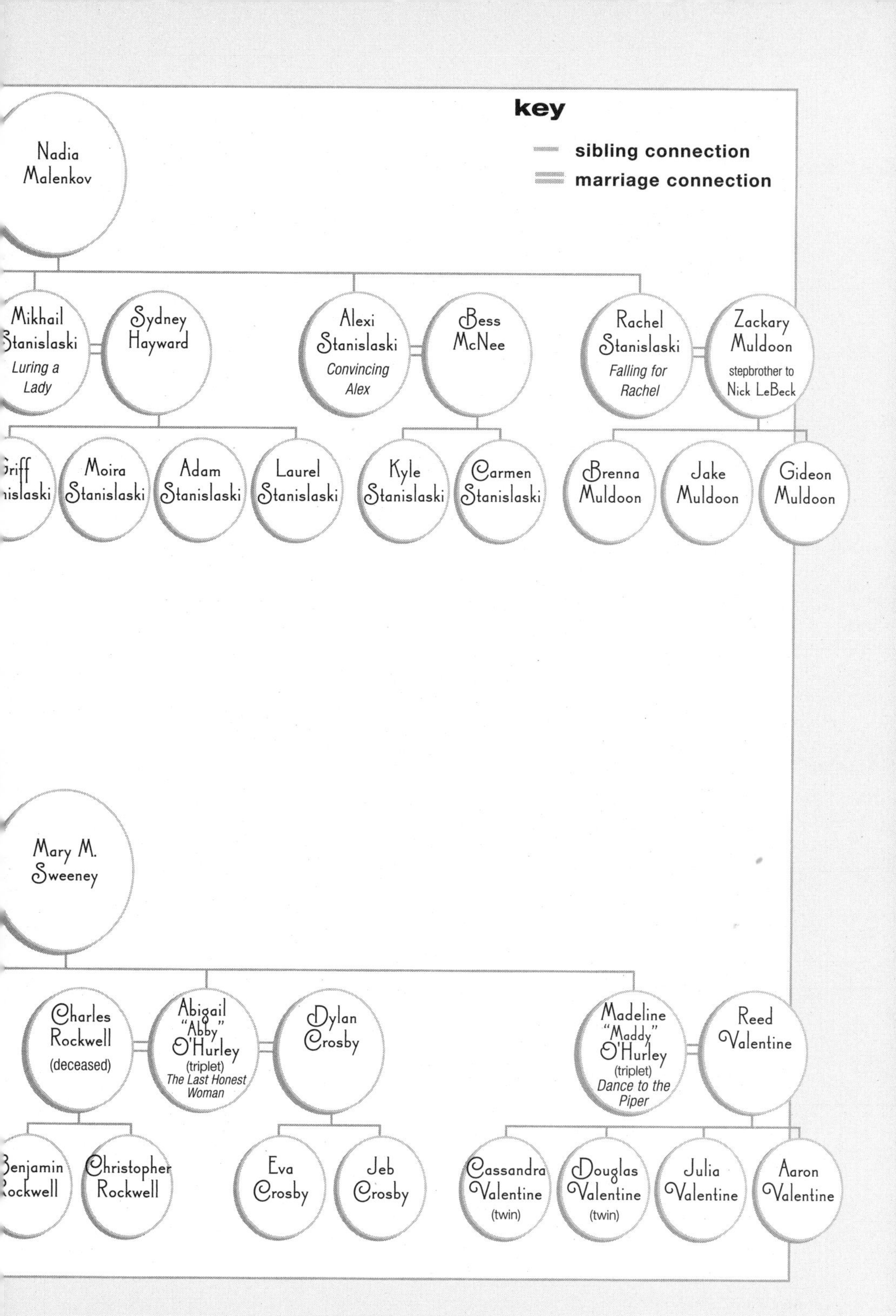
key
sibling connection
marriage connection
Nadia Malenkov
Mikhail Stanislaski
Luring a Lady
Sydney Hayward
Alexi Stanislaski
Convincing Alex
Bess McNee
Rachel Stanislaski
Falling for Rachel
Zackary Muldoon
stepbrother to Nick LeBeck
Moira Stanislaski
Adam Stanislaski
Laurel Stanislaski
Kyle Stanislaski
Carmen Stanislaski
Brenna Muldoon
Jake Muldoon
Gideon Muldoon
Mary M. Sweeney
Charles Rockwell
(deceased)
Abigail "Abby" O'Hurley
(triplet)
The Last Honest Woman
Dylan Crosby
Madeline "Maddy" O'Hurley
(triplet)
Dance to the Piper
Reed Valentine
Christopher Rockwell
Eva Crosby
Jeb Crosby
Cassandra Valentine
(twin)
Douglas Valentine
(twin)
Julia Valentine
Aaron Valentine

"An absolutely terrific summer read. Excellent character definition . . . sweet, passionate."

—*The Philadelphia Inquirer* on TRUE BETRAYALS

traveling

PART SIX

with nora

ALTHOUGH NORA DOESN'T like to tour, she loves to travel all over the world for her vacations. She's been to practically every part of the United States, as well as Europe, Japan, and even Australia for both work and pleasure, and when she can she e-mails travelogues of the places and people she's met. These travelogues are as wonderfully vivid as her novels, and nearly as fun to read.

What's even more fun is to see Nora's travel turn up in her books—in the following travelogues, you see the Venice of *The*

Villa, the city of Prague from *Three Fates*, and the Ireland of many of her books. Will the Cayman Islands be the setting of a future book?

(By the way, *BW* refers to Nora's husband, Bruce Wilder.)

venice

june 11, 1999

A storm came in last night with the drama of lightning over water. We went to sleep to the sound of rain. But first, we had a tremendous meal in our room. Amazing pasta, salad so fresh it deserved to be slapped. We watched *The Van* and laughed our butts off. The Gucci party down below seemed fairly restrained. Music, a little chatter, then they moved to another area of the hotel, I suppose, as the rain was fierce for awhile.

Slept wonderfully and woke to the metallic clang of the guys taking down the platform they'd put up for the reception. And more rain.

There's a wonderfully sort of sinister look to Venice in the rain. At least from across the canal. All those grays looming and the water coming in irritable little chops.

We lazed around, had our breakfast, then braved what was then a drizzle to go over. We headed toward the Basilica, and as I needed a pair of gold hoops to replace the ones I'd broken, I window-shopped along the way. Found the perfect pair, and snagged a great ring. Wide white gold band with a square-cut citrine. Really loved it. Started to pour while I was in the shop, so we scooted out, hit the church.

Nora in Venice

St. Mark's Cathedral is fascinating. I think the Venetian guys got together and said: Hey, those guys up in Florence think they're so damn cool. We can do more. Let's just throw in lots more stuff. More columns, more mosaics, more gilt. More, more! It's an ornate, yet oddly dreary place with no grace whatsoever. Crowds pack in, gaping up at the many-domed mosaic ceiling with their pounds of gilt and garish colors. You can't help but stare and wonder. One part of the floor—all of that's mosaic too—looks like it was designed by Peter Max. You get dizzy walking over the circles of it. LOL.

Still, I enjoyed the walk through. Then it was on to the Accademia to look at art. Long queue there, but under an awning so we stayed dry. Wonderful old wall and ceiling panels heavy, natch, on the Madonna. Particularly the Annunciation and the Coronation. And as always, lots of the long-suffering and arrow-filled San Sebastian, with his baffled, melancholy face. But some gorgeous Bellinis. It's a large building with many rooms and you can stroll through at your leisure once inside. It is not the grand, heart-wrenching art of Florence, but some of it was lovely.

At the end was a Leonardo exhibit, full of his sketches. This was wonderful. You get a real glimpse of the man's genius.

Nora in Venice

Outside, in a deluge, we bought an umbrella and walked back to San Stefano Plaza for a very, very nice lunch of pizza while we watched the rain and those running through it. I watched an angel-faced toddler with curly hair charm every waiter in the place. His parents would sit him down and two seconds later he'd be up just wandering. Our waiter was so delighted, he took the boy by the hand and let him come back into the main restaurant with him. Seriously adorable.

Nora having dinner cruising through the canals

We window-shopped some more, and I hit on a nice little glass shop. Found my mother's Christmas present, my mother-in-law's birthday present, and scored a beautiful wineglass for me, and a pretty crystal perfume bottle.

The rain let up and the sun came out. Lovely, lovely light with a fresh breeze. We'd been heading home, but decided to stay and enjoy it. We walked over a bridge and watched gondolas row by, with families and accordion players. Back to San Marco to eat gelato and watch the people and pigeons. Millions of pigeons who enjoy lighting on people who buy little bags of corn to feed them. Some of these birds are so fat you can't believe they could fly. They barely waddle. You cannot even think Alfred Hitchcock during this scene or you'll run screaming.

Across the square a little orchestra was playing. I heard my favorite song, "Only You," and BW and I danced in the square among the pigeons.

One more glass shop on the way to the dock, and a couple more Christmas presents are in the bag.

We came home, had a drink by the pool, and will just relax until it's time for dinner.

It's brilliantly sunny now, but still breezy. Promises to be a beautiful evening.

Nora

the cayman islands

friday, june 15, 2001

We're up early, BW for his dive lesson, me for a workout. His is undoubtedly the more interesting of the two.

They give the lesson in the pool, putting on the equipment, explaining it—giving a lesson in physics as well. He tells me they do this in a kind of circle, kneeling on the bottom of the pool at another hotel. They learn how to breathe through the regulator, the underwater hand signals, the dos and don'ts.

While he's learning to be Lloyd Bridges I write for about an hour and a half. Felt very good. To reward myself, I go down to the pool for a regular-type swim. I get my towel, scope out two chaises. Quite a crowd at the pool today. As I dump my stuff, the woman in the chair next to mine says: Excuse me. I look over and she turns up my photo on the back of her book. You look an awful lot like this picture. I'm a little taken aback because without makeup, wearing my sunglasses and I'm-on-vacation straw hat, I

Nora and Bruce out for a romantic evening in the Caymans

don't think I look much like the picture. Plus I'm not used to getting recognized. Plus I so rarely see anyone in real life reading one of my books.

I say something bright and charming like: Ah, yeah, I guess I do. LOL.

She is delighted, thrilled, and very sweet. She's with her brand-new husband—they're from Charleston, WV—practically neighbors. They are Jody and Jim. We chat. I sign *Carolina Moon* for her. Then she shouts across the pool to a couple of women. One of them is holding *Heart of the Sea*. Second woman is from Pittsburgh, and tells me she LOVES my books, and that she met my dil [editor's note: daughter-in-law], Stacie, over the weekend. Stacie spotted her reading another of my books and went over to talk to her. This woman is a national sales rep for PepsiCo, so now we can rhapsodize about each other's product. LOL. I sign her books, and we all chat. She's Nancy, and she and Jody and Jim have made pals over the last several days.

They ask a few questions, but it's all very friendly and casual. I take my swim. We chat a bit more in the pool, and BW returns, notes this and is surprised—as I am not Chatty Girl. I introduce him, and

Nora signing The Villa *in the Caymans*

Nancy fetches another of my books for one of her traveling companions.

BW and I go have lunch on the restaurant terrace, and when we're done, the waitress tells us it's on Nancy. Well, my goodness. I look around for Nancy, and she comes over to the table with THREE more of my books. The woman's gone on vacation with no less than five of my books. She works for Pepsi. How can I not love her?

Guess who showed up at Nora's signing? Dick Francis! Dick lives on the Cayman Islands.

Nancy's off to the airport and Pittsburgh, BW and I are back to the pool. Chat a little more with Jody and Jim. Jody shows us her finger where a stingray mistook her digit for a squid. They don't have teeth, but the cartilage is strong enough to have left a mark.

BW's off for his first dive. I finish my next book. Robert Parker this time. It's been years since I read Parker, but I read *Potshot* at the beach last month, and I'm hooked on him again.

On the pool terrace and the beach, they're setting up a banquet for some convention. A lot of tables. Gonna be some party. BW returns and we sit on our terrace and have a drink while he tells me about his dive. A different kettle from snorkeling—spookier and a lot of fun for him. They were down 40 feet, buddied up and with an instructor to explore another wreck—a banana boat that was a front for drug smuggling—unbeknownst to the crew. When the crew found the pot and wanted their cut, the captain flipped them off. So they flipped him off—right off the boat. But they didn't know how to operate the boat, damaged it trying to get into George

Town. Cops burned the pot, and the story goes that the wind blew the smoke for two days and everyone got a free high. LOL. A dive company bought the damaged boat, and sank it for wreck dives.

The convention-goers—some Internet group—begin to arrive for cocktails.

Tonight's sunset is a show in itself. I've seen a lot of gorgeous ones, but this is amazing. Layers of clouds hulked over the horizon, and with the sun sliding behind them, they look like they're etched on blue glass. Tones and textures. Shapes and shadows. Rose, gold, mauve, reds. Huge billows of clouds, like a Maxfield Parrish painting. You almost expect to see some goddess rear out on a winged horse. It goes on and on, with those tones changing as you watch. Deeper golds, a long God-finger of cloud underlit in brilliant white, a volcano spewing deep red smoke.

Then it all goes purple and silver and gray and the sea's like a huge silver platter with a few boats set on it. The long sunset turns into that fingersnap twilight that becomes tropical night.

On the beach, the party crowd livens up. The band plays . . . guess what? Yes, it's yet another rendition of "Margaritaville." God bless Jimmy Buffet.

Nora

Nora, her mother, Jason, Dan, and Stacie all enjoying the Caymans

prague

june 11, 2000

We've seen the sights. They picked us up at ten, for a reputed three-hour tour. Time is different here. Drove down Paris Street with its fabulous shops—sorry I missed that on foot and with credit card at the ready. On toward Prague Castle. First stop a church. Loreta, with many exquisite chalices, reliquaries. Amazingly ornate and so filled with gilt I needed my sunglasses. I am comforted by seeing a painting of the reliable St. Sebastian—or Sebastianus here, I believe—with his usual expression of baffled sorrow and body full of arrows.

The castle itself is more palatial than castle-like. Silent uniformed guards a la Buckingham Palace stand in front of the entrance. This is the official office of the president, though he lives in a villa elsewhere. Grand open courtyard with a big fountain. We were told that during the Communist regime you could be hauled away to prison for touching the water. Today people all but play in it.

Nora and Bruce in Prague

We go through the treasury with its lovely old jewelry and antiques.

They change the guards every hour, but at noon daily do it with pomp and ceremony for the tourists. It's brutally hot, and I wonder how those guys can stand out there in the heat with those heavy uniforms, all full of braid, the white gloves, the boots. The band stands in a window and plays and the guards parade around a courtyard. Very militarily. This draws a real crowd for the fifteen minutes or so it goes on.

We walk to a little café and get drinks. Then down a narrow road with tiny Snow White cottages, which were once the home of alchemists. Charming crooked road of brick and stone, little houses with low doorways now little shops with handicrafts. I could've wandered there quite a while, but we're on a schedule.

Back up again and a quick stop at the Basilica. Much more simple, more quiet and reverent than the church. Stone walls, faded murals, simple altar. Then on to the huge Romanesque cathedral. You step in and it steals your breath. This is definitely the jewel of this tour. The grand arches and fluted columns are so perfectly aligned that they give the optical illusion of going on forever. It's cool and quiet despite the hordes of tourists. There are deep, bold colors in the stained-glass windows, and above them leaded windows where the light streams in pale gold.

There's a huge organ with gleaming pewter pipes, ornate silver work, glossy marble, and lovely murals.

Since we're on tour we join the horde going down windy steps to view the tombs of Czech kings. I wonder as I shuffle along with the crowd why people of all cultures seem compelled to look at the places of the royal and holy dead. What I see through the little window when I get up there are some big caskets. I suppose I'm just not drawn to such things. I preferred the walk through, the musty smells, the old stone and little passageways closed off to the public.

We take the long, long walk down to the Charles Bridge. A lovely walk, though, through yet another section of the city which I'd have enjoyed if there'd been more time. The bridge itself is quite lovely. Street artists line up there as they do along Jackson

Square in New Orleans. There are wonderful views of the river and the heart of Prague beyond it.

But by now it's nearly three, and we need to get back to the hotel to meet the pickup for the box we're shipping home. We say good-bye to Marcella here. Karel will be here in the morning to see us off to the airport. Or perhaps he'll go with us. We are arranged here. LOL.

We have a nice, light lunch at the outdoor cafe at the hotel, and watch the people walk by. Corn on the cob on a stick is a big walk-around treat here.

Young women wear capri pants, black, midriff tops in black or white, and clunky platform shoes or sandals. It's almost a uniform. You hear every language imaginable.

I've had a short nap and our banana box is on its way back home. We'll have dinner here at the hotel and organize for our flight tomorrow.

Can't wait for Ireland. Nothing but free time. No interviews, no schedule. No pantyhose.

Nora and Bruce on the street in Prague

irish eyes are smiling . . .

It's very obvious that Ireland holds a special place in Nora's heart, and that love shines in the Ireland travelogues included here, and permeates much of her fiction. In fact, Nora's affection for Ireland is so well known that the Ardmore Council of Ardmore, Ireland (the setting of Nora's magical Irish trilogy), contacted Nora for assistance when a proposed development threatened the historic center of the village. Nora immediately enlisted the aid of her fans, contacting them through her website and asking them to write to the Waterford County Council protesting the development. Here is the entire original message Nora received from Andrew Cockburn of Ireland, Nora's response, and the decision from the Ardmore Council:

from andrew cockburn:

OVER THE PAST few years we in Ardmore have become used to visitors from around the world who have come to know our village through Nora Roberts's Ardmore trilogy, and we make them welcome. They find that Ardmore is indeed a magical place, full of that same Irish mystery that recurs in the books.

The problem is that the magic of the village is being threatened by ill-considered development, crowding around our historic thousand-year-old Round Tower. Up until now the spiritual heart of the village, a holy site known as Declan's Well, has been left undisturbed on its cliff ledge looking out over the bay and the Celtic Sea beyond. Legend has it that St. Declan built his first church here in A.D. 314, when he arrived (before St. Patrick, we like to point out) to convert the Irish, but it seems clear that the well has been a sacred site for far longer.

But the peace of this place is now being threatened by a proposal in front of the Waterford County Council, the operative authority in such matters, to rezone the area adjacent to the well for commercial development. This will in practice result in a large apartment block next to the little Cliff Hotel, complete with car park and overloaded sewage system right next to our beloved well and the remains of Declan's church.

Given all the other problems of the world, this may seem like a small matter. But it is not small to us. The entire village is united as never before in opposition to the proposal. Much of our beauty has already been spoiled by unchecked development, and we are determined to preserve this special corner.

We are asking the help of Nora Roberts, who once said that "Ardmore in reality was very much as Ardmore has been in my imagination," to come to the aid of a place that she has portrayed with such feeling. Apart from a statement of support from Nora herself, we would welcome suggestions on how we could acquaint her legion of fans to the threat of Ardmore, home of the Gallaghers. Time is short, as the crucial vote by the council on the proposal is due to take place on May 31, 2002.

nora's statement:

When I received word of this proposed development in Ardmore, I was stunned and saddened. There are rare and special places in the world, and Ardmore is one of them. The beauty of the village, the cliffs, the beach and bay make up one of the truly special and unspoiled spots of Ireland. Added to that, the history of a place, the traditions, the magic of it should never be discounted in the name of progress. There is no progress, no meaning to it, without respect and appreciation for tradition. When we rip out our roots they can never be replanted.

Once, I sat with an old woman and her little dog on a bench on the cliff ledge near Declan's Well. I've never forgotten the place, the feel of the air, the view—or the woman and her dog, and the few minutes of quiet conversation we shared.

I set three books in Ardmore because I knew it was a place steeped in beauty, tradition, community and magic. In my way, I tried to transcribe onto the page what can really only be fully appreciated by seeing it firsthand. Since that time, I've received letters from many readers who tell me they've visited Ardmore to see for themselves, and were charmed and delighted to find it as I'd described.

My own family roots are in Ireland. I own land in County Clare. Twenty acres of lovely hills and fields. I have no intention of developing it, but instead want to preserve this small piece of land for its beauty alone. How much more important is it to preserve the heart and soul of a village with such great history and vital tradition as Ardmore?

It would break my heart when I return to Ardmore, as I hope to one day, were I to find the charm, the beauty, and yes, the magic, has been lost in a spot where I once sat with an old woman and her little dog in the sun.

Nora Roberts

I'VE SENT THE above statement to the Waterford County Council, with the hope it may have some weight in their decision. I imagine if some of you feel as I do and e-mail them as well, it may have impact.

Let's not let this happen without at least trying to stop it.

Nora visits Ardmore

nora's support and call for action resulted in this response from the ardmore council:

Thanks to the enormous volume of submissions (a pile reportedly nine inches high, thank you, Nora) the crucial council vote had to be put off to July 8, 2003. I myself have been away from Ardmore for a while—I will be back tomorrow—but I understand that on July 8 a possibly acceptable compromise will be offered, making the area around St. Declan's an untouchable "green area," including the spot where the enemy wanted to build his apartment block. This still leaves open the possibility of construction on the site of the present hotel building, but for that the enemy will have to apply for planning permission, and we will be ready.

All in all it seems to have been a very successful campaign, thanks in very large part to you and the worldwide host you alerted. (I heard that for the first few days of your readers writing in, the council were completely mystified at the flood of e-mails from Mexico, Canada, the Philippines, Moscow, etc.) I also hear that you went on Irish TV to great effect—it really made the whole thing a national issue in a way that the press did not do.

So a happy ending, in vintage Nora Roberts style!

Nora doing a radio interview in Dublin

cork, ireland

june 14, 2000

A bit cooler and overcast when we started out this morning. Headed south to Kinsale. Minutes out of Cork City and the fields take over. This is what draws me back here, again and again. Those lush hills, that soft light. There are gold squares in the green I think must be hay, and the patchworks are bisected here with thick, rough, dark green hedges. Clouds thicken and the wind kicks up. Queen Anne's lace dances by the roadsides and there are spears and spears of foxglove. Tangles of honeysuckle in the hedgerows. Amazing calla lilies in cottage gardens, the cream-colored cups huge and glossy.

Mist rolls in as we near the sea, and mist becomes nearly fog with little scattered sprinkles. We drive the ridiculously narrow and windy streets of Kinsale—adorably pretty—and opt to come back through for lunch and drive now to Old Head. The *Lusitania* sank off the coast here. Farmland spreads out, and holiday homes—many quite big and lush for this part of the world—snuggle in. Kinsale's been discovered, we're told, by film people and others with money.

Nora by the ruins of an Irish church

An old stone tower looms out of that swirly mist and we're at the entrance to the private golf course that takes up most of the Head. We'd pay the admission and drive through, but the mist is so thick now we wouldn't see any of the reputedly excellent views from the cliffs or the lighthouse. Instead we drive back a ways, pull off the road across from an old ruined keep. Out in the mist and wind and across the field. I can hear the foghorns as we walk and are blown about. Marvelous.

We just drive a bit. More windy, narrow roads, incredible glimpses of the hills, and the sun begins to break through a little to chase away the mists.

Nora and Bruce in an Irish cemetery

We find parking in Kinsale and begin to walk, looking for a restaurant that suits us in this the food center of Ireland. Restaurants abound but many are open only for dinner. Ultimately we find a roomy pub, more modern than the usual with bright blue upholstery and lots of dull silver metal. I get a burger, American style, and BW the fried scampi that is really just fried shrimp. Both are very tasty. I order tea and fish out the bags before it's strong enough to walk out on its own. Most of the pubs advertise live traditional music, so we may work our way back here.

Head toward Inishannon, and on the outskirts of Kinsale see beautiful little houses, all cheerfully painted and neat as pins. Bigger, more contemporary houses farther on, then the road narrows and it's forested as it follows the river. Hedgerows of fushias, yellow gorse, more foxglove.

There's an old cemetery in Inishannon and the ruins of a church or abbey. No one tends the graves here as they do in most of the Catholic cemeteries I've seen. This Anglican one is atmospheric and rather stark with its overgrown grass and wildflowers and time-worn stones. Pigeons roost and coo in the ruins.

One of the stones carved in the 1800s asks God to have MARCY on his soul, and when the carver ran out of room, he'd pop the last letter of the word over the word. Somewhat like a crossword puzzle.

By now the sun is back, though it's much cooler than yesterday and still a bit breezy.

Home to the hotel for a drink in the bar and a recommendation for a pub with music for tonight. Found a little Italian restaurant in the guide for dinner. I think pizza's in my future.

Nora

traveling with friends

Ruth Ryan Langan has traveled with Nora many times and to many places, including Ireland, and she shares her experience here.

Nora, Ruth, and Ruth's husband, Tom

IN 2000 MY husband and I went to Ireland with Nora and her husband. Take it from me—these two know how to travel. They choose the best hotel (or in this case—castle) to park the luggage, then leave each day to different locations to take in the sights. We managed most of the highlights, returning each night to our humble castle quarters to refresh ourselves before starting over the next morning. Whether visiting ancient stone circles, or seeing the country's most famous landmarks, or simply shopping, Nora does it all with such enthusiasm that it can't help but rub off on those around her. It was a fantastic trip, and we left knowing we would have to return to that green island of our ancestors. To ensure that she would always return, Nora bought property on her last visit. A fair exchange. Now Nora owns a piece of Ireland and Ireland owns a piece of Nora's heart.

Nora, Ruth, and Tom by standing stones

ireland 2002

galway

june 19, 2002

After a late start, and with the weather looking promising, we decide to drive west to the O'Flahertys' great stronghold of Aughnanure. This rather fierce family managed to hold on to the castle pretty much straight through its history, due to inventive fortification, positioning, brutal battling, reputation, treachery and whatever it took, until they turned it over to the Irish government in the last century. Much of the original structures are intact, and there's been careful restoration as well.

You have to walk down a long path, over a natural arch stone bridge, to get there. On the way we see a family and a little girl they're encouraging to pet the pretty buckskin mare who's got her head over the stone fence. Katie's desperate to pet the horse, and her grandmother rips up some long grass for her to offer. She does, but each time the mare turns her head to take the grass, Katie clutches and yanks it back.

The fortress is on the river, and at one time the river came right up to the door. The original walls surrounding it remain as do some of the inner defensive walls. And the enormous keep is six stories. There's a separate banquet hall—party time for the O'Flahertys and their guests—but half of it fell, undermined by the river. There remain wonderful carvings on the windows, and the original stone floor.

It has every defense I've ever seen in the keep including murder holes, trip stairs, slot windows, trapdoors and secret rooms. Battlements—Irish style—that afford full-length protection for soldiers so they could rain rocks or pour boiling oil or pitch—a favorite of the O'Flahertys, we're told—on invaders.

In the great hall is a fireplace so big you truly could have roasted an ox in it. They've rebuilt the balcony in the chieftain's chambers above, where the visiting bards would play. The reasoning for the balcony, we're told, is as bards traveled widely, staying with many families or settlements, they might've carried diseases and were separated from the chieftain so they couldn't infect him. The secret room here is just off the main chamber, in back of a thick door. It's really just a very deep hole where they'd toss captured invaders and let them starve to death. The clan wasn't known for its compassion. The chieftain also had his own privy, in addition to the main one on the floor below. An early master suite.

There's a squat round tower across from the keep, built in such a way that if the munitions inside blew, it would hold rather than explode outwards. An amazing and ingenious beehive shape with thickly layered stone.

The great Grace O'Malley married one of the sons at 16, and the pirate queen outlived him to marry twice more.

While I'm wandering about a bit on my own a little spaniel puppy comes up. Oh God, cute puppy! I have to play with him, and he with me. He trots off, stops, looks back at me. Sits and waits. So I have to go over and pet him again. He repeats this, and BW joins us on our way out. At the gate I have to urge him to go back—the puppy, that is—and his boy shows up and calls him. We stop along the path to admire the mare again, and the puppy gambols up to me. I walk him back to his boy.

We're going to take the western loop of the lake, up into Connemara, maybe stop at a couple more sights. The weather's holding up pretty well, a couple of sprinkles only. Dark clouds layered over pretty white ones, blue sky in patches, and all of it sailing in the brisk wind. Lough Corrib is such a sight, with its little nubby

Nora in Cobh

islands floating on it, the water shining blue or going silver depending on the clouds.

As we head west, fields go to moors and moors to bogs where I see stacks of cut turf piled among the high hillocks of rough grass. The wind, I know, dries the bricks of peat, and the farmer will turn them regularly until they're cured. The sun strikes through the clouds and the light takes on that indescribable glow that turns the green to something beyond color. It's this quality of light and landscape that doesn't just dazzle the eye, but the heart as well.

And there, ahead in the distance, are the magical misted silhouettes of the Twelve Bens. Clouds smoke across them, then move on to leave them standing against the sky.

They go up and up, dominating the landscape with their high rounded peaks and long dips. And seem to go on forever. The sheep grazing on the bases look like white dots.

Nora stayed at Dromoland Castle Hotel in County Clare in 2000.

We follow the Joyce Country road, and miss a turn, ramble up, then back the skinny roads lined with high hedgerows of fuschia with tall purple foxglove growing around and through them.

At Cong we stop to look at an old abbey and cemetery—more Sweeneys here. Wonderful carved arches, and intact steps you can climb up. It starts to rain a bit, so it's back to the car, and we wind our way home. *Quiet Man* business here, the bridge is near and I see the thatched roof cottage used in the film. I also see shorn sheep for the first time, and at first glance take them for oddly shaped pigs. They look so strange and vulnerable when they're naked.

It's been a long day, so we decide to stay in, have room service. We both go for the enormous and delicious burger and have a bottle of champagne to go with it while we watch the pretty pathetic golfers on the little course between us and the lake. They're still playing at ten, with the light holding. The days are long here, with a soft, subtle twilight coming late and leading to utter dark.

Today we'll get another late start—total vacation mode now—and have no idea what we might do.

Nora

"Doyenne of the bestseller lists, Roberts may have achieved her personal best in this tense Southern gothic. As atmospheric and unsettling as a Tennessee Williams play . . . this is romantic drama at its best."

—*Publishers Weekly* starred review for CAROLINA MOON

the book

PART SEVEN

sellers

the family bookstore

ALTHOUGH NORA ROBERTS goes on book-signing tours more often than most authors, and visits many cities each year during the course of touring and attending writers' conferences, not every fan lives close enough to the places Nora visits to get a personally signed book. But there's one place that always has signed Nora Roberts titles in stock. Furthermore, readers can get them personalized, and even order the books from the comfort of their own homes. That place is Turn the Page Bookstore Café, a real bookstore with an extensive virtual presence, one that any fan can reach via the Internet.

Turn the Page is a wonderful independent bookstore owned by Bruce Wilder, Nora's husband. Opened in July 1995, the store sits just beyond the town square in historic Boonsboro, Maryland. For readers who can't get there physically, the store has a website at http://www.ttpbooks.com.

Did You Know . . .

Nora originally met her husband, Bruce Wilder, when she hired him to build bookshelves for her house.

Housed in a beautifully restored pre–Civil War town house (I've often wondered if some of the prose in *Considering Kate* has its roots in the experience of bringing Bruce's bookstore to life), Turn the Page sells new books—romance, mystery, and science fiction—and also features an extensive collection of books about the Civil War.

But more important to Nora's legion of fans than the ambience, though that is charming, is the service the store offers to anyone interested in buying personalized, signed copies of her books from their favorite author. For those lucky enough to visit the brick-and-mortar store, they'll find an assortment of Nora's books, all signed. The store also offers signed volumes from many other authors, including such bestselling writers as Patricia Gaffney and Ruth Ryan Langan.

Bruce Wilder and Nora Roberts sit on the porch of Turn the Page before the TTP first anniversary signing began.

On the Turn the Page porch. Nora with her son Jason (author Elaine Fox is over Nora's left shoulder).

Nora Roberts and her pal Patricia Gaffney at Turn the Page

For those readers who can't get to Maryland, they can participate through one of Turn the Page's "virtual book-signings." Upcoming autographing events are posted regularly on the website. Readers can log on and choose the events they are interested in. Fans can order or preorder Nora's books and those of other visiting authors. Preorders can even be personalized for a specific reader. The on-line store is set up to offer customers either onetime sales or the ability to continually preorder all of Nora's releases, signed, via its "direct ship" option.

The store's close proximity to Antietam National Battlefield as well as other historic sites makes it a natural to handle Civil War books. Bruce has an extensive selection of titles, including both new releases and old favorites. Research buffs will revel in the variety of titles about specific military campaigns of the war. Turn the Page's stock also includes many hard-to-find small press titles.

Did You Know . . .

Having a bookstore in the family is one of the best ways to do research, according to Nora. "I just tell my husband, Bruce, to order anything I want to read, then, when it's in, I go and steal the book. What's he going to do to me? It's a great system."

Every year, the bookstore hosts an annual event in July for Nora's fans. Dedicated Nora Roberts readers from across the United States and many other countries gather at the small store to join together, to put faces to names they know from their on-line friendships, and to bring a sense of physical reality to the virtual community they share on the Internet. To learn more about or be a part of the next gathering, check the TTP website.

For Nora Roberts fans who are in western Maryland, it's worth a stop at Turn the Page Bookstore Café just to browse the well-stocked shelves, sip a cup of coffee, and talk with other fans who gather there on a daily basis. The store is open from ten A.M. to six P.M. Eastern Time, Monday through Saturday. The store is located at:

turn the page bookstore café

18 North Main Street
Boonsboro, MD 21713
(301) 432-4588

Directions: From Washington, D.C., take the Washington Beltway to I-270 toward Frederick, Maryland. From Baltimore, get on I-70 toward Frederick. For both, once past Frederick, take the Braddock Heights exit #49 or Alternate 40 (40A). At the light go left, or north. This is the road the bookstore is on. Stay on 40A for 11 miles, until you come to the light in Boonsboro. The Turn the Page Bookstore Café is 1/2 block past the light, on the left at no. 18.

On the floor, in front of Nora, is Sue Noyes; on the chair and going around are Nina (aka Wymzee) Friedman, Debby Moran, Carolyn Smith, Jaci Hanna, Diane Noyes, and Tracey O'Donnell.

an interview with tommy dreiling

Romance Buyer for Barnes & Noble

by Susan C. Stone

NORA ROBERTS IS a law unto herself. In a field that, despite its acknowledged popularity, is often dismissed or disrespected, she has achieved worldwide acclaim for both her many series and her stand-alone books. Her work also spans an extraordinary range of styles and genres, from so-called category romances for Silhouette to mainstream women's fiction to mystery. And when Nora Roberts writes, the divisions between those categories often blur. Her mainstream fiction and her mysteries frequently include romances and women's issues, as well as elements of magic or the paranormal, and her category romances have also long been praised for their innovative elements and compelling characters . . . particularly in her many popular series of interconnected books. On top of all that, she writes an extraordinary number of new books each year and her publishers maintain an active backlist, without any sign of either exhausting the market for her work or compromising its superb quality. I asked Tommy Dreiling, romance buyer for Barnes & Noble and B. Dalton, to share a major chain bookseller's perspective on Nora Roberts's extraordinary career.

SUSAN C. STONE: *Have you ever met Nora Roberts?*

TOMMY DREILING: Yes, publishers often arrange for buyers to meet authors when they are in New York. It's one of the best parts of being a book buyer. I first met Nora a few years ago, and by that time she was already a very big-selling author. I got several very strong impressions from that first meeting. First, I was surprised to learn that Nora was still doing such extensive publicity tours to promote her books. Despite her level of success, and the extraordinary number of books she was writing each year, Nora is still going full steam on the tour circuit. Second, I learned that, although she revealed that she enjoys a good afternoon of shopping, she otherwise seemed to be unaffected by her fame and fortune. And third, I realized that Nora still really likes to write. It's clearly not just a job for her, or just a way to make more money.

One of the main ways our Barnes & Noble and B. Dalton stores let fans know about upcoming books is through our very popular *Heart to Heart* newsletter, which we e-mail to our readers every month. We do reviews and excerpts of books, and interviews with authors and letters from them. Over the years, we've done several pieces about Nora Roberts's books, and Nora has been willing to take time out of her busy schedule to do interviews and write special pieces to tell readers about her books, as well as to make personal appearances. This is an area where she puts in time above and beyond the call of duty. I think that it's another way she shows how much she appreciates and respects both her readers and her booksellers.

SUSAN C. STONE: *What is your first memory of working with a Nora Roberts book as a buyer?*

TOMMY DREILING: My first memory of working on a Nora Roberts book as a buyer was with the Born In trilogy. Experience in the bookselling field told me that most trilogies or series drop in sales with each successive book, as some readers just choose not to go on, but the numbers on the Born In books actually increased with each book. I saw that as the point when Nora really started to break out as an author.

Sign announcing booksigning at Barnes & Noble

SUSAN C. STONE: *Have you noticed anything different about Nora Roberts's readership, compared to that of other writers in the romance field? Do you think that her books appeal to a broader readership—more mystery readers, more men, more mainstream readers?*

TOMMY DREILING: I think the thing that is most different about Nora's readership is that it is so broad and so loyal. Large numbers of people have been willing to follow this author, even when she has chosen to write in new subject areas as she did with the J. D. Robb futuristic police procedurals, or to add paranormal elements to her romances as she did in the Donovan series, her Irish trilogy (*Jewels of the Sun, Tears of the Moon,* and *Heart of the Sea*), and her Three Sisters Island series. Books like that are generally seen as "niche" subjects and have a very small readership, but not when Nora writes them. I have to admit that I was very skeptical about

Matt and Kristin Gilbreth and their daughters, Tarah and Jolie, meet Nora at a booksigning.

the first J. D. Robb book when it was presented to me, because futuristic romances have a loyal but *very* small following. But, as happened with the Born In series, each J. D. Robb book increased in sales as readers responded to the compelling quality of Nora's writing.

SUSAN C. STONE: *What do you see as Nora Roberts's greatest impact on the category romance field? And what about her impact on the mainstream fiction field?*

TOMMY DREILING: I think Nora's greatest impact on category romance comes from the fact that she *still* writes them. There are several best-selling authors out there who started in romance, and once they achieved success in the mainstream, chose to distance themselves from the romance genre. Part of the reason for this undoubtedly comes from the general bias in society against romance as a genre. A lot of people, especially among those who don't read romances, try to say that if it's a romance it must be badly written—that if it's really good writing it's fiction. One thing I've learned in my time as the romance buyer is how truly misogynistic our society can be. It seems that all too often, if a book is about men's fantasies, it's called literature, and if it's about women's fantasies it's called trash. When an author as universally respected as Nora Roberts chooses to continue to write category and mainstream romances, and to identify herself as a romance author, that is a tribute to the genre that helps to highlight the strengths of one of the most diverse, dynamic, and popular genres in today's market.

SUSAN C. STONE: *Has Nora Roberts had an impact on how Barnes & Noble sees (and sells) category and mainstream romances, and women's fiction in general?*

TOMMY DREILING: Absolutely. The extraordinary sales of Nora's books, the diversity and scope of her writing, and the support and loyalty of her customers, all have helped to make Barnes & Noble more aware of and responsive to the romance market. Nora's contributions to the field, along with the contributions of some other top authors, have helped to bring romance out of the shadows and into the storefront. Better cover art from the publishers has also helped overcome the stereotype of romance as a category of "trashy" books. Nora's books have helped to set a precedent for publishing romances with covers that may differ little from those on books published as mainstream novels. People often do judge books by their cover, at least at first, and it's clear that this new cover approach has made many romance fans more comfortable picking up the books they love, and made a broader spectrum of mainstream readers more willing to explore this exciting genre. As booksellers, we try to display books that have visual appeal. That's why you can now see the books of Nora Roberts and other top romance authors displayed prominently in our stores, when I don't think I need to say that this was not frequently true five years ago.

SUSAN C. STONE: *What do booksellers like best about an author like Nora Roberts? And what's the hardest part about handling a writer with such a varied and prolific output, who also has such an active frontlist and backlist?*

TOMMY DREILING: The main challenge of buying an author as prolific as Nora is keeping up with all of the reissues, while giving proper attention to each new book as well. The other challenge is determining how much to buy of the reissue. Once an author becomes a bestseller, there is always a demand for their earlier work, but that demand can vary greatly from author to author. In this again, Nora is in a league of her own. Nora attracts so many new readers each year, that some of her oldest titles, especially those which have been out of print the longest, when reissued, can sell almost as well as a brand-new book! If you haven't read it, it's new to you! One of the most exciting new trends I've seen in romance is that readers seem open to longer books. I think that's one reason for the success of some of the recent reissues from Nora Roberts's backlist that collected several of her short category romances and republished them in a single volume, for example the omnibus edition of her paranormal romance trilogy, *The Donovan Legacy.*

SUSAN C. STONE: *Do you think Barnes & Noble has had any impact on Nora Roberts's career? Has the chain done anything special to promote her work?*

TOMMY DREILING: Many people think that buyers, particularly chain store buyers, determine what gets read and what becomes a bestseller. As a buyer I know it's the customers who determine that. I can think of many books over the years that I personally thought were good—books that I liked and that I bought a lot of. But when the readers didn't agree with me, those books went nowhere. I can also think of other books that struck me as nothing special when the publisher's sales reps presented them, that really took off when they hit the stores and I had to scramble to do reorders in order to keep them in stock. As a buyer, it's my job to put books in the stores that people want to buy. That means I try to "buy into a trend" when I can see one, be it a kind of book, like romantic suspense, or a specific author, like Nora Roberts. Nora is certainly a "trend" that I have bought into over the years. I think that during that time Nora and B & N have been very good for each other. In fact, I'd say Nora Roberts has been a great success for everyone concerned—the bookstores, the publishers, and, I think most of all, the readers.

Jennifer Webster-Valant meets Nora at a signing.

Tommy Dreiling's career started in B. Dalton stores in Overland Park, Kansas, and the Kansas City area, then he became a store manager in Wichita. Wanting to become a buyer, he interviewed for jobs in New York. Shortly after following a divisional merchandise manager's suggestion to transfer to a New York store, he was offered an assistant's job. Later, when a spot opened for a buyer in mass-market fiction, romance, and mystery, he jumped at it. He has been the romance buyer for eight years now and continues to enjoy the challenges of this diverse and dynamic genre.

Susan C. Stone is a freelance writer and editor. Being paid to read books was always her dream job. For the past twenty years, since she accepted her first job in publishing, she's found a variety of ways to make that dream a reality, both in-house as an editor of science fiction and fantasy, romance, and suspense, and as a freelance writer of fiction and nonfiction, a copyeditor, and an editorial consultant. Among her other freelance projects, for nearly ten years she wrote and edited the Barnes & Noble/B. Dalton *Heart to Heart* newsletter.

appreciating nora

A Talk with Sharon Kelly Roth at Books & Co.

SHARON KELLY ROTH has worked at Books & Co. in Dayton, Ohio, for more than eighteen years. Part of her job as director of public relations is to coordinate and prepare for author signing events. Sharon is an avid reader, and a big fan of Nora Roberts's books. Naturally, she has an enthusiastic reverence for all books, and works to make every signing she oversees a success, but after many years of handling autographings, she believes Nora brings something special to every appearance. Here's what she had to say about it.

DENISE LITTLE: *When did you first meet Nora Roberts and how?*

SHARON KELLY ROTH: I've *always* known Nora. I've been reading her books for years. We met in person about ten years ago when she first came to visit us at Books & Co.

DENISE LITTLE: *What are favorite memories and anecdotes of Nora with her fans?*

SHARON KELLY ROTH: If Nora were not a writer, she could be a stand-up comedienne. She enthralls the audience with her quick and easy wit as she answers their questions and makes them feel right at home with her. Indeed, she makes everyone feel like they are best friends coming together for a chat.

The last time she was here, she made arrangements to have dinner with a group of her fans before her signing. Isn't that a friendly thing to do! And it's not one that most authors would think of.

DENISE LITTLE: *How do you get ready for a signing?*

SHARON KELLY ROTH: We make the first announcement that we've got Nora for a signing in our newsletter, which is mailed to our large customer list. Then we prepare a two-by-three-foot poster to hang in the store over her book display that promotes the event. We notify romance clubs, as well as our TV and radio stations and newspapers. Notices of our events are regularly printed in area newspapers. We distribute flyers to target groups. At least two staff members are assigned to host the event and to handle any details that may need attention.

DENISE LITTLE: *How do you spread word to her fans that she is coming to town?*

SHARON KELLY ROTH: Our mailed newsletter and our webpage (booksandcompany.com) announces the event as do local newspapers. Romance groups get special notification.

DENISE LITTLE: *What kinds of reactions do you get from readers when they hear Nora's coming?*

Mary Kay McComas, Nora Roberts, and Patricia Gaffney share a laugh with Vicky.

SHARON KELLY ROTH: They are eager to make plans (or change plans) so that they can come to her signing. They come from states all around. Some people travel six or eight hours to get here. She's worth it to them.

DENISE LITTLE: *Are Nora's signings special or different from other authors' events?*

SHARON KELLY ROTH: Nora is a model visiting author! She appreciates each one of her fans and lets them know that without them, she couldn't have the phenomenal success she has.

She takes time to talk with each person coming through her autograph line, and makes every one feel it was worth their time and effort to come meet her. She is happy to have her photo taken with her fans, too.

In her presentation before the signing, Nora often shares her thoughts and feelings about her family and personal life, including her husband and his bookstore. People feel that they "know" her because of that style of communication, and they appreciate it.

DENISE LITTLE: *Why does Nora inspire such loyalty in her readers?*

SHARON KELLY ROTH: Nora writes well-plotted stories and never repeats herself. She writes quickly, so there is always a new book for her fans to enjoy. Since some of her characters reappear in other stories, readers develop a personal interest and friendship with them and like to follow them into another book.

DENISE LITTLE: *Are you a Nora Roberts reader?*

SHARON KELLY ROTH: I surely am a Nora Roberts reader. My favorite book is always her newest book. I pick it up with great anticipation, and am never disappointed.

DENISE LITTLE: *What do booksellers like best about an author like Nora?*

SHARON KELLY ROTH: We appreciate Nora's respect for her fans. She welcomes them to her events and makes them feel valued. Her presentations are friendly and casual and a mutual love-fest.

DENISE LITTLE: *How do you choose books for the signing?*

SHARON KELLY ROTH: We try to bring in a sampling of all her backlist. You can be sure that we are never without a large supply of Nora Roberts titles.

DENISE LITTLE: *What is your perception of the romance genre?*

SHARON KELLY ROTH: Books & Co. has great respect for the romance genre. It is one of our bestselling sections, so we keep it very well stocked.

DENISE LITTLE: *What can other writers learn from Nora?*

SHARON KELLY ROTH: We love it when our visiting authors show appreciation for their readers and thank them for coming to their signings. A friendly author who takes time to make eye contact and speak to each person coming through the autograph line is a joy to booksellers.

We find that if authors post their book-signing schedule on their website, people come from far and wide to attend the event. That outreach effort is very effective and augments our own publicity efforts, and is appreciated by all.

DENISE LITTLE: *Do you have any words of wisdom from watching Nora in action?*

SHARON KELLY ROTH: Nora is the quintessential pro! She is enthusiastic about her signings and conveys that to her audience.

Sharon Kelly Roth has been director of public relations for Books & Co. at 350 E. Stroop Road in Dayton, Ohio, for more than eighteen years. The store has a busy visiting-author schedule, with authors arriving nearly every day (sometimes more than one author a day). Sharon is responsible for organizing these events. One of the things Sharon likes best about her position is reading the books of the authors before their visits. She says, "It keeps me on my toes and gives me the opportunity to read broadly; since in any given week, our visiting authors may have written on such varied topics as science, cooking, romance, current events, fiction, gardening, business, children's books, history, etc. It's such an honor to meet these talented authors after having read and appreciated their work." When she is not reading, Sharon enjoys gardening and art projects.

selling nora

An Interview with Anne Marie Tallberg, Former National Romance Buyer for Waldenbooks

ANNE MARIE TALLBERG was the national buyer for Waldenbooks for many years, and as such, she was responsible in large part for what romance readers in America were reading. Her choices determined how many copies of what titles flowed into each Waldenbooks store in America. Naturally, given that she dealt with every romance produced, she has some strong opinions on romance and Nora Roberts. A personal and professional fan, Anne Marie took the time to talk about Nora's success in the bookstores of America.

DENISE LITTLE: *Have you ever met Nora Roberts?*

ANNE MARIE TALLBERG: Several times, each time finding her gracious and very good company. But the first time I met Nora was at the Romance Writers Association Conference Awards luncheon. Each year at the RWA, Waldenbooks gives out awards based on sales performance that are highly prized in the romance writer community and Nora (winner of several Waldenbooks awards already) had won the Bestselling Original Contemporary Paperback award for *The MacGregor Brides.* Nora—as usual—was extremely busy at the conference and was not scheduled to attend the luncheon. When she learned she had won a Waldenbooks award, she rescheduled her day so that she could accept the award in person. During the luncheon, I announced Nora Roberts's award. She walked up the aisle from the table where she had just arrived, accepted her award and thanked me sincerely, then walked out of the room, on her way to another meeting, another interview. This first meeting made quite an impression on me, as I think it really showed her dedication to showing appreciation to the people who help her to be successful at what she does.

DENISE LITTLE: *Have you noticed anything different about Nora Roberts's readership, compared to that of other writers in the romance field? Do you think that her books appeal to a broader readership—more mystery readers, more men, more mainstream readers?*

ANNE MARIE TALLBERG: Nora is 100 percent committed to creating real, believable, fully fleshed characters. This focus provides a broad and solid base from which to work and, by having the relationships grow organically from the characters' situations, doesn't force the romance genre on readers. In itself, this

Nora hands back a signed copy of The Reef.

is not so different from what some other romance writers do. What is unique about Nora is her breadth of story line. She does not shy away from writing historicals, contemporaries, category romance, science fiction, suspense—she really writes something for everyone. I do believe that this gives her a broader readership than many romance writers. In fact, I have talked to several romance fans who must fight their husbands for the first read of a Nora Roberts book, something I don't really hear about with other authors.

DENISE LITTLE: *What do you see as Nora Roberts's greatest impact on the category romance field? And what about her impact on the mainstream fiction field?*

ANNE MARIE TALLBERG: Nora Roberts has given category romance a shelf life of longer than four weeks, and that's quite an achievement. By continuing to write category romance, Nora shows that she won't hide her romance roots and that she respects this often maligned subgenre. Category romance has always been very important to Waldenbooks and I'm thrilled to see an author of Nora's stature continue her series romance career. As wonderful as this is for booksellers, Nora is also a very savvy businesswoman. By continuing to write for Harlequin/Silhouette she can have some control over their reissue publication schedule. In this way she can keep her series backlist in check, something in her best interest since she has at least one book release each month.

DENISE LITTLE: *Has Nora Roberts had an impact on how Waldenbooks sees (and sells) category and mainstream romances, and women's fiction in general?*

ANNE MARIE TALLBERG: Romance has always been a signature category for Waldenbooks. We have a strong, loyal romance customer base. So the impact is less on how Waldenbooks sees romance than on how fiction readers and other romance authors see romance.

So many ambitious romance authors see romance as a stepping-stone to the "Promised Lands" of suspense and women's fiction. Nora has shown the world the diversity that romance can provide. She has legitimized staying in the romance category—or the "category romance" category—and reaching across the aisle to the fiction reader, and has proven that readers will cross the aisle for a good story, well told. She has shown authors and readers alike that you can have it all without leaving romance behind. And by doing that, she helps to remove any stigma there may be in writing for, or browsing in, the romance category.

DENISE LITTLE: *What do booksellers like best about an author like Nora Roberts? And what's the hardest part about handling a writer with such a varied and prolific output, who also has such an active frontlist and backlist?*

ANNE MARIE TALLBERG: What booksellers like best: She spoils booksellers! What other author can provide a new release or a huge reissue every month of the year? Her writing is of such quality that just about anything she writes is a guaranteed good read. And she is so prolific, writing such varied stories, that there is a Nora Roberts book to please just about anyone! There are very few authors who can support that claim.

The hardest part about handling such a writer: "Prolific" is not a problem, but "varied" is. It means booksellers need to know a little bit about every book—at this point nearly 150 titles. To add to the challenge, Nora publishes basically a book a month, but some are new releases, some are reissues. Although that's difficult to keep straight, it's vital information for booksellers who are hand-selling to customers.

DENISE LITTLE: *Do you think that Waldenbooks has had any impact on Nora Roberts's career? Has the chain done anything special to promote her work?*

ANNE MARIE TALLBERG: Waldenbooks is many romance fans' first stop on their book-shopping spree, so we do tend to have quite an impact on a budding author's career. Waldenbooks has been there for Nora since the beginning, hand-selling and promoting her books enthusiastically. She has been promoted in every marketing vehicle we have—and we are constantly coming up with new ways to spread the Nora gospel. Thankfully, Nora makes this easy by offering exclusive letters and stories—sometimes when we put in a request she has something good ready in mere *hours*.

Of course, Nora is heavily promoted in-store. Beyond that, she has been featured in the "Romantic Reader" section of our print newsletter, *The Walden Book Report*, so many times that she deserves her own retrospective issue. We create postcard mailings to our Preferred Readers, and now that the Internet has become a viable vehicle for promotion, we can send e-mails to her fans to let them know about her latest books.

Here are some of my favorite promotional stories:

✦ In early 1998, I was assigned a new, non-romance-reading assistant buyer. Her first romance assignment was to read the just-published book *Sea Swept*, the first in the Chesapeake Bay trilogy. She loved it, of course, and suggested that we ask Nora to write a Christmas story featuring the Quinn family. Nora graciously obliged, penning a fifteen-hundred-word story that was so amazing that I made everyone in the department read the piece (picking up new fans for Nora along the way). "Christmas with the Quinns" came out in the December 1998 issue of *The Walden Book Report* and quickly became our most requested back issue. Now the story is available on Nora's website.

Suz McErlain with Nora Roberts

- ✦ Long before the public unveiling of J. D. Robb, we mounted our own internal campaign at Waldenbooks to make sure our booksellers knew the famous name behind the Robb books. It was a personal crusade of sorts, since the In Death series is my personal favorite and we were seeing incredible sales growth. We quizzed readers with signs and bookseller pins: "J. D. Robb writes as what other bestselling romance novelist? Ask your bookseller!" And for *Conspiracy in Death*, I asked Nora to allow an interview with Lt. Eve Dallas. The interview was conducted by e-mail and I could swear that it was really Eve typing answers into a crummy New York Police and Security Department–issue computer, being her fabulously terse, prickly self. The Dallas interview ranks as one of my favorites.
- ✦ With the Irish trilogy, featuring the Gallaghers, we became more ambitious, expanding the idea of an exclusive short story to a ninety-six-page exclusive-to-Waldenbooks sampler book. The book contained exclusive short stories, an interview, and a preview of *The Villa* and was available to customers with the purchase of the conclusion to the Gallagher trilogy, *Heart of the Sea.* It was a beautiful and very special Christmas 2000 gift to thousands of fans. If you missed them, the stories are now available on Nora's website.

DENISE LITTLE: *How is Nora different as a writer from most romance writers—what sets her apart from the pack and makes her so special?*

ANNE MARIE TALLBERG: Nora Roberts has a huge dose of the gift that most authors—of any genre—desperately strive to develop: she makes a reader like her characters. Nora often describes her books as character-driven and that's what truly sets her apart. She brings individuals to life, makes them so real that readers recognize themselves and those they love in the pages of her books. The story itself naturally evolves from the characters involved, which makes the reading experience feel both natural and comforting, never forced. When a reader takes a break to make dinner, she (or he) wonders just what so-and-so is up to now. . . . Even for those who don't love the romance genre, they often acknowledge that Nora's books are a satisfying read.

DENISE LITTLE: *Many of Nora's books are written as series. How do you think this impacts Nora's career?*

ANNE MARIE TALLBERG: Series can only bolster her career. A family saga or a trilogy makes sense on every level for a writer like Nora Roberts. She's a prolific writer; a series or trilogy provides her enough space to create a fuller story. And because her books are so character-driven and fans tend to fall in love with everyone in the books, there is greater satisfaction for the fans to learn more and more about their favorite characters. At the same time, Nora can build readership—as well as book sales—by luring customers to buy more than one of her books. I mean, really, who could read *Sea Swept* and not then rush off to buy *Rising Tides*, and then *Inner Harbor*?

DENISE LITTLE: *Do you have any personal favorites among Nora's books? What are they and why?*

ANNE MARIE TALLBERG: Fan to fan, I absolutely adore the stories she writes as J. D. Robb. Eve and Roarke are such a perfectly matched couple, I never tire of spending time in their company.

bookseller's corner

A Talk with Beth Anne Steckiel

BETH ANNE STECKIEL owns and operates an independent bookstore in Colorado Springs, Colorado, called Beth Anne's Book Corner. A strong supporter of local and national authors, Ms. Steckiel has watched her store grow in stock and in reputation as the years have gone by. In 2000, Ms. Steckiel was named Romance Writers of America's Bookseller of the Year, the first independent bookstore winner of this prestigious award. Major publishers now include the store as a signing location for their authors on national tour, which is quite a coup for a store that sells both new and used books. One of the most popular authors to visit the store on a regular basis is Nora Roberts.

I had a chance to sit down with Ms. Steckiel in the big chairs by the store's very inviting fireplace and talk about her encounters with Nora.

LAURA HAYDEN: *When did you first start reading Nora's books?*

BETH ANNE STECKIEL: The first Nora Roberts book I read was *Night Moves.* It really hooked me. After that, I started going back and reading her older books. They were hard to find, even then. When I opened my store in early 1988, I already knew that Nora Roberts's books, both new and old, were going to be important to my customers.

LAURA HAYDEN: *Do you have a favorite Nora Roberts book?*

BETH ANNE STECKIEL: Nope. I like 'em all. [*Editor's note: And despite prodding and wheedling, I couldn't get Beth Anne to commit to one favorite book or series. However I did discover she has an almost complete collection of Nora's books.*]

LAURA HAYDEN: *When did you first meet Nora?*

BETH ANNE STECKIEL: We first met in Savannah at the *Romantic Times* convention in 1992. I'd introduced myself as a bookstore owner and we were sitting together, talking, in the lobby of the convention hotel. Suddenly Michael, one of the convention coordinators, came running up, all excited. "Nora, Nora! Do you want to be on television?" He explained that *Entertainment Tonight* was there to cover the book signing and she could be interviewed on national television.

When she told Michael, "No, thanks," he was totally shocked. She explained, "Find an author who has one or two books out and let them interview her. I don't need this sort of thing. A new author could really benefit from something like this."

I realized very quickly this wasn't a case of her wanting to impress anybody. It was just Michael and me there. It was simply Nora being Nora. Where so many authors would have grabbed that opportunity, she was willing to forgo the chance because it was something she really didn't need. It's so like her to give the limelight to someone else who could really benefit from a chance to shine. Even if she wasn't trying to impress me, she sure did. I realized very early on what sort of really neat, down-to-earth person she really is. And best of all, she hasn't changed to this day, ten or so years later. As big and successful as she is now, she's still that down-to-earth person.

LAURA HAYDEN: *What do you think her appeal is to her readers?*

BETH ANNE STECKIEL: She always gives them a good read. Whenever you buy a Nora Roberts book, you always get your money's worth. It's a matter of being assured you'll get a quality book—her books are never a waste of money. And they're always different. There are some authors who give you the same book every time—they just change the names and the location, but the plot is pretty much the same. Not with Nora. There's even a discernible difference between her categories and her general fiction. She plays with her category romances—using lots of paranormal. She has such a following in the category that it gives her a real freedom in her general fiction.

LAURA HAYDEN: *Do you see crossover to Nora's category books from those who read her general fiction?*

BETH ANNE STECKIEL: I have male readers who, having read her single titles, now buy her category romances. She's really the first author who has gotten people to cross over from fiction to category romance. Before Nora, nobody really went back and read an author's romance if they were now writing suspense or some other type of noncategory. Because of her, mystery readers are trying Intrigues and Intimate Moments. Readers aren't as hesitant in trying the category romances because Nora has proven that they're good. She's the reason why more romance books are making the *New York Times* bestsellers list. She's opened the list up for all sorts of category romances. And more crossover means better sales for everyone.

LAURA HAYDEN: *Do you see crossover from romance books to her J. D. Robb books?*

BETH ANNE STECKIEL: I do, but it's hard to explain the series to some readers who read only romance. When I try to describe the futuristic story line, I tell them it reminds me of the movie *Blade Runner* with its gritty, futuristic tones. In terms of genre, it's not really science fiction, but it's definitely a mystery. I tell readers that they need to read the first three books in order. Also, if the reader doesn't usually read mysteries, I tell them to read at least half or three-quarters of their first J. D. Robb before making any decisions. Romance readers aren't used to such a totally different writing style and story construction. Plus, throw in the *Blade Runner* atmosphere and you've got something totally different from Nora's romances.

I always remember a comment that Eve/Nora made in the first book. It's something to the order of—even if you make today's drugs legal, tomorrow people will find newer, more powerful illegal drugs and want those. Take guns out of the system, people will still find ways to kill other people. That's why a lot of readers are taken back by the J. D. Robb book; it deals with lots of gritty, dark things. But you have to look at the series in perspective. The same problems, the same vices are going to be there in the future, no matter how much change the world has gone through. In my opinion, Nora really has carved out her own niche with the J. D. Robb series.

LAURA HAYDEN: *Why does it work for her and not other authors?*

BETH ANNE STECKIEL: Nora is able to come up with story elements that are totally believable. Even when it comes to paranormal elements, she makes it all believable. When she wrote *Divine Evil*, she was the only person who could have pulled off that book with its witchcraft element. She's not afraid to deal with a whole host of paranormal elements.

LAURA HAYDEN: *So, tell us about the typical Nora Roberts book-signing.*

BETH ANNE STECKIEL (LAUGHING)**:** There isn't one. Not a typical one, at least. You never know how many people are going to show up—usually lots!—or how much fun you're going to have. One time, she was scheduled here for a signing, but she had to show up early because she had to do a radio interview. Do you know how hard it was to not tell anyone she was going to be there early? So there she was, hiding in my back room—which isn't all that big—on the phone, doing a radio interview. No one could know she was there so we had to sneak her in and out the back door. That was a lot of fun and she was a great sport about it.

You know, she's such a great storyteller, even in person. She can take the smallest story and just make you fall over laughing she tells it so well.

The first time she came to sign at the store was because she was speaking locally at the Pikes Peak Writers' Conference. I pulled out the ARC [advanced reading copy] for *Naked in Death* and she got excited. As it turned out, this was the first time she'd ever signed any material as J. D. Robb. So it was a big moment for both of us. Another time, when she was at the store to sign *Montana Sky,* she brought red bandannas as promotional materials. We made my son wear one the entire time and he still won't let me forget it.

Nora and Ruth Langan with Laurie, aka Jewells, in front

LAURA HAYDEN: *You have quite a collection of items from her various promotions.*

BETH ANNE STECKIEL: They're very special to me. The most interesting promotional item is a small piggy bank that she sent out to advertise *Hidden Riches.* I don't keep it at the store because too many people want it! My second favorite is the binoculars. *[She points to a pair of red plastic binoculars hanging high on the wall.]* They were for *True Betrayals,* for watching horse racing.

[Beth Anne reaches to a wall of certificates and pictures and pulls one off and reads it aloud.]

> *"Dear Bookseller, In lieu of sending you a gift to announce the publication of my latest novel,* River's End, *I've requested that one tree be planted on your behalf. I hope that you share my enthusiasm in making this a greener, more beautiful and healthier place to live.*
> *Best Wishes,*
> *Nora Roberts."*

[Beth Anne proudly pulls out several other promotional items.]

- ✦ A small burlap sack full of popcorn. Printed on it in green letters is BURSTING WITH IRISH LUCK and advertising the Born In books: *Born in Shame, Born in Ice,* and *Born in Fire.*
- ✦ Four small "sticky" notepad cubes, one each advertising *Loyalty in Death, Witness in Death, Judgment in Death,* and *Conspiracy in Death.*
- ✦ A wind-up alarm clock with "Sweet dreams from Nora Roberts" imprinted on the face, and advertising the three Dreams books: *Holding the Dream, Finding the Dream,* and *Daring to Dream.*
- ✦ A large white coffee cup advertising *Sanctuary.*
- ✦ A large notepad cube advertising *Private Scandals* and *Honest Illusions.* Each sheet includes a quote from reviewer Rex Reed, saying, "Move over, Sidney Sheldon, the world has a new master of romantic suspense and HER name is Nora Roberts."

- ✦ A box of tissues advertising four of the MacGregor books. The bottom panel includes the entire series and the top panel says, "Don't cry. The MacGregors are back."
- ✦ A book-shaped notepad decorated with the original *Naked in Death* cover. It reads: "For the dark sides of love, passion and ambition, *Naked in Death*—J. D. Robb."
- ✦ A pair of navy blue mittens that have the name J. D. ROBB knitted into them. They're bound together by a white ribbon that also reads J. D. ROBB/NORA ROBERTS and also included a gift of hot chocolate.
- ✦ A gold "centennial" bookmark mounted on a card that reads, "Please accept this commemorative bookmark as a small token of my appreciation for your warm enthusiasm over the years as I look forward to the publication of *Montana Sky,* my 100th novel. I welcome your continued support."
- ✦ A black cauldron advertising *Born in Shame* and once upon a time filled with something delicious, long since consumed.
- ✦ A collection of signed cover flats and pictures, book dumps, and T-shirts from various book tours/promotions.

LAURA HAYDEN: Any last anecdotes?

BETH ANNE STECKIEL: One more. It took place at the Romance Writers of America conference. I was in the elevator and I started talking to a husband and wife who were riding up with me. They told me they were from overseas, in town for another conference. The man admitted that his wife made them stay in this hotel because she'd heard that Nora was staying there because of the RWA conference. But unfortunately, the woman had missed the big literacy book-signing where she'd hoped to meet Nora and get a signed book. So the woman went out to a bookstore and purchased *Irish Hearts* in hopes of stumbling into Nora somewhere in the hotel. But eventually she decided it'd be a real long shot to run into Nora by chance.

I told her that Nora was around, somewhere, so there really was a decent chance she might run into Nora. And if she did, to not be afraid to go up and ask Nora to sign the book. I assured the woman that Nora would gladly do that. But the woman said she'd be too self-conscious to ask, even if the chance arose.

Lo and behold, the elevator door opened and there stood Nora in the hallway. I pulled the couple out of the elevator and introduced them to Nora, explaining how the woman had missed the book-signing. Sure enough, Nora stopped what she was doing, spent some time talking to the couple, signed the book, personalizing it, and then to their utter surprise, she thanked them in their native language. Talk about impressive! Afterwards, the man came running back to me and thanked me profusely. "Do you realize you've made my wife's year?"

But I knew if I saw Nora, that she'd gladly sign a book for a fan, especially considering the circumstances in this case. Sometimes there are authors you can't approach, but Nora is totally approachable and so available for her fans. That's what makes her special, as a writer and as a person.

"You can't bottle wish fulfillment, but Ms. Roberts certainly knows how to put it on the page."

—*The New York Times* on THE VILLA

a circle of

PART EIGHT

friends

nora in their own words

ONE OF THE special talents Nora has as a writer is her ability to bring to life the friendships between women—the way they talk, laugh, cry, fight, and bond about life, family, work, and, of course, men. And for Nora, this is truly a case of art imitating life, because she has been blessed with the friendships of a group of truly terrific women, who all happen to be fellow writers. They have known each other for years, and all of them were happy to share with us another glimpse of Nora, the great friend.

The friends and authors of the Once Upon anthologies (L to R): Jill Gregory, Marianne Willman, Ruth Ryan Langan, and Nora

say, was your father a traveling man?

I FIRST MET Nora at a conference aboard the *Queen Mary,* drydocked in Long Beach, California. Nora was working the registration desk when my buddy and roommate, Ruth Ryan Langan, introduced us. We were all newbies back then, and so excited to meet other writers we could hardly stand it.

Marianne Willman

The *QM* was hosting a bizarre combination of conferences simultaneously—the American Association of Orthopedic Surgeons, the British Rugby Team, and fledgling Romance Writers of America. If there had been a competition to see who enjoyed the weekend more, the writers would have won hands down. The surgeons were quiet and so well behaved we hardly knew they were aboard. The rugby team was a bit more colorful. Every night the Brits took over the ship's lounge and sang the entire score from some musical. In harmony. We sang, too. They shushed us. We sang louder.

I don't remember laughing so much in my life. Nora was witty, intelligent, friendly, and very, very funny. I couldn't know back then that she would be a publishing phenomenon, a true legend in her time. I just knew that I bonded with her from the moment we met. I felt, as I had with Ruth, that I'd found a long-lost sister.

And I still do.

Marianne Willman

Nora and Ruth Ryan Langan in Ireland

Nora may be one of the best-known writers in the world today, but she's also a mom. The year was 1984. RWA's annual conference was being held in Detroit, and I invited Nora to bring her boys to stay with my family while she and I attended the conference. When we were leaving for the hotel, Nora gave her sons, Jason and Dan, what she termed her "hairy eyeball" while cautioning them to be on their best behavior. Then she warned my husband, Tom, that he'd have his hands full with these two.

When we returned three days later, Tom was singing the praises of her two sons. Nora seemed pleased, but later, when she got Tom alone, wanted to know what he did to get them to behave so well. Did I mention that we own a bowling center and pizza parlor? All he had to do was promise that as soon as their chores were finished they could bowl, play pinball games, and stuff themselves with pizza, and they couldn't do enough. Empty the trash? Wipe down tables? Vacuum? Not a problem.

To this day, Jason and Dan proclaim that visit as one of their fondest memories.

Ours, too, since it cemented a bond between our families that has held throughout all these years.

Ruth Ryan Langan

Babies and Dogs

WHILE NORA is extremely self-disciplined in her writing habits, she does have her weaknesses. One of them is babies. Nora can smell a baby at 300 feet. I swear. She will accost young mothers at a busy mall—anywhere really—and ask if she can *pleeese* take a peek at their baby. What's the baby's name? How old is it? What did it weigh at birth? Pat Gaffney and I know this is going to take a while; we go off for a drink, come back a half an hour later, and Nora and the mother are swapping diaper rash remedies. We're very glad she has her very own granddaughter now—however, she also has four dogs and she's this very same way around anything canine. They must be petted and fawned over . . . except Pat has a thing about dogs, too. So there I am at the bar, drinking alone.

Mary Kay McComas

george washington has nothing on us

OUR FORMER HOUSE was a converted barn, and the staircase to the upper floor was steep and narrow, with a right-angled turn at the bottom. One day, when Nora was staying with us, she lost her footing and went tobogganing down in her bathrobe. Luckily she wasn't hurt, but it gave us both a scare. The next morning we posted a sign at the foot of the stairs: NORA ROBERTS SLIPPED HERE.

Marianne Willman

(L to R) Mary Kay McComas, Pat Gaffney, and Beth Harbison are on hand to celebrate Nora's birthday in 1997 in Shepherdstown, West Virginia.

Sometimes my friendship with Nora, which has been going strong for about fifteen years now, seems like one long adolescent slumber party, and I mean that in the best possible way. When we're together, we regress to the kind of relationship I associate with college roommates, not middle-aged matrons.

It helps that we have so much in common. We both had brothers but no sisters, we grew up in virtually the same middle-class Washington, D.C., suburb, we're Irish Catholics, both writers, we both married tall, handsome carpenters-turned-entrepreneurs. Seems odd that we didn't meet sooner—where *was* she all my life before 1987?

We have the same tastes in entertainment, too. Talking, eating, drinking, and shopping—that's our mutual idea of a Good Time. It's our friend Mary Kay McComas's idea of a good time, too, so whenever we can, we do these things together.

And ideally, all at the same time. Hence, the *ultimate* for us is the pre-Christmas weekend shopping getaway. We drive to the biggest mall in our area and stay overnight in a motel that has suites. Here's where the dorm-room dynamic really comes into play—or maybe it's more like high school. We've never actually dropped ice cubes from the balcony on the people in the lobby, never actually crammed ourselves into a while-you-wait photo booth, but that's the mood we're in on our shopping weekends. Girls just wanna have fun.

One year we all got glasses. I forget who started it, but once one of us bought new glasses—frames, I mean, the six-hour kind—the other two had to have glasses. That same day we all got facials, another spur-of-the-moment choice; we were just lucky the beauty shop could take us. But we *always* have good luck on these trips, it's like the shopping gods are smiling down on us, elbowing each other in the ribs, saying, *Aren't they cute?* Store clerks are charmed by us. "Are you all friends?" they ask, as if this is somehow remarkable. "And you're just out for a nice time?" Yes, we say, we're great friends and we're just here to play. We revert to adolescent shopping mall pleasures—cosmetic makeovers, flashy costume jewelry purchases, as many hot fudge sundaes as we can eat—but with a difference: unlike during our real adolescence, now we can *afford* them.

It was on one of these weekends, Saturday evening after a long, satisfying day of Christmas shopping, that we three had our one and only fight. We were kicking back with a glass of wine in the bar of a nice Italian restaurant, waiting to be seated for dinner. As usual, Nora and Mary Kay lit up. Maybe it was the wine, maybe it was the ten years or so I'd held my tongue about what a stupid, self-destructive habit smoking is—who knows, but for some reason I let 'em have it, and with all the self-righteousness of the formerly addicted. Words were exchanged. It was two against one, and I lost. Hurt silence lasted for the length of a trip to the ladies' room, and that was that. Fight over.

I'm still mad, though. Because they still smoke.

I believe that was the same weekend we all bought melatonin. We'd never tried it, and we'd heard it had wonderful sedative qualities. At evening's end we each took a pill and retired to our separate rooms, anticipating a long, restful sleep. At one A.M., the alarm went off. Fire drill! Ever put your coat on over your nightgown and wait in a freezing parking lot for half an hour with two hundred strangers? While doped up on melatonin? Not that we needed it, but that was a bonding experience.

I can hardly remember it, but my life must've been a lot duller before Nora came into it. I introduced her to my mother, and afterward Mom said, "I liked her a lot. She's not like any of your other friends, is she?" No. She's not. She's the only person I know besides my husband who does dogs' voices—that's just one thing, and it's not insignificant, that I love about her. In a lot of ways she's the sister I never had. She was famous when I met her, but now it's ridiculous, she's a household name, an icon—and still exactly the same funny, generous, outgoing, shy, opinionated, fiercely loyal friend I made fifteen years ago. I want to tell you about the time we drove back from New York with the brake on, or the time Nora drove *ninety miles an hour* all the way to the airport because I'd gotten the time wrong and made us late for a plane to some conference or other. So many stories. Or the time she called up a fellow author who'd dissed one of my books in public and just *blistered* her, reduced her to sputtering, apologetic incoherence—all because she loves me.

Like a sister. That's the way I love her.

Patricia Gaffney

Nora with Pat Gaffney

Nora and I have roomed together so often we know each other better than sisters. Nora's a night owl. I'm a dawn riser.

Several years ago we checked into our suite, only to discover that we'd be sharing a king-sized bed. Okay, we thought. We could do this.

One night Nora crawled into bed hours after I'd gone to sleep. As she was settling in, she heard me whispering in my sleep. She managed to decipher just enough to have her intrigued. Next day she told me about it, and I tried to recall what I'd been dreaming about. No luck. That night she stayed up really late, and when she crawled into bed, I woke and decided to play a trick on her. I started whispering again, and she moved closer, hoping to decipher what I was saying. I almost had her believing I was asleep until I started giggling. The two of us were awake for hours after that, still laughing.

Ruth Ryan Langan

New York, New York!

ONCE NORA, Ruth Ryan Langan, and I booked a suite at a posh hotel. The people in the suite decided to stay on and refused to move out. The hotel was undergoing renovations. The three of us ended up in a long, narrow room that looked like a run-down college dormitory. No bed, just a pull-out couch and a cot. We flipped for the cot. I lost.

Despite our disappointment in the room, we had a marvelous time, talking half the night and giggling like three sisters sharing a bedroom. We exchanged news and gossip, read each others' manuscripts-in-progress, took turns putting on makeup in the hankie-sized bathroom. At night we'd lie awake talking over our hopes and dreams, while taxis honked and ambulances wailed and the energy and excitement of New York swirled around us. We were there in The Dormitory when Nora's editor called to tell her she had her first fantastic review in *Publishers Weekly*, and celebrated the occasion with pizza and champagne. Hmmm. I sense a theme here. Whenever we get together we always seem to wind up with wine and pizza. In a way, the two sum up Nora pretty well. Nourishing and down-to-earth, yet sparklingly sophisticated. A world-traveling bestseller, who will always stop to autograph a book, speak to a fan, or give encouragement to a struggling writer; yet Nora is never so happy as when she's home surrounded by family and friends, her dogs and cats and gardens. (Not to mention a very snappy collection of earrings, shoes, handbags, and rings.)

Marianne Willman

Nora, Pat Gaffney, and I have been good friends for about fifteen or sixteen years. We live about an hour driving time from one another and every two or three months we get together for "lunch." That's what we still call it, although it has long since morphed into many other things—like lunch, shopping, and dinner, too. There's nothing we like more than being pampered, so we frequently go to a day spa and get facials, manicures, haircuts, and massages and *then* do lunch, shopping, and dinner. In early December we "lunch" at Tyson's Corner, a huge shopping mall outside Washington, D.C. We meet at noon and . . . have lunch, of course, then we Christmas shop . . . till we drop, have a late dinner, rent adjoining rooms at the Embassy Suites for the night, get up, shop some more, have lunch *again,* and go home.

You see the pattern here? We like to eat and shop . . . and drink. But we never shop drunk—we're very serious about our shopping. Although we have made some impulse buys that would make you wonder. One of our favorites is to—spur of the moment—get new eyeglasses. In and out in an hour . . . all three of us. We've done that several times, in fact. Another time we all bought *huge* sets of luggage, and after that it was cell phones. My husband shudders when I tell him I'm having "lunch" with the girls.

Another thing we *luuuuv* doing, but usually with a larger group of our writing pals—say, late one night during a conference when we can all get comfortable in our play clothes or jammies—is to beg Nora to do a "reading." We never have to beg very hard. We give Nora a book and she reads it to us, acting out all the characters in the story!—including the secondary characters which are usually the funniest anyway. Her writing talent doesn't hold a candle to her acting abilities. (Well, maybe one candle.) We particularly like to have her read historicals to us as there's usually more dialect in them. She is a *magnificent* Scottish Highlander—except that they sometimes sound exactly like her Ohio River riffraff from a western novel . . . but we never complain.

Mary Kay McComas

Nora, Jaci Hanna, Mary Kay McComas, and Pat Gaffney

Take My Husband. Please.

WHAT CAN I say about a woman who has, over the years, shared hotel suites and limos and adventures with me? Not to mention her spiffy Italian shoes, her office, and her husband. "Generous" doesn't begin to describe her.

I suppose I should explain that last one. One day as I was writing I heard the gentle sound of rain beyond my windows . . . but much louder than usual. In fact, it sounded as if it was coming from my office cabinets. It was. I opened the door and rain was dripping inside them.

My husband fixed the plugged gutter that caused the problem and repaired the roof damage, then went blithely off to work in Massachusetts. Six weeks later, while Ky was away, I scooted my chair back and sank down into a hole like a moose in quicksand. The leak had rotted out the floor beneath the carpet. My husband was still in Massachusetts and I had a problem. Nora's husband, the estimable BW, had time on his hands and Nora had a deadline. (When does she not?)

We decided we could help each other—after all, what are friends for? So BW drove all the way to Michigan and fixed my floor, then turned an unused enclosed porch into a library. He didn't get home to his Nora again for two weeks.

See what I mean about generous?

Marianne Willman

"John Grisham, watch your back."

—*Entertainment Weekly* on SANCTUARY

"Roberts is indeed a word artist, painting her story and her characters with vitality and verve."

—*Los Angeles Daily News*

PART NINE

the fans

WHY DO SO many readers love Nora Roberts? In their own words, self-confessed "Noraholics" talk about why they love Nora's books and how Nora has touched their lives. From every part of the country, and from around the world, here's what they have to say. . . .

This was the "original group" that helped to start the TTP pilgrimages. Back row: Tracey O'Donnell, Nora, Sue Noyes, Carolyn Smith, Wendy, and Debby Moran; front row: Nina (Wym) Friedman, Jaci Hanna, and Diane Noyes.

When I think of Nora Roberts, I think of relationships—of love and friendship. And I'm not talking about her wonderful stories; I'm talking about the incredible friendships that I have made since I first had contact with Nora back in March of 1997.

Through on-line message boards, chats, e-mails, instant messages, signing events, and other special occasions, I have met some of the best people in the entire world—and I know that others feel the same way. We all started with one thing in common: our love of Nora's stories.

Nora has created an incredible legacy that goes far beyond her stories.

Sue Noyes, Owner, ADWOFF.com

From a pair of mother-and-daughter fans:

My name is Jean K. Brightcliffe. I currently reside in Philadelpha, PA. I'm a 74-year-old grandmom and even became a great-grandmom in the past year. After spending most of my life being a wife and mother, I never got the opportunity to do much traveling other than taking the kids to the shore. However, since I raised my children and became a widow, I started reading Nora Roberts's novels. She has whisked me all over the country and even the world. I've visited Ireland many times and even walked along the streets of Venice! Thank you, Nora! I look forward to our next journey together.

My name is Jeanne M. Brightcliffe. I'm 50 years old and a resident of Philadelphia, PA. I've been on Disability Retirement since the age of 48 and I don't know what I'd do without Nora Roberts and her wonderful books. She not only writes intriguing stories but creates characters who stay in your heart and mind forever. In fact, you wouldn't mind having them over for a visit since they become so "real" for you!

There are a couple of things I really appreciate about Nora Roberts. First, and most important, is her consistency. I *know* when I pick up a "Nora" book, I won't be disappointed. I know I'm in for an enjoyable experience.

I really love the way Nora interacts with her fans. The way she puts herself out there for us is amazing. I don't know of many other (or any other) authors who would so consistently put up with our questions, shenanigans, etc., with such grace and humor.

As a result of reading Nora's books, and participating in several message boards about the books, I have also made many what I hope will be lifelong friendships with people all over the country.

Thanks, Nora, for all the good times.

Elaine Schmoock, Pennsylvania

My name is Renee McNeil and I live in Long Island, NY. I am 26 years old.

I started reading Nora about 6 years ago with *Montana Sky*. I've been hooked since. Nora's books make me feel like I have traveled to Ireland, Montana, Maryland, and all the other places that she describes so well. There are not enough words to express how much I appreciate Nora's writing and storytelling abilities. When things get bad, I've been known to pick up *Montana Sky* and reread the book. I can probably repeat the entire book, with the amount of times that I have read it! I am glad that the companion is going to be published so that other readers will discover what a wonderful author Nora is.

In front of Ruby Tuesdays in Frederick after dinner. In the background are Nina (Wym) Friedman, Tracey O'Donnell, Carolyn Smith, Wendy, and Jaci Hann. Nora, of course, is in her way cool car!

Nora never forgets a fan, she has, in my humble opinion, a way of making each one seem special. And seeing how many of us there are, this is amazing. She has added to my life not only great books to read but worldwide acquaintances/friends. Nora Roberts (and her willingness to share herself with us) may be the reason people were originally drawn together on the Internet, but these friendships have become a real part of everyday life. Thanks Nora.

Jill Purinton, Lamar, MO

Having read just about everything Nora Roberts/J. D. Robb has ever written I feel safe to say that her storytelling ability has eased the wear of everyday life from my mind. The magic of her words creates a cocoon around the reader that keeps you warm and entertained for hours. In the three years since I discovered Nora Roberts's books, I have made a point of collecting as many as I could. They become like old friends who are always around for a quick visit or a long leisurely read. She has the remarkable ability to take the oldest story (man meets woman) and make it new again. She enthralls her readers not with overblown and complicated plots but rather with quiet and stalwart characters. Each of these amazing characters comes to life under her careful guidance; their hopes, fears, dreams, and realities become our own. In the end I would have to say that in my opinion, Nora Roberts is a master wordsmith who provides endless enjoyment and whose work can always be counted on to lift your spirits and warm your heart.

Tara Wong, Nova Scotia, Canada

Nora just received a folder from Phyllis Lannick detailing all of the "baskets" that various people had raffled off to help earn money for Nora's foundation. Behind Nora, to her right, are JB Brightclivve and Jill Purinton; to Nora's left are Vicky and Debbie Rogers.

Top Ten Reasons Why I Love Nora!!

10. She created Roarke.
9. She releases more than one book a year, thus feeding my addiction at regular intervals.
8. She writes trilogies. (I'm a sucker for a good trilogy.)
7. She hasn't strangled any of her fans for asking the same questions over and over. (Example: Where do you get your ideas? When is Eve going to have a baby? Any plans to revisit one of the trilogies?)
6. She is the only author I can read while happily ignoring the messy room in which I am sitting.
5. She is the only author I can read while happily ignoring my children who are sitting with me in the messy room. (Ummm, Disney movies *are* considered educational, aren't they?)
4. Did I mention Roarke?
3. Thanks to her I've met so many great people through ADWOFF [www.adwoff.com, a fan website].
2. Thanks to her I've traveled to a glass workshop in Ireland, a winery in California, a ranch in Montana, a futuristic New York City, and so many other places without leaving the comfort (or mess, as the case may be) of my home.

And the number one reason why I love Nora:

1. SHE CREATED ROARKE!!!

Kirsten Cheskey

My name is Lalitha Sundaram. I am originally from India and came to the U.S. about twenty-two years ago as a student. I started reading Nora in 1994. I picked up *Hidden Riches* and *Sacred Sins* for a long plane ride. To this day, they are two of my favorite books. They opened to me a world of Nora books and I went on a binge. I have not missed a single one since.

When you read a Nora Roberts book there are some definite guarantees: You *will* get a great story. You *will* get a set of believable characters. You *will* get a heroine who is not a pushover and, like all romance genre, you *will* get a happy ending. In addition to her characters, Nora's dialogues are witty, funny, and simple conversations that one of us would have. Nora knows her men and does family interaction like no other author. I am in awe of her imagination, be it her contemporary romance, romantic suspense, or her futuristic suspense.

Nora Roberts has been called the Queen, the Goddess of romance writing, the Doyenne, the Wordsmith of our times, to name a few. To me she is all of the above and more. Thanks to Nora, I am proud to be a Noraholic.

I started reading (romance novels, mysteries, etc.) about five years ago. I am a 30-year-old woman that used to think that sitting down with a book had to be very boring. My mom is the one that got me to reading. J. D. Robb's "In Death" series were some of the first books that she got me to read. Since the books were set in the future I really didn't want to read them. But my mom stayed after me for over a year to read these books! I finally gave in and read the first book, *Naked in Death,* and I have been a Nora fan ever since!

Nora Roberts has given me and my mom something that we have in common now . . . the love of reading. My mom has always been the reader of the family. Now I can share that with her.

Cindy Sims, Tennessee

At the Bavarian Inn. This is a shot of the second group that attended the Turn the Page anniversary signing.

I have been reading Nora's books since I was in college—I was away from home and somehow I got signed up for Silhouette's Reader's Service. Some of the books were good, some not so good, and some exceptional. I always looked forward to the months when Nora's books were included. After I left college to start life in the real world, I didn't have time to read as much so I stopped the Reader's Service. However, I was hooked on Nora so if I saw one of her books in the store it was an automatic purchase. It seemed as the years went on her books just kept getting better and better, and I started tracking release dates and buying her books almost as soon as they were released. Nora's writing has helped me get through some tough times. When the real world threatens to overwhelm, it is amazing that I can pick up one of her books and get lost in a world she has created and make the real world go away for a time. By the time reality intrudes, the time of peace is enough to make it easier to deal with life.

Then in the spring of 2002 I sold one of Nora's books (a duplicate copy, of course) on eBay and the woman that I sold it to told me about ADWOFF and that Nora posted there! Well, I couldn't believe it. I had been to her website many times and read her guest book, checked out her publishing schedule, and read some of her travel reports, but I didn't really believe that an author could be as accessible to her fans as I was told. So, I decided to check it out. I lurked for a while reading posts, and I was amazed at how open she is and how much of life she shares with her fans. She doesn't seem to get tired of answering really stupid questions, she has a wonderful sense of fun, she shares her joy over being a nana for the first time, she commiserates with those who share their sorrows, and she is more than just a writer to her fans—she is a woman who understands the day-to-day joys and trials of being wife, mother, daughter, sister, and friend. I have never met Nora in person, although I hope to one day be able to make it to one of her book signings at her husband's bookstore in Maryland. However, I can say that through her work and her posts on the board, I feel like I have been given a glimpse into her world and that if I am ever lucky enough to meet her, I will be meeting a friend.

Susan Faber

I started reading Nora Roberts books early on in the Silhouette line and followed her books on an interested but casual level. Then in 1996 my sister, Crystal, fell seriously ill and I spent three solid weeks at the hotel watching her battle for her life. I spent the days in her room and the evenings at an on-site guest room and had virtually no escape from the situation. One evening I picked up a book at the gift shop—*Naked in Death* by J. D. Robb—having no idea that J. D. Robb was Nora Roberts until later. That book in so many ways saved my state of mind, providing me an escape from the real world and characters to care for that were in a healthy, strong place in their lives. I quickly went back to the gift shop and picked up two more J. D. Robbs as further escape and have not missed a Nora book since. No other author or series of books can hold the emotional attachment and meaning these do for me. Though my sister later lost her battle, I feel a connection to her when I read the J. D. Robb books and a connection to Nora for providing me that feeling. What a powerful gift.

Jennifer Tucker, Seattle, WA

Nora Roberts's stories are superlative sketches of the human spirit. With intelligent heroines and tough-yet-lovable heroes, Nora paints extraordinary portraits of struggle, faith, hope, and, of course, love, with precision humor weaved throughout.

Her dynamic characters compose some of the most enduring fictional families ever written. Each page turned is a memorable opportunity to visit such families as the Quinns, who raise a troubled youth to be an honorable man; the MacGregors, who find love thanks to a meddlesome patriarch; the Gallaghers, who find time to fall in love while composing Irish music, running a pub, and conversing with a faerie prince. These families are just a few examples of the depth and range of Nora's characters, which demonstrates how exceptional a writer she is.

After the last page is turned, there's a sense of joyous completion at being allowed to witness such an emotional journey. Thanks to Nora Roberts and her tales of love, the world is a better place.

Christyna M. Hunter, Lovettsville, VA

The first time I read a novel by this talented lady, I could immediately see that the depth of the characters and events were of a caliber I had not yet experienced. I was able to envision the story in three dimensions and with such clarity! Nora's characters have hopes, dreams, fears, insecurities, idiosyncrasies, and personalities that endear them to the reader. Her stories can pull out a variety of emotions in the reader, as well as make you think, teach you something new, and offer you a perfectly safe escape into the possibilities of life and relationships as Nora sees them. Her characters become like friends and family to her fans, and her novels are devoured and reread by those of us who claim to be "Noraholics." As for Nora herself, she is gracious, friendly, funny, smart, and so accommodating to her fans. We love her, and as long as she has a story to tell, we will all be happily waiting to read it!

Dawn Ball, Charles Town, WV

(just a quick drive to Turn the Page Bookstore)

"When Roberts puts her expert fingers on the pulse of romance, legions of fans feel the heartbeat."

I've seen this *Publishers Weekly* quote on quite a few book covers recently. To me, this is one of the statements that goes some way to explaining why so many people read Nora Roberts's books, why she is an "auto-buy" for us. Why I snatch up her books when they first appear in the store, or click "add to basket" without a second thought. I know that 98 percent of the time I will close the book feeling completely satisfied, having watched the characters move towards their inevitable "happily ever after," while feeling real twinges of sympathy at whatever obstacles they face and literally cheering when they triumph. I read romance for the sense of escapism that comes with setting my own life aside for a while and diving into a book that will grip me; with characters that move me; and which will take me on an interesting, exciting, funny, moving ride that ends—of course—in a "happily ever after." Nora's books do that for me.

Tak-Hui Chow, London, England

As an English major, I read a lot. Books, poetry, drama, all genres—mostly classics. So I'm pretty picky about what I read for fun in my spare time. I was always a little of what you might call a "literature snob." I had favorite authors and specific genres of popular fiction that I was willing to read for fun, but turned my nose up at anything that could possibly be construed as "romance novels." My mistake.

Then one day, after much grief from a friend, I finally agreed to pick up one of Nora Roberts's novels. I will be eternally grateful. For the last two years I've been quickly working my way through anything and everything that Nora has ever written. She has an incredible style of writing that becomes highly addictive and has completely obliterated all misconceptions I had about the romance genre entirely. Nora doesn't just write "sex novels." She writes love stories, mysteries, family sagas, and stories that make you examine your own life. Her characters are real—with fears and doubts and faults just like everyone else. They laugh, they cry, they love, they grow—and she takes you along for the ride. I finish every book of hers with a great big smile on my face, and count down the days until the next is published.

Nora has also broken down my views on what a "famous author" would be like. Having met her at several book signings as well as communicated with her on ADWOFF (Internet message board), she's everything that I didn't expect in a world-renowned author. She's unpretentious, down-to-earth, incredibly kind, and funny, and she opens her life and herself up to her fans in a way that makes you feel like you're really seeing her as she is. She's accessible rather than coming across as a well-created publicity figure, and that makes her even more special to her readers.

Nora's opened up a new world for me. I reread her books time and time again, falling in love with her characters over and over. I'm no longer ashamed to be found in the romance section of the bookstore. "Don't knock it till you've tried it" is my new favorite motto where books are concerned, and I will give her books to anyone and everyone who are willing to try them. I've gone from being a "literature snob" to being a "Nora snob" because I'll tell you that "nothing beats a Nora"! I can't thank her enough for every book, every moment of enjoyment and escape that she's offered me. At ADWOFF, we call her the Queen, and she truly deserves the title!

Kelly E. Fenton, Columbia, MD

Nora holds a drawing given to her to commemorate Turn the Page's second anniversary in 1997.

Hi. My name is Chris Plank and I live in St. Louis, MO, USA.

I'm a Noraholic.

I have been reading romance books for a long time. One of the first books that I picked up was a Nora Roberts book. I enjoy the way that Nora writes—she makes the characters come to life for me.

The J. D. Robb "In Death" series are some of the best books that I have ever read.

I had never read this type of book before—a friend told me about this series and that I had to read them. I was hooked from the first page of the first book and the rest, as they say, is history. I can hardly wait for the next installment in the series.

Thanks, Nora, for all the wonderful hours of reading enjoyment that you have given me.

Nora at one of the local jewelry stores in Danville. Patricia Gaffney, Katie Dunneback, and Mary Kay McComas all focus on the Queen of power shopping.

Nora's really amazing. She can make simple things very special, common people alive and vivid, and her stories remind us of the good things we sometimes forget, like values, true friendships, family, and pets.

We love you, Nora! Keep them coming!

Rhea Luz Hernandez, Metro Manila, Philippines

Nora's writing blows me away.

When I read about the sinking of the *Lusitania* in *The Three Fates,* I was so in awe, I literally went "Wow!" That's what I like about Nora.

She has a way of pulling you into her stories so that you are there experiencing it right along with the characters. She draws you in and keeps you until the very end. For me that is the ultimate, to be able to immerse myself so deeply in a book that I wonder, at the end of a loud argumentative scene, if I was the one actually doing the yelling.

When I read her books I find myself laughing at the silly and sweet, or crying at the sad and sentimental; I feel the anger during an argument. Reading a new book by her is like visiting with an old friend I haven't seen in a while. Sometimes the characters are people we both know and she's catching me up on how they've been doing. Other times she's telling me about some new people she's met. And I always feel like I know them personally.

Reading is a part of me. And to be able to trust an author's writing, like I do Nora's, is very important. I like knowing that I can pick up one of her books without knowing the story and that I will be entertained completely. I get a great story, great characters, love, suspense, the whole nine yards. Every time.

It's hard to adequately describe why I like Nora, except to say any book by her is definitely a keeper.

Debbie Bailey, Alpharetta, GA

I've always been an avid reader. Murder mysteries, suspense, fantasy. However, I never read romance novels. I was turned off by their Fabio or bodice-ripper covers. But when I was 45, I read my first Nora Roberts novel. I quickly learned that Nora doesn't write romances. Her books give a glimpse into the lives of real people in real situations. Yes, they fall in love but they also laugh, cry, and argue. They live.

Since reading my first Nora Roberts novel, I've collected all of her books, including the out-of-print titles.

Reading one of her books is like meeting new friends for the first time. The only good thing about finishing one of her books is the excitement of looking forward to her next one.

Ani "goddessani" Kendig, Poulsbo, WA

From the moment I learned to read, books became an escape for me. I loved to "get lost" in a great story.

One day I picked up Nora Roberts's *Homeport*, an intriguing novel of romance, mystery, and suspense. Nora drew me into that story from page one, and I remember thinking, "Man! This Nora chick can tell a really great story." I could not put the book down. Just one more chapter and then I'll go to bed, I'd think. But one more chapter became one more chapter and then one more chapter. . . .

I began to seek out other novels written by Nora Roberts, and in my searches I came across a website dedicated to Nora that is known as ADWOFF.

Through the ADWOFF message board I have made friends that are very dear to me. Together, we talk, we laugh, we cry. We are held together by a common thread. That thread is Nora and her novels.

A love for Nora and the mesmerizing stories she tells has brought together thousands of people from all over the world. We discuss Nora's books, but we also talk about our lives and our friendships with one another. Several of us have met in person and we have such fun times with each other when we do.

Whatever my mood, I know that I can immerse myself in a Nora Roberts novel and feel comfort and understanding.

If I need to escape from my life for a little while, I know that I can do so with one of Nora's books.

The following is a poem I wrote for Nora. I gave it to her the first time I met her at a book signing. It was simply my way of giving a little something back to her for all the wonderful stories she has told me. A way to make her laugh. A way to just say "Thanks."

In a small town in Maryland in the winter of '79,
A young woman struggled to keep from losing her mind.
The chocolate was scarce, the snow was deep,
All she really wanted to do was snuggle and sleep.
But with two young boys and no school for days,
She felt like a mouse trapped in a maze.
So, armed with a #2 pencil and a spiral notepad,
She began to write and realized it was not just a fad.
She wrote when she could, at home and away,
The release she felt helped see her through the day.
Page after page, the momentum built.
She wove a story as some might a quilt.

With passion, persistence, and perseverance she led,
In time she was rewarded with Irish Thoroughbred.
She no longer felt the need to flee to Bora Bora,
Romance had a new name; and the name was Nora.
The MacGregors, the Gallaghers, and oh, those Quinns!
All of Nora's men keep me on needles and pins.
Whether set in Ireland, Italy, or America's own shore,
Nora always takes her readers on a hell of a tour.
When you thought she couldn't get any better, a new story she began to weave.
Along came J. D. Robb who gave us Roarke and Eve.
Nora and her writing may have had a humble start,
But her stories and characters will always touch your heart.

Suz (a.k.a. Suzanne a.k.a. da Raisin) McErlain, Holland, PA

I've been a devoted "Noraholic" since 1989 when, under stress from college midterms, I went to a bookstore and discovered *Sweet Revenge*. I was hooked! And was lucky, too, since that was when many of her older books were being reissued as the Language of Love set, so I now own every story she has published.

Nora Roberts's books make me laugh out loud and sometimes cry when her words so realistically describe someone's pain. I can get lost in her words, and forget about my little problems for a while. It's a great gift she has—storytelling—and I'm so glad Nora is a very prolific writer.

As for the J. D. Robb books, let me say that I resisted at first. I was like, "I don't care for mysteries." But once I finally read *Naked in Death*, I found out how much I love reading a continuing series with characters I've really come to love and identify with.

And, last, because I love Nora's books so much, I became part of a great cyber community at ADWOFF.com. Discussing your books, asking Nora "stoooopid" questions, and just chatting about life in general has been a great part of my life. It's because of Nora Roberts that I now have a bunch of fantastic new friends.

Nora Roberts truly is *my* Queen!

Robyn Beckerman, Rockaway, NJ

A wise woman told me to write from the heart. The heart is never wrong.

When it comes to Nora Roberts's books, that's what it's all about. Heart. Nora writes amazing stories of hearts and lives joining together to make something not necessarily perfect, but absolutely beautiful. And believable. Not only that, but because of the reach of Nora's books throughout the world, women from all walks of life, all ages and races, have come together to one place and with their love of Nora's writing in common, created friendships that will last a lifetime.

I've read Nora's books for almost seven years, and every time I pick up a new one the same anticipation fills me, because I know that no matter which book I'm reading, as long as the cover says *Nora Roberts*, I'm getting a story that will bring me laughter and joy and a very happy ending.

To me, Nora isn't just a talented woman and writer, but a link that has brought something special to the lives of readers everywhere.

Melissa Rivnie (a.k.a. Mel), Bozeman, MT, USA

At a restaurant to help Nora celebrate her birthday late. Nora is holding the Liberty Bell, a gift from JB and Mama Jean Brightcliffe.

In 1981, bedridden during a pregnancy, I discovered Silhouette romances. Initially, I bought the new releases each month, but after my husband made noises about wallet sizes, I began to narrow my choices to a certain few authors I looked for each month.

Nora Roberts headed that list. Her stories were filled with people I wanted to meet, heroes I fell in love with, and heroines I admired for their honesty and spirit. Her romances are tender, but never mushy, and filled with humor and a quiet joy.

In over twenty years, I haven't missed one.

Carol Holko, Pittsburgh, PA

My first Nora was *Brazen Virtue.* It was published as a part of a series here—something like "Venus—Books for Women." After that came *Hot Ice,* and then nothing for a long, long time. I got really hooked on Nora when I was in the U.K. for two years as an au pair. When I went to the local public library to find something to read her name was familiar so I borrowed the book titled *Born in Ice.* I really enjoyed it and continued to check out her books from the local library, or bought them when I saw one was published in the U.K. They are really special stories for me, not just because she is a gifted storyteller and I can get lost in the world of her novels, and forget about my little problems for a while, but I also learned a lot about the English language through her. When I came back home to Hungary I gave away all the books I acquired in England, except the Nora Roberts novels.

I did the same when I was in the States. Since then I try to get all I can from her. I read most of her single titles either in English or in Hungarian. I am really grateful that I speak English as I have double the chances to get hold of a Nora book. And I am also glad that she is a prolific writer because I hope that I will never run out of her stories.

When I start to read a Nora Roberts book there are a few things I know for sure: I'll be seduced by strong men and women, I'll be reading and dreaming about great adventures and interesting relationships, and I will feel the magic. Reading Nora helps you believe there is magic in this world.

I am really grateful for the Internet and to the ADWOFF site and I also think that Nora is a generous person as she takes the time to interact with her fans from all over the world.

In the last two years she became very popular in Hungary. Since last autumn J. D. Robb is available and they (the local publishers) are really fast because now we are at *Holiday in Death* and they promise to publish more this year.

Tünde Gabriella Lepp, Budapest, Hungary

Nora does for writing what the *Mona Lisa* did for art. She opened it up to the masses. Where else can you find a writer that can write so quickly and so expertly? Not with just one genre, but with at least three. Where else will you find such a different array of fans? Every walk of life has read at least one of Nora's books. She has heroines that make you proud, and heroes that make you *hot*. Every author can write; not every one can spin a tale like the great Nora Roberts! When you open a Nora Roberts/J. D. Robb book you become a part of the story. You start to care about the characters as if they were long-lost friends. Thank you, Nora, for giving us so many books to escape into.

Kimberly Mitchell, South Carolina

I can't tell you how much Nora's books mean to me. There just aren't words to describe it. She just captures human emotions so well and tells a story that is genuine, warm, and funny all at the same time. Her books about families are just how a family should be. The books touch on the squabbles, the affection, and the respect most families have for one another. The books set in Ireland teach us something while at the same time making us feel that we are actually there experiencing it.

What amazes me the most is that despite her popularity she is so approachable. On the ADWOFF message board she takes time to answer all of our questions, no matter how stupid they are!

She should be a role model to all writers out there. I know she is to me. The story about the blizzard and being stuck with her children gives all of us hope that if she can do it, we can too. It brings her down to earth and makes her real.

Melanie Jenkins, Olney, MD

A guarantee. That's what I get from every book by Nora. Great story? Guaranteed. Believable characters in believable situations? Guaranteed.

I was a Noraholic long before I even knew the term. I have at least one copy of every story she's published. I'm not a fan because Nora's a fun and skilled writer who also indulges her readers with her time and attention—even though she is and she does. I buy and read Nora's books for one simple reason. I never have to wonder whether my money is well spent. Nora's work is guaranteed enjoyment, every time, from cover to cover.

Carla R. Garnett, Hyattsville, MD

I've been reading Nora's books basically since the start. I believe the first book of hers I read was *Song of the West*. I enjoyed this new author, her style of writing, her characters, and their stories so much I would buy her books any time I would see a new book on the newsstand. Well, I've been doing that ever since. Anything Nora writes I buy—the story basically doesn't matter as her writing is so amazing that the actual story is secondary.

I say it all the time—she's ruined me for other authors because when I just finish a new Nora book I end up going back and rereading other books she's written as I just can't let it go.

I personally don't have a Nora story as such because I've never met her and have never been in her bookstore for a book signing (I'm not exactly close by) but from what I can observe on ADWOFF she's a pretty special person just by the fact that she comes on the board and chats with us and answers more questions than you'd think it possible to ask. But I think she's a great sport (for doing that), she has a wonderful sense of humor (which is visible in her books) and an amazing brilliant writing talent, and she's a lovely lady.

Being that I've been a reader and fan of hers for about twenty years it's a great feeling to be able to come on ADWOFF and check in with her and her numerous fans and make friendships with other Nora fans on the board. I feel there's a *real* connection between reader and author. I honestly can't imagine too many authors of her caliber doing the same.

Oh, I can't sign off without saying I truly believe the most amazing characters Nora ever created are Eve and Roarke in the J. D. Robb books. I cannot articulate how amazing these characters and those books are. Nora has created something truly, truly incredible. Seriously, her talent truly astounds me and I can't imagine my life without her books!!!

Lisa Blackler, Newfoundland, Canada

I first "met" Nora Roberts out of sheer boredom while roaming around Target. I stumbled on *Rising Tides,* the second of her Chesapeake Bay trilogy, and fell in love with the characters, the lives they lead, and the stories they hold. Since then, I've sunk into dozens more of Nora's books and my reaction is the same every time I turn that last page: a contented sigh of longing to be part of that story and for the story to continue.

Of course, every time I finish one of Nora's "In Death" books the reaction is a bit different. I have the sudden urge to kick some ass, beat up a computer, cut my hair myself, and search for Roarke.

And one of these days I'm going to find him.

Thanks, Nora, for being a warm blanket when it's cold, a shoulder to lean on when the day isn't going so well, and a constant companion who reminds me that the sweetest things in life are only a page turn away.

Sarah Kissell, Burbank, CA

One day about five or six years ago, I was looking for a book with a happy ending. What better source than the romance department of my local bookstore? I was overwhelmed by my choices, but I finally made a decision that would change my life. I picked up a book called *Honest Illusions* by an author named Nora Roberts. Why did I pick that book? It was a silly reason, really, but one that I've never regretted. My choice was based on the fact that I share the same first and last initial with this author, N and R. Maybe it was fate, maybe just dumb luck. But Nora's gift for storytelling hooked me immediately. I fell in love with reading. In that first year I went from reading two to three books a year to reading over a hundred books a year. The love affair continues almost six years later.

Nancy Rairden, Arcola, IL

I started reading Nora's books in 1998 when my sister, who has been a fan since 1981, gave me the Chesapeake Bay trilogy as a gift. I was immediately hooked and spent the next year or so working my way through her impressive backlist. When her 2000 *Carolina Moon* tour schedule was posted on-line, I was thrilled to see Nashville listed. I decided to fly my sister to Nashville to attend the signing with me—the perfect gift for her upcoming fiftieth birthday. A few weeks before the signing, I contacted Nora via e-mail, told her about my sister's birthday, and invited her to have a drink with us before the signing. To my surprise, she accepted!

My sister was impressed and loved her "gift" but I think the person who was a little overwhelmed, in the end, was me. Not only did I get to meet and spend a little time with someone I admire a great deal, but due to Nora's generosity, I got to share that experience with my much-loved big sister. The same sister, in fact, who fostered my love of reading from a young age, introduced me to Nora's books, and has always been my best friend.

I worried about meeting Nora. Heroes are hard to come by and what if I was disappointed? Nothing could have been further from the truth. What really stood out for me was that this is a highly talented, hardworking, and staggeringly successful woman who puts on her pants one leg at a time, just like the rest of us. Her level of success isn't due to coincidence or luck. Nora has taken a natural gift for storytelling and driven it home with hard work and discipline. The fact that she wraps all of that in a warm, friendly, down-to-earth manner is the truest gift she gives her readers.

Annette Gerst Brown, Nashville, TN

The first Nora book I ever bought was her first published novel, *Irish Thoroughbred*. I've bought every book since. The reason? Simple. She weaves words into consistently enchanting stories with credible characters, honest dialogue, and gentle humor. Thank goodness. I need her stories. Especially now. In a world seemingly gone mad, there is no better gift than the ability to lose myself in the pages of a magical book where good triumphs over evil and love conquers all. Nora's stories help keep me sane.

Wymzee (a.k.a. Nina Friedman), La Jolla, CA

Close-up of the quilt honoring Nora

I read my first Nora Roberts book when I was 16 years old. A typical teenager, I was all attitude and insolence. A friend dared me to read *One Man's Art.* The gauntlet at my feet turned out to be a hook in my mouth. I was captivated by Nora's ability to cast dreams, and weave emotion, with her stories.

I think about the choices we make. How timing and circumstance play major roles in our lives. Without that subtle challenge from a friend, I would not have spent the last twenty years absorbed, and entertained, by the work of this exceptional writer. Her stories are as precious to me as my own memories.

At such a pivotal time in my life I found someone I could respect and admire. The strength and resolve of her heroines not only made it okay to be a strong woman, they made it a necessity.

An intrinsic part of myself has always felt empowered by Nora's words, as well as engrossed in her stories. The opportunity to escape into the world of Nora Roberts is a gift I continue to treasure.

Tonya Wood, Stoutsville, OH

I have been reading Nora Roberts books for years. I started when she was just writing categories (Silhouettes), and I remember so clearly when I discovered what I think was her first "non-category"—*Hot Ice.* I was in a bookstore in Orange, CA, where I lived at the time. I remember getting so excited that she was doing a bigger (i.e., longer) format of book. I immediately bought it, and couldn't wait for more.

Then, many years later, after moving to Colorado, I signed up for the Internet finally, and I found the boards where I could read about authors and their books and have discussions with other readers. Lo and behold, I actually got to post notes to Nora herself. I thought this was just super.

While posting on these boards, I met not only Nora, but a group of women who were also fans and readers. I actually traveled to Maryland for a Nora signing event and met in person these women I had just communicated with on the Internet. In the years since, I have stayed friends with these women, getting together off and on. And have had many other opportunities to meet and talk with Nora.

What all this means to me is this: In meeting a "personality" that I never dreamed I would have a chance to ever meet—let alone dine with or spend time talking with—I met a wonderful, creative soul who uses her heart to create books loved by so many. We tease Nora about being "the Queen," but she does illustrate a queen's better qualities—dignity, class, compassion for the people around her, a sense of humor, and the ability to make a reader from Denver feel special. And Nora—via her time with us on the Internet and in person—has given me a connection to a group of women I feel privileged to call friends.

For my friends, her stories, and her time—I will always thank Nora.

Debby Moran, Denver, CO

My name is Denise Lewis. I am a 34-year-old Nora Roberts fan. I was in love with books until I was in the fourth grade. My teachers and parents would not allow me to read books that were of interest to me, so I stopped reading altogether. Today I realize why, but that does not change the fact that reading became a burden instead of fun.

Three years ago I was between jobs and feeling under the weather. My mother brought me a goodie basket with several Nora Roberts books. Reluctantly I decided to read one of the books. I picked up *Inner Harbor*. I could not put the book down and finished it in one day. I picked up a book by another author and could not keep interested in it. I made a trip to the library and checked out *Rising Tides* and the next week checked out *Sea Swept*. I soon learned that I read the books in the wrong order, but that did not matter. I loved reading Ms. Roberts's books. Soon I had checked out and read all the Nora Roberts books the library had. I then began purchasing the ones I had read and the new ones. I fell in love with books for the second time in my life. It seems like an eternity waiting for Ms. Roberts's books to be released.

I try to introduce Nora Roberts books to everyone I know. When I'm at the bookstore and I see someone looking for a book, I grab the newest Nora book and offer it to them. Many have since become Noraholics also. I would like to take this opportunity to thank Ms. Roberts for bringing reading back into my life.

What does Nora mean to me? Above all, she means wonderful, readable, enjoyable stories, with characters that are so real I almost forget they're fiction. But that's not all. I started reading romance because of Nora, met a lot of wonderful people because of our shared love of her books, and found an enjoyable hobby in managing on-line communities of other fans that's kept me active and involved in spite of a chronic illness. As if that were not enough, Nora is one of the most accessible authors, always making fans feel welcome and appreciated. She's truly one of a kind.

Darla Stokes, San Antonio, TX

Nancy DeRousha explains the gift of the quilt as Nora and Ruth Langan listen.

Nora stands with the quilt Laura Helvie made for her.

I've written and presented an academic paper on Nora's "Dream" trilogy. Her repeated use of communities of women fits in with elements of French feminist thought/theory. I am in the planning stages of a further study, which would be extended to include other communities of women—namely M. J. O'Leary, Bailey James, and Grace Fontaine (of the Stars of Mithra trilogy). Another project would examine her communities of men—the Quinn brothers and the MacKades. Nora was very helpful and answered all my questions. Having a direct quote from her in my paper made people at my conference take my paper on romance novels seriously!

Kelly Rivers, student [She got an A on her paper.]

Nora's books were a big part of choosing the itinerary we did for our trip to Ireland in the fall of 1999. I went with my friend Jody, another romance reader and Nora fan. . . . Jody and I drove off the beaten path and visited Ardmore [the location of Nora's Irish trilogy]. We also spent several days in County Clare and one of the reasons I wanted to visit County Clare so badly was from reading the "Born In" series—one of the first times reading a book has really encouraged me to visit a particular location.

My husband and I listened to the unabridged version of *Montana Sky* while driving across Montana in 1997. How very enjoyable to be in the setting of the book while listening to it!

Maudeen Wachsmith

I once had the good fortune to hang with Nora and her friends at a conference. She found out it was the cocktail waitress's birthday, so Nora slipped into a gift shop and bought the waitress a lovely bracelet and a card, and had all of us sign. Then Nora quietly presented them along with an autographed copy of *Montana Sky*, I think, to the waitress. The woman was overwhelmed and moved to tears. It was typical of Nora, whom I've seen be both generous and gracious again and again. No matter how tired or under pressure she is, she always has time for her fans, and that's not the only time I've seen her do some act of great kindness without any fanfare. . . . She's not only immensely talented and hardworking but a true class act.

Jean Brashear, author

This was the Michigan gathering of Board Broads/Noraholics.

Nora was doing a book signing celebrating her one hundredth book, *Montana Sky,* at the Tattered Cover Bookstore in Denver. This was also during the time the MacKade Brothers series was being published. After Nora read from *Montana Sky* she asked for questions, and a young girl rose and asked her, "Why aren't the dogs Fred and Ethel in the MacKade series neutered and spayed?" It was obvious Nora was surprised at a question she'd never heard or answered before, but she recovered quickly, saying, "Fred and Ethel are going to have puppies and good homes will be found for them. *Then* Fred and Ethel will be neutered and spayed."

Robin D. Owens, author

My name is Susan Heimann and I'm a Noraholic. While some addictions can be harmful to my health, I believe that I have only benefited from this one. I realize that Nora has, too. I've probably spent enough money on her books to enable her to send her kids to college.

I've been reading Nora Roberts's books for years. And when I say years, I really should say from the start—*Irish Thoroughbred.* In the beginning, I would read the back cover and then buy the book. After a while, I just picked up anything that had her name on it. I'd probably buy her grocery list!

Over the years, my Nora collection has grown. I have a habit of rereading her books, so I even have multiple copies of some of them. God forbid that I wear out a copy. Of course, I have to have a paperback copy to go along with the hardcover. This part of my addiction developed because I couldn't wait for the paperback to come out. Now, recently, publishers have made a hobby of changing the covers of her books. I can't stop myself from buying the books with the new covers. I also have to factor in the Nora books that I lend out. People never want to give them back. That's when I pat myself on the back for having multiple copies. Of course, then I have to replace the strayed books. . . .

Recently, I went on a road trip. I took "Nora" along with me. I listened to one of her books on tape. When I ran out of something to read, I went to a bookstore to scope out the new books. Nothing caught my interest, so I walked out with a Nora Roberts book. (Of course.)

My friends won't be doing an intervention. I'm afraid that I have passed this addiction on to many of my friends—even the ones who thought they would never read a romance. Nora Roberts has such a wide variety of books that it's easy to hook mystery and other genre readers. It requires a sneak attack, but it can be done.

There's a whole world addicted to Nora. When we find someone else who reads Nora Roberts, we compulsively start naming books that we love. There are telltale signs: our eyes light up; we talk faster; and we sigh, saying, "I'm going to have to read that one again. . . ."

As a bookseller, I honed my art of spreading the Nora Roberts addiction. I would check out the customer, glance to see what kind of books that they were looking at. I would run and get Nora's newest and casually stroll over to the customer. "Hi. I see you're looking at (insert bestselling book here). Have you ever read Nora Roberts?" Five minutes later, I had my hooks in them. Maybe I wouldn't sell them the newest title, maybe it would be one of her backlist titles, but nearly every customer I dealt with would go with at least one—and nearly all of them came back for more.

In my effort to spread this joyful addiction, I didn't limit myself to just one state. No, I crossed state lines. I went from chain bookstores in Texas to an independent in New Mexico. I no longer officially sell books, but I have not been able to overcome the urge to spread the word. While I'm browsing in bookstores, I have a compulsion to strike up conversations about Nora's books with complete strangers.

I can't stop reading her books. I can't think of one good reason why I should. She is one of the few authors who always writes a good book. I know that as I'm reading, I'll feel a wide range of emotions. I know that her characters will become friends that I will want to revisit again and again. I know that I will never be disappointed.

I know that I'm not going to give up my addiction. I know because there's just something about Nora Roberts.

Susan Heimann

Mary Kay McComas, Nora, and Patricia Gaffney admire the pencil drawing that Nancy (Ottis) Rairden did of Turn the Page.

"Roberts is in peak form with this combination of historical romantic suspense and contemporary ghost story. . . . Roberts has cleverly crafted an enticing tangle of times and relationships. . . . To add to the pleasure, tastefully choreographed, highly erotic scenes are seamlessly woven into a novel that exemplifies storytelling at its finest."

—*Booklist* on
MIDNIGHT BAYOU

PART TEN

by net

connecting nora's fandom

THE INTERNET HAS played a strong role in Nora's connection with her fans. Put her name in a search engine like Google (www.google.com) and you'll get a list of over twenty-four thousand hits. Many are references to her books, but a staggering number of them are interviews and websites devoted to her.

The most prominent of all is Nora's own official site, www.noraroberts.com. Designed and maintained by Eileen Buckholtz, the site is the first place any Nora fan should visit on the web. We asked Eileen a few questions about the site.

LAURA HAYDEN: *When did the site debut?*

EILEEN BUCKHOLTZ: January 1996. It really gave Nora a chance to get even more close and personal with her fans. Today her website at www.noraroberts.com receives over 12,500 visitors a week from the United States and almost every country that has Internet access. The site has won many awards as one of the best author websites on the net.

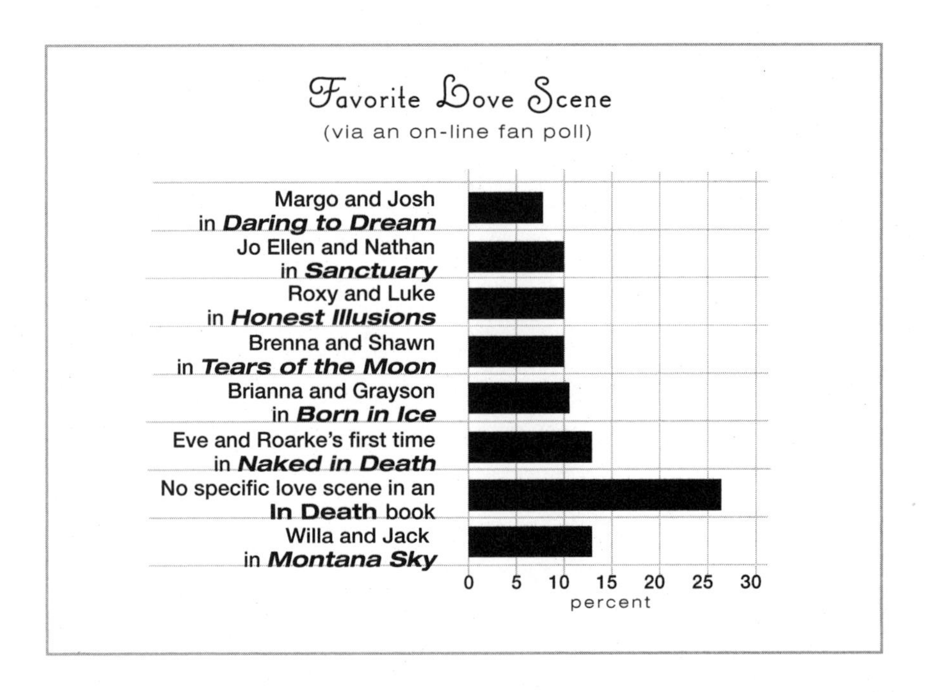

LAURA HAYDEN: *So what would a fan find at the site?*

EILEEN BUCKHOLTZ: Readers can leave messages for Nora on her guest book and sign up for her electronic newsletter, "Nora's News," which has over twenty-six thousand subscribers. Noraroberts.com contains:

- Biographical information at "About Nora"
- News about upcoming books at "What's New"
- Frequently Asked Questions at "FAQs"
- A complete book list
- A list of audiobooks
- A list of trilogies and series

- ✦ Information on book signings and appearances
- ✦ A list of review quotes in "Kudos for Nora!"
- ✦ A "Free Stuff" page
- ✦ Info on the In Death series in "Meet J. D. Robb"
- ✦ Information about the MacGregor series in "About the MacGregors"
- ✦ A link to Nora's on-line store
- ✦ A photo gallery
- ✦ "In the News"
- ✦ A list of recent on-line media interviews
- ✦ A link to Turn the Page Book Café
- ✦ Links to Nora's publishers
- ✦ Her guest book
- ✦ Sign-up page for her newsletter

The Turn the Page Book Café, www.ttpbooks.com, is run by Nora's husband, Bruce. There, readers can order autographed copies of books by Nora Roberts and J. D. Robb. On the "Free Stuff" page, visitors can send in for free bookmarks, booklist calendar magnets, and other goodies. Nora's store on the site sells T-shirts, book bags, and many other items made especially for Nora's fans. One of the most popular pages on the site is the list of book signings and appearances. During Nora's spring tours, this page is updated daily to let fans know exactly when and where they can meet Nora.

Nora on tour in New Jersey with Edith Chiong and Arlene Miklovic

LAURA HAYDEN: *What sort of notes do the fans leave?*

EILEEN BUCKHOLTZ: Visitors often leave notes on the guest book on how Nora's books have changed their lives, helped them get through difficult times and illnesses, and always about how much they love Nora and her books. Comments from the past guest books include "You are my favorite author," "Can't put your books down," "I am a huge fan," "Absolutely love your books," "Your books are fabulous," and "Your stories have a way of wrapping themselves around my mind and heart." Other messages include pros and cons of Eve and Roarke having a baby in an upcoming story and suggestions for more MacGregor books. The guest book gets hundreds of entries a week.

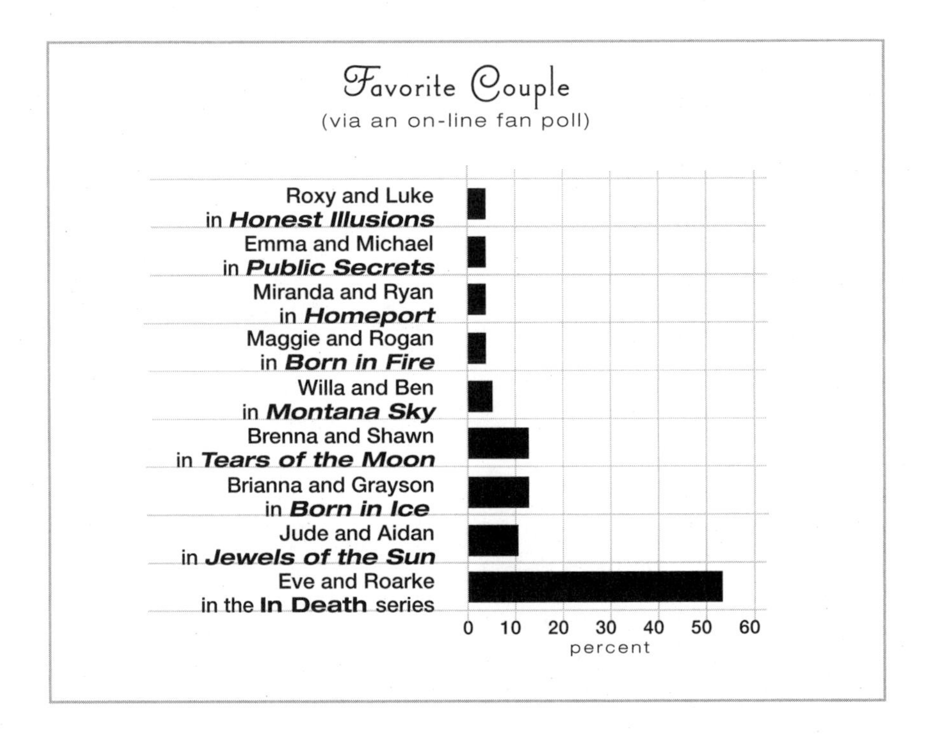

Nora's books have inspired many readers to travel to Ireland to see for themselves the lovely settings that she describes in her books. Fans often send in requests for books about secondary characters from previous books. And readers are quick to find any typos or omissions on the website. They send in corrections within minutes of any mistakes being posted. Nora's readers are always polite and appreciative. We even get thank-you notes from hundreds of subscribers every time we send out the e-mail newsletter.

LAURA HAYDEN: *We know Nora is the genius at the front of the website, but who are the sharp minds behind it?*

EILEEN BUCKHOLTZ: I've maintained the site since its inception in 1996. I'm a computer scientist and author of over fifty books including a great number of romantic suspense novels. I also manage the ever-growing newsletter list "Nora's News." Content for the website is provided by Creative Promotions.

In addition to Nora's official site, there are many unofficial sites on the web, maintained by fans. The most popular of these is ADWOFF: A Day Without French Fries (www.adwoff.com), which opens with the following quote:

> Barb, how can one live without French fries. Not well, I say. In fact, I've been known to say a day without fries is like a day without an orgasm.
>
> —Nora Roberts

Designed and maintained by ultimate Nora fan Sue Noyes, it's obvious that the site is a labor of love. ADWOFF is also the home of the largest concentration of "Noraholics"—or those readers who are (as defined by the *Romance Reader's Dictionary*)—"committed to faithfully ignoring the realities of life (i.e., work, marriage, family, etc.) in order to read, reread, and sometimes memorize

(L to R) Tracey O'Donnell, Wendy, Jaci Hanna, Nora, Carolyn Smith, and Sue Noyes

every book written by the author who personifies and transcends the very best the romance genre has to offer: Nora Roberts."

The website features several sections:

- M.O.M.: An ADWOFF staple from the very first issue, members are asked to nominate a "Man of the Month" from one of Nora's books.
- ROARKE: Members are asked to nominate individuals who have demonstrated an act of kindness that reflects what Nora stands for: integrity, compassion, humor, openness, generosity, honesty, passion, romance, time, etc.
- BOOKIE: their resident gossip columnist
- WYT & WYZDOM: the wit and wisdom of columnist Nina Friedman, otherwise known as Wymzee
- THE PHANTOM: reports from the field about members who have "approached strangers in bookstores across the United States (and the world!) and recommended stories by Nora / J. D. Robb."
- NORA'S BOOK LIST: a list of Nora's work
- NORA'S TRAVELOGUES: written commentary from Nora while on various trips:

- The Caymans (2001)
- Europe/Ireland (2000; includes travelogues from Ruth Ryan Langan)
- Italy (1999)
- Ireland (1998)
- Australia/Japan (1997; notes originally sent to Mary Kay McComas)

✦ ADWOFF'S PHOTO ALBUM: including pictures from Nora's travels, book tours, TTP events, fan gatherings, weddings, and member pictures

✦ ADWOFF'S MESSAGE BOARD: where members can discuss Nora, her books, her friends, ask questions about stories, look for books missing from their collections, and more

✦ THE NORAHOLICS: a list of members and their on-line nicknames

✦ RECOMMENDED AUTHORS: links to the official websites of Nora's closest friends: Mary Kay McComas, Patricia Gaffney, and Ruth Ryan Langan

✦ ROMANTIC SITES: links to other websites of interest

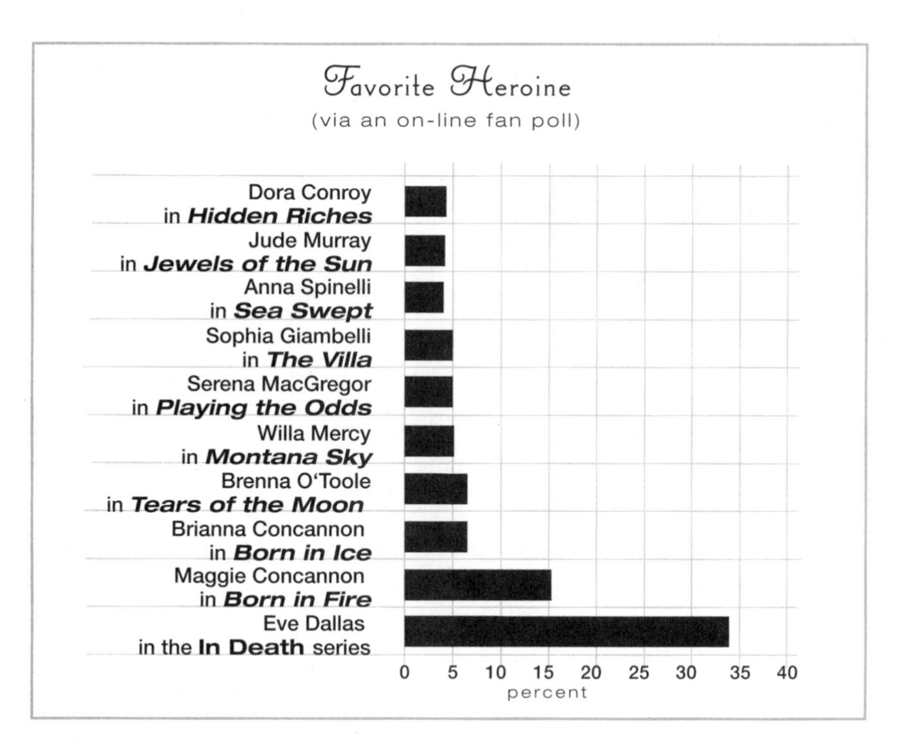

Amazed by the site, we asked Sue Noyes to tell us more about ADWOFF and its origins.

LAURA HAYDEN: *In your very first ADWOFF newsletter, you mentioned the circumstances that caused you to be exposed to Nora's books. ("Little did I know back near the end of February that by attending an online chat for Dean Koontz I would ultimately be led to another terrific writer, Nora Roberts. On March 8, I entered Nora's folder at The Book Report (on AOL) and posted a challenge to fans of Nora's to 'convince me' that I should read her books. Not only did I receive replies from many of her fans, but I also received a reply from Nora.") Can you tell me more about this? What metamorphosis did you go through from not knowing her work and becoming such a fan that you started the ADWOFF website?*

SUE NOYES: As I mentioned in the first ADWOFF, it was via a Dean Koontz chat that Nora's name first came up; I had also been posting at Tami Hoag's board on AOL, and various people kept mentioning Nora. So, when it came time to try out a new author, it was between Nora and Patricia Cornwell. I went into the two authors' boards, and I asked their readers to "convince me." Needless to say, having the author herself respond was quite an attention-grabber!

Not only did I try a couple of Nora's stories (*Sacred Sins* was first) and enjoy them, but I also started to read and hang out at this board of Nora's on AOL called "Sanctuary." A group of ladies would get together in chats (which Nora would also from time to time drop in on), and then they started an e-mail deal that would go out every single day (mostly gossipy stuff like we did on the board—I guess it took it to another level).

Well, as you can imagine, our mailboxes were stuffed with these e-mails, and soon we had little time for chats, the boards, etc. So, as quickly as it started, it ended. Since I was having such fun with the board, the chats, the e-mails, etc., I felt a little down. I didn't want it to end. So I approached Nora with the idea of creating this on-line newsletter creating a kind of "fan club" of sorts. She told me that she was very flattered, amazed that I'd want to do such work, that she'd help out as much as possible, etc., etc.

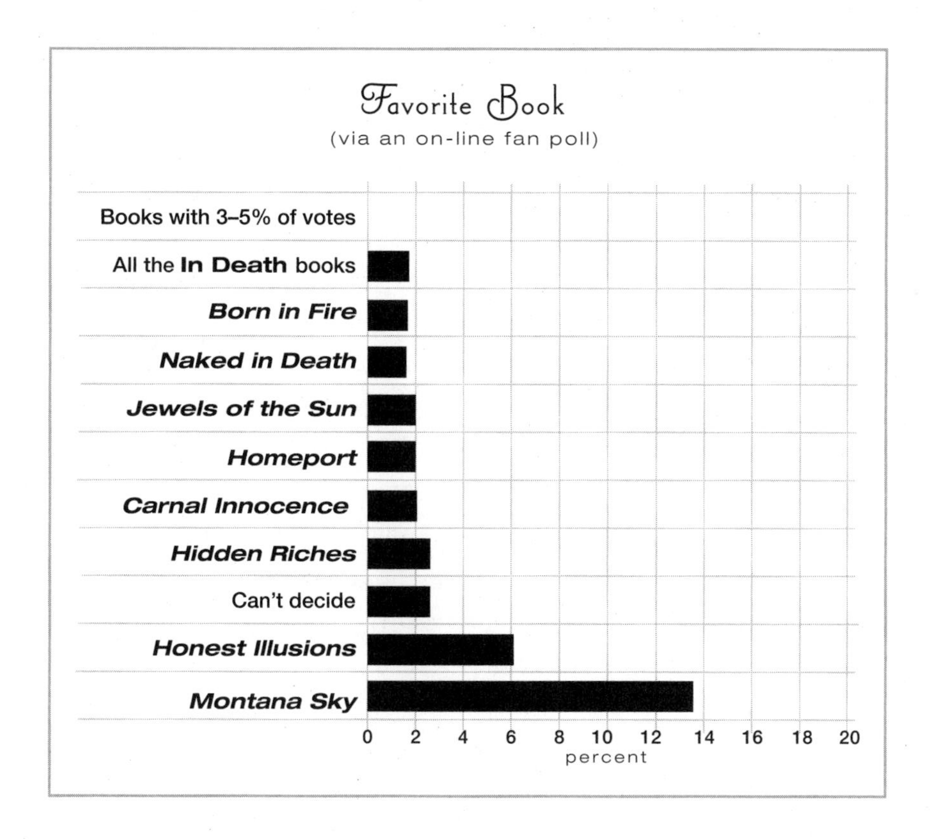

Once I had her blessing, I then called upon others, and ADWOFF took off. Had that initial e-mail deal not have gone bad so fast or had Nora not been so accessible, I honestly don't know if ADWOFF would have been born. But once it was, we just had too much fun with it not to continue.

LAURA HAYDEN: *Your website features the "French fries" quote by Nora Roberts. We realize that "ADWOFF" stands for "A Day Without French Fries." But who is Barb and what led Nora to make such an astute comment?*

SUE NOYES: Barb is just a person who posted on one of Nora's boards; I think "Diets" was a topic, and she obviously said something about cutting out fries. For me, Nora's reply back was pure Nora—the side of her personality that we embrace so much. I mean, who would expect a person of Nora's stature to say such a thing? And since we had so much fun with sexual innuendos (especially in the early days of posting at Nora's board), it was something that I knew I had to use.

LAURA HAYDEN: *You refer to yourself and other Nora fans as Noraholics. Who first coined the phrase "Noraholic"?*

SUE NOYES: This is a good question. I'm not sure if I coined it or someone else did. I know that after a while, some ladies in another group took "issue" with it—feeling that it had negative connotations (i.e., alcoholic, etc.). Whenever something like that happens (like with Pat Gaffney and Nora calling her "the Lying Slut"), I go directly to the source and ask her how she feels about it. So I asked Nora if the phrase "Noraholic" bothered her, and she emphatically said that it did not. After that, I freely used the term—especially in regards to the group of ladies who revolved around ADWOFF. *[Editor's note: The word "Noraholic" is gaining popularity. We recently saw it used in the Barnes & Noble romance book newsletter.]*

LAURA HAYDEN: *How has running this website changed your daily life? Has it segued into any professional success for you?*

SUE NOYES: Changed my daily life? Well, I wish I could say that it segued into professional opportunities for me, but so far it hasn't. Basically, it's changed my life in that it's a responsibility that I can't ignore. People have come to depend on the ADWOFF site almost (well, not almost, but you know what I mean;-)) as much as they depend on Nora's next book.

LAURA HAYDEN: *I also know that cyber friends can become very good friends in the "real" world, too. Have you developed close friendships because of the website?*

SUE NOYES: Probably the neatest thing about ADWOFF is that it has brought readers of Nora's together—and friendships have developed. We call Turn the Page Bookstore Café's anniversary event in July "TTP"—and this year will be the fifth year that ladies from all over the world will have gotten together—not just to celebrate Bruce and Nora's store and Nora's stories, but also the friendships that have been developed.

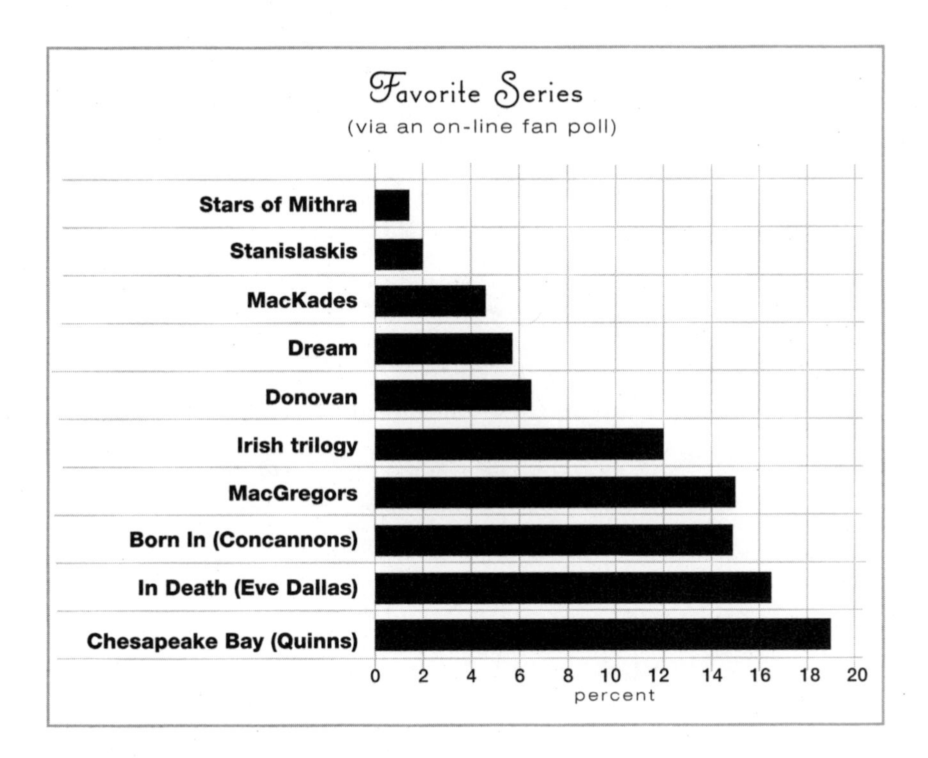

In 1997, a group of ten of us—one each from California, Colorado, Washington, Wisconsin, Michigan, New York, Pennsylvania, Virginia, and two from Maryland—traveled to Maryland for TTP I. The following year, all but one of the original ten returned and around a dozen more came for the first time.

We call ourselves "the board broads" or "broads" or "BB/N" (board/broad/Noraholic). As the years have passed, more and more women attend this event, and different groups of friendships have evolved (like the "Brats"). So yes, many friendships have developed from the creation of ADWOFF—which I think is its greatest legacy.

LAURA HAYDEN: *Nora may have been the reason why you found each other, but there's a real sense of community and camaraderie on the message boards and reflected in the newsletters. Any stories you can relate about friendships within the community?*

SUE NOYES: Oh wow. I think if you check out the ADWOFF site, you'll see little gatherings that we've had which are so typical of the community

Some of these ladies came as far away as Wisconsin, Illinois, Michigan, and New York, to attend this event at That Bookstore in Danville in Danville, Pennsylvania. In the back (L to R): Linda, Pat, Katie Dunneback, Mary Kay, Diane Noyes, Nora, Elaine, Bonnie's friend, Bonnie, and Arlene Miklovic. In the front (L to R): Sue Noyes, Edith Chiong, Jaci Hanna, Tracey O'Donnell, and Nancy DeRousha

created from ADWOFF and the "Nora connection." For example, I moved from Virginia to Pennsylvania to work for Jaci Hanna—at her bookstore—after getting to know Jaci through the boards and TTP and ADWOFF. In New Jersey, Arlene is working for Edith—another relationship that sprung from the ADWOFF/Nora connection.

We've even had a marriage! One of the BB/Ns was introduced via cyberspace to the son of one of the BB/Ns in San Diego. A romance evolved, and Lisa was married to Keith two years ago this month. Last summer, a "Brat" came to the United States from Australia, and she toured the U.S. with another Brat—before eventually heading to TTP. On and on it goes.

LAURA HAYDEN: *How much time did it take to build the initial website and how much time does it take to update it? (And the time involved moving it to the new site!)*

SUE NOYES: Another good question! First, understand that the very first ADWOFF was delivered in an e-mail. Then, when we sent out the second one, it was so big that it was causing everyone's computer to freeze or crash when they tried to open it up. Since I knew that ADWOFF was going to keep getting bigger, I knew I needed to come up with an alternative. AOL gives each screen name 2MB of web space, so I invested in a web page program and set about learning how to create web pages and upload it to the Internet. Initially, it was a grand learning experience. All in all, once the articles are collected, it usually takes anywhere from two to three weeks to get the new "newsletter" ready for on-line presentation—that's working on it several hours each night of the week.

Through the years, I quickly outgrew AOL's 2MB of space, so I had to use all of the screen names AOL makes available (seven in all), take advantage of a special offer when AOL created its "homepage" site (by participating in its beta testing, you could get up to 10MB more of web space per name), and beg my boss, my sister, and another friend for some of their screen names so that I had enough room for ADWOFF.

Needless to say, when I had the opportunity to switch ADWOFF to its own domain, I jumped at it! I started the conversion in the beginning of May 2001, and two months later, it still hasn't been all converted. That's working every day of the week—oftentimes until the wee hours of the morning. Needless to say, I learned some stuff about organization and its importance.

LAURA HAYDEN: *Got any good anecdotes?*

SUE NOYES: I think my favorite "Nora story" occurred at the first TTP event. It took place at the dinner I mentioned earlier. Nora had agreed to meet with the group for dinner, so we arranged to do so at around five P.M. The group I was with arrived a little late because we were looking for birthday presents for Jaci, so when we got there, we discovered that Jaci had had what we refer to as a "blonde moment." She locked her keys in her car's trunk; they had to call a locksmith to open it up.

When we pulled into the restaurant's parking lot, we were right next to this hunter green BMW convertible. It had to be Nora's car, we thought. In awe, I circled it, admiring it. And then I noticed that she had this funky thing in the ignition. I, being the naïve person that I am, thought it was some kind of an antitheft device.

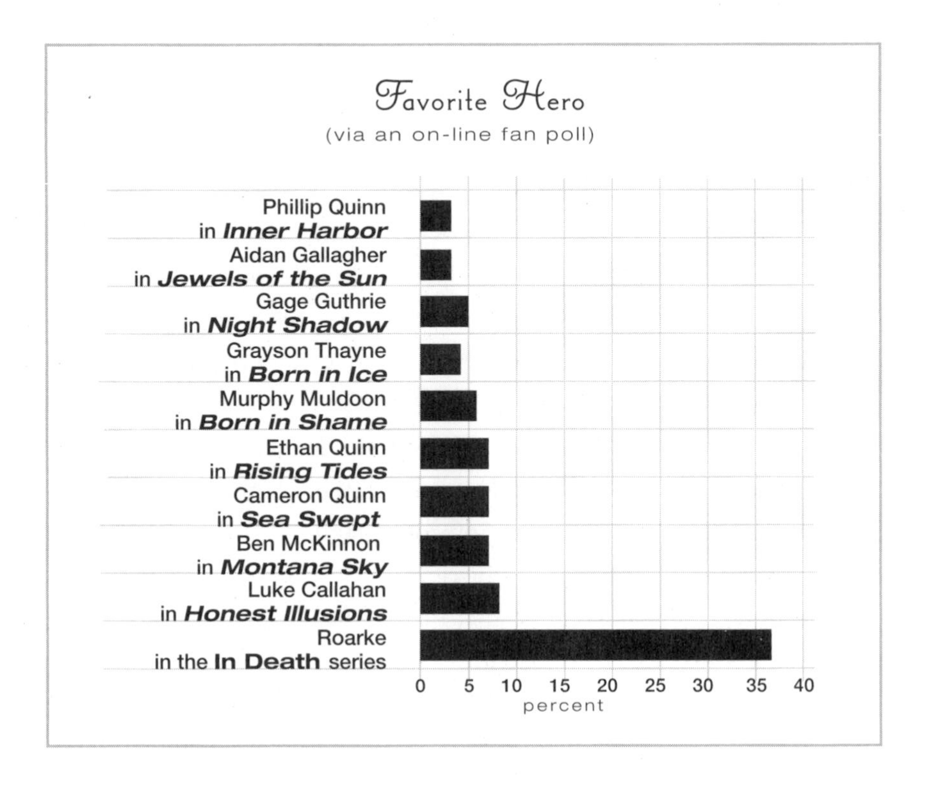

When I mentioned this to Nora inside, she turned rather pale. It wasn't an antitheft device but her actual car keys! And not only had she been so distracted when she pulled into the restaurant that she left her keys in the car, but she also parked in a handicapped parking space!

I think seeing Nora interact with her buddies, Ruth Ryan Langan, Pat Gaffney, and Mary Kay McComas, is the other highlight of knowing her. It is obvious that these ladies have such affection for one another—and the ability to razz one another without worrying how the other will take it. Some of ADWOFF's better pieces over the years have included interviews with these ladies and actual meetings with them.

Nora's famous BMW!

Not all Nora Roberts fan sites are created by American fans. Isolde Wehr may be Nora's greatest fan in Germany. When searching the Internet for interesting Nora-oriented web pages, we found Isolde's extensive romance novel review site (www.die-buecherecke.de) to be a real standout. A twenty-six-year-old secretary working in Germany, Isolde has amassed over nine hundred reviews of romance books in general, including sixty reviews of Nora's books, many in both English and German.

LAURA HAYDEN: *When did you first discover Nora's books?*

ISOLDE WEHR: My very first Nora Roberts book was *Ein König für Schottland* [*Rebellion*], which I read in the early '90s. At the time I thought Nora Roberts was a historical author because shortly after that, I read *Eine Lady im wilden Westen* [*Lawless*]. A couple of years later, I saw a contemporary novel by Nora in a bookstore and after a while, I bought it. I never regretted buying this first contemporary novel because I quickly became hooked and bought every one of her books that came out in German. At the time I didn't know that she also wrote for Harlequin (Cora publishes this type of novel in German).

LAURA HAYDEN: *What is it specifically about Nora's books that intrigues you?*

ISOLDE WEHR: She is a dream for every reader who reads as much as I do because she writes so quickly. Her books are fascinating, I love the wonderful characters, and not one of her books is boring!

LAURA HAYDEN: *What sort of feedback do you get from fellow Nora fans because of your website?*

ISOLDE WEHR: Actually, I'd like to think I converted hordes of normal German romance readers into devoted Nora Roberts fans. Nora Roberts wasn't really very popular in Germany at first, but my homepage introduced her to a lot of readers and provided information about her and her books, not to mention that I have nearly sixty Nora Roberts book reviews on my homepage. So what else could they do but to buy her books and they love them! At least that's what I always hear.

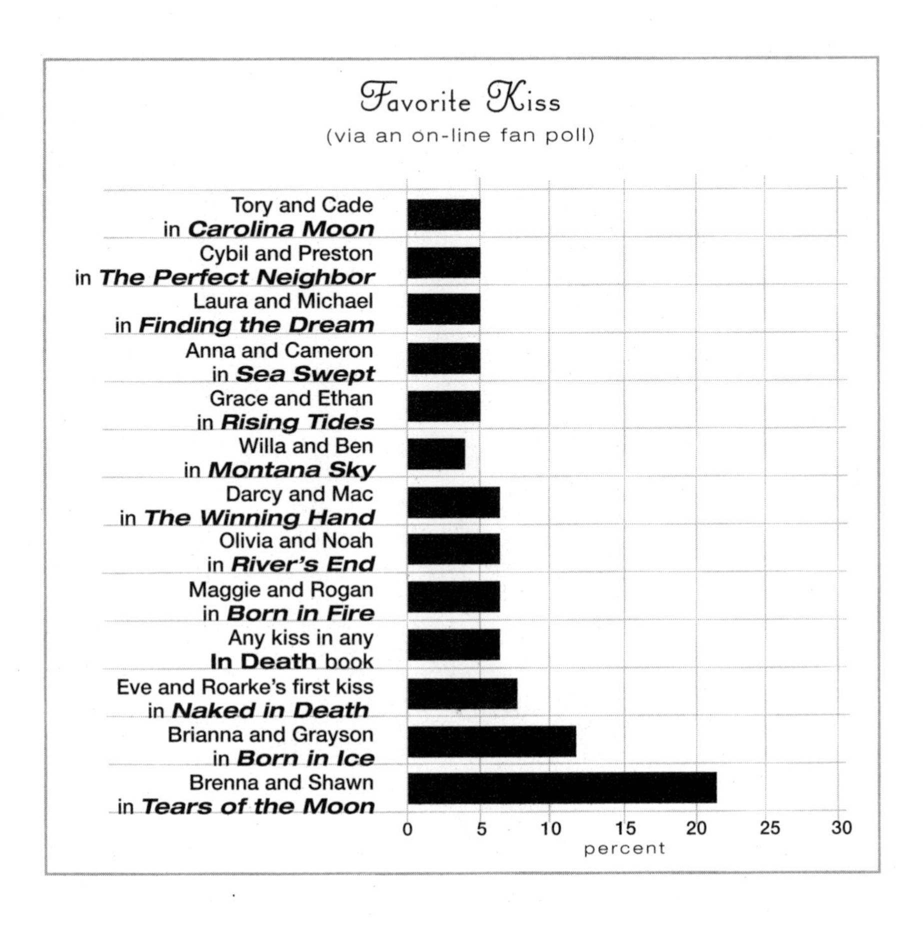

LAURA HAYDEN: *How much time have you spent building the site and maintaining it?*

ISOLDE WEHR: My website went on-line in 1996 and making updates, writing reviews, etc., requires most of my free time.

LAURA HAYDEN: *Have you ever met Nora?*

ISOLDE WEHR: Unfortunately I've never met Nora Roberts. I haven't had the opportunity to fly to America just to meet her. But when I started doing interviews with American romance authors, a friend of mine asked, "Why don't you interview Nora Roberts?"

I was shocked and said, "She is so famous, I couldn't do that. She would never answer me." Well, my friend finally talked me into it and I agreed to try. My hands were shaking when I wrote Nora the e-mail

Nora with her British publisher, Judy Piatkus, of Piatkus Books in a bookstore in England

and in a very short time, I had my answer. I nearly fainted because I didn't know what to ask her. Well, I managed to put together a few questions and I was so excited that I got my answers and I still am, because I can't believe how friendly she is to her fans.

[Editor's note: This interview can be found at www.die-buecherecke.de/roberts2.htm]

LAURA HAYDEN: *I understand that you had a direct role in getting the J. D. Robb books translated into German. Can you tell me how this happened?*

ISOLDE WEHR: I have a good relationship with a few German romance publishers. I also have a message board on my homepage. Often Nora Roberts fans complained that no German publisher seemed to want to risk translating the J. D. Robb books. One day I got an e-mail from Blanvalet, a well-known German publisher. The editor, whom I had known for some time, asked me to explain what was so special about the J. D. Robb books. I told her that I'm addicted to the series, that I love Roarke (and will not share him with anyone), and that the idea for a science fiction crime series is simply wonderful. Not long after that conversation, I got another e-mail from the editor and she wrote, "You did it and we did it." She explained to me that she was now also addicted to Eve and Roarke and was willing to take a chance of translating the first book *Naked in Death* for the German market. To make a long story short, Blanvalet made me, and all the German readers who can't read English, extremely happy.

[*Editor's note: The German translation of* Naked in Death *was released May 2001, as* Rendezvous mit einem Mörder.]

LAURA HAYDEN: *I understand that you have a new position as the editor for a German-based romance club. Can you tell me more about this?*

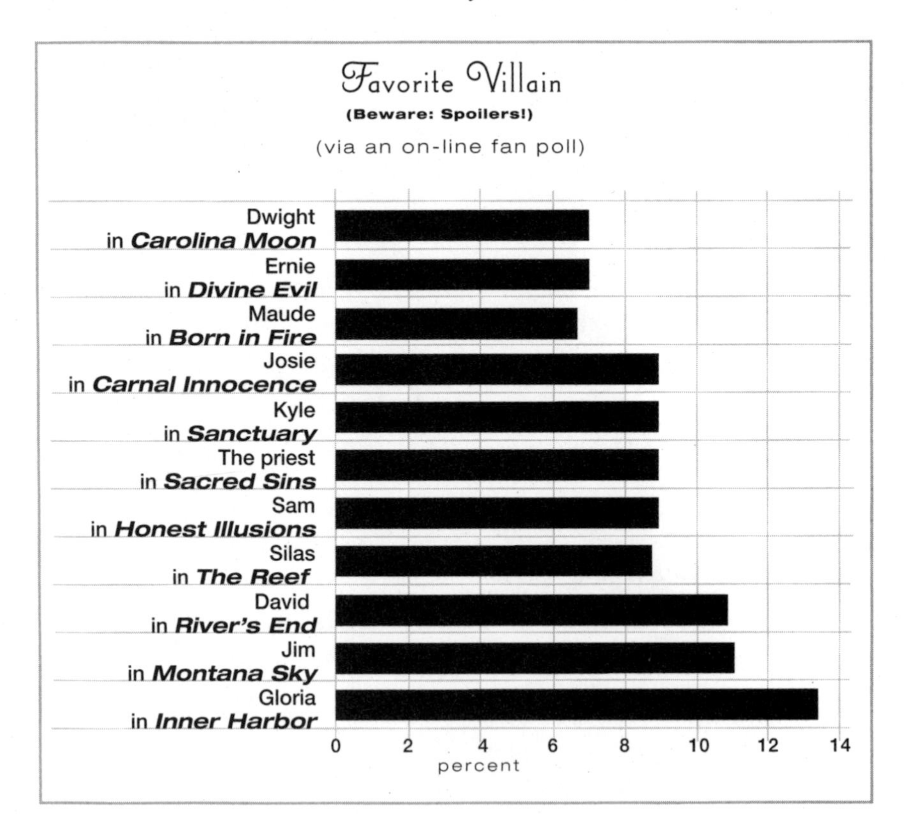

ISOLDE WEHR: In February of 2001, Bertelsmann (one of the largest German publishers) decided to start specialty book clubs. They wanted their first club to be a romance club. They needed somebody to select the program for the club and since I am Germany's most famous romance reader, they decided to try their luck with me. When I got the phone call from Bertelsmann offering me the job, I couldn't believe what was happening, because it has always been my dream to work with romances. Now the dream has come true.

Other notable web pages include:

- ✦ Nora, Nora, and . . . ummm . . . Nora!!!: www.geocities.com/deansdenise/
- ✦ Notoriously Noraholic for Nora Roberts: www.geocities.com/jens_noraholics
- ✦ There's Something About Nora: www.writerspace.com/somethingaboutnora

Happy web surfing!

"HOMEPORT is vintage Roberts. The prose is taut, the story is well-researched, and the . . . sex scenes . . . are steamy. Roberts, whose last bestseller was SANCTUARY, is fond of titles that suggest refuge. After flirting with danger, that is just what her heroine hopes to find—home, herself and the man of her dreams."

—*People* magazine on HOMEPORT

a last word

PART ELEVEN

from nora

NORA ROBERTS DOESN'T confine herself to the fictional world when she's writing. The *New York Times* asked Nora to write an editorial on the 2000 presidential campaign, and the following appeared in the *New York Times* on August 23, 2000. Though the election turned out to be too close to call, she made some very valid points.

The Votes in a Kiss

BY NORA ROBERTS

SEX AND POLITICS always make an intriguing couple, but, usually what we hear and read about are illicit sex and dirty politics. When it's sexual zing between a happily married and political couple on national television, apparently we don't know what to make of it.

When Al Gore planted a big kiss on his wife, Tipper, at the Democratic Convention, it wasn't the nice, firm and friendly peck it appeared she, and the rest of us, were expecting. It was, to me, sweet, sexy, amusing and romantic all at once. That's a lot of punch from one kiss.

You go, Al.

Despite the endless speculation in the days since that this was all about Mr. Gore showing the world he wouldn't be involved in any Monica Lewinsky–like scandals, what I saw in the Gores' kiss was a man and woman, married long enough to be grandparents, embracing at one of the high points of their personal and professional lives.

The kiss came after a taped montage of their life together and directly after Tipper introduced Al as the man she fell in love with at first sight. A good strong kiss seems pretty appropriate to me at such a moment.

If I'd been writing the internal dialogue of Al Gore, so often described as a cardboard man, when he pulled Tipper into that clinch, it would run something like this: "This is our moment. Look where we are, after all these years. Look what we've achieved. Together. I love you."

The love in that kiss speaks to me as a woman, as one who appreciates both intellect and romance. This was a man who, at one of the pinnacles of his political career, felt compelled to show his wife his love, his need and his gratitude.

What could be more romantic?

And it is the romance that seems to have eluded all the political commentators, despite their endless search for new angles to analyze. But I'll bet it wasn't missed by the nation's women.

I can only assume that there were a great many women watching, as I was, who would hope they would be as important, as essential to a life mate at a crowning moment in his career, as Tipper was at that moment to Al.

I think Mrs. Gore was, initially, a bit taken aback. But she rallied, put her arms around him and was as much a part of that moment, of that kiss, as he was. The embrace after the kiss was even sweeter, even more intimate, to my mind, than the kiss itself. This made them a team, demonstrated a passion between them and from them that I think women voters will admire and respect.

But will those women voters show that admiration in the voting booths? None of the women I know would be swayed in their political judgments merely by the sight of a guy locking lips with his wife on TV, any more than a man would cast a vote for a candidate based on his ability to throw the perfect sinking curve ball. We are not quite that simple.

But while a kiss has nothing to do with platform or policy, it does speak, very clearly, to human nature. Love matters, even in politics, or we as women—as voters or as candidates—should hope it does. Candidates can make promises or sling mud, and will, endlessly. But show me the heart of the candidate, and I—as a woman—will pay more attention to that candidate's words.

We had a glimpse inside the heart when Mr. Gore embraced his wife before he addressed the world as the Democratic presidential nominee. That heart took one long, public moment to express love for a woman. A lot of us may pay more attention to Mr. Gore's words because of that quick, endearing and romantic impulse.

Will it add up to more votes in November? If we like what we hear, maybe it will.

about the editors

LAURA HAYDEN

Laura Hayden is an award-winning author who has been published primarily in the romantic suspense category, including several books for Harlequin Intrigue. She has also collaborated with former First Daughter Susan Ford on a hardcover mystery series, the most recent of which is *Sharp Focus*, released in July 2003 by St. Martin's Press. She has written successfully in a wide range of settings and story lines as well as in multiple lengths and formats.

Laura graduated from The Brook Hill School in Birmingham, Alabama, and from the University of Alabama with a degree in industrial engineering. She is married to a colonel in the U.S. Air Force, and they are currently settled in Colorado Springs.

Laura has nine published novels and has several more under contract. *A Margin in Time* (March 1995) won the Golden Heart Award from the Romance Writers of America. Her other novels include *Stolen Hearts* (September 2001), *Through the Eyes of a Child* (May 1998, as Laura Kenner), *Hero for Hire* (February 1997, as Laura Kenner), *Chance of a Lifetime* (July 1996), *A Killer Smile* (March 1995, as Laura Kenner), and *Someone to Watch over Me* (February 1994, as Laura Kenner). Other projects include short fiction for *Murder Most Romantic*, "Twelve Days," *Guardian Angels*, "Guardian of the

Peace," and *Dangerous Magic*, "Nine-Tenths." She has also done an original audiobook called *Star of Kashmir* for Audio Entertainment.

Laura is an accomplished scriptwriter, as well as a novelist. Among her credits in this area is a script she wrote for an episode of *Remember WENN*, an Emmy and CableAce Award–winning show on the American Movie Classics Channel, which aired in November 1997.

DENISE LITTLE

Denise Little worked for Barnes & Noble/B. Dalton Bookseller for nearly fifteen years—for more than ten years as a bookstore manager, then for four more years as their national book buyer for romance, science fiction, and fantasy. She was selected as Bookseller of the Year by *Romantic Times* and by the Virginia and the New Jersey chapters of Romance Writers of America. She launched and wrote B. Dalton's genre magazine, *Heart to Heart*, for the first two years of its existence. She joined Kensington Publishing, where she ran her own imprint, *Denise Little Presents*, as well as editing fiction and nonfiction projects throughout the list, including books by a number of bestselling authors. Two of the romances she edited and published under her imprint were nominated for RITA Awards by the Romance Writers of America. Since 1997, she's been executive editor at Tekno Books, working for the legendary Dr. Martin H. Greenberg. Her books, published and forthcoming, include *Witches' Brew* (with Yvonne Jocks), *Words of the Witches* (with Yvonne Jocks), *Alien Pets*, *Perchance to Dream*, *Twice upon a Time* (winner of the New York Public Library's 100 Best Books of the Year Award), *Dangerous Magic*, *Constellation of Cats*, *Creature Fantastic*, *Vengeance Fantastic*, *The Magic Shop*, *Realms of Dragons*, *The Quotable Cat*, *Murder Most Romantic*, *Mistresses of the Dark*, *Alaska: True Adventures in the Last Frontier* (with Spike Walker), and *The Valdemar Companion* (with John Helfers). She lives in Green Bay, Wisconsin.

copyright notices

photo credits

Photograph (top) on page vi by Dale
Photograph (bottom) on page vi © 2002 John Earle
Photograph on page 60 courtesy of Kathy Onorato
Photograph (top) on page 277 courtesy of Jodi Reamer
Photograph on page 295 courtesy of Tiffini Scott
Photograph on page 303 courtesy of Kathy Onorato
Photograph (top) on page 310 by Dale
Photograph (bottom) on page 310 courtesy of Mark Youngblood
Photograph on page 315 courtesy of Tom Langan
Photographs on pages 356–358 courtesy of Sue Noyes
Photograph on page 362 courtesy of Laura Hayden
Photograph on page 364 courtesy of Laura Hayden
Photograph on page 368 courtesy of Tiffini Scott
Photograph on page 372 courtesy of Tiffini Scott
Photograph on page 375 courtesy of Sue Noyes
Photograph on page 382 courtesy of Sue Noyes
Photograph (top) on page 390 courtesy of Sue Noyes
Photograph (bottom) on page 390 courtesy of Scott Willman
Photograph on page 393 courtesy of Sue Noyes
Photograph on page 395 courtesy of Sue Noyes
Photograph on page 398 courtesy of Tiffini Scott
Photograph on page 404 courtesy of Sue Noyes
Photographs on pages 406–407 courtesy of Sue Noyes
Photograph on page 410 courtesy of Sue Noyes
Photograph on page 413 courtesy of Sue Noyes
Photograph on page 414 courtesy of Tiffini Scott
Photograph on page 418 courtesy of Tiffini Scott
Photograph on page 424 courtesy of Sue Noyes
Photograph on page 427 courtesy of Sue Noyes
Photograph on page 429 courtesy of Sue Noyes
Photograph on page 431 courtesy of Sue Noyes
Photograph on page 437 courtesy of Sue Noyes
Photograph on page 440 courtesy of Sue Noyes
Photograph on page 446 courtesy of Tiffini Scott
All other photos courtesy of Wilder Family collection.